The Sea Detective

The Sea Detective

Mark Douglas-Home

W F HOWES LTD

This large print edition published in 2012 by
W F Howes Ltd
Unit 4, Rearsby Business Park, Gaddesby Lane,
Rearsby, Leicester LE7 4YH

1 3 5 7 9 10 8 6 4 2

First published in the United Kingdom in 2011
by Sandstone Press Ltd

A CIP catalogue record for this book is available
from the British Library

ISBN 978 1 47120 433 3

Typeset by Palimpsest Book Production Limited,
Falkirk, Stirlingshire
Printed and bound in Great Britain
by MPG Books Ltd, Bodmin, Cornwall

For Colette, Rebecca and Rory

For this book I have invented an island and two settlements on the north coast of Scotland to avoid imposing a fictional story on an existing island or communities which have rich histories of their own.

I owe a debt of gratitude to Toby Sherwin, UHI Professor of Oceanography at the Scottish Association for Marine Science, for his time and advice. If there are errors in any of the passages dealing with the movement of the sea they are mine alone.

My thanks also go to Maggie Pearlstine, my agent, for all her support and guidance; to Colette, my wife, Rebecca and Rory, my children, for reading the drafts and for their suggestions and encouragement; and to everyone at Sandstone Press who made it happen.

I should also acknowledge the research of Anuja Agrawal in her book *Chaste Wives & Prostitute Sisters: Patriarchy and Prostitution among the Bedias of India* which provided context and detail not available in the published journalism on the subject.

CHAPTER 1

The cold wind made the girl shiver. She flared her nostrils, inhaling with short bursts, sniffing for clues, trying to fix the smell. Was it the sea? Her heart began to beat faster. Was this the path to the sea? Was this the way home? She stopped struggling and trembled again, now with excitement.

The woman carrying her, scolding her, tightened her grip. One arm was clamped around the girl's back, the other behind her knees. The girl's tongue pushed at the rag in her mouth, trying to force it out, to gulp a lungful of fresh air, to test whether it tasted as it smelled, of freedom. She'd all but abandoned hope of that. She was young and time had passed slowly for her. Hadn't her father been right? Be obedient, Preeti, and be patient, he'd said.

After the money had changed hands, her father had seen the sudden little-girl-lost panic in her eyes. 'He'll return you to us, Preeti, in a week or two. It's the custom,' he whispered to her, adding, 'when he tires of you.'

She'd said, 'What if he doesn't tire of me, father?'

1

He'd given her an indulgent look, the one he sometimes gave to let her know the depth of his experience in these matters. 'He will.'

'Even a man who has paid 60,000 rupees?'

Nobody had ever paid 60,000 rupees for a girl from her village. The previous record had been 40,000.

'Particularly a man who has paid 60,000 rupees . . .'

Preeti frowned. She did not understand. Hadn't her father said she was the most beautiful girl he had ever seen? Hadn't the truck drivers stared at her with more longing and desire than at any of the other girls? 'Why father? Won't I still be beautiful?'

'Yes, Preeti, you will always be beautiful, but a man like this desires variety. He can afford to buy another beautiful girl and another after her.'

The woman stumbled on the path and Preeti clung to the coarse cloth of her jacket. Again the woman said something angry which Preeti did not understand. They were going downhill, the woman hurrying, Preeti feeling her urgency. Now they were on steps: the woman descending them sideways, quickly, one at a time. Preeti's feet banged against a railing, making the skin above her ankles rub painfully against the knot of the rope. She wriggled and the woman squeezed her tighter still. Then they were out of the wind and the woman's feet crunched on gravel. Ahead was the splashing sound of water washing against a shore. When

Preeti had heard it the last time (how many weeks or months ago?) it had filled her with foreboding. Where was she being taken? Why was she tied, gagged and blindfolded? Why had this rich man paid so much for her only to treat her this way?

Now the lapping water thrilled her. When the woman put her down, Preeti felt the rough wood underneath her and the sway of a boat rocking. Wasn't this the boat which had brought her here? Wasn't she going home?

Her head filled with a kaleidoscope of colours, faces and scents: the pinks, reds and greens of saris, the happy dirty faces of her younger sisters Nita and Meena, the wood-smoke, the hens scratching in the dirt, the grit and dust from the Jaipur road, the sound of trucks stopping and starting, the smell of diesel in the hot air, men bargaining over girls.

She had vivid flashes of memory: her mother sitting outside their hut, singing and cooking over a fire of Tamarind branches; her mother's raindrop tears when Preeti, in her pink sari and jewellery, was taken to the roadside; her mother wrapping her arms round Preeti and saying, out of the hearing of her waiting father, 'forgive me' and Preeti saying proudly, hiding her fear, 'There is nothing to forgive. I am a Bedia girl and this is what Bedia girls do'.

Sitting in this boat, she made a promise. As soon as she returned home she would take her father aside and ask if she could buy presents for her mother with some of her deflowering money. It was the custom for all of it to be spent on a feast. But wasn't 60,000 rupees more than enough for the biggest feast the village had ever had?

How she'd dreamed of the celebration.

Whenever she'd been with a man she thought of nothing else, her head brimming with its brilliance and noise. She would wear gold jewellery and with her father's permission she would buy her mother a dark pink sari of Mysore silk as well as cotton saris for wearing every day, a new cooking pot and a mattress for her bed.

The boat buffeting against a wave suddenly interrupted the girl's dreaming. She wished the woman would take off the blindfold. She wanted to see the ship that would return her to her family. It would be waiting in deeper water, as it had when she'd been taken ashore. Would she again be locked in an airless cabin? There would be no need on the return journey, Preeti thought. Whoever had bought her no longer had a reason for shutting her away from other men. She wasn't a virgin any more. Preeti had a better understanding of these things now.

When the car had slowed at the roadside in her village, shiny black bodywork, blackened windows, a flutter of satisfaction had travelled through her little frame. No car like that had ever stopped for a girl from her village before. She remembered how the truck drivers had ceased their bad-tempered haggling and had stared sullenly at the car knowing this beautiful girl would not be theirs, not then, maybe never if she went to work in New Delhi, Mumbai, or even Dubai. They had heard stories of exotic girls like that who earned many tens of thousands of rupees for their families every year. Preeti had watched as the car window slid open a few centimetres. Her father had approached it uncertainly and spoken through the gap, stooping to it in deference.

When he returned to her side, she'd asked, 'Was he handsome, and clean?' Her father shook his head and smiled like someone who had just been blessed. 'A man who spends 60,000 rupees on a girl will be clean.'

'60,000 rupees,' she'd gasped, and her father's smile broadened into the widest grin.

'Did you see him father? Was he handsome?'

'A man who spends 60,000 rupees on a girl doesn't drive his own car.'

That was something she didn't understand. Why would a man have a Mercedes if he didn't drive it himself? She didn't want to show disrespect for her father so, when she was in the car, she said to the driver, 'Are you the man who has paid for me?'

He guffawed at the idea. 'Where would I be able to find 120,000 rupees?'

'But you only gave my father 60,000 rupees.' (Preeti considered 'only' a surprising word in such a context.)

'I did and soon I will give another girl's father

5

60,000 rupees. It is another man's money. I am just his driver.'

Preeti fell silent, in jealous pique. Was there another Bedia girl so beautiful she could be worth 60,000 rupees also? Hadn't her father told her she was the most beautiful girl ever born to Bedia parents?

No more than ten minutes later the car stopped at another village and the driver lowered the front passenger door window a few centimetres, as he had done for Preeti's father.

The driver passed a roll of money through the gap to a large man with a round face and white, even teeth – Preeti's mother had taught her that good teeth in a man were a sign of wealth and breeding. Then the car door opened and a girl in a green sari sat on the tan leather seat beside Preeti. She was tall and beautiful with thick lustrous dark hair, wide eyes and full lipstick-red lips. She was crying. Preeti's jealousy drained from her. She clasped the girl's hand and asked her name.

'Basanti,' the girl replied.

'How old are you Basanti?'

'I am 14.' Her wet eyes stared at Preeti. They were pleading for help.

Basanti was one year older than Preeti.

'Are you the oldest child?'

'No, I am the youngest of my family.'

Now Preeti understood her tears. Whereas Preeti, being the oldest girl, had been prepared for the *dhanda*, the sex trade, Basanti had not, not yet. Basanti's tears were for the marriage she would never have and for the husband she would never have, for her new life as a *dhandewali*, a prostitute.

Preeti hugged her.

The journey took many hours and Preeti held on to Basanti all the way. At one point Basanti fell asleep on Preeti's lap. The younger girl stroked the elder's hair, marvelling at why a man would need two such girls and which he would find more appealing. Basanti was long and slender, with narrow hips, an elegant neck and wide eyes. Preeti was small and graceful like a dancer, with pronounced cheek bones and a finely drawn mouth.

Preeti thought she had never seen a girl as beautiful as Basanti.

After they had been driving for what seemed like half the night, Preeti tired of the headlights of approaching cars and trucks. She asked the driver, 'Are we nearly there?'

He replied kindly, 'Try to sleep and the journey will be quicker.'

Preeti said she could not, but she closed her eyes and awoke with a start when the driver braked sharply before turning into a back street.

He heard her stir. 'We have arrived,' he said stopping outside a warehouse with metal bars on windows blacked out with paint. 'We are in Mumbai.'

'Is this where the man who bought us lives?' Preeti asked. Basanti had woken too and tightened her grip on Preeti's hand.

The driver shook his head and let the girls out. They preceded him up some stairs to a door with a grille built into it where another man, wearing a white suit, white shoes and sunglasses, was waiting for them.

'Is this the man?' Basanti whispered to Preeti.

'I think so.'

Neither of them had seen such expensive clothes before. This man looked as though he could afford 120,000 rupees for two girls.

Preeti and Basanti were taken along a corridor to a room which had a single bed and a chair. It was lit by an overhead light and the blind was drawn across the window. A woman with a pock-marked face was sitting on the chair waiting for them. She stood up as Preeti and Basanti came into the room, said something Preeti didn't understand to the man in the white suit. After he'd closed the door, she held their hands: Preeti's right in her left, Basanti's left in her right, and regarded them appreciatively. 'Beautiful girls,' she said in their dialect and beamed with pleasure. Preeti and Basanti smiled too, though they were uneasy at feeling the rough calluses on her hands. Afterwards, she helped Preeti and Basanti out of their clothes telling them, 'You must wash . . .'

But she saw the worry on the girls' faces and didn't continue her sentence.

'Is the man in the white suit the one who has paid for Basanti and me?' Preeti asked.

The woman said nothing.

When they were naked they felt shy with each other.

Basanti touched Preeti's arm and said 60,000 rupees was too little money for a girl as lovely as Preeti.

Preeti said, 'And too little for a girl as lovely as you . . .'

'We are worth 70,000 rupees each,' Basanti said.

'More . . . 80,000, 90,000, 100,000,' said Preeti.

Then Preeti talked of the hundreds of thousands of rupees she and Basanti would make for their families from the *dhanda*, of the rich men they would still be attracting many years from now. Would any Bedia girls ever have earnings like theirs?

The woman left the room, shaking her head at these girls who thought only of money, and returned with some water in a bowl. She washed them down, first Preeti, then Basanti, turning them round as she did so. Preeti splashed Basanti and the girls laughed nervously together because they were fearful of what would happen next. The woman went out of the room a second time before bringing food, pav bhaji, and new clothes, western clothes; blue jeans, tee shirts and a choice of gold or silver pumps.

While they ate and dressed, the woman told stories about Bedia women and their warrior blood, how brave they were, how the *dhanda* was noble work for girls as beautiful as them. She knew from experience that Bedia girls liked these lies. Weren't they told them by their good-for-nothing fathers who were descended from bandits, robbers and thieves?

'Have you ever been on a plane before?' the woman asked.

Preeti and Basanti shook their heads.

'Or a boat?'

They shook them again and giggled.

'The men who have bought you live a long way away. You will travel to them when they have paid for you.'

'Haven't we been paid for?' Preeti asked. She had seen the money. What did this woman mean?

The woman didn't answer but Basanti inquired, 'Has more than one man paid for Preeti and me?'

'Yes, more than one.'

'Not the man here, the man in the white suit?'

The woman hesitated. '. . . No.'

'Where are these men? Are they here?'

'They were watching you when you were washing and changing your clothes.'

Preeti said, 'There was no-one watching us. The door was closed.' She looked at the window to satisfy herself the blind was still drawn. It was.

The woman pointed to the corner of the room where the ceiling met the wall. A camera was suspended there. 'The men were watching you a long way away and bidding for you.'

Preeti and Basanti exchanged worried glances and hugged each other.

Basanti said, 'Where were these men?'

'In other countries . . .'

They'd heard of girls going to somewhere called Dubai. Was it another country?

'Are we going to Dubai to see these men?' Preeti asked.

The woman shrugged. 'Yes, Dubai . . .' But because of the casual way she said it neither girl believed her.

'What is happening to us, Basanti?' Preeti asked. Basanti was crying again.

After they had dressed, the man in the white suit opened the door and waited by it. The woman hugged them saying 'there, my pretty Bedia girls' and led them along the corridor to the door with the grille and down the stair to the car where the driver was waiting.

They drove to an airfield outside Mumbai.

Half a dozen other girls were there, not Bedia, but girls like Basanti and Preeti, who would never marry because their virginity was being sold, whose destiny was to earn money for their families in the *dhanda*. They were led to a plane with a white fuselage and twin propellers. Preeti and Basanti shared a seat at the back and when it took off, engines screaming, Preeti willed herself not to cry. Didn't she have to be strong for Basanti?

It landed after an hour, perhaps two. Preeti had lost track of time. Now every second had enough

11

worry for a minute; every minute enough fear for an hour.

Preeti and Basanti were the last off. They climbed into the back of a black van parked beside the aircraft's wing and saw the frightened faces of the other girls who were already inside. Preeti said a prayer, aloud. Two of the girls began whimpering. Another retched at the smell of aviation fuel. Then the doors slammed shut, imprisoning them in pitch darkness. The whimpering became anguished cries. The retching girl vomited, filling the van with its stink. Preeti said another prayer, silently, and held Basanti tight to her.

Soon the van stopped and the doors opened. Preeti saw they were on a quay in a dockyard. A large ship was beside them and a man in dark glasses and blue overalls was shouting at them to get out. Preeti and Basanti were first up the gangway. Two men took them down metal stairs, along a narrow passageway to a rusted door which opened on to a small cabin with no window or porthole. It had one bed, a toilet and a shower.

They never saw the other girls again.

Their food was brought to them once a day by a man who wore a hood. He was their only visitor, from the first day of their journey to the last.

How many days were they on the ship? Long before they were taken off, Basanti thought it had been about two months. Preeti wasn't sure. It could have been more, or less, who could tell? After that, Basanti scratched the wall every time the man brought their food. One evening he told them not to sleep, to pack up their few belongings and be ready to go ashore. Basanti counted the scratches on the wall. There were 27.

They were blindfolded before they left their room. No light seeped through to their eyes when they were out on deck. 'Is it night?' Basanti asked Preeti.

'I think so.'

The cold was what struck them. Where were they? What country had they been brought to? They were taken to the side of the ship where Basanti was guided to a ladder. She cried out, letting Preeti know what was happening to her. All Preeti heard was Basanti's terror. Then there was a shout from below – a man's voice – and a crewman nudged Preeti to follow Basanti. He lifted her on to the ladder and held her until she'd found a foothold. Her hands gripped the metal sides as she began to descend. She trembled so much she feared she would fall, but after a dozen steps rough hands grabbed at her from below.

Her wrists and ankles were secured with rope. One person tied her, another held her. A cloth was forced in her mouth. When they'd finished with her, Preeti was put to sit with Basanti and the two girls pressed against each other for warmth and reassurance. Preeti choked on the dry gag in her small mouth. She swallowed until her throat was raw. Then an engine roared, the boat's sideways rocking stopped and the breeze dried the nauseous slick from Preeti's face.

Twenty minutes later the boat bumped gently against a pier.

Basanti was taken ashore first, then Preeti. Preeti could tell a woman carried her because she was held across her torso, against her slack breasts. The woman said nothing. The only sound was the lapping of the sea and the crunch of feet on gravel. They climbed what seemed to be steps and suddenly Preeti was taken indoors. Now the only sound was the woman's feet echoing off the floor. Where was Basanti? When the woman untied her and took off her blindfold and gag Preeti saw she was in a bedroom without any windows. The woman, who was wearing water-proofs and a balaclava with slits for her eyes, opened a door to show Preeti the bathroom. She said, 'You'll like it here, pet. I know you will.' Then she left.

Preeti cried for Basanti, sweet, frightened Basanti, and for herself.

Later the first man came to her. He was short, fat, pallid and wore a mouse mask. His voice was kindly and he took Preeti to the bathroom and washed her all over with special soap before carrying her to the bed and turning out the light. She heard him take off his clothes and then she felt the bed sinking under his weight and his face pressing against hers as he kissed her. He had taken off his mask.

14

She lay still, as her father had told her, forcing herself not to flinch when it hurt.

After he'd finished, he fell asleep, snoring, and she went to the bathroom to wash the bitter smell of his sweat from her and the trail of blood from the inside of her thighs. That was the first occasion she had filled her head with the swirls and sounds of the party she would have when she returned to her village. How many more times had it filled her head? A hundred, two hundred: she lost count.

Sometimes the men stayed a night. Sometimes the same man returned night after night. Some men stayed for an hour or two and never came back. Sometimes nobody came for days. It was after one of these times that the woman entered her room, wearing her balaclava as usual, but shouting at Preeti which was not. She stuffed her few clothes into a bag and tied and blindfolded Preeti, hurting her in her hurry.

Something's wrong Preeti thought.

Then she smelled the sea, heard the crunch of the woman's feet on the gravel and dared to believe she was going home. What more proof did she need than this boat? Wasn't it the boat which had brought her ashore?

Once it was in deep water, the woman moved in the stern. She was coming towards Preeti. Her boots thudded on the planks and the boat rocked from side to side. She untied the rope at Preeti's legs, then the one binding her arms and pulled the cloth from her mouth. Preeti gulped the salt air. It tasted of freedom, sweet freedom.

When the woman took off the blindfold Preeti stared around her. It was dark. The only light was the white fluorescence on the waves rippling past the boat. Where was the ship? Where was freedom?

The woman put her arms under Preeti's legs and around her back. She was lifting her. 'Goodbye, pet,' she said. Then Preeti was falling and splashing into the sea. The shock of submersion and the cold of the water made her gasp, silencing her cry of fear. When she came back to the surface, choking and retching, the noise of the boat's engine was already fading. Preeti screamed but her voice was lost in the vastness of the ocean and in the sharp wind. She cried for her mother, her father and Basanti. She begged to see her sisters again. One of them would be sold for the *dhanda* if Preeti did not return. Please, no.

She began to sink, gulping water into her lungs. Her throat and windpipe burned. Her chest felt as if it would burst. She lunged again for the surface, taking one more frantic breath before dipping back under the waves.

Now she was playing *Kabaddi*. She was running and running, sprinting for the line where her team-mates were calling for her, cheering her on, urging her to go faster. The opposing team was chasing close behind but she was fast. She had twenty paces remaining. Could she cross the line without taking another breath? One more step. One more step. One more step. Was she there? She had to breathe.

She gasped for air but cold sea water rushed in swamping her tired lungs.

CHAPTER 2

Rule number 1: know your escape route.
Did he? Did he hell.

When the sensor detected him and the floodlights blazed, Cal McGill ran on impulse towards the now brightly illuminated boundary wall. On top of it was a paling fence, erected to protect the new Environment Minister's garden from the prying eyes of neighbours or curious passers-by. Each plank had been cut to a point, giving the fence a saw-tooth appearance. Cal leapt at the wall but the sudden klaxon wailing of an intruder alarm made him hurry. His foot slipped on a wet stone and he fell, arms flailing, on to the fence, one of the posts stabbing his rib cage. He cried out, threw himself sideways and tumbled into the dark of the back lane. The hard impact of the grass verge knocked the breath from him. He grunted. A pain seared at the side of his ribs.

The base of the wall was lower in the lane than in the minister's garden. From here, the alarm sounded muffled and distant. Cal lay dazed, wiping grit from his hands, and groaning until an approaching police siren raised him unsteadily to his feet. He attempted to run, but every step tore at his wound and he resigned himself to hobbling along the cinder lane, aware of a sequence of events unfolding behind him.

The police siren gave a final strangulated whoop as the patrol car arrived at the minister's house.

The klaxon intruder alarm went silent.

A dog howled: an eager lupine baying, the kind of noise Cal imagined a trained hound emitted when it first nosed the scent of its fleeing quarry.

He swore, lurching away. At the end of the lane was a gateway and he passed through it into what seemed to be a field. The ground underfoot was even but his injury made him unsteady and the darkness disorientated him. After stumbling twice, he twisted his right ankle. On a different occasion he might have broken his fall with his hands. But, as he toppled sideways, another stab of pain came from his ribs and he held his arms tight to him for protection. His right shoulder crashed against a stone and the side of his face pushed into mud. He grunted again.

Now he was alert, listening, barely breathing.

The police dog would soon be upon him: running softly, sure-footedly in the dark. He imagined the rhythmic plop of its pads on the damp earth; its relentless intensity of purpose, its jaws hanging with sloppy webs of saliva. He drew in his legs, covered his face with his arms and waited for the shock of its teeth. Seconds passed, a minute. Now the only sound was the wailing of another approaching police car and he dared to think the baying had been a village dog disturbed by the commotion of alarms and sirens. He pushed himself to his knees, still half-expecting a canine missile to lunge at him from the dark. He listened for a moment longer, then stood and staggered away, leading with his left leg and dragging the right after him.

He crossed one field and climbed a fence into another where the land started to fall away steeply. He followed its slope and soon the lights of a village appeared ahead of him, half a dozen at first, then more stretching to his left and right. Cal felt in his anorak pocket for his mobile phone and turned it on, shielding it to conceal the green glow from its screen. The time was 11.48pm. It would be dawn in about five hours. Then he'd have to trust to his only piece of pre-planning. He'd searched the local bus company's website and found the late night service. It departed the Environment Minister's village at 11.40pm, eight minutes ago. Just in case, he'd also checked the early morning services. A bus visited all the villages in this area between 7.30 and 8.15, picking up schoolchildren. This was his contingency. Another time, he'd work it out better. Why was it always another time?

The village lights were no more than 200 metres from him now, a field away on the other side of a hawthorn hedge which was silhouetted against the sky. Cal crawled under its branches and rested his back against a stump. His left hand instinctively reached for his side. His fingers found the tear in his anorak and felt the stickiness of congealing blood on his tee shirt. He decided not to try to clean it. His hands were grazed and dirty from falling and anyway it was too dark for him to see what he was doing. He pressed the fabric softly against the wound, staunching whatever bleeding there was, before finding his iPod in his anorak pocket and shutting off the outside world.

It was unusual for him to sleep badly outside. At any season of the year he'd go to the islands and bed down on the sand if the weather was fine or under canvas if it wasn't. But this night he fretted about missing the pre-dawn. He wanted to be on the move before daylight for his approach to the village, in case the police were out hunting for him. He woke three or four times, checking the time, searching for the sky lightening behind the village, cursing when it was as dark as the last time. Then he fell into a deep sleep, lying on his left-hand side, muffling his phone alarm, and was woken by two pigeons fluttering noisily in the hedge beside him. His eyes flicked wide. Light washed the surrounding fields and hedges with the bright greens of May. Cal swore and opened his phone. It was 7.20, only ten minutes before the bus made the first stop on its morning schedule.

He twisted around to where remnant wisps of mist were lifting above the village, a neat collection of two dozen houses around a church and what looked like a hotel. The field between him and it was a football pitch, bordered on the short side by a stone wall which extended close to Cal's resting place. He crawled to it and climbed over, jarring himself when he landed on the other side. With stiff fingers he probed at his wound. The blood was dry to touch. Then, crouching, he made his stumbling advance towards the village. Half way there he peered over the wall. A terrace of cottages stretched to his right. The bus stop was outside the hotel which had Craw's Nest in black gothic script above its door. Cal ducked down and continued to the road-side fence. As he reached it he heard the sound of an approaching engine. It was a car, a red Volkswagen, not the bus arriving early or a police patrol. But standing by the bus stop were a child in school uniform and a man with a tweed cap; father and son, he assumed. They had their backs to him. He put his right foot on top of the fence and jumped into the road. The jolt of the tarmac forced from him a stifled cry of pain. He looked up anxiously but neither man nor boy had noticed him.

Cal pulled his anorak straight, brushed the tops of his jeans and crossed to the pavement. He was only 20 metres from the bus stop when father and son saw him. The man shot Cal an unguarded look of suspicion. His hand went protectively to the boy's shoulder.

'Good morning, fine day,' the man said, his country manners overcoming his wariness. His voice croaked and he coughed to clear it. Cal noticed his hands. They were big and his fingers were swollen red. His trousers were tucked into labourer's boots.

'It is, it is,' Cal mumbled and put his head down to discourage further conversation. He stepped back on the pavement to keep his distance.

Four more children, three girls and a boy, were coming towards the bus stop. When they saw Cal they squinted slyly at him. The tallest girl whispered something and all four put their hands over their mouths and giggled. Cal turned away. He didn't want them giving the police a description apart from what was obvious and unhelpful: male, 5'10, wearing black North Face anorak, black hood, dirty jeans and walking boots. He pushed the zip on his hood to tighten it and pulled it forward so the rim extended over his eyes and beyond the sides of his face.

When he turned back the man was looking down the road but his son was staring, eyes wide, at Cal's right thigh. There was a stain of dried blood, the size of a fist, on his jeans. Cal swivelled his hip to hide it just as the bus appeared round the corner. It slowed with an exhalation of brakes. When the door opened, the children raced up the steps to the back seats.

The father waved to his son and took a few uncertain steps along the pavement before stopping and glancing back at Cal. He seemed torn about leaving his boy on a bus with this stranger. But he turned and strode off, as if he'd decided that nothing bad could happen at 7.45 on a beautiful May morning in a village which last bothered the crime statistics seven years before when a joy-rider ran a stolen car into the side of the Craw's Nest.

The bus driver, a red-faced bald man, who had greeted the children cheerily by their first names, noticed Cal when he was on the bottom step. 'Lovely morning,' he called out.

Cal, his head down, asked if the bus was going to West Linton.

'Aye, that's where we go in the mornings.'

'Where do I get the connection to Edinburgh?'

'That'll be the stop by the school.'

Cal found a two pound coin in his pocket, collected his change and sat behind the driver. As the bus climbed uphill and veered left at a fork in the road, Cal noticed the signpost, swore and slid in his seat. The bus was returning him to the Environment Minister's village, to the scene of his crime.

The first houses were soon visible through flowering chestnut trees. The minister's house, a former Church of Scotland manse, was at the far end of the single street. Cal pulled his hood further over his head. A police car was parked at the gates of the property, a three storey Georgian building surrounded by flower beds with neat lawns and gravel paths lined with box hedges. The height of the bus allowed Cal a view over the wall to the saw-toothed fence. He saw where he'd skewered himself – one of the palings had snapped. Then he noticed the floodlights above the porch door and on the gable.

What puzzled him was why it had taken so long for the sensor to detect him and the lights to flash on. The delay had caught him off guard. He'd been in the garden for almost three minutes before he'd triggered the lights or the alarm.

Now Cal searched for the alarm box but instead he saw something which sent a shock of apprehension through him. On the first floor, between the two lights, was a small black camera on a wall mount. It ranged slowly backwards and forwards as Cal watched it. Why had he looked up?

Rule number 2: wear a hood. He had.

Rule number 3: never look up. He had; the moment the lights blazed; his face a pale, reflective moon with a startled expression staring into a camera.

Why?

Detective Inspector David Ryan's day started badly with a phone call at 5.30am. It was the control room at headquarters with a message from the Assistant Chief Constable ordering him to take charge of a 'politically sensitive case'.

'There's been an intruder in the Environment Minister's garden . . .' the duty Sergeant began. 'It was last night . . . it's taken a few hours to filter through from division.'

Ryan swore. Already it sounded like a short straw.

'. . . The ACC wants you out there as soon as possible because of the significant political risk to the force.' Anticipating Ryan's temper, the Sergeant added a quick disclaimer. 'His words not mine.'

'Was anything taken, was there any damage?'

'Apart from a bit of broken fencing, not a blade of grass was harmed as far as the local boys can tell.'

'So it could have been a drunk, straying off course.'

'It's possible.'

Ryan swore again. 'Where does this minister live?'

'A couple of miles outside West Linton . . .'

'Text me the address and post-code,' Ryan snapped.

He showered, put on his clothes and drove to the by-pass, programming his sat-nav at the first set of red lights. There was so little traffic he'd cleared Edinburgh and was skirting the Pentland Hills to the south-west of the city in less than 20 minutes. No more than 10 minutes later he was driving through the minister's gates. Then there'd been delay after delay, some of it routine and unavoidable, some of it not. Ryan had stopped distinguishing between them during the minister's wife's harangue about the muddy police footprints on her hall and drawing room carpets.

Short of offering to clean them himself what was he supposed to say?

At first he tried appeasement. 'I'm sorry madam.' Hadn't the officers in question been checking the house for intruders? Hadn't their concern been madam's safety?

Madam this, madam that.

But on she went, about her book group meeting later that morning, about the forensic team 'cluttering up the place' when her guests arrived, about the police making more mess in the garden than the intruder.

When, at last, Ryan extricated himself he drove to the local police station. He spent an hour waiting for the officers who attended the scene the night before to drag themselves out of their beds to answer his questions about their (inadequate) crime report. He didn't mention their footprints on the minister's carpets. In his opinion it was the only thing they did half right; taught that bloody woman a lesson.

The return journey to headquarters took another 40 minutes and tried his patience some more. Ryan idled angrily in one rush hour traffic jam after another. Now, he was snatching a late breakfast of tea and a cheese sandwich in the canteen when a civilian technician handed him a file. Inside were a mug-shot and a record sheet. The face recognition programme had identified the intruder caught on the minister's security camera as a petty offender cum political activist called Caladh McGill with an address in south Edinburgh.

Ryan swore again.

Everything about McGill smelt small time, way below where Ryan set his radar.

CHAPTER 3

The last hurrah of the Edinburgh property boom was a former whisky bond on the road between the old port of Leith and the harbour at Granton where the sailing crowd kept their boats. The buy-to-let investors who bought off plan in July 2007 and stumped up their deposits had baled out before completing their purchases six months later. By now, The Cask, the building's refurbished name, was showing its neglect. The red and white banner which proclaimed '1 & 2 bedroom luxury penthouses for sale' was grimy with exhaust fumes. Underneath it was another, loosely flapping, which announced 'For rent/may sell 25% reduction for quick completion'. It was erected last spring for the upturn in the market which never happened. There had been no buyers. There had been no viewers.

Instead the developer had done a deal with a social housing association to deter the bank, now majority owned by the British taxpayers, from repossessing the property. The association signed low rental leases on four of the 20 flats: 'transition homes' for teenagers coming out of care. The only other occupant was Cal. The developer let him live rent free in a 'studio penthouse' with views of the abandoned flour mill across the waste ground opposite in lieu of payment for caretaking duties. Cal's 'grace and favour' flat, as the developer liked to describe it with a heavy inflection of sarcasm, was on the top, fourth, floor where the lift now deposited him with a final judder.

His apartment was at the far end of the landing. Recessed ceiling lights flickered on ahead of him. Cal dropped his chin to his chest to avoid their glare. Despite his weariness, the irony of it forced a wry smile: why hadn't he done the same last night when the lights blazed in the Environment Minister's garden?

His door, bearing the sign, 'Cal McGill, Flotsam and Jetsam Investigations', opened onto a large airy studio separated into living and sleeping areas by shelves on a metal gantry two metres high. Cal turned left past the sleeping area to the bathroom, descending the three steps slowly, holding his side. He untied the laces of his mud-stained boots, kicked them off, undid his belt and let his jeans and underwear fall to the tiled floor. His legs were muscular and white with a purple scar below the left knee, the result of a sea diving accident two months before. He unzipped his anorak which dropped from his shoulders revealing a blood stain on his tee shirt stretching from under his right arm to his hip. Cal pulled at the fabric but it stuck firm and he

30

went to find scissors before padding flat footed into the rainstorm shower.

The first deluge of water was ice cold and made him gasp. As it warmed, he cut away the tee shirt until all that remained was a circle of bloodied cotton glued to his flank. He teased at it, loosening it in the stream of water, finally exposing a livid, ragged tear of flesh five or six centimetres long. Cal turned off the shower and dabbed at the wound with tissues until water and blood stopped flowing. Towelling himself, he climbed the stairs to the sparsely furnished sleeping area. A mattress was on the floor with a crumpled duvet across it, and at its foot was a trunk with the lid open from which he took a pair of white boxers. He put them on with one hand while holding on to the gantry of shelves with the other, taking care not to disturb any of the 273 (at the last count) artefacts and curiosities washed up by the sea that he stored there.

The discovery he valued most was on the top shelf: a 1.2 metre-long green turtle shell he'd come across while walking the long ribbon of beach on the Atlantic west coast of South Uist. It had been half buried by sand after an October storm. He'd hauled it to the road and thumbed a lift back to his tent. That night he'd opened up his maps and imagined the seas the turtle had travelled and by what freak of weather or orientation it had ended its journeying on the Outer Hebrides. As with his other finds, a label recorded the date of discovery and the relevant coordinates. (Like an antique collector, provenance was important to him.)

Cal rummaged again in the trunk for a clean tee shirt. He put it on and went to the kitchen which was opposite his sleeping area in an alcove with a spiral staircase to the roof. Cal leaned against the iron banister rail, waiting for the kettle to boil. He made coffee, black, and carried his mug to his work table which filled the living area. Either end of it was laden with oceanography books, rolled maps and files. The middle was taken up by his computers: two desk tops and a laptop which travelled with him on his research trips. Between the desktops were a telephone and a double photograph frame. On one side of the frame was an old sepia portrait of a weather-burnished young man wearing a woollen hat. On the other, in colour, was a photograph of a white gravestone by a curved stone wall and an azure sea beyond.

Cal sat at his swivel chair. Two maps were on the wall behind him, between large windows. One was of the world's ocean currents. Cold currents were in darkening blues, shaded according to temperature. The warm ones were in oranges and deep reds. The second, smaller map was of the North Atlantic and the Arctic. Different coloured pins were stuck into it with pieces of string leading from them to newspaper cuttings attached to the wall. Each told the story of an unidentified body which had been washed ashore or retrieved from the sea. The largest of them reported the discovery three years before of a young Indian girl whose remains had become entangled in the nets of a fishing boat near the Island of Scarba off the Argyll coast.

Cal touched his left hand against his wound, checking it for bleeding, and with his right he switched on his desktops. Then he logged on to googlemail and scanned his inbox. There were 28 new messages. He opened one from DLG. 'Hey guys, listen in to the radio news. Severed foot found at Seacliff beach. Mad eh?'

Cal clicked on the BBC website. There was a brief story on the Scotland news page.

'The remains of a human foot were found this morning by a woman walking her dog on a beach in East Lothian. Police are searching the area for more body parts.

'A spokesman for Lothian and Borders Police said, "Our inquiries are at a very early stage. We'd like anyone who saw anything suspicious on Seacliff beach, five miles east of North Berwick, to come forward."

'Seacliff is a well known beauty spot close to the ruins of Tantallon Castle.'

Cal slid the keyboard of the other computer towards him. It was his reference library. At the last count he'd stored 48,422 pictures and hundreds of folders and documents containing maps, research papers and ocean data collected by marine scientists around the world.

His search for 'foot Columbia' brought up seven

files, one for each of the severed feet which washed up on British Columbian and US Pacific shorelines between August 2007 and November 2008. Cal remembered most of the details because they were bizarre even for someone like him accustomed to the sea's habit of throwing peculiar objects on to the shore.

All the feet had been encased in lightweight trainers; there had been two matching pairs. Only one foot had been identified – it belonged to a depressive, a male. The theory was he drowned himself. According to local speculation, the other feet belonged to the passengers of a light aircraft which had crashed into the sea near the discoveries.

What Cal couldn't recall was the physiological explanation. He found it in a file, named Kirkland, after the island where the fourth foot had been discovered. There was a comment from British Columbia's chief coroner, Terry Smith. 'This may very well be nothing more than the results of a natural process of decomposition in water and the combined effects of predation by aquatic scavengers.'

In another report of the time, an unnamed medical expert described the process as 'disarticulation'. He told CBC News how the ankle joint could separate naturally from the leg once the body had reached an advanced stage of decay. 'What seems to be happening here is these disarticulated feet are being brought to the surface by the buoyancy of the shoes. There's a natural explanation for this though how so many bodies got into the water is harder to explain and may have a criminal connection.' Cal read the remaining three files. By the time he'd finished DLG had mailed again. 'The foot was found at about 7.30am. The woman's dog brought it to her!'

Cal replied, 'Thanks, DLG. Send me anything you hear. I'm interested.' He checked his wind data: a light easterly had been blowing for a day or two. Then he traced his finger down his tide chart. High tide that morning at Dunbar, the nearest reading point to Seacliff, had been an hour and ten minutes ago, at 11.44am. The foot probably came ashore the previous night when high tide was at 23.34, about the time he'd been escaping from the Environment Minister's garden.

A map of the North Sea now filled Cal's screen. He magnified the area around the Forth Estuary and the East Lothian coast where a whorl of arrows displayed the direction of the currents. He considered the possibilities: the foot could have travelled long-distance down the east coast on the southerly flood of Atlantic waters which poured through the Fair Isle channel between Shetland and Orkney, or it could have been washed eastwards along the Forth. Cal looked at the file recording bodies beaching on the estuary's coastline. There'd been six in the last nine months: five were suicides and the last, a yachtsman, had a heart attack and fell overboard.

How many more were lying submerged was anyone's guess. They could remain on the bottom for years if the water was deep enough and undisturbed by storms or fishing boats. Had the foot disarticulated from a corpse lying in deep, calm, estuarial water? It was possible.

He opened an email from WWF Scotland inquiring about Cal's investigation into a cluster of fishing nets found floating in the Moray Firth, near Inverness. Four bottle-nose dolphins had become caught in their mesh and drowned.

Cal replied, 'I'm making progress. The variety of net is used widely by the Spanish fleet. I'm waiting for information from the net distributor.'

Then he emailed DLG. 'Do you know if there was a shoe?'

DLG emailed back. 'What do you mean?'

'Was the severed foot at Seacliff beach wearing a trainer?'

'Why?'

'It could make all the difference. If the foot wasn't wearing a trainer, it's more likely it was dumped there.'

Cal sipped at his coffee which had gone cold. It matched his mood. Why had he looked up? It rankled still. What would the camera have caught: his mouth, his nose; perhaps not even his mouth? What use was that to the police?

Somehow he didn't feel reassured.

Next time he'd plan it better.

CHAPTER 4

Detective Inspector David Ryan lit another cigarette, his third in twenty minutes. After inhaling once, he dropped it to the pavement, squashed it under his heel and glanced again at his watch. It had gone 2.30pm. They'd already been standing there more than an hour: five officers wasting their time, because Detective Constable Helen Jamieson didn't know the meaning of the word urgent. He sighed and kicked at another discarded, half-smoked butt which skittered smouldering across the concrete slab. The Procurator Fiscal said everything was arranged: a sheriff would sign the search warrant at 1pm. Ryan had made the call and set it up for Jamieson. All Jamieson had to do was collect the warrant from the fiscal's office 'any time after 1.15'. How long did it take to drive from the Fiscal's office to Granton, for Christ's sake? Ryan's worry now was the story breaking in the media before he'd made an arrest. How long before the Environment Minister told his colleagues in the Scottish Parliament or his whiney wife the entire fucking world?

'Come on Jamieson.' He sighed again. 'Hurry up, you ugly bitch.'

Ryan had already wasted time knocking up what turned out to be the wrong house in the city's south side. It was owned by McGill's father but let to tenants who hadn't seen Caladh McGill or Cal as they called him for nine months, perhaps more. No, they didn't have a forwarding address, though the letting agents might. The letting agents said McGill senior was abroad teaching in Swaziland and the only contact they had with McGill junior was a mobile number. It had taken another hour and a half to trace the phone's signal to a converted whisky bond in the north of the city. Now, the hold-up was the search warrant. Ryan had rung Jamieson four times and each time he'd been told it was on its way. Christ, where was the fat cow?

Leaning against a warehouse wall, sheltered from the sea-breeze, Ryan lit another cigarette and stared impassively across an empty car park. His mobile beeped. He flipped open the phone. 'About fucking time,' he muttered angrily.

It was a message from Jamieson. 'I'm by your car with the warrant.'

Ryan shut the phone without replying and crossed the street to stay hidden from McGill's flat on the top floor of The Cask. Ryan's car was 100 metres along the road on the forecourt of an abandoned petrol station. Jamieson watched her senior officer's progress in her rear view mirror.

There was something ungainly about him at a distance which amused her: the imperfect David Ryan. Either his thighs were too big or his lower leg too short. Whatever it was, when he was walking like that, with his chest thrust out, his feet flicking purposefully forward, his body looked too big and his legs too short.

Would she?

It was a question she asked herself occasionally.

Would she, if she had the opportunity?

Jamieson had tried to warn the new Detective Constable about Ryan over coffee in the canteen. 'He hits on every woman sooner or later.'

Which wasn't strictly true, since he hadn't hit on Jamieson.

But in DC Tessa Rainey's case it would be sooner, not later. She was a tall, slim brunette with a bob and a pretty oval face. One of the other female detectives, Sandra Paterson, interrupted Jamieson mid-caution. 'All you need to know Tessa is he's six foot, cropped brown hair, handsome face and narrow eyes, a mysterious green. And . . .' she licked her lips provocatively, 'he's hot, a dish, always dresses in single-breasted blue suits and white shirts, no tie, two buttons undone, always two.'

'Sounds good to me,' said DC Rainey.

Jamieson had smiled weakly and sipped her coffee. When the conversation drifted to another subject she leaned over to Rainey. 'Wait till you meet Ryan and you'll see what I mean.'

Rainey gave her the kind of pitying look she'd

suffered so often before. In one exaggerated and contemptuous sweep, it took in Jamieson's thinning curly hair, her red face and her size 18 bulges. 'Can't wait . . .'

Jamieson flushed some more.

Then Paterson chipped in, 'Just because he doesn't want to shag you Helen . . .' and the new girl Rainey had laughed.

Jamieson was angry with herself for minding and for letting it show. Rainey didn't have an IQ of 173, or a first class degree in law, or an MSc in criminology. Nor could she speak three languages. Jamieson had. Jamieson did, Jamieson could. Jamieson had read Rainey's file. She was bright enough but not in Jamieson's league. Sometimes she wanted to scream it aloud. *I'm not the person you see. I'm someone else, someone better.*

Still, DC Rainey was an innocent by comparison to Ryan, a silly kid. Someone had to warn her off. 'Listen Tessa . . .' Jamieson's kept her voice low, to impress Rainey with her sincerity. 'Ryan's a ruthless bastard. Watch out for him.'

Her final piece of corroborative evidence – Ryan's continuing bachelorhood – she decided to keep to herself. She'd already said too much. Ryan was 39 and no woman hung around him long enough to marry him. There had to be a reason apart from the congestion around his bathroom mirror.

Rainey and Paterson had exchanged glances after Jamieson's warning; and Paterson winked at the new girl. 'The best ones are bastards. Don't you think, Tessa?' The two detectives sniggered and Jamieson excused herself, inelegantly as usual. Her hips stuck on the arms of her chair and when she stood it rose with her.

Would she? No, she wouldn't. But somebody, some time would be nice.

Ryan was on the garage forecourt when Jamieson stepped out of her car. She patted her shoulder bag.

'Got it, boss.'

'About bloody time.' he said, passing her without looking at her.

She started to explain the delay. 'The sheriff spends half his lunch-time in the bookies . . . the fiscal had to wait.' But Ryan wasn't listening. He'd gone to the back of his car, opened the boot, removed his suit jacket and was putting on body armour.

When he re-emerged, Jamieson said, 'McGill's not dangerous is he sir?'

'Oh, I doubt it, Jamieson.' Ryan looked at her as if he'd achieved high enough status to be spared close proximity to a plain woman. 'I'm sure he's harmless. Stick by me and you'll be safe enough.'

Here lies Helen Jamieson, the only female detective constable who was safe with Inspector Ryan.

Jamieson reddened. 'That's not what I meant sir.'

Ryan shrugged. 'Well, it's what you *asked*, Jamieson.'

He ignored her and walked to the white Audi in front, banged twice on the roof and leant down at the open window. 'Ok, let's go.'

The front doors opened and two uniformed officers emerged. They wore helmets, with the visors up. The taller and squarer of the two carried a black metal tube enclosing a battering ram. Jamieson trailed five steps behind them. Two more officers, Detective Constables like Jamieson, were watching the front and back of the building. They were in jeans, trainers and sweatshirts.

It had been Ryan's decision to go mob-handed even though McGill's record suggested he was a small-time political activist who strayed incidentally into minor criminality. He had two previous convictions, both on the same day in 2003. He'd been arrested and charged with breach of the peace during a rowdy demonstration in Glasgow against the Iraq War. After a body search, the second charge had been added: possession of cannabis. The cases were heard together at Glasgow Sheriff Court. He'd pleaded guilty and was fined – £180 and £250 respectively – for each offence. He was 22 at the time and studying for a degree in marine science at the Scottish Marine Institute at Dunstaffnage near Oban. A mug shot taken then had provided the match for the face in the minister's security camera.

The next entry in McGill's file was July 2005 when he was described as a self-employed research student. He'd been arrested with a crowd of demonstrators who broke through police lines at the G8 Summit at Gleneagles Hotel, Perthshire. He was released without charge. There'd been no new entries for the past four years, nothing until last night. Which begged the question: had McGill changed from small-time agitator to something more worrying?

Ryan doubted it, but still. The Chief Constable was taking an interest. The media wouldn't be far behind. Small-time or not Ryan had to arrest him, and quickly. If he screwed up, he knew what the headlines would be. There'd also be questions in the Scottish Parliament. 'Does the Justice Minister have complete confidence in the Environment Minister's local police force?' Ryan's application to transfer to the Scottish Crime and Drug Enforcement Agency would be in jeopardy if this became a media circus.

As Ryan approached The Cask, one of the watching detectives left his position at the corner of the building and pointed up. 'McGill's flat is top floor right, sir.'

Ryan went in, crossing the tiled hallway, and checked the lift, opening the outer door to prevent anyone above using it. He motioned to the other officers to follow him up the stairs. '. . . in case he's on the way down.'

On the landing before the top floor, Ryan held back and asked Jamieson, 'All right, Jamieson?'

'Yes sir.'

'Stick by me, ok.' Ryan grinned.

Jamieson, reddening again, said, 'Thank you, sir.'

Ryan went down the corridor first. The overhead lights flashed on as he approached McGill's apartment. He glanced at the 'Flotsam and Jetsam Investigations' sign, arched his eyebrow and whispered, 'Chris'sake, he's a nut.' Jamieson pointed to the key which was in the lock. Ryan turned it slowly and the door swung open on to a bright room filled with a long table, maps, books and assorted piles of paper. A young man with short dark hair, wearing a black tee shirt and white boxers jumped from a chair behind a group of computers. He let out a shout of surprise.

'What the fuck . . .'

His hair was shorter than in the 2003 mug shot, but it was the same face, the same slanting nose.

'Caladh McGill?' Ryan said coolly, looking around. 'Are you Caladh McGill?'

Cal nodded.

'My name's Ryan, Detective Inspector Ryan, and these are police officers. We need to talk.'

One of the uniformed officers ran past Ryan and ordered Cal to put his hands behind his back. He leant forward and the officer cuffed them.

'See, what did I say?' Ryan turned to Jamieson. 'Harmless enough . . .'

'Yes sir.' Jamieson scowled.

'Caution him, Jamieson.'

When she'd finished, Ryan held up Cal's front door key. 'Yours, I presume. Lucky no-one let themselves in with it.'

Ryan put it on the table which he walked around, the fingers of his right hand trailing across the books and files, leaving a line in the dust. 'Flotsam and Jetsam Investigations; what does that mean, Mr McGill?'

Ryan studied the shelves containing Cal's artefacts.

Cal shrugged. 'It's what I do?'

'Well I'll have to take your word for that Mr McGill. What does it involve?'

'I work for environmental organisations tracking back on oil spills, containers which have gone overboard, fishing nets. They use me to find polluters.'

'How?'

'You can work it out from wind speeds and data on ocean currents.'

'So . . .' Ryan was now behind McGill, looking at the ocean maps on the wall. 'What ocean current or wind took you to the Environment Minister's garden last night?'

Cal said nothing.

'Suit yourself.' Ryan turned to Jamieson. 'Show Mr McGill the search warrant.'

Ryan had seen the spiral staircase leading to a small landing and a half-sized door in the roof. 'And try up there, Jamieson,' he said, settling into the armchair in the corner under the window by the shelves. Beside it, on the floor, was an untidy pile of books. Ryan lifted two titles off the top and put them on his lap. The first was 'Science of the Seven Seas' by Henry Stommel. The other, by the same author, was called 'The Gulf Stream: a Physical and Dynamical Description'.

Ryan held them up to Cal. 'Who's this guy, Henry Stommel?'

'He's an oceanographer.'

'Anyone special?'

'You could say that.'

'In what way?'

'For his work on the thermohaline circulation of the oceans . . .'

'The what?' Ryan pursed his lips. 'Help me out Mr McGill. I'm just an ignorant policeman.' There was a sneer in his voice.

'It's the system of ocean currents which distributes heat around the globe.'

Ryan looked at the ocean maps. 'So why does someone who reads "Science of the Seven Seas",' he held up Stommel's book, 'spend his nights in someone else's garden? That shouldn't be so hard a question, should it now?'

Cal said nothing and Ryan watched Jamieson climb awkwardly up the stairs. She stopped at the top, red and embarrassed, feeling her senior officer's unspoken disdain. Her skirt was too tight.

'All right Jamieson?'

She heard the amusement in his voice.

Ha bloody ha, sir.

'Yes sir. Why wouldn't I be sir?'

Ryan stood up, putting the books behind him on the chair. From the table he picked up a buff-coloured file labelled 'Flotsam/Jetsam 2006'. He flicked through its contents in a casual, uninterested way before replacing it. He walked along the shelves peering through them at Cal's unmade bed when he noticed the open door of the bathroom. He went to take a look. Blood-stained tissues were strewn across the tiled floor. A bloodied section of tee shirt lay outside the shower.

'That's quite a lot of blood Mr McGill. What happened?'

'I cut myself.'

'Did you now? I wonder where.'

'It was nowhere.'

'It must have been somewhere Mr McGill.'

'Nowhere special is what I meant.'

Jamieson re-emerged on the wooden landing at the top of the spiral stairs.

'Anything Jamieson?'

'Some pot plants. There's a kind of roof garden up there.'

'Very nice too. Was there a fence up there Jamieson?'

'No sir.'

'Did you know that someone broke the Environment Minister's new fence last night, Mr McGill?'

Cal shrugged.

Ryan sat on the edge of the table and reached into his pocket. He unfolded a copy of the security camera photograph of Cal and showed it to him. 'You see we know you were there. We just don't know why you were there.'

A slow smile spread across Cal's face.

'I was doing some gardening ok?'

'Well that's better Mr McGill. What time?'

'About 11pm.'

Ryan looked at the print-out. '11.23 and 20 seconds Mr McGill. Is that where you hurt yourself?'

Cal nodded.

'You're under arrest Mr McGill.'

Ryan turned to Jamieson. 'Get the doctor here. I don't want Mr McGill moved until he's been examined.'

'That's not necessary,' Cal said.

'It is, you know. I want your injuries recorded by the doctor before we move you. I wouldn't want you claiming police brutality. So we might as well get to know each other while we wait, mightn't we?'

Jamieson finished speaking into her mobile. 'The doctor'll be half an hour sir?'

'That's fine. Half an hour should be time enough for Mr McGill to come up with a good story.'

Cal didn't react.

'Jamieson, start going through his stuff,' Ryan commanded. 'See what you can find.'

He pointed to the computers. 'We'll want those . . . might as well take them away now.'

Cal began to protest. 'I need them for my work.'

'Well Mr McGill, you should have thought of that.'

Jamieson was beside Cal at his computers. She tapped return on one of the keyboards. The screen-saver of waves crashing on a beach cleared away. In its place were seven pictures of trainers. They were in two rows, four on the top and three on

48

the bottom. Each picture was captioned. The file name was 'British Columbia: severed feet.'

'Sir,' Jamieson said. 'Want to have a look at this?'

As Ryan walked round the table, Jamieson hit the return key on the other machine. Cal's email inbox appeared on the screen. She clicked on Cal's conversation with DLG. 'Sir, you'd better look at this too.'

Ryan leaned across Jamieson to read the emails.

'What do you know about the foot found at Seacliff?'

'Nothing.'

'It doesn't look like nothing.'

'I know a severed foot has been found. That's all.'

'Why did you ask if a shoe had been found?'

'It might make the difference.'

'To what?'

'It makes it more likely the foot came ashore on the tide rather than it being dumped on the beach by someone.'

'Would you like to explain?'

Cal told Ryan and Jamieson about the severed feet in British Columbia and the process of disarticulation.

'So if the foot's wearing a shoe, it floats away when the body decomposes,' Ryan said.

'If it's wearing a shoe with a buoyant sole, like a trainer, it can do, yes.'

'Who's this guy DLG?'

'I don't know him.'

'Come on Mr McGill. He's emailing you. You seem on good terms.'

49

'I know his email address, but I don't know his real name.'

'Well you know DLG?'

'Yes, but it's just a name he uses.'

'What does it stand for?'

'Doctor Long Ghost.'

Ryan put both hands on the edge of the table and lowered his head until it was at the same level as Cal's. 'Don't screw around with me, Mr McGill.' The menace was unmistakeable.

'I'm not. DLG's a member of a beach-combing society. All the members have pseudonyms. I don't know their real names. They help me out with my research work.'

Jamieson had resumed searching through Cal's recent emails. 'Is there a Mack?' she asked.

The question irritated Ryan and he stared contemptuously at his subordinate. 'What's that got to do with it?'

Cal didn't pick up on Ryan's annoyance. 'Yeah, there's a Mack. He's the leader of the group.'

'Like in the book,' Jamieson said.

'Can someone let me in on this private conversation?' Ryan sounded exasperated. 'What are you talking about Jamieson?'

'Sir, we're talking about *Omoo*, an autobiographical novel by Herman Melville who wrote Moby Dick, sir.'

'Why?' Ryan snapped.

'Well sir, Doctor Long Ghost is one of the characters in it, so is Mack. Omoo is supposed to be the first book in the English language to use the word beach-comber. But it's Mr McGill's story . . .' Jamieson half bowed to Cal, thankfully passing him the baton of Ryan's contempt.

'Yeah,' he said, 'the book's an account of Melville's time on whaling ships in the south-seas. Its title comes from a Polynesian word for a man who roves from one island to another. Mack was the leader of a gang of rovers or beach-combers described by Melville; and DLG or Doctor Long Ghost was the doctor on board a whaler called *The Julia.*'

Ryan shook his head in bemusement. 'What's that got to do with a foot on an east Lothian beach?'

Cal shrugged, 'Only that Omoo is the name of the beach-combing group to which DLG belongs. It's a kind of a listening post for anything interesting that washes ashore all around Scotland.'

'And they get in touch with you.'

'More often than not, they do. It helps me with my computer modelling and I can help them.'

'How?'

'Tracking back and finding out where any flotsam they discover might have started its journey.'

'What's your pseudonym Mr McGill?' Jamieson asked. 'Bembo?'

Cal smiled. 'No. I'm not dangerous.'

'The Environment Minister might disagree,' Jamieson said.

'Enough . . .' Ryan glowered with irritation. 'Who or what is Bembo?'

'Bembo,' said Jamieson, 'was the harpooner, who was "remarkably quiet, though something in his eye showed he was far from being harmless".'

It was clear to Ryan she was quoting from the book, a book what's more he'd never even heard of. 'I'm in a madhouse,' he muttered under his breath but loud enough for Cal and Jamieson to hear. Ryan brushed the track of dust from his trousers where they'd rested against the edge of the table. 'Well thank you for that little diversion around the South Seas Mr McGill but I'm much more interested in what you were doing in a government minister's garden.'

Cal replied immediately and matter-of-factly. 'I was planting a Dryas Octopetala.'

As if it was obvious and the question was unnecessary.

'A what?'

'It's a type of arctic flower.'

Ryan looked at Jamieson for help. 'I suppose you know what he's talking about this time too.'

'No sir. I don't.'

This was the fifth time.

The first time Basanti had screamed at its unexpectedness. She had tried to twist away from him but his weight on her shoulder trapped her in her chair while his right hand groped at her breasts through her shirt. Then he heard a noise outside in the corridor, the sound of the outer door opening, and he broke away frightened of being caught by the men who owned her and who employed him, an Albanian, without the proper papers, without any English. He gathered up his things, a bucket, a mop and a vacuum cleaner and hurried away without looking at her.

The second time, she'd been in the chair in front of the mirror drying her hair. He'd finished cleaning round her bed and she noticed him glancing at her furtively before going to lock the door. She watched the reflection of the dangling keys in the mirror as he leaned across her and groped at her breasts. She didn't scream, nor did she twist away from him. Be brave; for Preeti's sake, be brave, she said to herself. She lifted her shoulder with lazy resignation which seemed to say to him 'All the other men do worse, much worse, to me and anyway you are too big and strong'. He grunted at the illicit pleasure his power gave him.

The third time she watched the keys dangling in the door, the tightness of the swarthy skin on his neck and a curly ginger hair below the lobe of his ear and the pulse beside it.

The fourth time, she felt for the pencil by her thigh, watched the keys dangling in the door and studied the way he lifted his neck when she turned towards him. Beside the ginger hair and the pulse was a faint subcutaneous line of blue. She saw it, but she also noticed the angle of the neck. The skin was taut enough but it slanted away from her, making deflection more likely.

The fifth time she felt for the pencil by her thigh

and checked the keys were dangling in the door. She sat facing the mirror, her back square to him. When he touched her she didn't turn away or towards him because this time she had to make him lean further over her shoulder than the other times. Yes, the skin had to be stretched but his neck had to be extended, his head in front of hers, looking down and distracted. She had to trick him into presenting his neck to her in this way before the fear of his employers catching him molesting her exceeded his desire to touch a young and beautiful Indian girl.

So, as she sat there, letting him fondle her, she opened the buttons of her shirt and after them the button which fastened her jeans. He grunted in the lustful way that he did and leaned far across her shoulder, first to gaze at her uncovered breasts, next to slide his stubby hand into her knickers, and it was then she gripped the pencil half way along its shaft to prevent it snapping on impact and plunged it through the stretched skin of his neck and into the artery by the curly ginger hair.

All the way up to her hand, and then she wrenched it out.

He screamed as it went in and again as it came out. A crimson spurt burst from his neck.

She ran for the door and for his bunch of keys which dangled from the lock.

CHAPTER 5

'Mr McGill, I'm not a fool.' Ryan's irritation increased every time Cal spoke. Jamieson knew why, and it entertained her, almost to the point where she'd snorted with laughter. She'd disguised it by feigning a sneeze. Back at police headquarters Ryan had listened to Cal's confession but hadn't liked what he heard. Could you charge someone with planting flowers in the gardens of dozens of MPs and MSPs including the Scottish Environment Minister and the Scottish Justice Minister? So far the only reported 'damage' had been one broken plank from the Environment Minister's fence. Nor had any of McGill's other 'victims' made a complaint: none of them had reported an intruder or a crime of any sort.

'It's just not believeable Mr McGill. Wasn't planting flowers just your cover? You had another more serious and criminal purpose.'

Cal looked up at Ryan, then down. 'What other purpose might I have had Detective Inspector?'

'I'm asking the questions Mr McGill.'

Ryan was getting riled, Jamieson realised with glee. In a few cases, where MPs and MSPs had country properties, he'd even threatened McGill with the Land Reform (Scotland) Act 2003. It granted rights of access over land though not over designated 'curtilage', the area of garden around houses.

Cal had considered Ryan's point for a moment before replying coolly, 'Well it's a technical matter isn't it? The *practical* issue is this: wouldn't it be an embarrassment for the prosecution and the police to waste money charging me and putting me on trial when, for all you know, some of the garden owners might appreciate my present of a plant. I'm told it thrives in rock gardens.'

He'd paused and lifted his eyes and looked at Ryan before lowering them again. 'I imagine some MPs or MSPs might even take the stand *for* me, the Lib Dems for example, or the Greens in the Scottish Parliament . . . or even the Environment Minister himself. It'll be a green cause celebre after all.'

A tic pulsed under Cal's right eye as he paused again.

'Anyhow, Detective Inspector, aren't the curtilage provisions of the Land Reform Act a civil, not a criminal, matter? Surely it would be a matter for the landowner to pursue in the first instance, not the police.'

Schadenfreude
A delight in the misfortune of others
Jamieson found herself wondering how schadenfreude was spelt. It was a word she'd never written before. Was it with a capital 'S'? Was it 'freud' as in Sigmund? Absent-mindedly, she wrote it on her

pad before crossing it out and glancing nervously at Ryan in case he thought she'd been writing him a note. Not that he would have been interested in any suggestion Jamieson had to make.

The Assistant Chief Constable had told Ryan to 'tie McGill in legal knots. We've got to stop him going on with this or it'll play badly for us, Ryan. We'll be a laughing stock.'

And now they'd be a laughing stock if they took him to court.

Schadenfreude

Jamieson reckoned there'd be a final 'e'. Didn't 'freude' mean 'joy' in German? Freud without an 'e' meant Sigmund and joylessness.

Ryan, unaware of his junior colleague's internal discussion about semantics, said, 'Tell it to me again, Mr McGill. When did you start this?'

'Last September.'

'And you say you've done one or two a week since then.'

'Sometimes more . . .'

'And always at night . . . ?'

'Mostly, though in December and January it's dark by four o'clock.'

'And in each garden you planted just one plant.'

'Yes.'

'What type of plant?'

Cal looked wearily at Ryan as if to say I've told you this before, my story isn't going to change. 'Dryas Octopetala. It's also known as Mountain Avens.'

'Describe it Mr McGill if you would.'

57

Jamieson's eyes widened. It was the first time she'd ever heard a Detective Inspector ask a suspect for a description of a plant. Would there be a computer-generated likeness of it broadcast on the BBC evening news?

Has anyone seen this plant? It is considered dangerous and must not be approached.

'It's a low-growing evergreen which has white flowers,' Cal replied. 'Normally with eight petals . . .'

'Which is why it's called octopetala. You've told me that already,' Ryan snapped.

'I'm answering your questions, Detective Inspector. I've also told you that it grows wild in the Arctic, Scandinavia, and the Alps as well as some mountain areas in the UK – Snowdonia and the Scottish highlands.'

'Thank you Mr McGill.' Now Ryan seemed irritated by Cal volunteering information unprompted by a question. 'By the way do you collect your plants from the wild?'

Ryan's tone lightened. He tried to make the question sound like conversation, as though he might have a personal interest in the answer, a gardener looking for a tip perhaps.

Jamieson sussed him. He was trying to get McGill for breaching the Wildlife and Countryside Act Section 13 which prohibits uprooting wild plants. McGill had sussed it too and Jamieson offered up silent applause.

'That would be illegal, Detective Inspector. I propagate them myself, from seed or by division.'

The sneer returned to Ryan's face. 'We'll make inquiries to make sure you're telling us the truth.'

Cal shrugged. 'I imagine you will.'

Jamieson smirked and opened Cal's file. She flicked through it but she'd seen what she wanted on the first page: his date of birth. He was 28, almost 29, two years younger than she was. Her internal voice was now musing about his girlfriend and in particular whether he had one. As soon as the thought entered her head, she scolded herself. It was typical of her, this flitting from intellectual word plays (*Schadenfreude*) to emotional trivia with a brief diversion around Scots law in between. At university, she'd heard two professors discussing the difference between a first and second rate mind. From the gist of their conversation, she'd realised (with a shock) that high IQ was not the distinguishing character-istic. No, apparently high IQ conjoined with something they referred to as a 'rigorous disposition' was what separated a first rate mind from a second rate one. Jamieson's habit of neural fluttering from one subject (high/low brow) to the next (low/high brow) in seconds was – she tried to persuade herself – commendable for its versatility. Though would the two professors have regarded it as a 'rigorous disposition' of the qualifying kind?

There was another unresolved matter which amused/bothered Jamieson depending on her mood. If she had a boyfriend, a settled, loving relationship of the type she read and often dreamed about, would it liberate her to concentrate entirely on intellectual thoughts and pursuits (surely, the hallmark of a first class mind), or would (and this was her worry) opportunity and availability make her think more about sex? It was Cyril Connolly who said 'There is no more sombre enemy of good art than the pram in the hall.' *With apologies to CC, was there no more sombre enemy of a woman's good mind than a man in bed? Stop it, Helen*

'And what is the significance of this plant?' Ryan, as ever, was oblivious to Jamieson.

'It thrived in the big freeze roughly twelve to thirteen thousand years ago. This period is called the Younger Dryas after the plant.'

'Is the plant noxious?'

'Do you mean poisonous?'

Ryan nodded. Jamieson prepared the charge in her head.

Mr Caladh McGill, you are charged with attempted murder by planting a poisonous plant in the Environment Minister's garden.

'I don't think so. I don't know, though I've read somewhere it can be used as a tea substitute.'

Nice cup of tea anyone?

'So you put these Dryas plants in the gardens of politicians or leading businessmen. Why?' Ryan carried on.

'It's an under-the-radar way of campaigning, as I've said. Each one is labelled with a warning about the prospect of another Younger Dryas, a new big freeze.'

'And you hope they'll discover the plant, be

60

surprised by it, look up Younger Dryas on Google or something and discover that it's associated with a . . .' Ryan glanced at his notes, 'catastrophic environmental event and give them pause for thought.'

'Yes. I'd like them to discover it for themselves and realise how close we could be to another trigger point.'

'And discuss it with their friends, Twitter, that sort of thing.'

'Yeah, I guess.' Cal winced and shifted in his seat. The stitches in the gash in his side were constricting and stinging. The local anaesthetic was wearing off. Ryan was unsympathetic: the detour to the Western General Hospital on doctor's orders had been another avoidable delay in his opinion; not that he'd accompanied McGill. He'd left that to Jamieson. He'd something else to do. Jamieson had an uneasy feeling about what it was. She'd heard about Ryan's methods with suspects who thought they were too clever for him.

'Sore?' Jamieson asked and looked flustered that she had spoken at all.

Cal smiled at her. 'It's ok, thanks.'

'Spare your sympathy Jamieson,' Ryan barked. 'It's his fault for fooling around on someone else's property at night.'

Jamieson flushed (at Cal's smile, not the reprimand) and studied the sketch Cal had drawn during his first explanation of thermohaline circulation. 'Wasn't that what Henry Stommel studied?' she'd asked Cal and Ryan had thrown down his pen (*his toys out of the pram*) and sighed with impatience.

'Henry Stommel – you picked up his books in Mr McGill's flat, boss,' she'd explained.

'Yes I know, Jamieson.'

If she'd understood McGill correctly, the big freeze occurred when the ocean conveyor of currents distributing heat from the Equator to the north Atlantic seized up. The result? Glaciers and ice moved south, conditions which few plants or mammals survived. In the big freeze, Dryas Octopetala was one them, one of the very few which thrived.

Now Ryan was studying a print-out from Cal's computer. 'So this is the list?'

Cal held the bottom of the paper and glanced at it.

'I've crossed off the names in the right hand column.'

'You've left a plant in each of their gardens?'

'Yes. The "to do" list is on the left . . .'

Ryan examined the 'to do' names and addresses. The Scottish First Minister was there; so were the Transport Minister and the chief executives of the transport companies Stagecoach and National Express. There were two dozen names and addresses, most of which Ryan didn't recognise.

'Well Mr McGill, you won't be going anywhere until we've checked out your story. Detective Constable Jamieson will be organising searches at the addresses you've crossed off.'

Will she? 'All of them?' Jamieson said. There were 63 addresses.

'All of them. In the meantime charge Mr McGill with vandalism.'

'Vandalism sir . . . to what sir?'

'To a fence, Jamieson.'

'Yes sir.'

Cal shrugged at her in complicit understanding. Then he smiled at Ryan. 'I won't plead guilty whatever the charge, Inspector.'

Ryan pushed back his chair. 'I wouldn't waste the court's time if I was you Mr McGill. You've admitted it after all.'

'That's not my point Inspector.'

'Well, what is your point?' Ryan was standing now.

'Just that I didn't commit a crime, any more than a political party canvasser breaks the criminal law by walking up to someone's front door to drop off a campaign leaflet.'

'A canvasser doesn't damage fences Mr McGill.'

'So I'll pay the Environment Minister civil damages for the repair.'

Ryan turned to the tape machine. 'Detective Inspector Ryan and Detective Constable Jamieson are suspending this interview with Mr Caladh McGill at 17.53 on Tuesday May 5.'

Gathering up his files he went to the door and knocked on it. A uniformed officer pushed it open. 'Mr McGill will need a cell for the night,' Ryan informed him brusquely and left the room.

With Ryan out of the way Jamieson blurted, 'Hope the bed isn't too uncomfortable', collected up her scattered papers, including his drawing of the thermohaline circulation system, and left the room flustered and blushing.

Stop being such a girl, Helen, for heaven's sake.

'The minister will be able to take your call at 6pm.'

The minister's assistant was firm about it. No, the minister couldn't leave the members of his local bowls club in mid-tour of the Scottish Parliament. No, he couldn't take a call on his mobile phone and catch up with the tour later. 'It's 6 o'clock or nothing Detective Inspector. He's got a black tie dinner starting at 7.'

Ryan put his head round Detective Chief Superintendent Jim Reynolds's door. 'Can we hold the meeting for 20 minutes? The minister can't speak to me until 6pm.'

Reynolds, a big man with a florid face and a shock of steel grey hair, replied, 'That suits fine David. The assistant chief's coming to sit in if you don't mind.'

Ryan said, 'No, of course not,' but there was sufficient inquiry in his tone for Reynolds to add, 'The top floor's worried. It's the politics of it, now that the Justice Minister's involved as well. You know the score, David.'

Ryan did. Recently the Justice Minister had announced an inquiry into the 'structure and funding of the Scottish police'. It was being led by a judge and the usual collection of great-and-good. Should Scotland's eight forces be merged to make a single national police force? Ryan would have phrased the inquiry's remit differently: should the gravy train for Chief Constables and Assistant Chief Constables be brought crashing off the rails? Of course the ACC wanted to be at Ryan's meeting with Reynolds. Any officer above the rank of Chief Superintendent jumped at the mention of the Justice Minister's name nowadays. Every ACC in Scotland recited the same mantra, 'It's important to retain the proud local traditions of the separate forces.' Blah, blah. It's important to retain the proud local traditions of large salaries and pensions for pen pushing ACCs was more like it, Ryan sneered.

But the wind was blowing and Ryan was happy to be blown with it. It was why he'd applied to the Scottish Crime and Drug Enforcement Agency. Its portfolio of responsibilities already included organised crime, people trafficking and drugs. Ryan was positioning himself for promotion at its next inevitable expansion.

As he walked back to his office Ryan's mobile rang. 'What is it?' he said irritably. Jamieson answered, 'Sorry to bother you sir.'

'Well?'

'Sir, we've identified the Dryas Octopetala in the minister's garden.'

'Which minister, Jamieson?' McGill had visited at least eight.

'The Environment Minister's, sir.'

'And?'

'Well sir, the minister's wife has asked if she can keep it.'

'Did you tell her it was impossible; that it's evidence in a criminal case?'

'I tried sir. But she said nonsense.'

'So where is the plant now?'

'It's still in the minister's garden sir.'

'Well dig it up, Jamieson.'

'Yes sir . . .' Jamieson let the 'sir' trail on as though she had something else to say.

'Well?'

'Well sir, the minister's wife thought the Dryas Octopetala was very pretty and she wondered if she could purchase two more from Mr McGill. She's got the perfect place for them in her rock garden.'

'For God's sake!' Ryan ended the call.

Ryan's conversation at 6pm with Alasdair Gordon, the Environment Minister, didn't improve his mood. It started badly – Gordon's assistant put Ryan on speaker phone – and deteriorated thereafter. Ryan spent most of the call trying to interrupt a private conversation between the minister and his assistant. He told the minister about Cal McGill's arrest and overnight detention which failed to draw any comment from either of his listeners. He reassured the minister that McGill wasn't a thief or a terrorist 'more of a beach-combing eco-nut really'. It was at that stage Ryan heard the assistant say something indecipherable after which the minister asked, 'And you say you've charged him with vandalism to my fence?'

Ryan heard the minister 'shushing' his assistant. 'Yes, Mr Gordon. It's a holding charge. We expect more serious charges to follow.'

Then the assistant addressed a question to Ryan. 'What about the perception of this, charges, a court case? Ok he shouldn't have been there, but he was making a political statement, one that the minister is in agreement with. Isn't there some other way?'

Gordon's grating voice added. 'Couldn't there be reparation for the fence – £10 or something – and that's that?'

Ryan forced himself to hold his temper.

'There are others Mr Gordon, the Justice Minister for example.'

'I understand the problem Detective Inspector. It's just a sensitive area of politics that's all.'

Once more the assistant said something Ryan didn't catch but Gordon said, 'Good point, Richard. Detective Inspector my assistant was reminding me that I've been invited to go to the Arctic in mid-September to see the impact of climate change for myself.'

'If we don't prosecute McGill,' Ryan said, 'what about the next intruder in your garden? It'll just encourage others – animal rights activists, anti-nuclear protesters.'

He realised he was wasting his breath. Law and order used to be at the top of the political agenda. Not any more. Protecting raptors, the reintroduction of beavers, carbon emissions, wind farms, biodiversity whatever that was: these were the new priorities in Parliament. God help Scotland.

Gordon sensed Ryan's disapproval. 'You must of course do what is right Detective Inspector. It's not for politicians to direct the police.'

'No sir,' Ryan agreed.

Reporting later to Reynolds and Assistant Chief Constable Ian Carmichael, Ryan didn't allude to the detail of his conversation with the minister. Nor did he mention the custody officer's report of McGill's story about the Justice Minister relieving himself into a shrub (a Viburnum Opulus, McGill said) while he'd been hiding in his garden. Instead he presented his 'caveats' about rushing to prosecute McGill as though it was his own politically-acute analysis.

'We can't get away from the politics of it, much as I know we'd like to. Imagine McGill's counsel leading supporting evidence from the Environment Minister or his wife.'

Carmichael paced the room in rumination. 'Damned if we do by the Environment Minister, damned if we don't by the Justice Minister.'

'*Possibly* damned if we don't by the Justice Minister.' Ryan doubted the Justice Minister would want to be anywhere near the witness box once he knew McGill's lawyer might blab his night-time ablution habits.

'Why do you say that, David?' Reynolds asked.

Ryan played safe in case McGill's story was bravado

or embellishment. 'Every politician wants green credentials nowadays. Can I make a suggestion?'

His senior officers mumbled assent.

'Send the papers to the Crown Office in the usual way and have a quiet word with someone senior there about the political risks of prosecution, the possibility of MSPs, ministers even, speaking for the defence.'

Assistant Chief Constable Carmichael nodded with approval.

'McGill will be in custody tonight, pending further inquiries,' Ryan continued. 'The Crown Office will book a sheriff for 10pm or so for an interdict hearing in chambers imposing a ban on him from going within 250 metres of any of the addresses he hasn't yet visited, or the ones he has.'

Carmichael looked at Reynolds. Both men were nodding now.

'And McGill?' Carmichael asked

'He'll be released tomorrow. Once we've checked out the addresses on his list. The last I heard we'd been to 14 and recovered plants.'

Ryan omitted another detail: six of the MPs and MSPs had asked if the plants could be returned to them if they weren't required as court exhibits.

'Fucking politicians,' Ryan said after Jamieson told him.

'Absolutely, sir,' she replied, turning away from him quickly, a smile stretching across her face.

Schaden and freude sir

CHAPTER 6

She'd meant it as a warning, but a warning of what? 'Be careful, won't you?' There was no undercurrent of threat; no 'or else' left unsaid. Her manner was kindly, her tone well-meaning, like a friend dispensing good advice. Be careful of what?

Detective Constable Jamieson had been in the front lobby at police headquarters sitting in one of the arm chairs. 'So they're letting you go are they?'

Cal had nodded, caught off-guard. Was she waiting for him? She'd seen the query in his expression and she'd said, with a nonchalant sweep of her hand, 'Meeting a friend for lunch. She's late.'

They'd smiled; her first, then him. He'd gone towards the door, awkwardly, not wanting to be rude, and she'd glanced at the sergeant manning the reception desk.

'Be careful, won't you?' She'd lowered her voice. It was for him to hear and him only. He'd mumbled something insincere about 'being good'.

Outside, on the tarmac, he'd looked back and she'd gone. Had she given up on her friend or had she been waiting for Cal? If the latter, 'be careful' now meant more than it had a few seconds ago.

He walked to Comely Bank, his stitches pinching at him with every step, where he caught the bus to Granton. Twenty minutes later, outside The Cask, it came to him. Had Jamieson been alerting him to the court order obtained by the police the night before? It prohibited him from going near any of the addresses on his list. Random blocs of Edinburgh were now a danger for him. Was she warning him not to stray accidentally? Was that it? Had Detective Inspector Ryan covertly changed his rules of engagement? Was this the way he planned to get him into court? If Cal infringed the banning order Ryan wouldn't need any politicians to take the stand for the prosecution; and nor would they. There were no votes in speaking up for someone who had broken a court order. Cal took the lift to the top floor, his aching side relegating the importance of his carbon footprint.

Was he overcomplicating things?

He slid the key in his lock and the door pushed open. It hadn't been locked and Cal noticed the bolt striker plate on the doorframe was hanging loose. The wood surround had splintered. His flat was in disarray. His books and papers were scattered everywhere. The shelves with all his beach-combing artefacts had been pushed over. If it hadn't been for Jamieson's warning he'd have assumed a burglar, one of the kids downstairs looking for drugs money. Now he thought of Ryan. Was this his doing, making it look like a break-in? Cal wondered if he'd led too sheltered a life. Did the police hand out extra-judicial warnings like this as a matter of routine?

Is this what Jamieson meant?

Be careful, because Ryan's a mean bastard.

It gave her the creeps, this old warehouse with its echoes and pristine emptiness: one floor after another of new flats and little sign or sound of habitation; now this.

The door at the end of the top landing was half open and the key sticking out of the lock. There was a noise coming from inside; a rummaging sound. Rosie Provan stopped to listen, one foot ahead of the other, in mid-stride. Her heart thumped, surely loud enough for whoever was the other side of the door to hear it, and her breathing became faster. She reached for her mobile phone, flipped it open and tapped in the news-desk number. At the first sign of danger she would press connect. Why hadn't she told anyone where she was going?

Her colleagues were accustomed to Rosie disappearing. The reporters called it 'Rosie glory-seeking again'. It infuriated them, the way the news editor cast a lazy eye at Rosie missing the start of her shift when everyone else had to be in on time. They bitched about it among themselves. In their view Rosie only got away with it because of her looks. The inference was of something sexual but unconsummated between Rosie and Dick McGhee who ran the agency's news operations.

'Ach bollocks,' Jimmy Armitage, the deputy news editor, said when he heard the others discussing it. 'Dick's soft on her because she gets bloody good stories for this agency. She pays your wages.'

Which was true, though would it be true today?

Rosie was beginning to have doubts about the wisdom of this little solo expedition and not because it was 3.17pm and her shift started at 3. The tip off had come from Sam's mate, Ewan, who worked in the Scottish Parliament.

Sam, her boyfriend, had teased her with it. 'I know a story you'd kill for Rosie.'

She feigned boredom. 'Not interested. It's my morning off.' She attended to unravelling the flex of her hair-straightening tongs and plugging them in. While she waited for them to heat, she painted her toe-nails and hummed along to *Mercy* by Duffy.

Sam kept up his teasing saying it was 'a cracker' and 'the scoop of the year' and Rosie said, 'Sam, go away I'm busy. You're scrambling my head.'

She'd played this game with him before. If she let him think she was curious he would say 'Ah, so you *are* interested. Well I'm not sure I'm going to tell you.'

Sam wrapped his arms round her and she hummed louder. When he began to tell her she hummed louder still until she was certain he was committed.

Ewan's boss had had an intruder in his garden, Sam said.

73

'So? Big deal.'

'His boss is the Environment Minister.'

Rosie shrugged.

The intruder was apparently 'some sort of eco terrorist' who left behind a plant which had something to do with climate change. 'Now,' Sam reported in anticipation of Rosie's wowed reaction, 'the police have discovered he's done the same thing in dozens of politicians' gardens.'

Rosie's police contact provided the rest, reluctantly. 'It's the talk of the steamie at the Parliament,' Rosie exaggerated. 'It's going to get out. You'd just be giving me a head start.'

He growled, grudgingly. 'You owe me a pint, Rosie.'

Rosie made a mental note to send him a bottle of malt whisky; something tasty. It was a good story. Sam was right, for once. His reward was a kiss and the promise of more when she returned from work.

Now the doubts were setting in.

Had her police contact given her the wrong address? Why would an eco-warrior live on the top floor of a made-over warehouse converted too late for more-money-than-sense-metro-executives? It didn't figure and it wasn't the only thing that didn't. The rummaging noise had become louder, like furniture being moved. There'd been a crashing sound and after it silence. Rosie took another step forward, head still tilted. Her new shoes – grey and white Converse with a yellow trim and matching yellow laces – let off mouse-squeaks on the shiny laminate flooring. The door was three metres away. Holding her breath, she approached it on the sides of her feet to muffle the noise of her soles. She glanced twice at 'Flotsam and Jetsam Investigations' on the notice by the door, disbelieving it the first time. In one way it was reassuring: at least she seemed to be at the right address. Still, it was weird, *seriously* weird.

Her hand hovered, about to knock at the open door. Instead, she put her head through the gap. The room in front of her was large, bright and in chaos. Papers and books were strewn across a plank floor; not that much of it was visible. A map hung by one corner on the wall opposite. Untidy didn't normally faze Rosie, but this was, well, something else. There was a large table in front of her, filling the middle of the room, and the rummaging noise came from underneath it.

'Hello.' Rosie knocked. 'Hello, anyone at home?'

A head appeared from below the table: male, dark brown hair, cut short. He was as surprised to see Rosie as she was to see him.

'Can I help you?' he asked.

He looked friendly enough, Rosie thought. A least he wasn't sleazy or a creep. In fact, on second glance, he was rather cute in a modern eco-chic kind of way: jeans, tee shirt, day-old stubble and a wide face made more interesting by the slight crookedness of his nose. Her heart beat slower.

'God, what happened here?' She stepped inside the door.

'You'd better ask the police.' His voice was educated, like a school teacher's.

'You've called them, have you?' He snorted as though that was the last thing he intended to do.

She seemed to be getting off on the wrong foot with him so she tried, 'Are you Cal McGill?'

'I am.' He looked at her fleetingly before resuming his search of the mess around him.

Rosie found it oddly disconcerting. Men usually paid her more attention.

'Has anything been stolen?'

'God knows.' He sounded irritated.

Rosie walked to the table and peered over the edge. 'Can I help?'

He spun round looking down at the hurricane trail of papers and books. 'There's a photograph frame . . .'

He didn't need to tell her it was precious.

'Has it gone?'

'I don't know; it's hard to tell.' Cal began collecting up papers. 'If I can just clear up some of this . . .'

'Who did it, Cal? Do you mind me calling you Cal?'

Get on first name terms. It was a card Rosie liked to play as quickly as possible.

Cal shook his head. Rosie wasn't sure whether the gesture meant he didn't mind or that he was still distracted looking for the photograph frame.

She knelt down as if to help him and picked up a book which was splayed open on the floor. It was called 'Essentials of Oceanography'.

'I see you go in for light reading.'

'Sorry, who are you?' His attention strayed from her again almost as soon as the question was out.

'I'm Rosie,' she held out her hand.

Cal brushed the back of his left hand against her fingers. She noticed him wincing. 'Are you hurt?'

'It's nothing; I gashed my side and had some stitches.'

'Gosh, you have been in the wars.'

Sympathy was the other card Rosie liked to play quickly.

'Well Rosie, it's nice meeting you but I'm not quite sure why you're here.' He gathered up a file which was spilling paper out of its ruptured spine.

'I'd like to talk to you.' Rosie made a show of rescuing another book. 'Heavens it's going to take you ages to clear all this up.'

'You want to talk to me. Why?'

'Didn't I say? Oh I'm always doing that.'

This was disarming ditzy Rosie. She handed Cal the book and said, 'Hi, I'm Rosie Provan. I work for The Reporting Factory.'

This was how she liked to do it. First, get over the doorstep. Second, establish a first name relationship. Third, say the name of the freelance agency but not its business. Fourth, say it's a news agency. In Rosie's experience the fourth stage was the trickiest. Some people reacted to it as though they'd been punched. Cal's expression, she was relieved to see, didn't change. 'What's The Reporting Factory?'

'Oh it's a news agency. We supply a lot of the London papers. You know *The Times* that sort of thing.' Top of Rosie's list of Don'ts was: don't say 'sell' as in 'Oh, we sell stories.' Next was: don't say red-top.

Cal just mumbled 'Mmmh' and resumed lifting up the debris.

Rosie said, 'What about me helping you and putting this here and then we can clear this mess up and talk at the same time?'

She balanced her digital recorder on the pile of books she'd tidied and switched it on.

Cal wasn't looking and didn't seem to register the recorder. Did he think she was just putting down another book? Well, she'd been upfront about it. What else was she supposed to do, draw his attention to it again? She might as well invite him to clam up.

'So, Cal, you're the talk of the political classes.'

'Am I?' He didn't seem surprised.

Rosie said, 'The world's in a real mess. We're ruining it for the next generation. It's people like you who force us to think about it.'

Cal stopped what he was doing. 'Oh come on, you don't really think that.' Her earnestness seemed to amuse him.

Rosie replied, put out. 'Sure I do,' straining for emphasis, 'Of course, yes. Why wouldn't I?'

'Yeah, sure you do.' Cal went back to his searching. Rosie was about to tell him she had enough to write a story whether he cooperated or not – it was a tactic that sometimes worked – when he stopped what he was doing.

'Look, Rosie, there's only one reason why I'd talk to you.' He looked her straight in the eye.

For the first time she realised he was fired up, angry.

'What's that?' Was it something she'd done?

'If you can promise it'll be published in a newspaper with more than half a dozen readers.'

'I think I can do that for you,' Rosie said.

'I want it in one of the big tabloids.'

'Ok.' Big tabloid suited her fine. It meant more money for the agency; more kudos for Rosie. At last he seemed interested by her. His restless searching for the frame had stopped. Now she realised his expression wasn't just anger. Rosie said, 'You look like you want to settle a score.'

He shrugged, 'Or something.'

Rosie shrugged too. His motives didn't matter to her.

'What about the *Daily Record*? It isn't the biggest – *The Sun* is – but the *Record's* got more clout with the political class, if that's what you want.'

The edge of his mouth flinched. 'I just want to make it difficult for people . . .'

'Which people?'

He looked at the mess in the flat as if it might contain the answer. 'It doesn't matter who . . .'

Rosie didn't want him drifting off so she said,

'I'm pretty sure the *Record* would be interested. They take my stories all the time.'

Pretty sure? They'd tear her right arm off for it. This guy didn't realise what big news he was about to become.

He stared again, briefly, making up his mind about her. Then he carried on tidying. She thought she'd lost him again but suddenly he said he 'might as well' start at the beginning, with global warming and how it had the potential to trigger devastating climate events; how he'd wanted to draw attention to its dangers in a new way. He'd bought some Dryas Octopetala, the plant associated with the big freeze which began about 13000 years ago, propagated others, and found the home addresses of MPs, MSPs and leaders of industry (all easier than he'd expected).

'You must have been good at it not to get caught for so long.' Rosie now had to keep him talking.

'I watched the Parliament channel and read the papers. I went to their homes when I knew they were somewhere else.'

'Still it was a risk . . . their wives or partners.'

'After the clocks change in October it's dark early. Once or twice I was challenged but I just said I'd got the wrong address. It's less suspicious when it's dark at 5pm and you go in the front gate. There's usually a bit of garden by the front path or the drive.'

'So how did you get caught?'

Cal told her the story, how his bus had taken

longer than he expected, how it was late when he found the Environment Minister's garden, how he'd triggered the alarm, how he'd escaped and boarded a bus the following morning only to find the route took him back through the village.

Rosie laughed. 'So you didn't have the Mission Impossible team working with you.'

'No, not exactly.'

'Is that how you injured yourself, on the fence?'

'Yeah . . .'

'I couldn't help noticing the door, Flotsam and Jetsam Investigations. Is it serious?'

He nodded and smiled half-heartedly at Rosie's incredulity. It was the expression of someone weary at answering the same question many times over.

'How does that work?'

'Let's say there's an oil spill . . . I can track back on it using wind, tide and current data and match it to shipping movements.'

'Find the oily fingerprints?'

'Kind of . . . Usually I provide a list of suspects: tankers that were in the right place at the right time.'

'Does it pay?'

'Not very much; but it keeps me going. It's funding my PhD.'

'About?'

He stared at her again, narrowing his eyes, as if he was deciding whether to tell her. She was about to try the standard journalist's line – 'the publicity might help' – when he said, 'I'm developing and trialling a program for tracking back on flotsam and jetsam; anything that's floating in the sea. I've focused it on the North Atlantic for the PhD.'

'And when you've finished it?'

'I'll compile data bases for other oceans using the same computer program. Marine labs and meteorological departments around the world are gathering information all the time.

'My ambition . . .' He paused, smiling self-consciously at the word.

'No, go on, it's interesting.'

'Well, I'd like to extend my work to other oceans with data streaming into my computers 24/7. I'd be able to work anywhere, track back on any objects anywhere.'

Cal picked up a jumble of papers to his left and dropped them in front of him. Rosie took the opportunity to check the time on her mobile. It was 4.20 and there was one missed call. It would be the news editor: an hour and twenty minutes late for her shift tested even the limits of his indulgence. Rosie thought it was time to go. Her interview was better than she'd expected. 'Can you just spell the name of that plant again for me?'

After Cal had done so, she said, 'One last thing and then I must leave you. Deadlines, you know.'

Cal said, 'Sure.'

'Would you mind . . .' Rosie feigned embarrassment, 'having your picture taken? It's been so interesting talking to you.'

In Rosie's experience this was always a difficult bit. She delved into her bag, bringing out a small silver digital camera. 'I'll just do it quickly now.' He hadn't answered her, but nor had he said no. She took two pictures. 'Perfect,' she said examining the viewing screen. 'Sorry I can't stay longer and help.'

She was about to stand up when something caught Cal's eye. 'Ah; at last.' He extracted a double photograph frame from under a file.

'Found it?' She leaned over. 'Who's that, an ancestor?'

'He's my grandfather. His name was William but spelt in the Gaelic way – UILLEAM. He died long before I was born, lost at sea.'

Cal turned to the map hanging off the wall. He stood up and pushed on the corners to stick it to the adhesive gum. 'Somewhere here.' Cal planted his finger in the blue expanse between Norway and the Arctic. 'His death was what got me interested in all of this.'

Rosie hadn't really taken any notice of the map or the newspaper cuttings which surrounded it. Now she saw they were reports of unidentified bodies washing up around Scotland. String led from each cutting to a pin on the map. Cal was pressing two of the pins back in place and tightening the string when Rosie said, 'Is that right?'

This had the smell of a story. Rosie went to stand beside Cal and began reading about an unidentified Indian girl, only 13 or 14 years old, whose body had been caught in the nets of a

83

trawler off the west coast of Scotland. The police had released a computer-generated likeness of her because her face had been damaged by a propeller. 'Pretty girl,' Rosie said.

'Her body was recovered three years ago. She drowned. Could have been an accident or suicide,' Cal said. 'The post-mortem showed she'd lost her virginity. There was vague talk of it being an honour killing.'

'I remember it,' Rosie said. 'Sort of . . . I was at journalism school three years ago.'

Cal said, 'No-one came forward to claim her. The theory was the Indian community in Glasgow knew more than it was saying. The police reckoned her body had gone into the water some way south of where it was found. The prevailing flow of the current did the rest, carrying it further up the coast.' He paused, looking at the map, checking the pin indicating where her body was found. 'Probably happened that way . . . yeah, it makes sense. I keep records of them all in case I come across something in my research which might help . . . some quirk in a current, anything.' Now he scrutinised the mock up of the dead girl's face. 'What's going on when a 13-year-old drowns and nobody claims her?'

Rosie made a sympathetic sound and retrieved the camera from her bag. 'Would you mind – just one more, with the ocean map and the newspaper cuttings in the background? It's more your context.'

Cal shrugged. 'I guess.'

84

When she'd taken the picture Cal went back to sit on the floor and picked up the photograph frame, wiping it across his tee shirt. She kneeled beside him, putting her recorder back in its place. 'Tell me about him?'

'My grandfather?'

'Yes.'

'He went missing during World War II, aged 21. He was on a fishing boat, a trawler, which had been converted to protect merchant ships from attacks by U-boats. He was lost overboard in a storm, swept into the sea, trying to secure a loose depth charge which was rolling about on deck. His body was never recovered.'

'My grandfather was killed in the same war, in France. He was 21 too.' Rosie heard the insincerity in her voice and blushed at it, not the lie. Cal didn't seem to notice. He opened out the frame so she could see the second photograph.

'This other picture is of a gravestone on the Ardnamurchan Peninsual on the west coast. My parents took me there on holiday, and that's where I saw this grave for the first time, when I was nine. There are three graves together, white stone and with similar inscriptions.'

Cal read from the photograph, 'A sailor of the 1939–1945 war. Merchant Navy. Found 19th December 1942.' Underneath an engraved cross was written 'Known Unto God'.

The words moved him still, Rosie noticed.

'It made a big impression on me, the thought of

these men floating ashore, anonymous, their families waiting for them never knowing really if they were dead or not, never having a body to bury. Still does.' He glanced again at the newspaper cuttings on the wall. 'Anyway that night, I dreamt that one of these graves contained my grandfather. I was convinced of it, even though I knew he wasn't in the Merchant Navy. When we got home I persuaded my father to buy me maps and charts. After a while, I worked out my grandfather couldn't have come ashore on Ardnamurchan. His body went into the sea a long way north-east of Scotland between somewhere called Bear Island and the Norwegian coast. With the prevailing currents and winds his body would have floated further north and east. I remember writing to the Norwegian government asking them to search for him . . .' He smiled at his naivety. 'I became convinced he'd been preserved in Arctic ice for the previous 47 years and that if only he could be found he could be unfrozen and he'd come back to life. The Norwegians sent me a very kind letter . . . it's here somewhere.'

Cal picked up the papers in front of him and let them flutter back to the floor. 'Well, it doesn't matter really . . . I doubt I'll find it. But it's what got me into oceanography and being interested in currents and floating objects.'

Rosie said 'Can I see him again?' and Cal held out the photograph frame to her. 'He looks like a nice man,' she said glancing at Cal. 'You've got his eyes?'

'So people say.'

Rosie put the photograph frame beside her on the floor. 'Show me again on the map where he went into the sea.'

When Cal's back was turned she held her digital camera over the photograph and pressed the shutter button.

'Do you see this dot, there by my index finger?' Cal asked.

'Yes. Yes I do.' Rosie dropped the camera into her bag.

'Well, that's Bear Island. My grandfather was swept overboard, him and another crew member, more than 100 kilometres to the south, somewhere down . . .' He checked the longitude and latitude. '. . . here.'

Long after Rosie Provan had gone, with everything returned to its rightful place, Cal sat at his table, the turtle's carapace in front of him, a tube of glue in one hand, a broken piece of the shell in the other. He dabbed at it and pressed the shell splinter back into place. He looked around the room, as if expecting to find something malign there. 'Fuck you, Ryan.'

Tessa Rainey wandered across the detectives' room with an exaggerated wiggle of her hips. Detective Constable Sandra Paterson swung round in her seat to watch the show. The two of them had been talking: 'girl talk' Jamieson assumed.

Jamieson didn't do girl talk, couldn't do girl talk.

87

'Helen, you're working with Ryan on a case aren't you?' DC Rainey asked.

'Yes.' Jamieson didn't look up. She was writing a report about what she'd unearthed in Cal McGill's computers (nothing much, if libraries of material about oceans and their movement could be described as nothing).

'Well, he says I'll be working with him on his next case.'

Jamieson looked up.

'And what will he expect from you in return?'

Rainey smirked and shrugged.

Paterson laughed. 'Don't be so coy, Tess. Tell her.'

'It's private,' Rainey protested.

'Ryan won't be expecting anything from Tess he hasn't had already.' Paterson spoke for her and both of them began laughing.

Rainey held up her two hands with her index fingers extended until they were about 20cms apart. 'No, it's bigger than that.' She corrected herself.

Paterson said, 'I told you he was a stud.'

Rainey regarded Jamieson with exaggerated pity and bent towards her. 'Helen you don't know what you're missing, really you don't.'

Jamieson flushed red and went back to her report. The next five words she wrote were 'fuck you Ryan fuck you'. Then she pressed delete.

She gave her a sweet: lime brittle on the outside, soft chocolate in the middle. Jamieson remembered the taste but nothing else about that day, except the ladder in Isobel Dalgleish's tights. She'd sucked the lime brittle away, finding it a little too tart for her liking, and she'd smoothed the chocolate (a little too sugary) with her tongue, all the while wondering if she liked this sour and sweet confection, whether she should spit it out or not. Someone must have told her about her mother and father, yet she had no memory of the moment, or of the voice informing her about the motorway collision which had killed them. Perhaps Isobel Dalgleish had told her; perhaps someone else had. Was anyone else even there?

What was vivid and certain was the taste of the sweet. She'd known they were dead all right. By the time she began sucking the lime brittle. So someone must have told her.

Helen Jamieson had been 'six and three quarters', a plump girl with wayward curly hair, a red face, wire-rimmed spectacles and a precocious manner which later developed into a habit of asking potential adoptive parents personal questions. (Why do you smell? I don't have hairs in my nose, why do you?) She lost count of the times her foster parents, a kindly enough couple, said to her how unusual it was for a girl (they meant a white girl) to be left on the adoption register. On occasions they coached her in advance of prospective parents visiting for tea. The gist of it was smile more, speak less. Their intentions had been good but Helen refused to play the adoption game, as she called it. Why would she want to live with people who didn't love her as she was? What hurt her most were younger, prettier, sweeter, stupider girls passing through the foster home. For them it was a temporary place of refuge until a childless couple and a better life beckoned. For her, it was the beginning of something permanent, an adult world which tended to judge her by her physical appearance and to reject her for it. Apart, that is, from Isobel Dalgleish who was a police inspector working in family protection; a motherly woman in her fifties, who had never married and had no children.

After the day of the crash, Inspector Dalgleish continued to visit Helen, once a month, sometimes more, taking her out to the park or the cinema, always ending up in the book shop. Auntie Isobel, as she had become, drank tea in the café while Helen browsed. 'A clever girl like you needs books, away and see what interests you,' she would say. To begin with she would choose a cheap paperback, and Auntie Isobel would send her back with 'away with you Helen; what use is that to a girl like you?' By the time Helen was old enough to leave foster care for her own half-way-house bed-sit, she was selecting four or five novels as well as two or three histories or political biographies every month. The more books she brought back the greater the pleasure it gave the older woman. 'Good. That's more like it,' she'd say. When Helen was 17, and about to leave school with six 'A' grades, she went to Auntie Isobel and asked if it was legally possible for a teenager to adopt a parent.

'And who might this teenager want to adopt?' Isobel Dalgleish asked, making light of it to conceal her nervousness.

Helen suddenly found a three letter word hard to say: 'You.'

Isobel, who was now 66, stared at her, cheeks reddening, a tremor beginning in her neck.

'Please,' Helen added quickly.

Isobel, as she became from that day, reached for Helen's hands. 'I can do better than that. I can adopt you. I've always wanted to.' Her emotion made her break off. 'They told me I was too old. That and the fact I wasn't married and didn't have a partner.'

They hugged, not speaking, her tears wetting Helen's hair; Helen's wetting her new mother's blouse.

Eventually, Isobel said, 'I would have asked you when you were 16, but I thought it was too late, for you.'

'No,' Helen said, blowing softly through her nose, tears beginning again. 'No.'

After school, she studied law at Edinburgh University. Her First was 'the proudest moment' of Isobel's life, followed soon after by another: Helen winning a scholarship to Florida State University's College of Criminology and Criminal Justice to study for a Masters. Before the end of her course Isobel, now 71, had a fall which caused bleeding in her brain. Helen caught the first flight home to care for her. In spite of Isobel urging her to return to Florida, she enrolled in a part-time MSc in criminology at Edinburgh University so she could also nurse her adoptive mother. 'It's my turn to look after you,' Helen said. A month before the two year course ended, Isobel died, leaving Helen, her heir, distressed and confused about her future. With the security of Isobel's flat in Comely Bank, close to Lothian and Borders Police HQ, and some money, she volunteered to work for an orphanage in India. She was 26 when she returned to Scotland to follow in Isobel's footsteps, joining her old police force on the Accelerated Careers Development Programme, one of only a few fast-track recruits in Scotland that year. She started as a beat officer in Wester Hailes, a 1970s estate in south-west Edinburgh, followed by a two year stint working in the sexual offence support unit. Last autumn, when she was 29, with promotion to sergeant in prospect, she began working in criminal investigations.

Was Isobel Dalgleish the reason she found Ryan so offensive? In Helen Jamieson's opinion he discredited the police and the rank of inspector, which Isobel had graced.

Or was it that he reminded her of all those years of rejection by people like him who judged a clever girl by her looks?

Fuck you Ryan.

CHAPTER 7

It was high up on the railway cutting, a construction of cardboard and branches, like a child's den. The commuter diesel sprinters between Glasgow and Edinburgh rattled 15 metres below: the west bound trains slowing towards the mouth of the long tunnel to Queen Street Station; the east bound ones accelerating from it. If any of the passengers had craned their necks to inspect the top of the embankment they would have seen the usual track-side urban detritus: a wild tangle of brambles and elder bushes, waste paper and broken prams. They would have returned to their newspapers or their text messaging oblivious to the rudimentary shelter which was built there or the teenage girl who was inside it, waiting for dark, waiting for the safety of night to go scavenging again.

Basanti was lying on a supermarket apple box, on her side, her knees together, staring at a pencil sketch which was propped against the shelter wall. The drawing was of a hill with a flattened top rising from a plain. The sides of the hill were ridged as though at some time in its history a heavy weight had pressed down on it. Half way up the left flank, on one of these ridges, was a lone tree. It was leaning at 45 degrees to the perpendicular, away from the hill, as if frozen in the act of toppling. She'd drawn this scene more times than she could remember and still she found her representation of it unsatisfactory. At first, she'd been frustrated by her lack of dexterity: her hand seemed unable to copy the brilliant and precise picture she held in her head. Either the shape of the hill (too squat, too narrow) or the tree (too flimsy, too substantial) was wrong; and there had been a particular difficulty over the corkscrew twist of the trunk. She had drawn it over and over again before she thought she had it approximately right. Now a different worry nagged at her: had she drawn this landscape so often that her memory of it had been replaced by all her self-made representations? Was the hill really as symmetrical or the tree really leaning as much? It unsettled her. Was she satisfied with this drawing only because her memory of the scene had altered? Was she producing a caricature which nobody else would recognise?

She closed her eyes and she could see the scene again, as vivid as the first time: the hill and the tree. Just as they'd been when dawn came and she'd glimpsed daylight and the outside world for the first time for many months and the last time for two, was it three years? How could she tell?

The man had carried her, tied, gagged and blind-folded to the base of the hill. He'd run all the way in the dark and put her in a shallow scrape, passing a chain between her wrists and attaching it to a metal ring embedded in the crack of a boulder. He'd locked the chain and left her there. She'd heard sirens and shouting; then it had been quiet and she'd rubbed the side of her head against the rock until the cloth around her eyes slid down to her neck. Then dawn came. The sun lit up the hill, the tree, and the bulge of rock below the tree. She'd fixed them in her mind, consciously, studying them for detail, closing her eyes, memorising them, opening her eyes and looking again: like a camera shutter each time taking the same photograph.

Before the sun had climbed much higher the man had come back for her. As usual he wore a balaclava with slits for his eyes. As usual, he shouted at her. When he saw the blindfold around her neck he'd slapped and threatened her, putting his face close to hers. She'd smelt his foul breath through the wool of his balaclava. Then, with her blindfold tied back on so tight she'd cried in pain, he'd returned her to her windowless room with its stale, still air.

Later that day she was put in the back of a van (it smelled of fish and the floor was slippery with fish scales). The journey was long, or so it seemed to her. All the way she thought of the hill, its ridged sides and the tree. How would she ever find Preeti again if she forgot them, forgot any detail of them?

When the van stopped she knew she was in a city. She heard the noise of traffic. The back doors were opened and the ropes around her legs were removed. Two men guided her inside, each one holding an arm. They took her down some stairs and along a corridor, their feet echoing. They'd passed through two doors – one at the top of the stairs and another to her room – before her hands were untied and the blindfold removed. (Each of the doors had been unlocked and locked behind them, she registered with panic.) Her room was a square box. The walls were covered with mirrors. The recessed lights in the ceiling cast a dull red glow (or, as she was to discover, whatever colour her clients preferred). The bathroom, en suite behind a mirrored door, was the same.

A man came to her that evening.

He became a regular, visiting her once a week. He had sex with her that first time but never again. After that he insisted on the same routine. He made her sit on his knee, him in yellow pyjamas with blue piping; her in a white cotton night dress which he brought. He brushed her long dark hair with his dead wife's mother-of-pearl brush. It lasted half an hour, 24 brush strokes a minute; 720 strokes in 30 minutes; precisely. Eventually, she asked him if he would bring her pencils and paper to draw on while he brushed. Her request pleased him. His wife, he said, had liked to read when he'd groomed her hair.

Only one other man didn't hurt her, didn't have

96

sex with her; didn't touch her, not ever. He was most particular about it. What gave him a thrill was watching her dancing, naked. He brought music, always the same, a CD of *The Blue Danube* waltz by Johann Strauss junior. She danced to it for every one of his dozens of visits while he masturbated. Afterwards he would watch her showering, drying herself and putting her clothes back on. Then she would stand in front of him, as he instructed, and he'd beg for her forgiveness, on his knees, pleading with her, rambling and incoherent. At first she didn't understand what he wanted.

When she did, she bargained with him.

She would pardon him only if he helped her to improve her English. She'd had a good tutor in India who taught her to speak the language, but her lessons had been interrupted before she could write it with the fluency she desired. He agreed with alacrity and thereafter he became her tutor, teaching her grammar and bringing her newspapers to read and pens and notebooks for her to practise composition exercises. One time, he came straight from his office before going home. He had a laptop with him, for a presentation the following morning. As usual, when she'd showered and dressed he'd pleaded for forgiveness and she'd said, pointing to the computer, 'Only if you will teach me?'

He brought the laptop for his next visit and every visit thereafter until she was proficient.

They were the only ones who didn't hit her or

spit on her, or take their pleasure by degrading her body in some other revolting way. The rest of them she detested.

Every day she watched for an opportunity to escape but none came until the change of cleaners. How many days, months, or years had that been? The surly Turkish maid was replaced by a squat, muscular Albanian man. Neither the Turkish woman nor the Albanian spoke any English but in every other way they were dissimilar. One contrast which Basanti noted was the bunch of keys at the Albanian's belt. The Turkish woman had never been trusted with them. An unseen man had let her in and out of Basanti's room and had waited in the corridor outside while she cleaned. Was the Albanian allowed keys because he was so much stronger than the Turkish woman, making Basanti's escape less likely? Another dissimilarity which she noted was the way he looked at her: she knew the desire it expressed. She had resigned herself to men looking at her that way. But when he groped her that first time, she cried out in anguish because, like the Turkish woman before him, he was her only visitor who was not entitled to touch her. Had she lost even that small respite? But the second time he groped her she saw him lock the door first and the keys dangling there and she tolerated it, seeing an opportunity, planning her escape.

The next day, she asked the man who groomed her hair with the mother-of-pearl brush whether she could have two new pencils, sharpened. He brought them at his appointment the following week.

One pencil was placed with her few other possessions in a canvas carrier bag on the back of the door, in readiness for the moment.

The other pencil she drove into the Albanian's neck with all the force of her pent-up hatred after she'd exposed herself to him and he'd taken the bait.

When she ran for the door, not looking back, she expected his hand to grab her at every step. She snatched at her bag and turned the key, removing it from the lock. Her heart beat so fast it felt it would burst from her rib cage. The corridor was empty. She let out a plaintive cry of gratitude and locked the door behind her to muffle the Albanian's screams and to prevent him chasing after her, if he still could. There were two doors on the same side of the corridor as hers. Were there other girls in them? Was Preeti here too? Had they been so close all this time? She stood and fumbled through the keys trying them in the lock of the first door, urging herself to hurry, the adrenalin coursing through her, warning her to run. 'Oh please, oh please, oh please, oh please,' she repeated in her panic until the lock turned. A black woman, wearing an orange robe with black stitching, looked up from the bed where she was sitting.

'Come with me; quick,' Basanti said.

The woman blinked, looked about her slowly, bewildered, and back at Basanti. 'Please, quick. Oh please.' Basanti retreated towards the corridor, as if her backward momentum would help to drag the woman with her.

For an instant it had the desired effect. The woman made to stand before slumping again. She closed her eyes and shook her head. 'I can't. They'll kill my father and my sister.'

Basanti asked, 'Is there anyone in the next room?'

The woman continued to shake her head, not answering.

Basanti left her door open and tried the keys in the lock of the neighbouring room. As she did so, she cried out, 'Preeti, Preeti.' When the last of the keys failed to turn the lock she knelt down at the keyhole. No light shone through. 'Preeti,' she called again. She listened for a response as long as she dared before turning and running to the door at the top of the stairs. She unlocked it and found she was emerging into a back lane, with rubbish bins and parked vans. She ran, dropping the keys, narrowing her eyes against the unaccustomed brightness of the light and breathing the fresh (to her) city air. Only then did she notice her shirt was undone, a spray of fresh blood across it, and her trousers were open at the top. She fastened them quickly and clutched at her canvas bag. She mustn't lose it.

Apart from a change of clothes and a pencil, it contained the drawing which was closest to her memory of the hill and the tree, the one that was now propped up in her make-shift shelter on the railway embankment. On the grass beside it was her hair, cut with a piece of broken glass she'd found by the bins in the supermarket over the wall where she scavenged food and cardboard.

If she was to find Preeti, first she must find the hill and the tree where they'd lost their virginity, where they'd lost everything.

CHAPTER 8

Rosie Provan called Cal late. When the phone rang he was leaning forward in his chair, a large street map of Edinburgh spread out on his table.

'Yeah . . .'

'Hi, it's Rosie.'

Cal said nothing. His finger was following the route he'd take. He'd checked it again for the third time. None of the politicians on his list lived within 250 metres of it. He didn't want to hand himself to Ryan, gift-wrapped.

'Did I wake you?'

'No.'

'The story's running in the *Daily Record* tomorrow. I thought you'd want to know.'

Cal paid attention.

'Front page, spread inside. You're big news. They'll all want a piece of you tomorrow, the other papers.'

'Thank you, Rosie.'

The line went dead. Cal had cut the call.

What's got into him? Rosie stared at her phone, eyes wide, her mouth a perfect, lip-glossed 'O'. Rude bugger, even if he was kind of cute.

What had got into him was the sudden thought he didn't have much time. Other reporters would soon find him. If he was going to put a plant on the doorstep of the First Minister's official residence – it hadn't been on the list that Ryan had, so it wasn't covered by the court order – he'd have to do it now, before the media circus began.

He crossed the room and climbed the spiral stairs, ignoring a warning voice about this being reckless. Hadn't he promised to plan it better next time? He reappeared holding a small plant in a plastic pot. The front door banged shut behind him.

It was 2.20am, more than two hours later, when he returned. The buzz of leaving a Dryas Octopetela on the doorstep of Bute House was fading but he felt good. Maybe it'd make Ryan's life a bit more uncomfortable. Maybe the First Minister would pay more attention to the environment. Maybe neither would happen. What mattered was he'd sent a private signal – it'd take more than his flat being turned over or a court order to make him go away.

Cal set his alarm for 7.30 and flopped on his mattress before rolling over to sleep.

At seven his entry phone buzzed; a long, loud blast. Cal grabbed at his alarm clock and, realising his mistake, stumbled from his mattress to the door. He was in jeans and a tee shirt; yesterday's clothes. 'Hi.'

'Cal McGill?'

'Yes.' His voice was only half awake.

'My name's Tom Baillie, Mr McGill. I'm from the *Evening News*. It's about this story in the *Record*.'

Cal ran his fingers through his hair until the heel of his left hand was pressed hard against his forehead. 'Listen; do me a favour, Tom. Come back later will you?'

'I'm on a deadline.' Tom left it hanging.

'Well, I'm not doing it now.'

'What time?'

'Eight thirty, nine would be good. If there's anyone else there tell them too.' Cal dropped the receiver and lurched stiffly towards the bathroom. He showered, shaved, squirted his wound with antiseptic spray – the rim of torn flesh was less livid than the day before – and rummaged in his trunk for clean clothes. He put on black jeans and a tee shirt and left the flat, taking the service stairs to the rear entrance. He crossed the lane and followed the path down the embankment to the pavement below. The Pakistani owner of the newsagent and general store across the street was putting out his display of fruit and vegetables. Cal bought two copies of the *Daily Record*, a litre carton of milk, some cereal and two filled ham rolls which were put behind the counter for the old beggar who collected them daily. 'How is he?' Cal asked.

'Same as ever, always complaining,' the shop owner replied. 'Says he'll buy you a drink when he has any money . . .'

'Won't be able to wait that long . . .'

Cal returned to his flat by the same route. He had coffee, made toast and boiled eggs, read the newspaper, scribbled some notes and ignored the entry phone which buzzed sporadically. When it went again, just before 8.30, he pressed the lock release. 'Come on up.'

The security guards at Bute House, on the north side of Charlotte Square, were relieving their end-of-shift boredom by itemising the differences between protecting Downing Street and the First Minister's residence in Edinburgh. The Downing Street list sounded like the index of a counter terror manual: car bomb barricades, metal security gates, luggage scanners, and armed police.

'And what do we have here apart from you and me?' said the tall, beaky looking guard. 'A couple of locks, a sturdy front door, a camera and a drunk who bangs on it at midnight asking the First Minister out for a dram . . .'

His colleague, a big bellied man in his fifties, every button straining to keep him decent, joined in, '. . . and a hoodie who dumps a house plant on the doorstep at 2.30 in the morning.'

The two of them laughed.

'Stole it from someone's greenhouse I bet,' said Beaky, patting his head, checking that the wisps of silvery hair which stretched across his otherwise bald crown were in their rightful place. 'Mind you, I'd rather have it this way.'

Big Belly nodded. They were killing time, waiting for the shift change, hoping their replacements would come before the First Minister's 8.30 breakfast meeting. Something about renewables and energy policy.

Beaky began to sort through the morning's newspapers separating them into different piles (one for the First Minister, one for the First Minister's wife, one for his special adviser, one for the Cabinet Room) and Big Belly glanced at the monitor on his desk. 'Here we go.'

Alasdair Gordon, the Environment Minister, was getting out of his car accompanied by his assistant. Big Belly crossed the small security room off the hall and opened the heavy front door, its brasses shining.

'Good morning Mr Gordon.'

'Morning, morning . . .' Gordon was brisk, businesslike.

'The First Minister's expecting you.'

'In the Cabinet Room . . . ?'

'Yes, Mr Gordon.'

Big Belly stood back to let the two men pass. He closed the door and returned to the security room but before he could sit at his desk Beaky beckoned to him. He was reading a newspaper front page, the *Record*, about an eco-warrior who left plants in politicians' gardens. There was a small picture of the plant with a Latin sounding name.

'That's it,' Beaky said. 'That's the plant.'

Beaky and Big Belly looked at each other but

before they could speak again the minister popped his head round the door. 'Forgot to say . . . My PA will be bringing some papers. Can you have them sent up to me?'

'Yes of course Mr Gordon.'

Big Belly moved to his left, attempting to insert his substantial frame between the minister and the plant which was on the windowsill. But the minister was already looking at it with a suspicious expression. 'Where did you get that?'

'The wife,' Beaky said, with a presence of mind that had suddenly deserted Big Belly. 'From the garden. Got green fingers she has. She can grow anything she can.'

'Oh,' said the minister, studying it again.

His exclamation continued to reverberate after the minister had gone and the click of his heels was receding across the hall. Beaky snatched up the plant looking for the label. Sure enough there it was. Some Latin name and a warning about a new ice age.

Just as the newspaper said.

'Dump it,' hissed Beaky, 'or we'll be for it.'

By 9.30 Cal's equanimity was draining away. His morning had become a confusion of reporters and camera crews with their questions, deadlines and demands. He'd lost track of who they were (except for the Scottish *Sun*'s crime correspondent who held Cal personally to blame for Rosie's news agency selling the story exclusively to his paper's rival, the *Daily Record*. For £25,000, he said, and 'Tell me Mr McGill, what was your cut?').

Cal sensed the others thought something similar. If it wasn't explicit in their questions, it was implicit in their tone. Did he know Rosie well? Had the story been some time in preparation? Had he/she held anything back for the Sundays, a second bite at the cherry? In every question there was the inference that he and Rosie had planned it together. It was what Rosie did, one of them said. Cut a deal for an exclusive with 50% of the proceeds shared between interviewee (Cal) and interviewer (Rosie).

Cal had bridled and had gone up the spiral stairs to the door to the roof. One by one the reporters fell silent and watched him. There was a murmur when he reappeared carrying a large wire tray full of plants, which he banged down on the table. 'Help yourself.' Cal began handing them out.

The Scotsman's reporter hesitated before taking his. 'Is it legal?'

Cal put one beside him. 'It's Dryas Octopetala, the plant I've been leaving in MPs' and MSPs' gardens. It thrived in the big freeze, and if we're not careful it'll thrive again. It's one of the possibilities, climate change disrupting the currents carrying warm waters from the Equator to the North Atlantic. Yes, you'll find scientists who say it won't happen, but why take the risk?'

The reporters shuffled awkwardly.

Cal said, 'Sorry about the lecture but that's the story not this crap about Rosie.'

A mousy young woman with an A4 notepad and a serious expression asked a question about the wild distribution of Dryas Octopetala. As Cal was answering, the others began to drift away and the camera crews packed up.

Cal didn't altogether blame the journalists. They'd had their fingers burned by Rosie before. Cal, too, felt scalded by her when he opened the *Record* for the first time.

The previous afternoon – it must have been when he was at the map – she'd copied his grandfather's photograph without him knowing. It was all over that morning's paper. The page 1 headline was what he'd expected if over-dramatic: 'Revealed: the eco-warrior who raids ministers' gardens.' The page 4/5 spread caught him by surprise: 'The making of an eco-warrior: I owe it all to my grandfather's tragic wartime death at sea.' His grandfather's smiling face stared out at him from the page.

He hadn't expected that. He shut the paper quickly, feeling a lurch in the pit of his stomach.

After he ushered out the last of the reporters, his mobile phone rang. He left it, ringing and vibrating on his table, and went for a long walk west along the Forth towards Cramond. Just to get away. The tide was turning when he arrived at the causeway to Cramond Island and he watched the sea lap over it before going to a pub where he played snooker and had lunch. It was mid-afternoon when he started back along the Forth to Granton, buying an ice cream on the way, killing time, watching children flying kites, enjoying the sun, delaying the moment he had to return. Would there be more reporters waiting for him, more questions?

He was angry with himself for telling Rosie Provan about his grandfather. Now all the papers would write the story. It was the picture he minded about most, the way it had become public property without his permission: Rosie's sleight of hand, but Cal's fault too, for saying too much, for trusting her.

It was after 5pm when he arrived back at The Cask. No reporters were waiting. His mobile phone registered four missed calls, but no messages. He didn't recognise any of the numbers and he checked his emails. Glancing down the list of 16 in his inbox, most seemed to be from media organisations of one kind or another. Two were from DLG; one from WWF; another from Greenpeace (which he registered as interesting because it might be more work), and one from his estranged wife, Rachel. He clicked on it. 'Cal, please ring.' She left her work mobile number and signed off 'Rachel xxx'. Three kisses were routine for her. It didn't signify anything.

He stared at her email, making up his mind whether to reply to it now or later, before typing 'why, what's up?' He made coffee and when he returned to his chair her answer was waiting for him.

'Cal, I've come across an old woman who grew

up with your grandfather. She saw his picture in the paper this morning. She'd very much like to meet you, Rachel xxx.'

Cal swore and dialled Rachel's mobile.

She picked up after the fourth ring. 'Cal?' She was nervous.

'Yes.'

'Don't be angry, Cal.' She did that often: telling him what his reaction was going to be before he'd even heard what she had to say.

'I'm not angry. I'm tired Rachel. I've had a difficult couple of days, all right.'

'I know I've been reading about it.'

It was typical of Rachel. Her standard response to his environmental campaigning was to say little about it, neither approving nor disapproving. But he knew by now what she thought: by always being on *that* side of the argument Cal restricted his clients to charities or public agencies when shipping and oil companies would pay more for his ocean expertise. He'd told her often enough: he didn't want to work for big business, for polluters.

Anyway it was none of her business. Not anymore.

'I meant don't be angry at what I'm going to tell you,' Rachel continued.

'Well what is it?' Cal tried to keep his rising irritation out of his voice.

'The woman who knew your grandfather is called Grace Ann MacKay. She grew up next door to him. They were friends, good friends by the sound of it.'

'Why should that make me angry? That's interesting.'

Rachel waited before answering. 'I wanted to see you.'

'Why?'

'To tell you about the TV series I'm working on. That's how I came across Miss MacKay.'

'You can tell me on the phone can't you?'

This was beginning to remind Cal of some of their conversations after the crack in their marriage widened into a breach. After a few exchanges, with her tip-toeing around him, he'd become bad-tempered, distant or unhelpful, exactly as she'd forecast he would be. He was starting to be it again: he couldn't stop himself. It had become a bad habit, one he couldn't break. 'Well can't you?'

Rachel sighed. 'It's about abandoned places, you know villages that were left deserted after the highland clearances, islands which had to be evacuated because they weren't viable, in one case a big house in England which was abandoned in the 1920s after a murder and has never been lived in again . . .'

She broke off as if expecting a response. When none came she added, 'We're planning a series of eight documentaries, two based in Scotland, the others south of the Border.'

Cal said, 'What should make me angry about that?'

'The thing is, Cal . . . the island is Eilean Iasgaich, where your grandfather was born.'

112

Cal didn't reply.

'Cal?'

'Why Eilean Iasgaich?' he replied, his voice flatter and louder.

'I knew you'd be cross.' She sounded resigned, deflated.

'Why do it then? There are other abandoned islands. What's wrong with St Kilda?'

'Cal, everyone's heard of St Kilda.'

He didn't reply.

She filled the silence. 'Eilean Iasgaich is less well known and it's a good strong story; all those men dying in the war; their widows and children having to start new lives on the mainland.'

Cal still said nothing.

'Well, you know the story . . .' she said. After another silence, Cal said, 'That's my territory, Rachel.' His meaning was clear.

'It's not *your* territory, Cal. You've never even been there,' she said.

'It's my *family's* territory. I don't want you on it Rachel.'

His tone communicated his distaste; his feeling that something underhand was going on, something calculated on her part.

'I didn't mean it to happen like this,' she said uncertainly. 'I mentioned it at the series planning meeting because it was a story I knew off the top of my head – and they liked it . . .' She broke up her speech as if she expected him to interrupt at any second, but everything she said was met with brooding silence. 'What was I supposed to do? Tell them it had to be another island, a less good story, because your dead grandfather was born there?'

Cal said, 'Back off, Rachel.'

She felt her temper rising, suddenly. 'Oh, get a life Cal.' She cut the call.

Later, she sent him a terse email. 'Her name is Grace Ann MacKay. She lives in Galashiels. She's 85, nearly 86, the oldest surviving resident of the island, and the only one left who was born there and grew to adulthood there. Until I met her she didn't even know of your existence. Nor did she know your mother was dead. She rang me today because the photograph of your grandfather in the *Daily Record* has made her anxious. After reading the paper, she knows how much your grandfather's death has influenced you, even though you never met him. It'd be a kindness if you contacted her or went to see her. She's worried about having another stroke and dying before she has a chance to speak to you. If you did contact her it'd stop her worrying. But of course you'll suit yourself, as always.' She gave Miss MacKay's address and telephone number and signed off 'Rachel xxx.'

Cal looked away from the screen after reading it and swore. Why hadn't he told her?

If he had told her about the affair, she wouldn't have anything more to do with him, she wouldn't have mentioned Eilean Iasgaich at the planning meeting, she wouldn't have emailed him. She'd hate him, instead of maintaining tenuous contact (ringing when her father died; sending him an e-card on his birthday), as if she sensed he still had something to say to her, an explanation that made sense of their split.

He clicked distractedly on the first of DLG's two emails. 'Well, haven't you become famous? In case you're still interested the severed foot was wearing a shoe, a man's trainer.' DLG's second email added, 'No manufacturer's name. Sorry.'

Cal replied, 'Thanks. I'm still interested.'

So the severed foot floated in on the tide.

Cal googled it and clicked on the Scottish *Sun*'s version of the story. 'Butcher or surgeon hunted in severed foot horror.' Cal read one sentence aloud in a despairing voice. 'The foot was separated from the leg so expertly that police suspect the culprit is someone with anatomical expertise like a butcher or a surgeon.'

He left it there and went to bed before 10pm, wanting the day done, feeling at odds with himself and tense after the phone call with Rachel. He didn't behave like that with anyone else.

Why hadn't he told her?

At the time, he didn't think he owed her an explanation. By then they were hardly speaking and when they did it was only to hurt each other, and hadn't she spent so much time away they might as well not have been married?

Cal and Rachel had met once since they'd separated 14 months before. It was the previous

August. She was in Edinburgh for the Television Festival. She rang him. Could they have coffee? Part of him dreaded seeing her, but he couldn't find it in him to be hostile. There had been enough of that already.

He arrived first and spotted her walking along George Street. She had a new hair cut, a half-fringe over her left eye, the colour a more lustrous brown than he remembered. Her clothes, too, spoke simple style: a blue shift dress and espadrilles, a linen jacket over her arm. When she joined him at a street table, as they'd agreed, her wide eyes creased pleasantly at the edges and she met his hesitation by saying, 'We can still kiss hello can't we?'

She presented one cheek, then the other. 'It's so good to see you,' she said, sitting down. His guard up, he said something awkward about how well she looked.

'Oh, it's my networking outfit; not really my thing as you know,' she said dismissively.

A waitress interrupted them and they ordered coffee.

'How are you?' Cal asked, wanting to deflect Rachel from inquiring after him for as long as he could.

'I'm well. The job's good. London's good.' She was still with the same company making television documentaries as she'd always done. She nodded, smiling, the sun lighting up her olive skin. 'Yeah, it's ok. I'm ok. And you?'

'Same as always,' he said, giving nothing away.

Like friends who hadn't seen each other for a while, they ran through the normal catch-up questions. She inquired after his father; he mentioned the death of hers, how was her mother coping? She asked about the flat – was he still in it? Her answers were longer than his. After they'd exhausted the obvious topics, conversation began to slow. During a gap, Rachel lifted her face to the mid-afternoon breeze. 'God, I'd forgotten the air here, the way it moves. In London it's stagnant. It never feels fresh, not like this.'

She breathed in deeply, before squinting again at Cal. She watched him, her eyes narrowing, as if searching for the explanation which still eluded her. An explanation she understood. Cal smiled back, 'You've forgotten about the cold winds from October to April,' but he was thinking meeting her had been a mistake. It reminded him uncomfortably of the past.

She laughed in a distracted way, leaning back in her chair. 'Isn't it odd,' she said, 'us talking like this?'

'Like what?' Where was this leading?

'You know, like strangers.' She shrugged. 'Don't you find that, well, sad?'

He shrugged too. He didn't know.

'What went wrong, Cal?'

He shook his head. He couldn't tell her, not there, not then. 'I can't do this Rachel.'

'Why did we let our marriage go?'

Cal didn't reply.

Rachel stirred her cappuccino before saying, 'Did you ever love me? I mean really love me.'

Her eyes studied his, alert for evasion.

Cal felt his arms folding. 'You were never here, Rachel.' It was how he'd justified his behaviour to himself at the time. Now, at this distance, out loud, it sounded weak, self-serving; hollow.

Rachel raised a hand to her cheek as if he'd struck her.

'I was trying to earn money so we could buy our own flat, a house . . . a home, so we could have children, be a family. And you . . .' She stopped herself throwing accusations back at him. 'Cal, one of us had to have a half decent salary and there wasn't any work for me in Edinburgh.'

The twin smile lines under her eyes now seemed to represent disappointment and the first sign of ageing. 'My God, I'm so fucking stupid.'

She twisted her mouth, picked her bag off the table, found her sunglasses, and slid them on. 'I've got to go, there's a reception.'

She pushed back her chair and left without saying goodbye. Cal was ordering a double espresso when she sent him a text. 'Bad day at the office . . . Suddenly it mattered someone had loved me. Wrong to burden you. It won't happen again.'

He didn't answer. What was there to say?

The affair, with a botanist he'd met on Knoydart, lasted a few months. It ended soon after Rachel moved south for good. There'd been two other

118

women since, short relationships. They'd all disintegrated the same way, with Cal going off on his own, escaping, finding space which wasn't shared.

Should he also tell Rachel that he was a loner who should never have got married in the first place? He hadn't known that then.

Had he loved her? Did it matter anymore?

The phone call had brought all this back. Cal kicked off the duvet and went to make coffee.

He wasn't going to get any sleep anyway.

After dark, Basanti crept from her shelter and waited by the wall, listening. On the other side was an expanse of tarmac. This was where she scavenged for food: in the bins of a supermarket service area, where the delivery vehicles came by day and the hungry by night. Usually, she was the last to forage through the boxes and ruptured bags of discarded food past its sell-by date. The others arrived soon after closing. Sometimes she heard them arguing and fighting. Other people frightened her; men who had been drinking scared her most of all. She ventured out only when everyone else had gone, to pick over what they'd fingered and left behind.

She climbed the wall, still watchful. The bins were across the tarmac under an awning. She ran across to them, a lithe figure with cropped hair, and started at the bin closest to her. The smell of rotting meat from it made her retch. She pulled out an empty cardboard box to use as bedding and moved on to the next bin. There were black bags of assorted food in it: over-ripe fruit, bread and fish which stank of the van which had brought her to Glasgow all that time ago. There was a pile of newspapers by the bin. She took one from the middle and laid it open on the tarmac to place the best of the fruit on it.

Then she saw the picture: a close up of a man standing against a map. Behind him, in the left-hand corner, beside the map on the wall, was a blurred small face she recognised.

She let out a wail of surprise and anxiety and held the newspaper up to the night-light above the bins, angling it one way then another, trying vainly to decipher the blurred text around the photograph of her friend.

'Oh Preeti, what has happened to you?'

CHAPTER 9

The bus from Edinburgh arrived at Galashiels in the Scottish Borders seven minutes late. Agnes, Miss MacKay's carer, was waiting for Cal as arranged by the baker's shop at the bus stop. She was 50-ish, small and overweight, with curly salt and pepper hair. Cal apologised for keeping her waiting.

'No bother at all,' she replied, cheerily, picking up the half-full carrier bag at her feet. 'I was doing Grace Ann's bit of shopping anyway.'

Agnes led Cal into a nearby street of two storey terraced houses at the far end of which was a group of four bungalows clad in cream coloured harling. She pointed to the right hand one. 'Grace Ann's lived here for a year or two now. She used to have a place on the Melrose road.'

Agnes made it sound as though that was *the* place to live in Galashiels.

Cal didn't pick up on it, instead inquiring after Miss MacKay's health.

'She can't really do for herself, not after the last stroke. The doctor says it won't take much to carry her away.'

121

Soon they were at the flagstone pathway to Miss MacKay's bungalow. Cal followed Agnes along it and into a small glazed porch with a wicker chair. The inside door was open, held by a rubber wedge. Agnes shouted ahead, 'Hello Grace Ann. I've a special visitor for you.' Then she turned back to Cal, lowering her voice. 'She's been agitated all day, don't know what's wrong. Something from the past – she spends a lot of her time there now. It happens when they're getting close . . .' Cal nodded, letting her know he understood what she meant.

The first opening off the hallway led into a bright rectangular room with white walls and blue curtains. It contained a sofa, two arm chairs, a pine mantelpiece with a little gold clock and Grace Ann MacKay sitting in an adjustable chair covered in a brown leaf-pattern fabric which didn't match the rest of the room. Her face was small and sharp featured, her grey skin stretched tight to the bone, her hair silvery-white and caught in a tidy bun.

She looked at Cal over glasses which seemed too big for her. She appeared confused, as if she had just woken up.

'So you're Uilleam's and Ishbel's grandson?' she said eventually.

Her speech had an unexpected and old fashioned rhythm.

'I am.'

She smiled quickly at him before examining his face for long forgotten memories.

'They call you Cal?'

'My proper name is Caladh. I believe it means harbour in Gaelic.'

Encouraged by Agnes, who whispered 'she'll settle in a minute or two', Cal went to the arm chair closest to Grace Ann. When he had sat down, the old woman said, 'I've been trying to remember. What was your mother's name? My feeling is I didn't meet her . . .'

'It was Eilidh.' Cal reached into an inside pocket of his jacket and brought out a brown envelope. He opened the flap, removed a faded photograph and handed it to Grace Ann who took it from him, her hand shaking. The photograph was of a young woman wearing a black hat with a black ribbon around it, and black clothes. A baby wrapped in an off-white shawl lay along her legs.

'It was taken after my mother's baptism,' Cal said. 'The woman is my grandmother, Ishbel.'

'Funny thing to wear black at a baptism,' Agnes said.

'She was in mourning for my grandfather Uilleam; he died before my mother was born.'

'The wee soul.' Agnes's sympathy was for the baby born without a father. She left the room, taking the shopping with her, and Grace Ann stayed quiet in contemplation of the photograph. The fingers of her free hand stroked the satin border of a blanket lying across her knees.

Cal asked, 'You knew my grandmother?'

'Yes. I knew both Ishbel and Uilleam though I

123

knew Uilleam the better of the two.' Grace Ann paused. 'What did your mother tell you of them?'

'Very little.'

She nodded as though it didn't surprise her. 'I was sorry to hear of your mother's death. Rachel told me . . . I forget her full name.'

'Rachel Newby.' Cal helped.

'Yes. You know her?'

Cal had wondered if Rachel had mentioned their marriage. It appeared she hadn't. 'Yes I do,' he said before changing the subject. 'My mother's death seems a long time ago. I was 17.'

Agnes returned with an enamelled tray on which were two matching mugs of tea and a plate of biscuits. She laid it on the table beside Cal's chair and put one mug on Grace Ann's trolley. 'That's me away now,' she said, touching the back of the old woman's hand. 'Mind, those wee boxes from your bedroom, they're on the stool beside you here.' Then she said to Cal, 'Pleasure to meet you.'

Grace Ann waited for Agnes to close the front door before speaking again. 'There are things I should have told your mother . . .' Her eyes flicked towards him and away, as if apprehensive about his reaction. Cal thought she seemed frightened. Perhaps she wasn't used to strangers. 'Things that I regret.'

He tried to reassure her. 'I can't believe that.'

Grace Ann picked up a small black Bible which was lying near her on the trolley. She put it on

124

her lap, plucking at a corner of it with her thumb, before saying, 'What do you know of the island?'

'I know its name, Eilean Iasgaich Mor; that it means Great Fishing Island; and that it's on the north coast of Sutherland, near a settlement called Eastern Township.'

'Have you been there?' Grace Ann was watching him again.

'No.'

'You haven't seen the memorial to the men who were killed?'

'No.'

'So you don't know then?' It was as much an exclamation as a question.

'Know what?'

Cal glanced at her and noticed her eyes were closed and her head was shaking as if she was upset. Had talk of the memorial brought it on, all those dead men? Rather than remain quiet and draw attention to her distress, he ventured, 'When did you leave?'

She looked towards the window. 'In October 1943.' Then back at him as though the event was still alive to her. 'There was such a storm blowing the island was hidden in spray when I reached the mainland. I looked back and it was gone.'

'Did you ever return?'

'So many times in my sleep.' She paused. 'If I could have gone back and put things right I would have.'

Once more she closed her eyes tight. 'God forgive me.'

125

'It's all right,' Cal reassured her.

'No, no it's not,' she snapped back.

'I'm sorry,' he said, surprised by the reprimand.

She picked at the satin trim of the blanket on her legs. A sigh came from her, then a thin, weak smile. She looked at him. 'You remind me so much of Uilleam, it brings it all back.' Her eyes were wet with tears.

She sipped at her tea and Cal let her settle again. Then she said, as if he had asked the question and she was answering it, 'There were eight families on the island – MacKay, Rae, Gunn, MacLeod, Murray, Sutherland, McIntosh. And of course Sinclair which was your mother's family.'

Grace Ann repeated the names counting them off on her fingers

'But if you ask me which families ran the island, it was the MacKays and the Raes. There were three brothers in each family. They ruled the roost.'

'They were your relations?'

'They were cousins. We were poor relations. Our circumstances were closer to your mother's family, the Sinclairs, who were our neighbours. There wasn't an able bodied man in our house; nor for many years had there been one in the Sinclair house.' She sipped at her tea. Cal did too, relieved she had regained some composure. Putting down her mug, she said, 'You see if you had a man on the boat you were all right. If you didn't, well . . .'

She reached down for a bleached cardboard box on the stool by her chair. She lifted the lid and offered it to Cal. He found himself looking at a wooden model of a fishing boat lying on a bed of cotton wool. 'Eilean Iasgaich' was painted in black on its side.

'My father carved it from an old deck timber,' Grace Ann said.

'Was it a big boat?'

'A proper trawler, 300 tonnes, it was. Other islands had boats but nothing as big as ours.'

The pride came through in her voice. 'It must have been something,' he said.

'It had a crew of 16 and every man of them came from the island. They wouldn't have it any other way even if they were short-handed. They thought a stranger off the mainland would bring them bad luck.' Grace Ann shook her head at the stupidity of it. 'A boat never had such misfortune.' After Cal handed the model back to her, she stared at it, momentarily forgetting herself. 'Did I tell you every crew member had an equal share of the boat's profits?'

'No.'

'Well, they did. So the MacKays and the Raes, with three crew members for each family, had six shares of the profits. But without a man on the boat, money was hard to come by. My family and yours, the Sinclairs, had to survive on whatever the land or nature provided: oats, fish, potatoes, eggs and as many seabirds as we could store.'

'Was there land to grow crops?'

'There was the green pasture between the island's two hills, Cnoc a' Mhonaidh and Cnoc na Faire, the peat hill and the watch hill. Much of it was boggy but other parts were dry enough and fertile. My family and your family had the two best strips.' She stared out of the window before adding, 'God knows it was the only blessing the island bestowed on us.'

Grace Ann's face had flushed purple. The colour looked livid against the silvery-white of her hair.

'Are you sure this isn't too much for you?' he asked, wary of provoking another reprimand.

She didn't answer, instead taking another sip of tea. After dabbing at her upper lip with a handkerchief, she said, 'My father was a MacKay, so the other MacKays looked after us now and again, but they wanted your mother's family off the island so their cousins the Raes could take over the Sinclair croft.'

She let out a snort. 'They hadn't reckoned on your great-grandmother who was determined to hold on until Uilleam, your grandfather, was old enough to inherit and to take his place among the boat's crew.'

Cal removed a photograph of his grandfather Uilleam from the envelope and gave it to Grace Ann. She examined it, becoming wistful. 'His mother used to say,' she shook her head, 'his smile could light up a room and his laughter could warm it; and so they could too.'

She seemed to become quite lost in her memories until Cal asked, 'Were you the same age?'

'He was older by three years,' Grace Ann replied. Then she hesitated. 'I believed I would marry him, but his eyes and his heart were set at another and that was that. What could I do?'

'Was that my grandmother?'

'Yes, Ishbel Stewart was her name then. She was from Aberdeen. Her parents moved to Eastern Township, the settlement nearest to the island on the mainland. They inherited the general store from an aunt. Uilleam fell in love with Ishbel the moment he saw her.' She rapped her knuckles on her Bible to emphasise the suddenness of it.

'It must have been difficult for you.'

Another thin smile, this one of disappointment, faded as quickly as it formed. 'It was hard seeing him so happy with her. We were living so close. I don't suppose I behaved as I should, but I'd grown up knowing I would marry Uilleam. The whole island knew.'

'I'm sorry,' Cal commiserated, realising with a shock that she loved Uilleam still.

She drifted off with her memories, talking softly to herself. Then looking at Cal, she said, 'My mama wouldn't say a word to him or Ishbel even though they were living next door. I was scarcely more welcoming, God forgive me.'

Cal noticed her lips trembling.

'You see, Ishbel wasn't from a fishing family and she was Episcopalian, not Church of Scotland like the rest of us. She didn't have the Gaelic. It set her apart. The MacKays and the Raes wouldn't speak to her, though they had their own reasons.' Grace Ann appeared distressed recalling it. 'When she was expecting a baby the Raes skinned a baby rabbit and nailed it to the Sinclair door.'

'Why?'

'They wanted to frighten Ishbel off the island. The Raes and the MacKays knew they'd never get the Sinclair croft if Ishbel had her baby and it was a boy.'

'The baby was my mother?'

'It was, and now even the bairn's dead.' Grace Ann stared out of the window.

After a while, Cal prompted her. 'The boat . . . didn't it become an anti-submarine trawler?' He knew it did but he wanted to keep the story going.

She nodded. 'I can still remember the day: the *Eilean Iasgaich* coming into the bay for the first time with her gun; the men all lining the deck; Hector MacKay, the skipper, leading his crew ashore. Oh, we were proud: our island sending a boat to war.' Her face said something different: what fools they'd been. 'The women and children stood on the steps to the pier and hugged the men as they passed by, all except Uilleam who walked untouched all the way to the top where his mother and Ishbel waited for him.'

Grace Ann laid her cheek against the back of her chair where her eyes were hidden from Cal. After a while her head rolled back towards him.

'If only I'd held him then. Everything would have been different.'

'He'd hurt you,' Cal said with understanding.

She gazed out of the window once more, her face etched with regret.

'When all the men had gone by us we cried; the women first followed by the children. My mama said it was a cold wind blowing from one generation to the next. I'll never forget her saying that.'

'How long after was it . . . ?' He didn't like to say 'the men died'.

Grace Ann shivered as though she felt that cold wind still. 'That October, after the first storm of autumn, the *Eilean Iasgaich* tied up at the pier. The news went round the island. Seven men had been lost. The boat had been to Archangelsk, with an Arctic convoy. Hector MacKay appeared alone on the track and the women ran for their Bibles. They closed their doors and begged for Hector to go to their neighbour's door, not theirs.

'My Mama and me prayed out aloud.' Now she pressed her hands together as if in prayer. 'And we listened for my brother Sandy's foot on the loose slab on the path, but it was Hector's we heard. My mama ran at him and beat him with her fists. How dare you come to my house? How dare you?'

She clenched a hand and beat the air with it.

'Hector, who was a big man, stood there letting her hit him, him not saying a word. Then she fell to the floor and Hector took me aside and told me, 'We lost him Grace Ann, we lost him.' I carried mama back into our house and the next thing there was a cry from Uilleam's mother next door. Uilleam had gone too. So had the Gunn brothers, Alexander and Sinclair, and Alasdair Murray, as well as Donal and Angus MacKay, Hector's two brothers. No wonder he let my mama strike him. He was half-deranged with his own loss, though it's said Sandy's death weighed heaviest with him because he was the youngest.'

She stopped again and Cal asked, 'What age was he?'

'Just sixteen he was with his blond hair and freckles. He joined the crew two months before. It broke my mama's heart, though any boy of 16 would have wanted the same, to be with the men at sea.'

'Mama,' I used to say when we stood on the cliff waving the boat off, 'He's with his cousins and with Uilleam. Uilleam will take care of him mama, you'll see.' Despite the difficulties between me and Uilleam, the two of them were like brothers, always looking out for each other, though my mama became angry with me when I said it. She had no time for Uilleam after he married your grandmother.'

Now it was Cal's turn to exclaim. 'So the Alexander MacKay who died with my grandfather was your brother?'

She nodded.

'I didn't realise.'

After a pause, he said, 'Wasn't the boat returning from Archangelsk when they died? Hadn't they gone to secure a depth charge which had broken loose?'

'Yes.' She followed it with a hoarse cry: what a thing to die for, it meant. 'Five were killed by German planes on the way out to Archangelsk. Uilleam and my Sandy died together on the way back. There had been a storm and Sandy had gone on deck and Uilleam went after him, as I knew he would. The same wave took them both away.'

Grace Ann held her Bible to her mouth and said in a whisper, 'God bless them both.'

Not knowing what else to say, Cal muttered 'Amen'. He bowed his head because it seemed the appropriate thing to do.

A minute passed, maybe more. He glanced at her and saw her eyes were closed again. Cal wondered if she was sleeping when without warning she began talking, softly, quickly, hurrying to finish her story, as if she'd rehearsed it so often she knew it off by heart, as if she was living it again.

'I had no rest that first night what with my own grief and my mama's crying. The next morning, I went to leave the house and when mama heard the hinge of the door, she shouted after me "Don't be wasting your sympathies on the Sinclairs. They killed my Sandy."

I ran back to her and said, "What are you saying?"

'She gripped me by the hand. "They killed him, Grace Ann."

'I couldn't bear to listen to her and I ran outside. Half way to the hill I came upon Ishbel. She was crying, her arms wrapped round her unborn child; your mother, Cal. Unlike me, Ishbel was a talker and something she said that morning didn't sound right.

'"Surely it was Hector MacKay, who came to your door," I said to her. She looked surprised at my interruption. "No, it was Hamish Sutherland as I told you."

'I didn't say any more for Ishbel, not being from the island, didn't know our custom. For as long as anyone could remember the skipper of the boat had delivered the news which made widows of wives. Why had Hamish gone to the Sinclair door when Hector MacKay had been to ours? I walked home with Ishbel, each of us going to our separate houses, and when I went inside my mama flew at me. "We've tragedy enough without you bringing disgrace on us too?"

'"Mama, Ishbel is a widow with an unborn child."

'She gave me a look I'll never forget. "Sandy would be alive today but for her husband," she said.

'Later, in spite of my mama's opposition, I visited the Sinclairs to pay my respects to Margaret, Uilleam's mother. She and Ishbel were sitting in silence and I sat with them too.

'In time Margaret said to me, "Why do they blame Uilleam for your Sandy's death?"

'"Why would they," I said, "for they died together, one 16, one 21, two brave young men?"

'Margaret replied, "They say the depth charge breaking loose was Uilleam's fault. They say he repaired the rack after the German planes had damaged it, that it was Uilleam's responsibility that it came loose, his job to go and secure it."

'"He did, with Sandy."

'"They say Sandy went to it first and when Uilleam followed him Sandy had already been swept overboard."

'I said, "Well, if that's what they say where's the fault between two brave young men like them? The war is to blame, not them."'

Grace Ann sighed, her eyes still closed, her head shaking. Hadn't Agnes warned him about her living in the past? He didn't like to speak, to disturb her in case she was sleeping.

He'd begun to look around the room when she started again. 'I thought these poor women were deluded by grief but they weren't. Hector MacKay wouldn't speak of Uilleam except to say he never wanted to hear mention of his name on the island again. The Rae brothers – all three of them survived – were the same. Two days after the tragedy Hamish Sutherland went to the Sinclair house and told Margaret and Ishbel they wouldn't be welcome at the memorial service on the pier.'

'Why ever not?' Cal almost shouted, forgetting himself.

Grace Ann's eyes flashed open. She looked at Cal, as if startled. 'I never knew for certain except that Sandy's death had to be avenged somehow.'

135

'Is that when my grandmother left the island?'

'It was. Ishbel went to live with her parents on the mainland in December 1942, though her mother-in-law Margaret pleaded with her to stay, for the baby to inherit the croft, so determined was she it would be a boy . . .'

Grace Ann broke off and Cal prompted her again. 'My mother was born early the following year?'

Grace Ann nodded. 'When your great grandmother heard the baby was a girl she left the island too, to go to her sister in Thurso. Murdo Rae and his family took over the Sinclair house and croft as they'd always wanted.'

Neither of them spoke for a few moments, Cal reflecting on what he thought was the end of the story, Grace Ann taking another sip of tea.

After returning the mug to the trolley, she glanced up at Cal and then quickly away. Suddenly she seemed nervous of him again. 'Did you know my brother's body was found?'

'No I didn't.' Cal sounded surprised.

'A letter came to my mother the following spring. It was from the Admiralty informing her Sandy's body had been washed up on the Lofoten Islands near the Norwegian coast. The commander of the German garrison there had identified Sandy by his wrist watch. He'd been buried where he was found, on the south-east coast of an island called Moskenesoy.'

'My mother never mentioned it.'

Grace Ann went on as if she hadn't heard Cal's comment. 'I hoped it would bring peace to my mama but she died of a broken heart by the autumn. The morning I buried her I left the island for good.'

She paused again, the emotion of the memory robbing her of words, before stretching her left hand to the stool. She picked up a small red box which had faded in parts to pink. 'My brother's watch was returned to my mama with the letter from the Admiralty.'

Grace Ann offered Cal the box.

She said softly, 'Your grandfather wore one too. All the men were given them when they joined the boat's crew.'

The watch, like the model of the boat, lay on a bed of cotton wool. The face was cracked and cloudy as if a sea mist was trapped inside it. Only the 1 and 2 in Roman numerals were visible on the hour dial. The leather strap was black, twisted and hard.

'Would you mind if I held it?' Cal asked.

Grace Ann shook her head and Cal picked it out and turned it over. 'Alexander MacKay, *Eilean Iasgaich* 1942.' He read aloud the inscription on the back.

'1942 was when he joined the crew,' Grace Ann said.

When Cal replaced the watch on the cotton wool, he said, 'It must be a comfort knowing he's buried and having his watch . . .'

'Yes.'

Once again the emotion seemed to overwhelm her. Warily, he attempted reassurance, expecting another ticking off. 'Thank you, for telling me this. It must be hard, going back over such painful memories.'

'Oh it's not finished,' Grace Ann said abruptly.

'I'm sorry,' Cal said.

Then she told him a story he knew already, though he didn't admit to it: how the depleted crew had continued anti-submarine patrols along the north coast and Orkney; how in 1944 the *Eilean Iasgaich* had come upon a U-boat on the surface attacking a boat-load of Norwegian resistance fighters, how it rammed the U-boat with the loss of both vessels. The last of the island's able bodied men died. 'Every last one of them,' Grace Ann said.

'The island was abandoned the following year wasn't it?' Cal said.

'The women tried to struggle on but without their men . . . well . . .' Her voice trailed away.

'Wasn't there quite a fuss? I've got some old newspaper cuttings.'

'There was a public appeal to help the widows and children build houses on the mainland. The Norwegian government bought them land along the coast from Eastern Township. I'm told you can see the island from it.'

'Did all the families move there?'

'Some moved away altogether but the Raes and

138

the MacKays settled there. They took legal title to the island.'

'They own it.'

'They do, and there's a shop and a museum on it, in the old schoolhouse, for the day trippers. Hector MacKay's log of the Archangelsk convoy is on display there. It was found among his widow's possessions when she died, wrapped around with prayers he'd written on to sheets of paper.'

Cal said, 'The memorial's by the pier isn't it? When I was a child I wanted to see it but my mother wouldn't take me.'

'It's to the heroes of *Eilean Iasgaich*, the nine island men who died in the U-boat explosion as well as the ones who lost their lives on the Arctic convoy . . .' she hesitated before looking straight at him, her eyes filled with anxiety. 'Cal. I couldn't tell you earlier. Your grandfather . . . his name isn't on the memorial.'

'They didn't leave it off?' Cal raised his voice in astonishment.

'God forgive them, but they did too.' Grace Ann said, closing her eyes and turning away, hiding from him in case he blamed her too.

If he'd lived Grace Ann's life he'd have gone a little mad too, he thought.

Between 5 and 6pm on a Saturday, Buchanan Street in Glasgow becomes a place of transition. The shoppers begin to go home, or rest in the coffee shops and wine bars in the side streets.

Teenage girls in flimsy mini-skirts and cheap white shoes with high heels emerge shrieking and giggling in expectation of the night's drinking and partying. The boys, in gangs, roam among them watching for possibilities. Everywhere people are moving, mingling, separating. Everyone is going somewhere. Everyone has a direction of travel, except on this Saturday at 5.43pm one slender girl who walks awkwardly and hunched to disguise her height. She stays on the margins of the crowds, her face half hidden by a stained, grey hoodie she found on the railway embankment near her shelter. A distant group of women wearing pink ear mufflers and singing, out of tune, 'Money, Money, Money' by Abba are heading towards her. She recoils. It is as if an unseen force travels ahead of the group, a force that only Basanti feels. Everyone near her maintains their course but she stops and turns as though buffeted by it. The women are closer to her now; their singing louder. Their arms are linked. They stretch across fifteen metres of pedestrianised street. They will barely notice her, despite her matted hair and the stains on her clothes. But she doesn't seem to know they will move aside for her. Their unseen force bears on her again, making her hurry back the way she has come, until she passes a lane. It pulls her in, a refuge. She walks half way up until she slumps on her heels. A wall is behind her. She feels the cold of the stone against her spine where her ill-fitting hoodie and loose shirt have exposed her skin. A black wheelie bin hides her from the street she has left. She hears the young women, more muffled now. 'It's a rich man's world,' they sing with a high pitch of tuneless shouts and cackles as they go to whichever venue is playing host to their friend's hen party. She shakes as they pass the bottom of the lane. She isn't used to crowds, or cities, or this country, or the hostility of the people: everywhere she goes hard, pinched faces stare at her. She's alone and now she seems also to be lost. She has to travel to Edinburgh. A shopkeeper has told her it is 80 kilometres away. She asks about a bus. 'Aye, hen, you'll catch it at the Buchanan bus station. D'ye not know it?' The woman tells her the way and when Basanti asks the cost of the journey, she replies 'Six, maybe eight pounds, isn't that so Billy?' The boy who is loading up the cigarette gantry says, 'Aye' without looking round. 'How do I get pounds?' Basanti asks the woman, lowering her voice. The woman laughs, a smoker's rasp. 'Ach, away with you,' she says, putting her hands on her hips, and nodding to the next customer.

The street at the bottom of this lane is Buchanan Street. Basanti has seen the sign on the wall. But where is the bus station? Where will she get the money for the fare?

She is exhausted. Her limbs are aching. Her stomach is tight. Her head is spinning with this unfamiliar city and its people. She is frightened. Since leaving her shelter on the railway embankment she has been tense with worry and fear. The men who own her will find her. The men who abused her will be in the crowds; somewhere. They will recognise her. The police who are patrolling the streets will arrest her. By now they will be looking for her, for stabbing the Albanian.

Only the thought of Preeti keeps her going. She is her strength. She is what makes her get up and walk along the lane. She is what gives her the courage to approach a man in white overalls sitting on a step, outside the back door of a restaurant. He is smoking and he watches her coming towards him with surly indifference.

She isn't looking at him when she speaks. She studies the space between them. There's a pigeon's feather floating in a pool of greasy water. She watches it. 'Please can you tell me the way to the bus station?' There is a tremor in her voice.

He detects her fear. He gives her directions. It's no more than five minutes walk. He says, 'Are you ok?' She hears what she thinks is sympathy so she asks him if he will lend her money. £8 she mentions. She's still not looking at him so she doesn't know he's looking at her, or the way he's doing it.

'I'll give you £10 if you do something for me,' he says and his voice changes, a tone she recognises. She feels her body go torpid, like a lizard's when the sun dips before night. It's a feeling to which she is accustomed. Isn't this how she has coped these past months, years?

As he penetrates her she makes a solemn promise.

No man will do this to her again, ever. But she needs the money. For Preeti. To travel to the address she's read in the newspaper, to find the man with a picture of Preeti on his wall.

He pushes into her. Basanti's face conveys no emotion or feeling. Her hand tightens around the £10 note. Otherwise she is quite still.

CHAPTER 10

There had been a reason after all.

Cal recalled his childhood complaint, 'Why can't we go to Grandpa Uilleam's island?' His mother answered him with more questions, a family failing. 'Why on earth would you want to?' or 'why waste precious holiday going all the way up there?' This response left Cal perplexed. Driving for hours to damp cottages on remote coasts was what they did for their summer holidays. Eventually his father said to him, 'Don't keep bothering your mother, Cal.'

Cal had asked why.

'Well, grandpa died before she was born and your grandmother's side of the family is all she's known. Aberdeen is where she's from, not Eilean Iasgaich. So let it drop, eh?'

There was an undertone of warning in his father's voice, and Cal did let it drop, though his mother's odd reticence and his father's caution only stimulated his interest. He was 11, and two years into his attempt to solve the mystery of his missing grandfather after coming across the unnamed graves in Ardnamurchan. All his calculations now pointed to his grandfather's body being encased in Arctic sea ice. The Norwegian government had to be notified, or so he thought, but he needed advice on the appropriate recipient of his carefully typed letter.

'Can I ask mummy?'

His father didn't answer his question, not exactly.

'Oh, can't I help you?' He'd sounded disappointed. 'After all, I'm the one who knows about coordinates, longitude and latitude and so on.'

Which, of course, was the case: James McGill was head of geography at the senior school of Edinburgh Academy – Cal was still in juniors. But once more there was that insistent undertone in his father's voice.

From then on he made sure he had his father alone whenever he discussed his latest theories about currents or the location of his grandfather. Recollecting it now, Cal appreciated his father's patience. A less sensitive man might have tried to dissuade him from the very idea of his grandfather's body still being intact and incorruptible so many years after his death. Cal's father never attempted to do so, nor was it strictly necessary. By then Cal understood the process of decomposition but he was so accustomed to regarding his grandfather as a benign and continuing presence that in his imagination he was still happy, smiling and wearing a hat like the photograph of him on his mother's dressing table.

Uilleam was like a make-believe friend: both real

and fantasy but most of all a companion for the solitary child Cal had already become. His father understood or at least recognised his son's need and indulged it.

Of course, he was also protecting Eilidh, Cal's mother.

Cal knew that now, after listening to Grace Ann. Once more, and only once more, had he tried to probe his mother for information. He must have been 13 or 14 and he was on an end of holiday break with her on Skye (on another remote coast). His father had stayed behind to prepare for the new school term. They were walking along the beach by their B&B when he said to her, 'Don't you love the sea?'

It was a sly question he hoped would lead somewhere.

'It's curious isn't it Cal? I was brought up in Aberdeen which is beside the sea and we live in Edinburgh which is beside the sea but I think of myself as someone who comes from the city, not the sea-side.'

'But you were born beside the sea.'

She didn't reply immediately. Cal remembered his anticipation of her response, hoping it would let him ask another question without making his intentions obvious.

'Yes, I suppose I was.'

He decided on another foray despite his father's warning.

'Why did you leave?'

'I suppose it was time for a change that's all. I was ten and my mother wanted to send me to a good secondary school. The one she knew best, where she'd gone to school, was in Aberdeen. My grandfather was ill by then and the shop wasn't the business it had been. My mother had friends and cousins in Aberdeen too.' They walked on for a few steps and she added, 'There's no mystery to it, Cal.'

Straight away she challenged him to a race along the sand and that was the end of that. As he lay gasping for breath by the rocks, while she gave up winded 20 metres before the finish, Cal thought he believed her. Its mysteriousness had lain in her silence but now it seemed ordinary, not mysterious at all.

The next year she was diagnosed with breast cancer and his father took him aside one day and said 'we must do all we can to avoid upsetting your mother.' So he hadn't attempted to broach it again, slyly or otherwise. She died when he was between school and first year oceanography. She was 53, coincidentally the same age her own mother, Cal's grandmother Ishbel, had been when she died, also from breast cancer. His mother's death left his father incapable and turned Cal into his unqualified counsellor. The reversal of roles made him resentful and intolerant of his father's fragility. They weren't emotions he'd expected. His father took bereavement leave from school and moped at home all day. When he pulled himself together, he announced he was going to join VSO and teach in Papua New Guinea. 'I'm no good to you like this Cal,' he said. 'I'll be back before you know it.' But other destinations had followed: the latest a two year stint in Swaziland. Cal's small family had disintegrated about him.

He had never seriously considered visiting Eilean Iasgaich since his mother's death. Something warned him against it. Perhaps it was loyalty to her or simply that her passing had severed his only living connection with the place. Whatever the reason, these vague half-feelings had deterred him.

There were other islands, other oceans, after all.

Now, in Grace Ann's bungalow, a different set of conflicting feelings assailed him: sorrow for his mother's unspoken memories which must have been too painful for her ever to confide in him; shame at the unintentional distress he inflicted on her every time he mentioned Uilleam's name; anger at the injustice of it all. There was another sensation too, one that had been dormant since his mother's death. Rachel talking about her documentary had disturbed its sleep; Grace Ann's story had awoken it. The island had an emotional pull on him again.

'Do you think my mother knew?' He asked Grace Ann.

Grace Ann was looking out of the window, distracted. 'I dare say she knew some of it,' she said after some consideration, without turning to Cal. 'She would have attended primary school in

Eastern Township. There would have been talk. But your grandmother and mother went back to Aberdeen after the war. The Raes opened a garage in Eastern Township, and then a general store. They put poor Ishbel's parents out of business. I heard her father had a stroke and her mother had to sell up to the Raes of all people.'

Neither spoke for a few minutes until Cal said, as though thinking aloud. 'It's odd my parents never mentioned your brother's body being found.'

Grace Ann still didn't look at him. 'The letter about Sandy arrived the spring after he died. By then Uilleam's mother had gone to Thurso and Ishbel, your grandmother, was on the mainland. No-one from the island had anything to do with her family after what happened so it's likely she never knew.'

Now her voice had an irritable tone which seemed to discourage more questions.

'You've been kind, telling me the story.' Cal said in case she had become impatient with him for staying so long. 'Thank you.'

He wrote his address and phone number on the notepad pad on her trolley. 'I'd like to come and see you again; talk some more . . .'

By then Grace Ann's eyes were closed tight, her Bible at her lips, her chin lifted, as if in defiance. Cal said goodbye but she seemed not to hear him. He tried goodbye again but still she didn't answer. He went to the door, closing it quietly behind him. On the way to his bus-stop he tried to rid himself of the suspicion she was behaving like that for a purpose. Was there something she wasn't telling him?

At low tide, at the base of Cnoc a' Mhonaidh, a beach of sand extends into the wide mouth of a cave. To one side of it is a rock, smooth on the top, with mussels and limpets clinging to its pitted flanks. Grace Ann observes herself, a young woman, sitting there. She feels the wind on her face. She sees how furtive her manner is: how she looks back at the hillside she has descended; her anxiety in case Ishbel is following her. Grace Ann shuffles backwards, crab-wise, on the rock until an overhang conceals her. She can no longer be spied on from above. She opens the book she is carrying: it is a Bible, the Bible which she is holding to her lips all these years later. She sees herself take from it a single sheet of loose paper. She unfolds it, reads it quickly, kisses it, folds it again and returns it to the book. She moves forward, observing the hill again. There's no sign of Ishbel, who was some distance behind her on the path. Grace Ann remains there for half an hour or more, never moving. She feels the thrill of possession as well as guilt at what she has done. Her eyes close as if she is in prayer. Suddenly, she leaps up and climbs the slope of the hill, cutting diagonally across it.

Long after Cal has gone, Grace Ann remembers all of this as though it is happening to her now.

She wonders at her jealousy of long ago, the continuing force of her unrequited love which has made her do such a terrible thing.

The Bible is now on her lap, the same Bible. Her hands shake as she opens it. She holds the same piece of paper in arthritic fingers. It is the colour of parchment, though flimsier. She reads it, folds it and returns it to the book which she closes and lifts to her mouth. She kisses its cover. She sits there with her eyes shut. Then she sighs, a long soulful sound. She berates herself as if her resolve is already weakening. 'You must tell him Grace Ann. You must.'

The warning bell for the start of the second act had rung. The smokers outside the Festival Theatre in Edinburgh had filed back to their seats. The café bar on the ground floor had emptied, arguments about the soprano postponed until the next intermission. Had the orchestra drowned her out deliberately or was her voice insufficient for the role? The exodus of opera-lovers revealed Cal sitting alone at a table by a window overlooking the street. The emptiness of the place seemed to affect him because he drained his coffee, said 'thanks' to the waitress who was clearing glasses from the next table and left the theatre by the side door.

He crossed the street before turning left into a terrace of Victorian tenements. Music was spilling from a house further along. The louder it became the slower he walked. He texted, 'Not sure it's my kind of thing, Kate. What about lunch next week?' Kate Simpson was a master's student in geophysics and meteorology at Edinburgh University, in the department which he visited every so often to collect historical weather data for his ocean tracking work. The last time he'd seen her he'd promised to 'look in' at the party her housemates were planning. On the journey from Galashiels to Edinburgh, she'd messaged, reminding him.

He'd replied, 'I won't know anyone.'

'You'll know me.'

Now he was standing outside the house. His impulse was to slink away before Kate saw him. He wanted to go to his apartment to mull over Grace Ann's story, look at an atlas and check out the Lofoten Islands. Something was wrong. He'd known it the moment Grace Ann had mentioned them.

His phone beeped. It was Kate messaging again. 'Where are you?'

'I'm outside, getting cold feet.'

'Come on Cal. Just for a few minutes. Please me.'

He groaned. He owed her. She'd helped him so much working through the department's old files. 'Where are you?' he texted back, looking apprehensively at the three storey tenement where every window seemed to be filled with light, music and drunk or stoned students. A banner flapping over the front door announced 'Tom, Fiona, Orlando and Kate welcome you to their FISH PARTY'.

'You'll have to find me,' she replied.

'Shit.' He put his phone away. Now she wanted him to play hide and seek.

Cal walked up the gravel path to the door of the house, sidestepping the smokers gathered there. A man in a long blond wig and wearing a mermaid costume was standing by the door, dragging on a cigarette he had cadged from someone returning to the party. 'I could have tried a bit harder,' Cal said looking at his jacket, tee shirt and jeans. 'I didn't realise it was fancy dress.'

'A *bit* harder? Doesn't look to me like you've tried at all.' The man in the wig was Australian. 'Don't worry mate. It wouldn't have mattered. You should see some of the other guys. There's a great white on the first floor and a sailfish on the third.'

The hallway led to a stairwell draped with fishing nets and lobster pots. As Cal climbed the stairs, he was assailed by a sickly smell of fish, chips, vinegar, tobacco and marijuana. On the first landing, he edged past four girls in silver wigs and cardboard sardine tin costumes. They were standing beside a table covered with plastic tumblers of wine with plastic fish floating in them. Cal took one and wandered slowly through the crowds looking for Kate. Every room was a babble of shouted conversations, music and dancing. A black female saxophonist in a shimmering gold body stocking moved through the crush. Cal followed her, breaking away after four rooms to go to the top floor. He was drawn there by cheering and clapping. Edging past a group of students gathered round a doorway he saw two young men, one dressed as a shark, the other (Cal thought) as a marlin, leaning over a bath. They were plunging knives into the water. Their target was a large trout which was swimming with frantic jerky movements round a metallic reef of cooling beer cans. The men took it in turns to stab at it. The crowd heckled every time they missed. Cal tried to leave but the jeering had drawn others to the bathroom and he found his exit blocked. It was then he saw Kate. She was sitting on a shelf between mounds of white towels. On her head she wore a home-made hat in the shape of a lobster. He waved and she saw him too, clapping her hands in pleasure that he'd found her.

Another cheer went up and Cal turned to see the marlin hold aloft the skewered trout. The blade had pierced its side. The fish's tail flapped and its mouth gaped. When marlin shook the knife, it fell back into the bath. A chant of 'Kill it, kill it' went up.

Cal was propelled forward by a surge behind him. More and more people were pressing into the bathroom, drawn there by the shouting. There was a tugging at his arm and it was Kate, smiling. 'You made it,' she yelled. Cal leaned towards her and said into her ear, 'I can't Kate, I'm sorry. Let's have lunch, soon.'

The last he saw was her disappointed face. He felt bad about it. Yes, he'd have to make it up to her. But as soon as the music faded behind him his thoughts turned to the Lofoten Islands. If they were where he thought, no way could Sandy's body have been washed up there. Not in a million years.

Ryan parked 200 metres from the entrance to police headquarters. He rolled down his window, lit a cigarette and waited for Tessa Rainey. She texted: *Just finishing a report. Meet at 11pm?*
He replied: *I'll be across the road from Waitrose*
Good plan.
Ryan liked that about her. She was pretty and smart with it. Smart enough to know the rules of this game. Don't hump in office hours. Don't kiss. Don't touch. Don't give each other knowing glances. Don't pick up outside. Park some distance away, as he'd done. Keep it cool around the office and hot away from it: in his flat, a penthouse with a roof garden in Leith. She understood that. He didn't need to tell her. They were two of a kind. They'd have fun while it lasted. No tears at the end; no regrets. That was the deal. Tessa knew that. Of course she did.
Ryan sucked on his cigarette and watched the Waitrose shelf-stackers through the side window. But his thoughts drifted back to Tessa to block out the frustrations of the last 24 hours: since McGill's media blitz Ryan had done nothing but take calls from politicians making their excuses. 'I'd like to help the prosecution but . . .'
Screw them.
After Ryan and Tessa had sex for the first time,

she had asked if she could partner him on a case and he agreed. Why not? He had worked with Jamieson and every other new recruit to criminal investigation. Wasn't it his job to guide them, show them the ropes? Everybody expected it. Wouldn't it be more of a signal in the office if he *didn't* let Rainey work with him? He could trust her to be professional about it. Tessa had been so grateful when he said yes – he'd remember what she did to him long into his old age, though he hadn't conceded anything at all, not really (not that he told her).

A movement across the road caught his attention.

A figure, female, was crossing the ramp entrance to the Waitrose car park which was in darkness. Ryan wondered if it was Tessa and hooked his finger round the headlight flasher to let her know where he was. But the figure was smaller than Tessa, and heavier, with none of Tessa's elegance. (It gave Ryan a buzz to watch the way she appeared to glide with her midriff, like a model or a dancer.) Soon the woman was in the pool of light from the supermarket's side window and Ryan recognised Helen Jamieson. His eyes followed her as she walked to the corner and crossed the road, his expression changing to disgust. A feeling of frustrated rage replaced his anticipation of another amorous night with Rainey.

What was Jamieson good for? Yes, she was clever. University clever. Book clever. Not street clever like him. Street clever was what you needed in the police. His temper was rising again now as it did every time he saw her. How did someone like her climb the career ladder quicker than guys who'd worked their way through the ranks from school, putting offenders behind bars? He wasn't against women in the force. Rainey, for example, was street-wise in the right way, athletic and physically strong. But Jamieson?

Ryan spat through his open window as if ridding his mouth of a bad taste. Yet she'd be a sergeant soon and an inspector by the time she was 33. He'd done it the hard way; in his opinion, it was the only way. He was three times the copper and he hadn't made inspector until he was 37, after 18 years service. Why did she get it so easy?

Because she had a law degree, an MSc in criminology and she was female. It made the Chief Constable look good. On paper. Not where it mattered. Ryan banged his fist against the steering wheel. Go back to university, get a job in a library; leave the police to people like him and Rainey. Christ, Jamieson wasn't even good for shagging.

'Lofoten Is, Norway. 48, C3' Cal turned to plate 48 in his Times Atlas of the World. He checked the map reference and planted his finger on an archipelago of islands jutting like a ragged dorsal fin from the Norwegian coast, south-west of Tromso. He found Moskenesoy at the south western end of the islands, and grunted as if in vindication. He wrote down the approximate co-ordinates and went to his big wall map of the north Atlantic and the Arctic. He put one index finger on 72°30'N, 18°03'E where his grandfather Uilleam and Sandy MacKay had been washed overboard, and found the Lofoten Islands. He double checked the coordinates and referred again to the atlas index, just in case there were two groups of islands with the same name in the north-east Atlantic. Lying back in his swivel chair he studied the map again. After staring at it for ten minutes, he shook his head and began to pace up and down the flat, occasionally stopping by the windows, or the wall map to check another theory. After an hour he slumped back into his chair. 'No fucking way,' he shouted.

Across the road from The Cask was a row of concrete garages with sloping and rusted corru-gated iron roofs. They were used by traders for storage and by men who liked to tinker with cars at evenings and weekends. Dog walkers also came here at night to let Buster or Rover roam the concrete waste ground behind the garages. Nobody cared what happened here. It was derelict, neglected buddleia-colonised land, which once belonged to the deserted flour mill on its far side. Here, dog owners were freed of the obligation to clear up after their canine charges.

Basanti lay on the garage roof long after the light had gone from three top floor windows in the building opposite. She had seen the man whose photograph was in the newspaper standing at one of the windows, and now she was lying on her back studying the few flickering stars which shone through the night glow of Scotland's capital city. Had her mother also gazed at the stars during these past months, years? Had she wondered about her lost daughter as her daughter wondered about her? Had her mother laid awake pleading for forgiveness even as Basanti meekly submitted to male desire and nightly renewed her vows of vengeance?

Against the men who abused her.

Against her rich uncle who ordered the sale of her virginity.

Against her mother who acquiesced?

Her mother's betrayal raised a storm of passions in the girl: rage, yearning, hatred, pity, even love. Her mother had been grief-stricken, newly widowed and besieged by her dead husband's creditors. Her mother had been weak. Her mother hadn't been able to envisage an alternative. How would she have provided for her other, crippled daughter without the protection of her husband's brother? The well-being of one of her daughters had to be sacrificed. Which one must it be?

Basanti had decided long ago not to take revenge on her mother, but nor would she forgive her. Even though she had hardened her heart, sometimes she longed for the warm wrap of her mother's arms. Lying here now she couldn't imagine anything more thrilling.

Basanti shut her eyes, blacking out the stars and cutting off a new and threatening flood of emotion. She inhaled deeply, finding unexpected solace in the darkness and in her solitariness. She'd have to move from the garage roof before the exposure of daylight. She'd have to find shelter away from the risk of haphazard encounters with men. But for these few minutes she would remain there, at last free, at last calm, at last a little closer to Preeti.

She had travelled to Edinburgh on a late bus. There had been random reasons for not getting earlier ones: an inebriated man bumping against her at the bus station; a gang of boys pointing her out; a leering driver; a girl telling her friends a joke about 'Pakis'.

The bus station crowds unnerved her and in her confusion she kept on making wrong decisions. She abandoned two bus queues almost at the point of boarding. Once she ran from the building only to encounter a police patrol car parked outside and she turned and went back inside. She knew she was drawing attention to herself but she was unable to control her urge to run when she felt the claustrophobia of a confined space with so many other jostling, threatening people. She joined the queue for the 11pm bus. Because she feared there wouldn't be another, she forced herself up the steps. To her relief, her matted, cropped hair and dirty clothes provoked little attention. Most of the passengers were too drunk, exhausted or

160

drugged to notice. The fare had been £6. She had £4 left.

In Edinburgh she waited for everyone else to disembark before asking the driver to direct her to Granton, 'a building called The Cask?' She showed him the line in the newspaper. 'There . . . The Cask, overlooking Granton Harbour.' She read it aloud for him.

'That's the place by Lower Granton Road, isn't it, by the old flour mill?' he remarked. 'I used to drive that route.'

'I think so,' she said uncertainly.

'Are you walking?'

She nodded.

'On your own?'

She nodded again.

He pursed his lips and shook his head. The risks kids took nowadays. 'At this time of night. You sure?'

'Yes.'

'Keep going that way until you reach the sea.' He pointed out of the side of the bus. 'Stick to the main roads mind, where it's well lit.'

She said she would, though she'd dipped into the shadows and dim side streets where she felt invisible and safe. She asked again for directions in a 24-hour store. She'd gone a little off course, but 10 minutes later she had found The Cask and the garage roof opposite.

Tomorrow night she'd find a way in. Now she had to scavenge for food and find somewhere to lie up during the day.

She wriggled off the garage roof and dropped into the darkness below.

It was daylight when Cal awoke. The arm of the chair pressed against the stitches in his side and he arched his torso, turning sideways, settling on his hip. He slumbered on, listening to the shrieks of the gulls and the passing buses. He'd slept badly, restlessly turning over Grace Ann's story in his head, wondering whether he had imagined her stubborn reticence at the end, or misinterpreted it. What bemused him more was the unexplained discrepancy over Sandy's body. Cal had spent a good part of the night trying to find a plausible explanation, at one point getting up to search his databases for any seasonal quirks of current in the area of ocean where Sandy and his grandfather had been swept overboard. He came across an Oslo University research chart displaying average October offshore winds and prevailing surface currents for the Norwegian, Greenland and Barents seas. He traced 72°30'N and 18°03'E, where Sandy and his grandfather had gone overboard on September 29 1942. It was more than 100kms south of Bear Island, which lay between the rest of the Svalbard archipelago to the north and Norway to the south. Then he drew a line from 72°30'N and 18°03'E to Moskenesoy, the most south-westerly of the large Lofoten Islands. This was where Sandy's body had been found, though on the island's sheltered south-east coast which only added another inconsistency. The line Cal drew cut across the shoals of arrowheads on the chart signifying the direction of current. His line went south-south-west. The currents tracked north-easterly, as he expected. Next he checked an archive of historical weather data, which he'd gathered for his childhood researches. It was as he remembered: there were recordings of frequent westerly gales in the North Atlantic in September/ October 1942. Like the currents, these would have pushed Sandy's body further east not south. Even allowing for occasional days of northerly winds, Cal found no explanation for Sandy's body travelling south across more than 300 kms of ocean, against the prevailing currents.

He'd jotted down three possibilities:

1. The body is not Sandy's.

2. It is Sandy's but he didn't go into the sea at $72°30'N$ and $18°03'E$. Given the prevailing currents/winds, he must have entered the water south west of Moskenesoy to beach where he did.

3. If Sandy didn't go into the sea at $72°30'N$ and $18°03'E$, did Uilleam?

Then he fell asleep but it must have continued to play on his mind. When the morning sun shone brightly into his apartment, he was conscious of having made two decisions during the night. He would go to Eilean Iasgaich, to see Hector MacKay's logbook in the museum and to build a stone cairn on one of the island's two hills, overlooking the ocean. Cal was the last of the Sinclairs.

If he didn't build a memorial to his grandfather on the island of his birth, who would? Who else would right the wrong? After showering, he packed his rucksack – jeans, tee shirts, two jerseys. He texted Kate. 'Sorry for running out on you last night. Had to sort something. Make it up to you with lunch next week. Cal.' He deleted 'Make it up to you with lunch next week' and sent it. She'd be pissed off, but what could he do? He didn't want a commitment.

He checked his inbox. DLG had mailed. 'Two severed feet found on Shetland, the first on Papa Stour two days ago, the second further south, near Walls, on the Shetland mainland today. Send you more when I get it.'

Cal replied. 'Yes, please.'

He considered for a minute. Perhaps the East Lothian foot had travelled further than he originally thought. The Shetland finds changed things. He'd run some simulations using wind and current data, work out whether all three feet, the two from Shetland and the other from East Lothian, could have followed the same ocean track west of Scotland before arriving at different destinations hundreds of miles apart. If so, they might have started from the same place.

Right now he had another mystery to solve.

CHAPTER 11

'Are these the ones you're after, Prof?'

A pathology lab assistant in a white coat held up a sealed see-through plastic bag in each hand. There was a single trainer in each.

The interruption irritated Professor Tony Maplin, a man of small stature and quick movements. 'In a minute, in a minute . . .' Maplin glowered at the assistant and let his eyes linger disapprovingly on the youth's pallid face and his lank hair trailing across his dirty collar. He sighed in theatrical exasperation. 'I'm sorry Detective Inspector, where were we?'

'You were explaining the onset of adipocere.'

'Ah yes. There were signs of it on both feet, as there was on the foot washed ashore in East Lothian. It can happen when bodies are in water for a long time.'

'How long would you say in this case?'

'It's guesswork I'm afraid. Certainly weeks, more likely months . . .'

Maplin's hands jerked up and down as he spoke and his eyes flashed between David Ryan and the assistant who had adopted a sullen, defiant expression since his ticking off.

'Oh for goodness sake,' Maplin suddenly exploded. 'Don't just stand there Thomas. Put the bags on the table.'

The assistant did as he was instructed with deliberate slowness and with a roll of his eyes at Ryan.

'I'm sorry Detective Inspector.' Maplin stared after his departing assistant. 'I can forgive anything in a place like this except a wilful lack of grace. I refuse to be reminded that we're dumb animals waiting in line for bodily corruption.'

There were six other tables in the room, in three rows. Ghostly grey-white corpses lay on the two closest. Ryan grimaced in sympathy with the professor's outburst. 'You were saying it could be many months, Professor Maplin.'

'Could even be years . . .'

Maplin threw both his hands into the air to make his point about the range of possibilities. 'Adipocere is a process which involves the fatty layer beneath the skin transforming into a soap-like substance. You might know of it as saponification. Its effect is to inhibit normal decomposition. There are recorded cases of saponified bodies surviving almost intact for years.'

'In this case . . . ?'

Maplin contorted his face and patted his unruly, wiry hair with both hands. 'Oh I do hate so much being put on the spot by you people.'

The tip of his tongue curled round the edge of his mouth. 'Ok, ok, if you want me to put my head

166

on the block . . .' He rammed both hands decisively into the pockets of his green tweed jacket.

'Something we can work with, yes.'

'Well, I'd say months, definitely months. The adipocere isn't as advanced as it might be . . .'

Ryan let out a grunt of disappointment

'I can't help it if you don't like it Detective Inspector. Really I can't.' Maplin's tone was petulant.

'No, no . . . You can only do what you can do . . .'

Maplin suddenly smirked. 'Though I have found something you might find interesting Detective Inspector.' He waited for a prompt.

'Go on.'

'Well the foot from that shoe . . .' Maplin lifted up the bag enclosing a trainer with red, orange and green bands round its side, the colours still bright despite its lengthy immersion in sea water. '. . . It belongs to the same body as the foot which beached in East Lothian.'

'Are you sure?'

Maplin beamed with pleasure at Ryan's shock. 'I'm absolutely certain Detective Inspector. There's not even a shadow of doubt.'

'But it never occurred to me . . . the shoe's different . . . the other one had a polka dot pattern.'

'Just so, Detective Inspector.'

'So you're saying the feet match but the trainers don't?'

Maplin beamed again, like a teacher proud at unexpected progress in his slowest pupil. 'That's exactly what I'm saying Detective Inspector.'

'Sure?'

Maplin arched his eyebrows in practised contempt. Did this pretty boy policeman in his well-cut blue suit, white shirt, stubble and tan doubt him? 'Of course it's up to you whether you want to avail yourself of my expertise Detective Inspector though I should imagine you'd want to.'

Ryan attempted to mollify the professor. 'No, no, of course . . . you've been very helpful. It was just unexpected that's all; extremely unexpected.'

The policeman paused to think. Maplin's face twitched with pleasure at the effect he'd induced.

'Did someone cut off the feet and put them in odd shoes?' Ryan was casting around for an explanation.

'No, all three were severed by disarticulation. The ankle separates as part of the routine process of decomposition.'

'How long does it take?'

'It depends.'

'On what?'

'Water temperature, the depth, disturbance . . . there are a number of variables.'

'Would the feet have disarticulated at the same time?'

'They might, they might not; and even if they did they wouldn't necessarily float to the surface at the same time. There are, as I say, a number of variables. It's all in my report.'

'Which you'll finish . . . ?'

'It's done Detective Inspector.' Maplin picked

168

up a brown envelope from the table and handed it to him. Then he gave Ryan the bags one at a time. 'We've done all we can with these.'

Ryan held them away from his body and Maplin remarked archly, 'Your nice suit's quite safe Detective Inspector. All the human material's been removed.'

Ten minutes later he was back in his office at Lothian and Borders Police HQ reading the message stuck to the telephone on his desk. 'Helen Jamieson will assist.' The writing was Detective Chief Superintendent Jim Reynolds's familiar scrawl. Ryan swore and crumpled it tight in his fist. His interview for the Scottish Crime and Drug Enforcement Agency was three weeks away and Reynolds had given him Detective Constable Jamieson when he'd asked for Tessa Rainey.

'Shit.' Ryan spat the word.

His lobbying with Ian Carmichael, the Assistant Chief Constable, had irritated Reynolds and this was his revenge.

'With respect sir,' Ryan had said standing at the opposite corner of the ACC's desk from Reynolds. 'This inquiry is better run from headquarters. The Shetland discoveries have changed the case completely. There's intense media interest . . .'

Reynolds snapped. 'One day wonder.'

Ryan ignored him, '. . . and Northern Constabulary has asked us to take the lead on forensics. The shoes will be flown to Edinburgh in any case. It makes sense for the same lab to deal with all the evidence.'

'And for our boys in East Lothian to run it,' Reynolds insisted, 'as they have been from the beginning when the first foot turned up.'

'With all due respect,' Ryan paused for effect. 'There's the potential scope of the investigation to consider. God knows where it's going to lead or how many more feet will turn up, or where . . .' Ryan glanced at his senior officer and Reynolds scowled back. '. . . It's a big coordination job and there are dangers . . . the media . . . at a sensitive time for all the Scottish police forces.'

Reynolds's already florid face turned scarlet with a rush of anger. Ryan was outmanoeuvring him, using the forthcoming review of Scotland's police forces to put the wind up the ACC.

'Wouldn't we all sleep easier if it was run from here?' Carmichael addressed his question to Reynolds but before he could answer, the ACC continued, 'I know I would, what with the politicians breathing down our necks. The review on the structure and funding of the Scottish police has its first public meeting in Edinburgh in a couple of weeks. We don't want any avoidable mistakes do we Jim?'

Reynolds shrugged. His argument was lost. 'I wouldn't push my personal interest over whatever's best for the force, of course Ian.'

It was a barb intended for Ryan.

'Well that's settled then. Good.' Carmichael clapped his hands together oblivious of the tension between the two officers. 'Who will assist you?' he said to Ryan.

'I haven't given it any thought sir, though the new Detective Constable, Tessa Rainey, is bright and could do with the experience. She's worked on missing persons before.'

By now Reynolds was moving to the door. 'I'll find you someone good David. No worries on that score.' He'd gone before Ryan could reply.

Detective Constable Helen Jamieson was Reynolds settling the score. Reynolds knew Ryan didn't like her.

Ryan clamped his fist around the crumpled message. How was he going to impress the SCDEA selection board if he had to work in tandem with Jamieson on such a high profile inquiry? His last case had made it big in the media but tackling organised crime or drug rackets it wasn't. Ryan had an unsettling feeling it wouldn't cut ice with his interview panel either, particularly if any of them had heard about the prosecution's struggle to find anyone prepared to lodge a formal complaint against McGill or even turn up in court. Arresting an eco-warrior for spending his evenings doing a bit of guerrilla gardening wasn't exactly crime-busting on the SCDEA scale of things. It had even caused a joke or two at headquarters. The one that still rankled with him was a snide shot by a detective on secondment from the Strathclyde force. 'That guy,' he said referring to Cal McGill, 'should be locked up in a greenhouse and the key thrown away.'

The other officers around the canteen table tried

to conceal their amusement but Ryan caught their disappearing smirks. Screw you, he thought, resolving to gatecrash another case to sway the SCDEA selection panel. 'The mystery of the severed feet', as the media described it, was the only realistic prospect for him. It was developing quickly and it was playing big on the BBC and ITN national news bulletins, not to mention the international networks. Ryan liked the thought of his face appearing on the ten o'clock news in the sitting rooms of his SCDEA interviewers for the next few days.

He'd jotted down a media plan. There'd be daily press conferences and briefings with selected crime correspondents, or editors if they wanted it. Of course, he'd make himself available for television. He'd do whatever it took. After a media blitz who would remember the McGill case, or his involvement in it, or that it wouldn't end in a prosecution (thanks to spineless politicians refusing to appear as Crown witnesses)? Now Jamieson would be a constant reminder of it, to him if to nobody else. He threw the crumpled message against the wall.

At that moment Jamieson put her head round his door.

'Mr Reynolds said you wanted me sir.'

'Did he?'

'He said you'd asked for me specially.' Jamieson sounded doubtful. *And pigs will fly.*

'Did he?'

'Yes sir.'

She picked up the discarded Post-it.

'Put it in the bin, Jamieson.'

'Yes sir.'

'Sit down Jamieson.'

'Let me guess sir – we're on the trail of a gang who've been taking unauthorised cuttings from botanical gardens.' Jamieson seemed startled and flustered all at the same moment. *Oh my God I've said it out loud.* 'Sorry sir,' she stuttered.

Jamieson had seen contempt on Ryan's face before but never like this. His eyes became hooded and his neck muscles tensed so tightly his head began to quiver.

'Are you serious about your career?' he said eventually.

'Yes sir.'

'Well act like it Jamieson.'

'Yes sir.'

'Mr Reynolds thought you should assist me . . .' which was Ryan's acid way of putting her back in her place.

'I see sir.'

'He thinks you can help me with this investigation into the severed feet that have washed up in East Lothian and Shetland.' Ryan made sure the emphasis was on the first word of the sentence: 'he'.

Jamieson flinched. Her expression deadened.

'What was it you wanted me to do sir?'

'Find out everything you can about the shoes.'

'Yes sir.'

'Don't screw up Jamieson.'

He threw the two bags containing the trainers towards her and dismissed her with a backward flip of his right hand.

'Oh right, sir . . .'

Jamieson picked up the bags. 'They don't match sir.'

'Yes, Jamieson, very observant.'

'I meant neither of them matches the trainer washed up in East Lothian. Two left feet, one right foot . . . and three bodies.'

Ryan thought: 'Two bodies, Jamieson. Two bodies.' But he didn't want her blabbing it and the story getting out before he was ready.

'Jamieson, your job is to discover something I don't already know. So go away and find it.'

'Yes sir.'

Six hours and forty minutes later Jamieson returned to the detectives' room. She was hungry and her legs were sore from pounding pavements tracking down Nike nerds as she now called them. These were (male and/or spotty) shoe shop assistants fluent in the design quirks of every Nike trainer manufactured since Adam Ant was a boy. She slumped at her desk. DC Tessa Rainey looked up and flicked her hair. 'Tired out?'

'Bushed.'

Rainey said, 'Big turn out wasn't it?'

'Excuse me?'

'For the press conference . . .'

'What press conference?'

'Ryan's – about the feet. He let me sit in on it.'

Jamieson tried to sound nonchalant. 'Yeah . . . listen I need to make a quick call.' She keyed in her home number and clicked on to the BBC website. There was a picture of Ryan looking man-about-town suave. 'Police reveal DNA match for severed feet found hundreds of miles apart.' She called up the story and read it.

Two left feet, one right foot and two bodies.

When she went to Ryan's office for the second time that day it was 6.55pm and he was lying back in his chair waiting for Channel 4 News.

'They match sir?' Jamieson let him know she was put out.

Ryan gave her a long-suffering look. 'What Jamieson?'

'They match, sir: two of the feet. They belong to each other.'

'Yes Jamieson.'

'Two left feet, one right foot . . . and two bodies; not three bodies as I'd said.'

'Looks like it Jamieson . . .'

'But the shoes don't sir.'

'What Jamieson?'

'Match sir. They don't match.'

'Yes Jamieson, very observant.'

'But sir . . .'

The Channel 4 News jingle began playing. Ryan held up his hand to silence her and turned up the volume.

'Not now Jamieson. Come back in ten minutes.'

It was the lead story, as it had been on the BBC

and ITN early evening news bulletins. 'A bizarre new twist in the mystery of the severed feet which have washed up on Scottish coasts . . .' the presenter lifted his eyes to the camera. 'Police reveal a foot found in Shetland matches the one discovered last week on a beach in East Lothian.' The screen flashed to Ryan at a table behind a bank of microphones, DC Rainey standing to one side of him. The camera angle was different to that of the BBC and ITN and less flattering. It made him look rather lantern-jawed. Ryan jotted down 'Channel 4 camera – better position' on a notepad. The page was covered with other observations for his debrief with the force's director of communications at 8.30 the next morning.

Jamieson knocked and put her head round the door. 'Is this a convenient time sir?'

'This had better be good Jamieson.'

'Yes sir.'

She took some steps towards him before stopping.

'Well . . .'

'Well sir, the trainers are all varieties of the same make, Nike Air Max. The left shoe from East Lothian is an Air Max 360, the 2006 model.' She looked at her notebook. 'The right shoe found in Shetland contained the matching foot?'

'Yes of course it was the right shoe Jamieson. How many people do you know with two left feet, apart from yourself?'

'It's an Air Max 95. The shoe we've got is a

recently restyled model. The remaining shoe is an Air Max Classic BW – BW stands for 'Big Window' sir – and it was introduced in 1991 though there have been different trims and adaptations since then. This one is a new version, last year.'

'Is that all Jamieson?'

'Not quite sir.'

'Well go on.'

'You might have noticed sir. There's no wear and tear on the soles. They're new, sir.'

Ryan frowned. 'Are you sure?'

'Yes sir.'

Ryan tapped his pencil on his notepad. 'So why would someone wear two odd trainers which were brand new?'

'I've no idea sir.'

Ryan sneered at her. 'No I don't suppose you do. Is that all you've got, Jamieson?'

Jamieson flushed in anger. She was damned if she was going to tell him now.

'Yes sir.'

No sir. The shoes are counterfeit sir.

Ryan was scribbling again.

The logo is wrong sir.

'Is there anything else Jamieson?' Ryan didn't bother to look up.

'Nothing sir.'

The labels are the wrong format sir.

'Jamieson, make sure you don't tell anyone about the trainers not matching. I mean no-one. Got that?'

'Yes sir. I've got that sir.'

Two can play this game sir.

The next morning Jamieson's pique had subsided. She went into police headquarters intending to tell Ryan about the counterfeit shoes but he wasn't in his office. When she went to the detectives' room she found he'd left a note on her desk.

'1. Where's your report on the trainers? By 11am urgent.

'2. Scottish Association for Marine Science at the Scottish Marine Institute, Dunstaffnage, Oban. Dr Tim Lenska, an expert on Atlantic and North Sea currents. You have an appointment with him at 3pm.'

At 10.37 Jamieson signed the three page report on the trainers and carried it to Ryan's office. She knocked on his door. There was no reply and she knocked again. His PA, a nervy temp with eaten away finger nails, called over to her from her recessed workstation half way along the corridor.

'He's gone out.'

'Oh . . . do you know when he will be back?'

'He's gone to East Lothian, Seacliff beach.'

'Oh, why?'

'Something to do with television. He didn't tell me exactly.' She pulled on her stringy blonde hair and let out a nervy giggle.

'No, nor me. Look can you give him this. He wanted it for 11. It's Joan isn't it?'

She nodded.

'I'm Helen.'

'Hi.' She took the report from Jamieson but something else also passed between them. It began with a look of desperation on the PA's face and it ended with Jamieson's expression of understanding. She patted her on the hand. 'Remember it's the good guys who win in the end, always.'

A flicker of a smile crossed Joan's face. Another of forlorn longing came into her eyes and another icicle dropped into Jamieson's heart. *My God he's screwed her too.*

On the way back from Oban, a three hour drive, Jamieson listened to Classic FM before switching to Radio 4 for the news at 6pm. It was the third item. 'Police try to solve a new puzzle in the case of the severed feet. Why was one of the missing men wearing odd shoes?' Jamieson stabbed her finger at the radio on/off button before Ryan's voice came on, misjudging a bend and swinging wide as she did so. She drove the rest of the way to Lothian and Borders Police HQ chastened and in a rage. On her desk was a note. 'My office ASAP.'

DC Tessa Rainey passed her as she was reading it. 'He put that there about 20 minutes ago.'

Jamieson remained silent.

'Looking dishy as usual.' Rainey growled with theatrical desire.

Jamieson said acidly, 'I've never seen the attraction of shagging a shit like Ryan but maybe you're just more used to it than me.'

Rainey put her hands on her hips and tossed her

hair. 'Well I'm certainly more used to being shagged than you . . . at least that's what I'm told.'

'Haven't you got better things to do Tessa?'

Two male detectives exchanged glances and jeered. Rainey walked towards them wiggling her hips. They whistled and jeered some more.

Jamieson covered her ears with her hands. The faint sound of laughter followed her through the closed door. Was she really hearing it or was her imagination conjuring up the noise she expected to fill every room after she'd left it? Ryan was sitting at his desk flicking through a sheaf of press cuttings. Jamieson stood in his doorway waiting for him to look up. 'Is this a good time, sir?'

Ryan kept on turning pages. 'That depends on what you've got, Detective Constable.'

'Can I come in, sir?'

'I can hear you well enough from there.'

'Dr Lenska wasn't able to be of much help sir. You see tracking floating objects isn't really a developed field of scientific investigation.'

Ryan stopped what he was doing. 'So you've got nothing for a whole day's work, Jamieson.'

'I didn't say that sir.'

'Well, I'm waiting.'

'Dr Lenska says marine science is more interested in salinity, temperature, whether currents are flowing faster or slower than in tracking objects. But there is someone who is expert at it, one of his part-time PhD students.'

'Well Jamieson, who is it?'

'Dr Lenska shares data with him and so does the Met Office. He's developed the best tracking program, the only one with complete data for the North Atlantic and North Sea.'

'So who is he?'

Jamieson waited to savour the moment. 'Cal McGill, sir.'

Ryan stared at Jamieson. His jaw muscles pulsed with tension.

'He's very good at it sir, highly rated.'

'Are you off your head?'

'I don't think so sir.'

'Are you seriously suggesting we go to a guy who has raided the gardens of half the politicians in this country, including the Environment and Justice Ministers?'

'If he can help us sir . . . ?'

'I'd be crucified. Can you imagine the headlines?'

'No sir.'

'Go away Jamieson.'

'Yes sir.'

When Jamieson returned to her desk Rainey and the two male detectives had gone. She clicked on her private hotmail account. She didn't want this email in the office system. She wrote McGill's address followed by 'Dear Mr McGill, Can we meet?' She signed it Helen Jamieson, not Detective Constable Jamieson. She stared at what she'd done, realising she was one click away from

181

something irrevocable. Then her nerve wavered and she saved it to drafts.

Walking home, she wondered what Isobel Dalgleish would have thought of her taking such risks with her career. She'd have advised against it, strongly, Jamieson decided. Back in her flat, changing her shoes, Jamieson glanced at the photograph of Isobel in her police uniform, on the chest of drawers. She picked up the frame and studied her adoptive mother's expression. There was pride there and in the lines around her eyes something that Jamieson hadn't noticed before. Was it disapproval at what her daughter was contemplating? 'Ryan's rotten, Isobel, a bastard. You don't understand. He's not like you.'

CHAPTER 12

She introduced herself as Mrs Ferguson and apologised to Cal for greeting him in her dressing-gown with the implicit reproach: 'I dare say you wouldn't expect anything else since it is well past midnight'. He mumbled something apologetic about the late train from Edinburgh and followed her to the Lavender Room, her last vacancy, on the third floor of the B&B close to Inverness station. At the penultimate half-landing she stopped to catch her breath.

'This is your bathroom.' She spoke in a hushed, impatient manner. 'You'll find towels in your room.'

'Will there still be hot water?' Cal asked.

Mrs Ferguson adjusted her hair net. 'There will of course, though at this hour I dare say my other guests would value their sleep more than your cleanliness.' Her disapproval hung in the air along with the smell of pine lavatory cleaner.

'Perhaps a small one,' Cal tried in conciliation.

'The morning would be more appropriate for bathing.' Mrs Ferguson pursed her thin colourless lips. A pale pink blush of irritation simultaneously appeared on her cheeks which were greasy with night cream. 'Your room is this way.'

She led him to the next landing and along a corridor panelled in dark wood. 'It's a comfortable room, and warm,' she remarked opening the door and switching on the light. 'It looks on to the river.'

The Lavender Room turned out to be painted pale green with a mushroom coloured carpet. A yellow fluted vase filled with dried lavender stood on the mahogany chest of drawers.

Mrs Ferguson went to the window and closed the curtains. 'Breakfast is from 8–9.30.' As an afterthought, she added, 'Punctual.'

'Oh, I have to catch a train at 8 . . .' Cal's exclamation trailed away leaving behind the unspoken suggestion of breakfast earlier.

Whether Mrs Ferguson detected it or not she replied brusquely, 'Indeed, ah well,' and bid him good night.

Cal propped his rucksack against a chintzy armchair, threw his jacket on to the bed before looking back round the door. Mrs Ferguson had gone. He went to the bathroom, closing the door quietly behind him. He was grimy and tired after his unexpectedly long journey: an obstacle on the line, whatever that meant. If he wasn't getting breakfast, he was certainly going to have a bath. When he turned the hot tap there was a loud gurgling, followed by a rush of water, and a distant clank of pipes. He imagined his landlady lying in bed, disapproving, lips pursed tight, and his mouth pulled right in a brief smirk. The bath was half full when he turned off the rush of steaming water. Before he could add any cold he heard the distant ring of his phone. He jumped up, opened the door, and went back along the dark corridor to his room. The mobile was beside his jacket on the bed. He grabbed at it and pressed answer without looking at the screen to see the caller's number. 'Hi,' he said.

'Cal, are you awake?'

It was Rachel. He swore silently.

'It's late Rachel.'

'I'm sorry. I couldn't sleep.'

'So you thought you'd wake everyone else up.'

'Oh, were you asleep?'

'I was about to have a bath.'

'Oh.'

Cal didn't feel like asking her why she couldn't sleep.

Rachel filled the silence. 'Did you go and see Miss MacKay?'

'Yes . . .'

'Did she tell you about your grandparents?'

'Yeah . . .' He knew it was grudging but he didn't want her thinking he was apologising for arguing the last time they'd spoken. She'd just have to make do with him sounding ungrateful.

'It's extraordinary they'd leave Uilleam's name off the memorial like that,' she said.

Cal didn't reply straight away. Then he said, 'What is it you want from me Rachel?' It didn't come out the way he expected. He tried again, 'I

185

suppose you're after permission to use my grandfather's story.' But the damage had been done. He knew it, and he couldn't bring himself to undo it.

Usually when he caught her on the raw, her speech became cold and distant. It was that way when she answered. 'I didn't think I needed your permission, and anyway that's not why I'm ringing.'

He closed his eyes and swore silently again. He hated what he became on the phone, talking to Rachel. Why did she ring him?

When he didn't reply, Rachel said, 'You always think the worst of me.' It was an accusation he'd heard before, often.

'How would you like it if I was grubbing around in your family?'

'I'm not grubbing.'

'What else do you call it?'

'I'm making a programme, Cal.'

'Well go on. Tell me you don't want to use my grandfather's story.'

'Cal, I wasn't ringing to ask you for anything.'

'Well, what else is there?' Cal regretted the question. It gave her an opportunity to open up the conversation, to talk about their marriage split. Before she had a chance to reply, he said, 'Can't you see it from my point of view? You doing a programme about Eilean Iasgaich . . . my family . . . ?'

'Why is it always about you Cal?'

'Well, tell me you're not doing it.'

'No.'

'Why not?'

'You know the answer.'

'You're being unreasonable, Rachel.'

'I'm doing my job.'

'Where are you?' he asked, suddenly suspicious.

'I'm in Eastern Township, at the hotel.'

Cal said nothing, another brooding silence.

'I haven't exactly made a secret of it, Cal. I'm researching the programme. So, I'm in Eastern Township. Ok. It's not big news.'

'Oh, of course you're not ringing about that.' Cal laughed. ''Course not.' Now he was angry again.

Rachel sighed. 'Do you really know want to know why I'm ringing?'

'Ok. Go on.'

'It's because I can't get to sleep and I thought you might like to talk to someone about Grace Ann MacKay and your grandfather.'

'Oh come on, Rachel,' he said. 'You know what this is all about.'

'Yes, yes I do. It's about you. It's always about you.' With that she ended the call.

'Fuck.' He fell spread-eagled on the bed. 'Fuck.' After a while, he rolled on to his side, flicked the switch by the side of the headboard which turned off the overhead light. He was still fully clothed. Sometime during the night he remembered the bath he'd run.

It was after 2am and the lane running along the side of The Cask was dark. A slender, girlish figure ran quickly to the back of the building. She rounded the corner and stopped by a rusted iron ladder. She clambered up it to a wooden landing from which whisky barrels once were lowered to the backs of waiting carts and, in a later era, lorries. She paused there, crouching, listening, before climbing the old industrial fire escape which rose from the landing. Near its top was a gully in the slate roof. She crawled into it. The gully was wide, with lead flashing in the bottom, which made walking easy. There were rows of plants there. They were all the same, in little plastic pots. Beyond them was a stairway with an iron handrail up to a small wooden door which was recessed into the roof. She listened at the door, pulled on it, opened it a fraction, then more until it was wide enough for her to squeeze through. Inside, she waited again, the whites of her eyes flashing as she searched the room. She was certain as she could be that nobody was there. She'd seen Cal McGill leave and the lights had been off all night. Still, she had a fear of being trapped. She paused, to calm her breathing, before descending the spiral stairs. The map she'd seen in the newspaper was on the far wall. It was lit dimly by the light from the street. The newspaper cutting was there too, in a shadow. She reached for it, easing it from the wall, taking it to the table behind her, beginning to feel nauseous with anxiety for Preeti. She clicked on the desk lamp and read the cutting quickly before turning it off. Now she was in blackness; her eyes still dazzled with the glare of the bulb and filling with tears. She fell to the floor. 'No, Preeti.'

Her beautiful friend, her gentle protector, had been dead three years and Basanti hadn't even known. Her sweet, lovely face had been cut by a boat's propeller blades. Basanti cried, curled up where she'd fallen, her body shaking with sobs. From the very first day they met, in the car with the blackened windows, Preeti had been her support. Even after their separation she knew Preeti would be brave and it made her brave too. Weren't they the most beautiful girls ever born to Bedia? Wasn't their blood warrior blood? Even apart they were together; strong, resilient. Except it was a fiction: Preeti was dead. Basanti's imagination flipped from one image to another: the fright in Preeti's eyes; her face luminous and lost in a vast ocean; the livid propeller slashes across Preeti's cheeks. Gradually the sobbing stopped. But she continued to lie there until her emotions turned cold and determined. Now she had to avenge Preeti. Now she had to be brave again. Wouldn't Preeti accompany her, just as she had these last three years?

CHAPTER 13

The early morning train from Inverness to Lairg arrived on time. The Postbus which travelled the remaining forty miles to Eastern Township was waiting at the station. Cal was the only passenger. He sat behind the driver, a woman in her mid-40s with a wind-beaten ruddy face, hoping it would discourage her from talking. She had other ideas. Her name was Sally 'and yes, I'm English before you ask'. He wasn't about to but he could hardly cut her dead now.

'What brought you this far north?' he said, as the Postbus gathered speed.

'Oh, a fellah, of course . . .' She erupted with laughter. 'It's always a fellah for a girl. But no sooner had I come up here than he went south. I was done with chasing him so I stayed.'

He grunted in sympathy.

'Where are you from?' she asked.

'Edinburgh.'

'A lowlander: the English are more welcome here than lowlanders . . .' She giggled. '. . . That's not saying much, mind. The English are the Poles around here. We drive the taxis and the buses; run the shops and the cafes. We're the builders, the carpenters, the plumbers and the electricians. I don't know what they'd do without us, and all we get is resentment and called names like white settler. Huh.'

Cal watched the scenery go by for a few minutes hoping his silence would end the conversation. But Sally wanted to chat. 'What brings you up here?'

'My mother's family came from Sutherland.'

'Oh, where?'

'Eilean Iasgaich, do you know it?'

She glanced at him in the mirror. 'The brave men of Eilean Iasgaich, the MacKays and the Raes?'

'You've heard of them.'

'Who hasn't?'

'My grandfather was born there, though he's dead now.'

'All the men were killed in the war weren't they?'

Cal said they were. 'His family name was Sinclair.'

She considered for a bit. 'I thought it was only MacKays and Raes.'

A long expanse of water opened up on their right. Cal watched the glistening water. Sally said, 'Loch Loyal. It gets its name from that,' and pointed to the left of the road where a mountain with multiple peaks loomed. 'That's Ben Loyal . . . it and the memorial to the men of Eilean Iasgaich are the big draws around here. Not forgetting the sun, the beaches and the blue seas . . .' She let out a long suffering laugh. '. . . Though maybe not the sun.'

'Today's good,' Cal said.

'It is indeed. This'll be summer, all of it.'

A narrow channel connected the northern end of Loch Loyal to another loch which Sally said was called Craggie. 'And along here a bit you should be able to see Eilean Iasgaich.'

The road crossed open moorland until a gouge of sea running inland – the Kyle of Tongue – revealed itself. It sparkled with greens and blues in the sun. Sally pointed out the landmarks. Below them and to their left was the village of Tongue. Further along the Kyle (Sally said it was two miles, though it appeared closer in the clear air) was Eastern Township, the old crofting settlement, and between the two settlements were tidal flats of sand and mud banks crossed by a curving causeway and a bridge to the Kyle's far shore. Beyond, where the Kyle widened and became open sea, there was a collection of islands. 'Your island's the one broadside to us, with a hill at either end.'

Cal hadn't given Eilean Iasgaich much thought since waking at 7 with an uncomfortable morning-after feeling. On the train from Inverness to Lairg, a cup of coffee chased away his sleepiness but the feeling hung on. If anything, it became worse as he preoccupied himself with Rachel, replaying the conversation of the night before, hoping for justification but not finding it; aware his bad temper then had as much to do with his guilty conscience about her as her documentary on Eilean Iasgaich. So when he saw the island it took him rather by surprise. He hadn't known what to expect: if not a dark, sinister place inhabited by ranks of black cormorants then certainly not a pleasant green splash in a bright blue sea. When the surprise passed, it was replaced by lingering resentment. A place which had caused his mother's family so much suffering and injustice had no right to look like this, enticing, pretty even.

Sally said, 'It's not always like this, of course.'

Cal asked, 'Where do I go for the boat?'

'By the slipway, at the causeway,' Sally said. 'It goes at noon and costs £12.50. You can walk along the road by the shop. Won't take you more than five minutes.'

Cal thanked her.

'I'll point you in the right direction . . . Oh and buy something to eat because there's nothing but sheep and birds on the island.'

A few minutes later the Postbus slowed and turned left. 'Well this is almost the end of the line,' Sally said. 'Welcome to Eastern Township.'

The Postbus entered the village, a collection of one and a half storey houses scattered along a single-track road. Cal watched for the hotel where Rachel was staying but Sally pulled up before he could see it. She parked on a tarred apron by a low-slung building. Outside it were two tables, some chairs and a rack of grey-blue Calor gas canisters. 'Rae Family Stores' announced the sign above the door.

'This is as far as I go.' Sally turned off the engine. 'It's the store, Post Office, café, you name it . . . You'll find the boat along there.' Sally pointed to a road which went between two large sycamore trees.

Cal thanked her again. 'Where's the hotel from here?' He opened his door, debating whether he'd try again to explain his reservations to Rachel about her documentary now, or later.

'Another couple of hundred yards, you can't miss it.' She pointed straight ahead. 'If it's full and you need a room there's a B&B opposite.'

Cal nodded acknowledgement and followed her into the shop where he bought rolls, tomatoes, ham slices, cheese, crisps, chocolate biscuits and a two litre bottle of water.

When he was at the counter paying he asked the shop assistant, a teenage girl with jet black hair and purple nail varnish, 'Is there another shop in the village?'

'Not really, not like this . . . There's the Sea Shop down the road. It does fishing gear as well as surfing and diving equipment.'

'Do you know if it used to be the general store?'

'A long time ago; before the Raes opened this. I don't know much more about it.'

'My mother was born here,' Cal said, 'and her grandparents used to run a shop here, during the war and after it.'

'Is that right?' The girl looked bored at the prospect of another tourist trip down family memory lane.

'Who owns the Sea Shop now?'

The girl arched her eyebrows as if the answer was obvious. 'The Raes of course. They own the village.' Cal thanked her for his change and went to the door, waving goodbye to Sally, who was at the Post Office counter at the back of the shop.

He looked at his phone. It was 11.34. Rachel would have to wait. The boat left in 26 minutes.

The road to the slipway curved left beyond the sycamore trees. A stone wall on his right soon gave way to fenced pasture and a view across the Kyle. The tide was coming in. There were fewer sand-banks showing now than when he'd first seen it from the Postbus. It was an observation made from habit and didn't occupy his thoughts. Those were concerned with Rachel and to a lesser extent with his own family's association with this road (was this where his grandmother walked, an outcast from the island, widowed and pregnant with his mother?). The road sloped gently towards the water and soon he saw the causeway curving across sand and scrub to the bridge which spanned the western sea channel, a fast flowing ripple of blue. A fishing boat was tied up close to the bridge, in a calm deep backwater by the stream. Someone in a red hat was lifting boxes on to the side of the road. As Cal continued walking, a stone slipway came into view on the near shore. A rigid inflat-able boat was moored there. It was orange and a man wearing a bright yellow jacket was leaning over its twin engines.

Eight passengers were waiting in a queue by the ticket booth at the top of the slipway. Cal studied them looking for Rachel but didn't see her. A small woman with greying blonde hair, a strained white face and a satchel over her shoulder asked him if he was taking the island tour. He nodded. 'That'll be £12.50,' she said. He slipped his rucksack off his shoulder, unzipped a pocket and took out his wallet.

With his ticket, she gave him a flyer announcing 'the opening of an island cafe/ restaurant later in the summer'. There was also news about an appeal fund for restoring the house of Hector MacKay, 'the famous skipper of the brave men of Eilean Iasgaich'. Cal wandered away from the booth reading about the various public grants the development projects had already attracted when he saw Rachel. She was sitting by the shore on the other side of the causeway, her back to Cal. He folded the flyer, put it in his pocket and crossed the road to the path which led to where she was. His feet slid on the gravel, but she didn't turn. Cal stopped a dozen paces from her.

'Rachel.'

She turned and looked at him through sunglasses, before turning away. 'It's such an amazing day isn't it?' There was no animosity in her voice, or none that Cal could detect.

He looked where she was looking, towards the mouth of the Kyle. Eilean Iasgaich was rising on the horizon. 'Yes, it is.'

She turned back, scrutinising him again, saying nothing.

He wished he could see her eyes. Her dark lenses reflected the causeway behind him.

'Can I just enjoy it?' Again, there was no hostility but neither was it a question.

He nodded.

'Yeah . . .' He scuffed some stones. He kicked at them again. 'Sure. Are you going on the boat?'

Her back was still to him when she spoke again. 'No arguments Cal. Not today.'

He took that to mean 'yes'.

'Ok,' he said. There'd be time to talk later, make her understand how difficult it was for him, without it becoming a shouting match.

She stood, bending to pick up her walking boots. Her socks were tucked into them. When she came towards him, bare foot, tentatively on the stones, he saw the lapping tide had wet the bottom of her jeans. She looked good, better than the last time, when they'd had coffee at the Television Festival in Edinburgh. Then she'd seemed manicured; today was how he imagined her: in jeans and a white tee shirt, a red over-shirt unbuttoned and flapping in the light breeze; her hair short and pretty, catching the light, not styled just-so as it had been then. Today, she was natural, more herself.

'Rachel . . .' he began. He was going to say, 'Can we talk later?'

But she shook her head. 'Don't.'

There was that brief brittle smile again. It told him she was resigned, not accusing. Would he have been the same?

'Ok.'

'No arguments today. Is that a deal?'

Cal held his hand out.

She contemplated it and said, 'Shake hands with the devil?'

'It's not that bad.' He knew it was. In fact it was worse than she knew. But what else could he say?

'Isn't it?' and she turned away. He withdrew his hand, feeling stupid for offering it.

She preceded him up the path to the road, stopping on it. 'I've found your grandfather's old house. Number 14. It's a bit of a ruin, but they all are.'

'You've been out to the island.'

'Yes, a few times; I'm trying to match families to houses, so that if we bring surviving relatives back to the island we know where to take them.'

He didn't say anything. The subject made him uncomfortable.

They crossed the road. The other boat passengers were gathered in a semi-circle around the man in yellow, who was handing out life-jackets while making his introductions. His name was Mike Thomson, 'but I'm Mike from now on'. He was ginger-haired with a broad smile and, Cal noticed, the same wind-whipped red face as Sally the Postbus driver. He'd started his safety spiel when he saw Rachel and Cal approaching and handed them the last two jackets. 'When you're ready, climb aboard,' he said. 'There's room for two on the bench up front for those who don't mind a bit of spray.' An elderly couple followed Rachel and Cal down the slipway to the *Rib*. The man was reading aloud to his wife from a guide book. He stopped when he saw Cal watching him. 'We've picked a good day for it . . .'

'Couldn't be calmer,' Cal replied.

'And so lovely and warm,' his wife added with a sweet smile.

'Tom and Sandra Parsons, from Wiltshire,' the man said.

Cal introduced himself and Rachel before Mike interrupted them. 'There's room for two more here and two at the back.' The seats were arranged in pairs: rounded saddles of black with padded back supports on tubular metal frames. Rachel sat behind the wheel seat and Cal behind her, his rucksack by his feet. When Mr and Mrs Parsons had settled, Mike untied the boat and let it drift from the shore before starting the engines. Rachel said to Cal. 'Looking forward to seeing it at last?'

'I think so.'

She looked at him quizzically. 'Only think so?'

The *Rib* accelerated, twin engines roaring, across a calm backwater. It sped through a narrow gap between sand spits and suddenly it was in the fast tidal stream flowing under the bridge. As the *Rib* appeared on the other side, the skipper of the fishing boat stopped lifting boxes and watched them go by, waving lazily. When they'd passed, Mike cut the engines and leaned back to Rachel. 'That,' he jerked his thumb back over his shoulder, 'is the grandson of the skipper who went down with the Eilean Iasgaich in the war.'

She leaned back to tell Cal. Both of them turned to watch his red wool hat bobbing up and down as he resumed unloading his catch.

Mike said, 'He's Hector MacKay too, like his grandfather, though everyone calls him Red because of the hat. He's never without it.'

Rachel shouted back to Cal. 'He won't speak to me.'

Cal didn't reply. He continued to watch Hector MacKay's grandson who belonged here, whereas Uilleam Sinclair's grandson did not, could not. Not without betraying his grandfather. Cal hadn't expected to mind quite so much.

The boat swung almost to the eastern shore where the channel split into two, divided by a sandbank. Mike steered the *Rib* within five metres of the rocks where the water was deepest. The rushing tide and the breeze whipped up waves.

'Hold on,' he shouted. The boat buffeted against the rearing water, showering spray over the passengers. 'Another one's coming.' Then the *Rib* was in calmer deeper sea. A group of small islands appeared on the port side: three hummocks of grass and rock.

Mike cut the engines temporarily. 'They're called The Rabbit Islands.' The boat picked up speed again and Cal stood. Ahead, lying broadside across the bay was Eilean Iasgaich. Mike shouted, 'We'll go round Eilean nan Ron, the Island of Seals first . . .' he pointed to starboard where a large grassy island had appeared. Ruined houses were silhouetted on its skyline. '. . . and then we'll go ashore.'

'It was occupied too?' Cal asked.

Mike shouted back, 'Yeah, it was abandoned in 1938.'

'Before Eilean Iasgaich?'

'Seven years before.'

'What happened?'

'The fishing was past its peak and the young men went looking for work on the mainland. Eilean Iasgaich stayed viable for longer because of the trawler: it had the range to go where the fish were; it could follow the cod and haddock.'

The engines roared again. Seabirds circled overhead as the *Rib* swept round Eilean nan Ron and approached Eilean Iasgaich from the east. A low outcrop of rock lay 20 metres off the main island. Mike cut the engine and let the Rib idle past. 'Eilean Iasgaich Beag . . . it means Little Fishing Island.' He shouted so all the passengers could hear. 'Only the tip shows at high tide. The main island is called Eilean Iasgaich Mor or Great Fishing Island.'

Now the *Rib* cruised sedately below suddenly soaring cliffs until, rounding a buttress, it entered a natural harbour. A pier jutted out into the sea and from it a line of steps ascended a rocky gully to the island plateau.

'It's deep here and sheltered from the gales and swell.' Mike said.

Cal wondered if this was why he had been called Caladh: harbour in Gaelic.

The *Rib* was now less than 50 metres from shore. From a shadow under the cliff, at the back of the pier, a sculpture began to emerge. It was a circle of men in bronze, linking arms, on top of a stone plinth. There was an inscription on it but the boat was still too distant for the words to be legible.

Mike noticed Cal paying attention to it. 'That's the memorial to the fifteen heroes of Eilean Iasgaich.'

'There were sixteen,' Cal snapped.

CHAPTER 14

The carved inscription read:

In memory of the brave men of the anti-submarine trawler *Eilean Iasgaich* who laid down their lives in the service of their country and their island.

On 17 September 1942, five men died protecting the North Atlantic convoys from German U-boats and fighter bombers.

On 29 September 1942, the youngest member of the crew was swept overboard in a storm returning from Archangelsk.

On 6 July 1944, nine men were killed in action east of Orkney after engaging a U-boat which had surfaced to shell a fishing vessel transporting Norwegian resistance fighters. The U-boat and the *Eilean Iasgaich* went down with all hands.

In June 1945, a month after the return to power of the Norwegian Government in exile, the nine were awarded posthumously Norway's highest gallantry decoration, Krigskorset med Sverd (War Cross with Sword), in recognition of their extraordinary heroism.

Let their deeds be remembered always.

Hector MacKay, skipper, aged 53, died 6 July 1944

Donal MacKay, aged 47, died 17 September 1942

Angus MacKay, aged 45, died 17 September 1942

Robert Rae, aged 45, died 6 July 1944

Iain Rae, aged 43, died 6 July 1944

Murdo Rae, aged 38, died 6 July 1944

Alexander Gunn, aged 35, died 17 September 1942

Sinclair Gunn, aged 34, died 17 September 1942

Duncan MacLeod, aged 29, died 6 July 1944

Robert MacLeod, aged 27, died 6 July 1944

Alasdair Murray, aged 26, died 17 September 1942

James Murray, aged 24, died 6 July 1944

Alexander (Sandy) MacKay, aged 16, died 29 September 1942

Hamish Sutherland, aged 49, died 6 July 1944

Donald McIntosh, aged 27, died 6 July 1944.

May God abide with them and may their
souls rest in peace.

Cal prayed for his grandfather. Uilleam Sinclair,
aged 21, died 29 September 1942. God abide with
him and may his soul rest in peace.

Mike was attending to the other passengers, who
had begun to climb the stone steps up the cliff from
the pier. Tom and Sandra Parsons from Wiltshire,
the least agile of the group, asked if they could take
it 'at their own speed'. Mike said he would follow
them up 'to catch them in case they slipped'.

'Can we stay here a bit longer?' Rachel read Cal's
mood.

'Sure no bother,' Mike said. 'Come up when
you're ready.'

Cal had been the first ashore. He had studied the
inscription and then stood with his back to it
looking out to sea as Mike told how the surviving
members of the MacKay and Rae families commis-
sioned the memorial in 1949, the year they took
title to the island, and unveiled it the following year.

'The Moderator of the General Assembly of the
Church of Scotland stood on this rock,' Mike
turned towards the sea, 'and held a service of
thanksgiving. The bay was full of boats at anchor
from all the surrounding townships and beyond.
The navy sent a minesweeper. The decks of all of
them were packed with people. The sun shone that
day, like it is today.'

It was here, Cal thought, the *Eilean Iasgaich*

moored when it returned from its refit as an anti-submarine trawler. It was here the men came ashore, Uilleam Sinclair among them, and climbed the steps where the island's women and children were waiting, his wife and mother separate from the others. How had Grace Ann described his progress past the islanders that day? 'Untouched': all the other men had been embraced as they went by, all except his grandfather. Cal read the memorial inscription again.

'I couldn't believe it either, when I saw it the first time,' Rachel said. She was waiting apart from him at the bottom of the cliff. By now the others were nearing the top.

'Will they be going to the museum?'

'I expect so. Normally they go there first and after that the houses.'

'The log book's there?'

'Yes.'

'I want to see it.' He was reading the inscription again. 'Then I'm going to build a cairn, for my grandfather. It's time he had a memorial.'

'Where?'

'Oh, on one of the hills, overlooking the sea. I don't know, away from here.'

'You could use some of the stone from your family's house,' Rachel had started to climb the steps. 'There's enough of it lying about.'

At the first turn, where the second flight started, she went behind a boulder. Cal looked again at the memorial, leaned close, and spat on it.

CHAPTER 15

From the top of the steps Cal surveyed the grassland which stretched across the centre of the island. It was slung like a hammock between its two hills, Cnoc na Faire to the east and Cnoc a' Mhonaidh to the west. Extending along the north side of the island were scattered ruins of houses in the shelter of a rising bank of heather. Many had lost roofs, some had collapsed gables, and others had become rubble. None was intact, or none that Cal could discern. For the most part they were single storey structures with a door in the centre and a window at either side. A few had a second floor, with two windows in the roof and a skylight in between. Around the houses were other geometric remnants of human settlement: a line of fence posts, a section of boundary wall, the course of a drainage ditch clogged with rushes. Rachel was walking along one of these when Cal next saw her. She'd gone ahead of him to finish her research on the houses. 'Come and find me once you've seen the log book. I'll show you the Sinclair croft.' It rankled that she'd been there already and he hadn't, but he let it ride.

The rest of the boat party was a long way ahead of him, below Cnoc na Faire, following a track up a grassy slope to the old school, a single storey building set apart from the others. Like them, it faced south with a window either side of the doorway. Unlike them, its roof appeared intact though matt in texture, not slate, and the windows reflected sunlight instead of being lifeless black holes.

Cal hurried to catch up, running along a path on the top of the cliff. When he reached the museum whose roof he now saw was thatched with heather, the others had been inside for five or six minutes. A sign was attached to the bleached wooden lintel: 'Eilean Iasgaich Museum', and underneath, 'Opened 23 May 1952'. The door, made from rough planks, was held open by a rope loop. Cal heard snatches of Mike's commentary inside describing the island's subsistence agriculture. He ducked below the lintel, following in his schoolboy grandfather's footsteps, and entered a passageway with a doorway on either side and uneven whitewashed walls which were cluttered with framed black-and-white photographs and modern paintings. All were depictions of island life. Cal stopped by a watercolour, about 20 by 12 centimetres in a deep frame of dark wood. It was of a fishing boat ramming a submarine. In the distance was another boat around which shells exploded. Cal read the printed card accompanying it.

'The heroes of Eilean Iasgaich by Elizabeth Rae,

whose father Robert was one of the nine island men killed saving a group of Norwegian resistance fighters from certain death. This frame was constructed from one of the trawler's recovered deck timbers. Prints can be purchased inside – £75 each.'

Next to the painting was a photograph of the Moderator of the General Assembly of the Church of Scotland blessing the memorial at the pier. Other photographs were grainier and even older: of family groups mostly, dressed in their Sunday best. The men and boys wore caps and the women and girls bonnets tied under their chins. Cal walked along them searching for something familiar about the faces: a likeness to Margaret, his great grandmother, Uilleam, or even Ishbel, his grandmother. Just as he was nearing the end of the corridor, Mike appeared at the doorway on the right. 'Ah there you are. I was just demonstrating the tools they used for growing and harvesting oats, hay and potatoes.'

Mike retreated into the room which was full of equipment such as fishing nets, creels, and tools for tilling the land, and a small boat like a coracle. He was about to continue his talk when Cal asked from the door, 'Is the log book here?' His tone was impatient, almost aggressive. The others noticed it and glanced at him.

'The skipper's log book?' Mike replied, put out by Cal's manner.

'Hector MacKay's, yes.'

'It's next door, in the glass case.'

Without a word Cal crossed to the room opposite. Some of the others began to drift after him, leaving Mike complaining peevishly, 'I thought I'd tell you about this first.'

The other room was arranged like a shop. There was a counter and a till by the door with racks of postcards of island scenes. More paintings and prints covered the walls except for the gable which had displays of souvenirs for sale. In the middle of the room were two glass cases. The first contained architect's drawings and models of the new cafe/restaurant and the restoration of Hector MacKay's house. The second, smaller case contained belongings of the man himself such as his pipe, prayer book and knife. These were arranged around an open leather-bound book, with yellowing, lined pages. Cal leaned over it. The book was open at 17 September 1942. The date and the boat's position were written at the top of the page. Underneath, in large, rounded handwriting, was a short passage of text.

'God bless those who died today – my brothers Donal and Angus, the Gunn brothers, Alexander and Sinclair, and young Alasdair Murray. They were buried at sea with blessings said over their bodies. God be with them always and with us tomorrow for whatever perils we face.'

Cal read it silently while the others gathered round him. Mr Parsons put on a pair of glasses and began to read aloud for the benefit of his wife.

There was a murmur of comment about the sto-icism of the author recording the deaths of his two brothers, yet he let no emotion show. Mr Parsons looked around for Mike, who had followed behind, reluctantly. 'I'd been expecting Gaelic.'

Mike said, 'Once the *Eilean Iasgaich* began anti-submarine patrols his logs were written in English. I don't know why; perhaps Navy regulations.'

A new hum of conversation followed as each visitor read the diary entry in turn. When everyone had seen it and after a contemplative silence, Mike said, 'You can buy facsimile copies of that and some other pages of the log for £1.50 a sheet.'

Cal asked, 'Is there a copy of the entry for September 29, when the *Eilean Iasgaich* was returning from Archangelsk?'

Mike shook his head. 'I don't think so.' He went to the counter and checked through the dated folders containing the facsimiles. 'No. No, there isn't.'

'In that case can you turn to 29 September?' Cal made it sound less a question, more a demand.

'I'm sorry. The pages can't be disturbed after all this time,' Mike replied.

'Two crewmen died that day . . . my grandfather was one of them.'

Another murmur started, sympathetic to Cal.

Mrs Parson said, 'Oh which one was he?'

'His name was Uilleam Sinclair,' Cal said.

Mrs Parsons mentioned something to her husband about not seeing a Sinclair on the memorial 'which was curious' when Mike interrupted her. 'Hector MacKay wrote each day on a new double page. It'd mean turning 12 pages. I'm sorry it's not possible. The paper's too fragile.' He moved towards the cabinet, inserting himself between Cal and the others.

Before Cal could speak again, Mike turned his back on him and said, 'Now if I might draw your attention to the other display case and the plans of the island's owners to build a cafe and restaurant as a glass extension to the museum and also to restore Hector MacKay's house.'

The boat party followed him obediently to the neighbouring display, leaving Cal on his own. 'If you would like to make a donation, there's a collection box on the counter.' Mike looked round as Cal walked out.

A path led downhill from the museum to a broad grassy track under-laid with stone. Cal went along it, passed the ruined houses, each one giving off its own atmosphere of desolation and abandonment. He found Rachel sitting on the remnants of a wall two thirds of the way along, before the base of Cnoc a' Mhonaidh.

'He wouldn't show you the page, would he?' She squinted up at him, trying to work out his mood.

'No.'

'What will you do about it?'

'Don't know,' he said. 'Who owns the museum?'

'The Raes.' Then she added, 'Of course.'

It happened every time the Raes were mentioned. The shop assistant had said the same, now Rachel, 'The Raes . . . of course.'

'I could talk to them.'

'You could.' Rachel's tone told him there wasn't any point.

'You've tried?'

'I've mentioned it.'

'Nothing doing?'

She shook her head. 'I would have told you before but I didn't think you'd want to hear it from me.'

He grunted. 'Yeah.' Then he said, 'Is this it, the house?'

'This is Grace Ann's: number 13. Your grand-father's is number 14.' She nodded towards the ruined building no more than ten metres across the grass. 'It's that one.'

Like Grace Ann's home, number 14 was a single storey cottage. They looked a matching pair since both had front walls constructed of rusted corru-gated iron into which had been cut the shapes of a door and two windows. But the roof and back wall of 14 had collapsed, whereas 13 still had much of its back wall intact. The gables of 14 had also crumbled leaving only the chimney breasts still standing and some stone around them.

'Grace Ann told me the corrugated iron made them hot in summer, cold in winter and noisy when it rained.' Rachel said.

Cal had crossed the grass and was standing by

the door to his family home. He went through it climbing on to the collapsed mound of stone, roof timbers and slate inside. Outside the air had been fresh: in there it stank of decay, damp and sheep droppings. Cal bent to pick up a flat stone. He threw it towards the doorway, and bent again to find another. He moved slowly around the rubble, testing each new step before trusting his weight to it. Every time he changed position he bent to pick up more stones. He rejected more than he selected but soon a pile was spilling through the doorway.

Rachel said, 'What are you doing?'

The next stone rolled on to the grass outside, and Cal followed it. 'They're for my grandfather's cairn.' He looked towards the top of Cnoc a' Mhonaidh. 'I'm going to build it up there.' Then he started to separate by size the stones he had collected.

When he stopped for a rest, Rachel went to sit near him. 'No arguments today, ok?' she smiled.

'Yes, I know.' He waited for what was coming next.

'This documentary . . .'

'I wondered when that was going to get a mention.'

'Something wrong happened here. You can still feel it, in the atmosphere, in these two houses, at the memorial . . .' She paused.

Cal crouched and plucked at some stems of grass.

'Cal, a television programme can't put it right but at least it can let people know a brave young man has been denied his place in this island's history, for whatever reason.'

He stared at her, his expression more pensive than anything else.

She added, 'It's not about you and me, what happened in our marriage.'

Cal went on plucking at the grass. Then he said, 'It's my fight, Rachel.'

'But I can help, let me.'

He shook his head. He was holding himself back. She saw it too.

'There's something I should tell you,' she said quietly.

'What?'

'You're not allowed to be angry,' Rachel said. 'You promised.'

'I won't be.' He plucked at another spear of grass.

'My producer was with Grace Ann MacKay today, filming. We couldn't take a chance on her dying.'

How could he make her understand how personal this had become for him? Until that day, he'd regarded the wrong done here as something historical, something that could be corrected by a grandson's homage, or its memorial equivalent, a cairn. Now that he was on the island, he experienced it differently. The wrong was active; being perpetrated daily, every time a boat load of tourists arrived at the pier and gathered around the memorial. Righting it was his responsibility, his alone.

It wasn't something he could put into words to Rachel. On the track from the museum he'd come to realise his fight wasn't with her. 'Yeah . . .' was all he managed.

While they had been talking, Mike had been leading the others along the grass track, on a guided tour of the township. Rachel saw them first.

'We're just going along to the end, to Hector MacKay's house,' Mike shouted.

She raised her hand in acknowledgement.

Now Mike was closer. 'You can catch us on the way back.'

Cal said 'Why?' and without waiting for a reply went back to sorting through his pile of stones.

Mike studied him before shrugging and saying to Rachel, 'The boat's leaving in half an hour.'

Cal, his back turned, said, 'I'm not going.'

'I can't leave you on the island.' Mike looked at Rachel, silently canvassing her for support.

Cal spun round, a stone in his hand. 'My mother's family lived here for generations. They worked this land.' His meaning was clear, even to those in the group ignorant of island culture. Mike was a blow-in, an incomer; what right had he to tell Cal, someone with island blood, where he could and couldn't go?

Mike tried again to recruit Rachel. 'The owners don't allow overnight visitors. That's the rule.'

Mrs Parsons remarked sotto voce to her husband. 'Well we have to get back. You've got your pills to take.'

'I'm going to stay,' Cal said.

'It's private property,' Mike answered.

Now Mr Parsons joined in. 'I think you'll find Cal's entitled, under right to roam.'

In an aside to the rest of the group, who had been listening to the exchanges in silence, Mrs Parsons said, 'My husband was a lawyer before he retired. He knows about these things.'

Mike flipped open his mobile phone and wandered away out of earshot, speaking into it. Cal continued sorting stones. A few minutes later Mike returned. 'Mrs Rae says it's all right for one night only. Her husband will come over in the *Rib* first thing tomorrow and he'll take you off. Ok?'

Cal said, 'I'll go when I'm ready.'

'You'll be leaving tomorrow morning like it or not,' Mike replied.

When Mike and the boat party were out of earshot, Rachel said 'quite the rebel' and Cal let out a nasal snort. He placed the stone he was carrying between his feet and crouched on it. Rachel took off her red over-shirt and put it in her bag, zipping it up.

'I've a couple of interviews to fix for the filming schedule.' She glanced after Mike and the boat party. They were now at number 19. She had a few minutes before they'd cut across the grazings to the pier. 'But I'll see you tomorrow. Have breakfast with me at the hotel?'

He didn't say anything at first. He plucked at the grass letting the sun warm his face.

Then he said, 'I'm sorry about the phone call last night. I don't know why that happens to me.'

Rachel smiled. 'Neither do I.'

Both of them laughed. Then Rachel confessed that one idea for a programme had been to re-populate Eilean Iasgaich with relatives of the last islanders to see if the modern generation could hack it better than their forbears. Cal let out a groan.

'Don't worry – it got killed off at the pass.'

Mike and the others were now crossing the grazings, making for the pier. 'I'd better go,' she said, getting up and tying her shirt around her waist. 'Be good.'

He nodded. She had begun to walk away when he said, 'Thank you.'

'What for?'

'For today.'

She smiled at him. 'It's been a good day, hasn't it?'

'Yeah, it has.'

As soon as her back was to him, his face fell into a frown.

He'd seen the hope in her eyes. He couldn't go on deceiving her.

CHAPTER 16

There were 67 stones, one for every year Uilleam Sinclair's death had gone without memorial. The first six, flooring slabs from inside the doorway of number 14, were the heaviest. Cal carried them two at a time and deposited them on top of Cnoc a' Mhonaidh. Then he quartered the plateau searching for a site to build his grandfather's cairn. He found it at the north-east corner where a spine of rock jutted above a sheer cliff. At the tip of the spine the ground flattened forming a natural platform which overlooked an uninterrupted sweep of the North Atlantic.

It took him another eight climbs of the hill to deliver the remaining stones to his chosen site. On each ascent he lugged one in each hand and more in his rucksack. When he completed the task after almost six hours his hair and shirt were soaked with sweat and he ached with exertion. His knees buckled and he fell to the ground, chest heaving. He remained like that until the sweat in his clothes grew cold in the evening breeze. Then he got up, stretched, and walked around the headland before placing the stones one by one until the cairn stood more than a metre high. Then Cal took from his rucksack a slate and a bent rusted nail he'd pulled from a collapsed roof timber. With it he scored onto the slate 'In memory of Uilleam Sinclair, 1921–1942, who died in the service of his country and his island.'

Underneath, after leaving a space, he scratched, 'Known unto God,' the inscription he found in the Ardnamurchan cemetery 19 years before, a form of words originally devised by Rudyard Kipling for marking the graves of unidentified First World War dead.

Cal propped the slate against the bottom of the cairn and wedged it there. By the time he'd finished adjusting the stones and removing heather debris from the area around the cairn, the gloom of evening had set in. As the last sprays of sunlight glinted copper against the underside of the clouds, Cal pulled his anorak around him.

For the hours of darkness he sat beside the cairn, sleeping fitfully, listening to the constant motion of the waves on rocks below him, peering half-blind into the night which dropped an opaque shroud of sooty-grey over the ocean. Twice he stood and stamped his feet to warm himself and to get rid of cramps. He ended the night as he'd started it: sitting, knees pulled up to his chest, arms wrapped around them, each exposed hand tucked into the other's sleeve.

When the sky to the east lightened, he pulled his rucksack towards him and took out the bag of food he'd bought at Rae's shop. He broke open a bread roll, put two tomatoes into it and squashed the two halves together. He ate it quickly, washing it down with gulps of bottled water. When he'd finished, he zipped his rucksack and rose stiffly to his feet. The place seemed to hold him for a minute or two: a grandson bidding farewell to a grandfather. Then he turned away, his rucksack hanging loosely from one hand, and descended the hill. Every so often he stumbled, partly because the detail of the ground was indistinct in the dawn light, partly because his stiffness made him clumsy and heavy footed.

At the bottom of the hill he found the grass track past the houses and followed it, glad at last of a level surface. The light was now coming quickly though not so bright that there was colour to the grass or the sea. The greyness combined with the stillness lent ghostliness to the dereliction he was passing. At number 14, his grandfather's home, Cal struck out over rough ground, across the grazings. In the improving light, his limbs looser, his stumbles less frequent, he was able to cover the ground quickly. Soon he was at the cliff overlooking the bay, watching out for the *Rib*, hoping it would come soon to take him from this hateful place.

Basanti yelped when her mother told her; the sound a wild animal makes when it is caught in a snare and it cannot make another because the wire has already tightened. Her mother, alternately sobbing and pleading, begged Basanti to understand. What choice did a sick woman with a dead husband and two daughters, one crippled, one beautiful, have? Basanti's father had only been gone a week and every day another creditor visited their door demanding money.

'But Mama,' Basanti said, 'you will have rupees when I am married next month. Can't it wait until then?'

Basanti had been promised in marriage for almost a year now. The wedding had been delayed because the groom required time to save for the bride price. He was a Bedia man who had gone to work in the city, who had noticed Basanti when he returned to the village to visit his bed-ridden father. At first he assumed a pretty girl like Basanti would be in the *dhanda*. When he heard she was not, not yet, he sought out Basanti's father offering 80,000 rupees and three goats for her hand in marriage. Her father had driven a hard bargain. 'My daughter Basanti is a beauty, the loveliest girl in this village, who will bring her family many rupees.' He took a sip of his drink and studied this city boy. 'It is the custom,' he said in the serious voice he kept for business, 'to compensate the bride's family in some small way for the loss of a daughter's earnings. In this case those earnings would be substantial, as you can see for yourself.'

After much negotiating, and some more drinking,

they settled on 100,000 rupees and five goats. Ten thousand rupees and the goats had to be paid within seven days, the rest one year later. The two men drank to the deal, with the groom-to-be seeking assurances from Basanti's father that Basanti would be kept from the *dhanda*, that she wouldn't be used to procure clients for the older women, and that she wouldn't dance in the provocative way Bedia girls were taught to dance. The older man had taken some minutes to reply. He'd wanted this city boy to think he was making a concession when really he was making none. Basanti's father, whose business was bootleg liquor, was prosperous, or had seemed to be during his life, and he'd decided long before to keep Basanti from the *dhanda*. At length, he said with an air of reluctance, 'I suppose that too is the custom when a Bedia girl marries. I agree.'

Basanti had been so happy when she was told. It didn't matter to her she had not yet spoken to her husband-to-be. She was to be married. She would live with him in the city and work in an office. Wasn't this what she had been brought up to expect? Wasn't this why she had been having English lessons? She would have children who would know their father. Few Bedia girls who went into the *dhanda* knew the fathers of their children, if they had children at all.

Then it had been stolen away, ripped from her.

Her dead father's prosperity had been built on the loans of investors who wanted their money back. His debts were rising every day – 287,000 rupees was the latest total – and still creditors came to their door.

After Basanti cried out, her mother wailed, 'What else can I do? Your sister is crippled and weak. She would earn a few rupees at most. I am sick and old. Your uncle, who is a generous and wealthy man, says he will pay off your father's creditors immediately and keep us safe from their threats. But his condition is that you give up your marriage and go into the *dhanda* to repay our family's debt to him. Basanti, I wish there was another way but there isn't. The money from your husband-to-be won't be enough. A good-looking girl like you can earn many hundreds of thousands.' Basanti had not spoken to her mother or sister again, even when they readied her for the roadside.

She watched the rising sun lighting up the sky to the east of Edinburgh. Where would she go since she couldn't go home? It was a question for another time, after she'd found Preeti's killers. Here, now, sitting by the entrance to the cardboard shelter she'd built on the whisky bond's roof, the light came quickly and Basanti felt her fear subsiding. Ever since her escape, when it was daylight, she made sure she could see to the horizon and the sky above. Her claustrophobia was the legacy of those months and years in underground rooms, trapped and at the mercy of abusing men. Now, only when it was dark outside could she venture inside. She'd spent last night in Cal

McGill's apartment. She'd spend the rest of the day here, by her shelter. When darkness came again she would go scavenging and she would once more climb the wooden stairs to the roof door. She'd wait inside for him. Another night. And another. And another. Until he returned.

Cal took out his phone and checked his emails. He had one from DLG.

'Cal, can you solve this one? One of the Shetland feet matched the one which beached in East Lothian. There was 250 miles between them, crazy or what?'

Cal replied, 'Not necessarily crazy at all.'

The sound of a distant engine took his attention. The *Rib*'s wake was beginning to spread across the Kyle. It would take another 10 minutes before reaching the pier below him. Cal packed his rucksack, put his phone in his pocket and went to meet it.

CHAPTER 17

Douglas Rae held up his raw-red paddle of a hand. 'Howdy doo.' Then he stepped back as though retreating behind an imaginary line of refuge. He was a big man, six feet five in his boots, with a square box of a head, a lopsided grin, and a mat of brown hair.

Cal said, 'Hi, I'm Cal McGill'.

'Howdy doo,' Douglas repeated, fidgeting. Everything about the man was uncoordinated motion. His boots scuffed at a mussel on the pier, his fingers wrapped and unwrapped round themselves like animated raw sausages, and his mouth twitched. 'Fine day, fine day . . .' Suddenly he was lost for words. The only immobile things about him were his eyes. They were fixed on Cal.

'Yes, it's a wonderful morning.' Cal continued the weather theme wondering whether his overnight stay had provoked the older man's curious behaviour. If it had, Cal wasn't about to apologise for it, not to a Rae.

'Indeed it's as fine a day as you'll ever want to see.' Now Douglas pulled at his ear and scratched at the hair above it. He took another step back

226

along the pier. 'Let's be getting aboard then, if you're all ready.'

The *Rib* had a smart black and red livery. As Cal stepped down into the boat, he commented on the newness of its appearance.

'It's for the day trippers,' Douglas said following him in. When he was at the wheel and about to start the engine, he added, 'The summer season's getting busier every year.'

'I noticed the plans for the cafe.'

Douglas's little eyes darted at him then away. 'Aye, and for that too . . .' He patted the wheel affectionately. 'She'll do the job all right.'

The roar of the twin engines brought their brief conversation to an end. Going back to the mainland Douglas pointed out landmarks and shouted their names. Just beyond the Rabbit Islands, the Rae family's other *Rib* passed them going in the opposite direction. Mike was at the wheel. Another, younger man accompanied him. Douglas waved at them and when the boats had crossed he shouted something inaudible in Cal's direction. Something about sheep, he thought.

When they were back onshore and walking up the slipway, Douglas resumed his fidgeting. It was accompanied by a succession of pronouncements, about the weather (again), the state of the roads, the best place for May bluebells, to all of which Cal replied with polite acknowledgements. He had the feeling Douglas was being voluble to deter Cal from talking to him. The only occasion when

Douglas asked Cal a question was when he was unlocking his Toyota pick-up and Cal had said, 'Thanks for the boat ride,' and raised his hand as a preliminary to bidding him goodbye.

Douglas's brow creased. 'Well, what about a bite of breakfast?' he said. 'Ellie, that's my wife, has eggs and bacon in a pan. She'll have put them on when she saw the boat going past.' All of a sudden his nervousness seemed to go away. 'Any way, there's something you should see.'

Until that moment Cal had wondered whether Douglas knew he was Uilleam Sinclair's grandson. Now it was obvious he did. It was in his tone of voice. Cal considered Douglas's invitation for a moment, shrugged and said, 'Why not?' managing to conceal his misgivings at accepting hospitality from a Rae. Perhaps Douglas wanted to show him something that would shed more light on his grandfather's death.

He texted Rachel. 'Coffee. 10am. The hotel?' It was just before eight thirty. He had time.

They settled into the pick-up, Cal's thoughts distracted by what he would say to Rachel, when she replied. 'Look forward to it.'

Cal asked Douglas, 'Where's your house from here?'

Douglas rattled the car keys and wound down the window before answering. 'Do you see that hill over there? Below it is New Iasgaich township.'

'It was named after the island?'

228

Douglas seemed not to hear Cal's question. He turned the ignition, busied himself looking up the road for approaching cars and took off with a spray of gravel.

Cal tried again. 'How many of the original island families live there?'

Douglas again ignored him. Instead of answering, he pointed out an inlet where he used to fish for mackerel as a boy. Next he showed Cal the best piece of land for growing potatoes followed by the cliff where peregrine falcons used to nest until egg thieves raided their clutch two years in a row. When they drove past a sign for New Iasgaich, Douglas said, 'There was no road here before the evacuation. The Norwegian government built it, as a thank you.'

'I thought they'd paid for the land only,' Cal said.

Once again Douglas didn't respond. Cal began to wonder if he had hearing difficulties. Just as he was about to try again, the Toyota breasted a rise and Douglas pointed to a settlement which consisted of eight houses built in a line along a single track road.

'There you are, New Iasgaich'.

Each house had its back to the hill and its face to a sward of green which sloped away towards a curve of beach. Beyond it, across the sea, was Eilean Iasgaich.

'So it is,' Cal acknowledged.

Douglas drew his attention to the last house in

the line. It was, he said, where the widow of Hector MacKay, the 'best skipper the islanders ever had', lived until her death, 'a fine age too'.

The house, like its neighbours, was similar in design to the larger ruins on Eilean Iasgaich: two windows and a door downstairs and two dormers and a skylight in the slate roofs. The difference, as far as Cal could tell, was the glazed storm porch with a pitched roof around the front door. All the houses had one, and all were clad in grey harling which gave them a drab, unwashed appearance even in sunshine. Cal thought it looked a forlorn place.

Douglas turned off the road at the third house along which had a double garage at the side and a single storey extension at the back. Lobster pots and buoys were stacked along the short driveway. 'Time for breakfast I think.' Douglas opened the door and swung his legs out. 'Let's see what Ellie's got cooking.'

Douglas loosened his boots on the boot scraper and Cal waited for him in the back doorway. The porch was pungent with the smell of bacon cooking. 'There's a hungry man here wanting his breakfast,' Douglas shouted towards the open kitchen door before propping his boots on the step. Cal dropped his rucksack beside them and followed Douglas inside.

The kitchen was a long bright room with a wood burning stove at the far end and an arm chair either side of it. An elderly woman with grey hair and dressed severely in black sat in the one nearest the window. She lifted her face and dropped her eyes when Cal entered giving her an appearance of watchful disapproval. To the left of the door was the cooker. Beside it was a small woman in her mid 40s, wearing blue jeans, belted, with a yellow shirt. She was standing over a frying pan of bacon and eggs. Her hair was greying blonde and caught up with a tortoiseshell comb. Her skin was white and stretched, and her manner similarly strained. Cal recognised her from the ticket booth at the slipway.

'Let me introduce you,' Douglas said to no-one in particular. 'Here we have Cal McGill and here we have two Mrs Raes; my wife Ellie and my mother.'

Ellie looked up from her frying pan. 'Oh there's only one Mrs Rae here. I'd rather you called me Ellie.' Something passed between wife and husband; a warning look from her; evasion from him. Cal registered it and Ellie saw he had. She gave him a reassuring smile of encouragement. 'Come on in. You must be hungry.'

Douglas was hovering in an alcove leading to another room. He waved one of his large hands, beckoning Cal to him. 'Come and see. There's a telescope here. The detail you can pick out on the island is a wonder.'

Old Mrs Rae looked away from Cal as he approached, her lips tightening in hostility. It was then he saw what was hanging on the wall behind the wood burner. It was a squared off piece of weathered timber. In its centre were two black shadows; two numbers, 1 and 4. It had been cut from the door of 14 Eilean Iasgaich. Cal stared at it. His grandfather's front door had become a decoration, a sentimental relic, in the house of his family's persecutors. Cal thought of his pregnant grandmother Ishbel closing it when she left the island to return to her parents in Eastern Township, of his great grandmother Margaret shutting it behind her when finally she abandoned the island, ending generations of Sinclair occupation. The dismay showed on his face.

'Here's what I want you to see.' It was Douglas beckoning him again; this time insistently. The man's great bat of a hand waved Cal into a sitting room. Caught off guard, he kept walking towards Douglas whilst glancing back over his shoulder at a piece of his family's history. 'Here, take a look,' Douglas said. He motioned Cal to the telescope at a broad window which overlooked the sea and Eilean Iasgaich.

'Have a gander through that.'

Cal bent to the eyepiece, hesitantly, his thoughts still on the remnant of door. The telescope was trained on Cnoc a' Mhonaidh where two men were in the process of dismantling his cairn. He watched as one, then the other, threw a stone over the cliff. 'Is that what you wanted me to see?' Cal pushed the telescope away in anger and Douglas observed him with a delighted oafish grin.

On his way back through the kitchen old Mrs Rae turned her severe face to Cal. There was a glint of triumph in it. 'So you're Uilleam Sinclair's grandson?'

Her voice rasped.

'Yes I am.'

She looked him up and down. 'Sinclair bad blood isn't welcome here.'

Ellie, who was at the table slicing open and buttering breakfast baps, cried out, 'Leave him be.'

Mrs Rae smirked at her daughter-in-law's naivete. 'What and have his trouble-making ruin the business we've built? All our hard work?'

By now Douglas had followed Cal into the kitchen. Ellie glared first at him then his mother, 'How dare you abuse my home like this. I warned you about it, both of you.'

Douglas was still smirking, a broad lopsided grin across his face.

'I think you'll find,' old Mrs Rae shot back, 'it's not your home and if Douglas has any sense in his head it never will be.'

The matriarch stared coldly at Ellie and then at Cal who by now had retreated to the end of the kitchen by the back door. Her look of contempt was the last thing he registered before exiting the house.

He walked briskly along the road, occasionally breaking into a run. At the end of the new road, he paused for breath and a car approached slowly from the direction he'd come. He stepped onto the grass verge which was chequered white, with daisies, and pink, with clumps of thrift. The car stopped beside him, instead of passing by as he'd expected.

A door opened and Ellie said, 'I'm ashamed that happened, Cal.'

He looked at her and then out across the bay, at the island. 'What are they frightened of?'

'Oh, they don't want you coming here, spoiling their myth.'

She let out a brittle laugh. 'The heroes of Eilean Iasgaich.' The same laugh. 'It makes me sick.'

She sighed twice, the second more despairing than the first.

'Don't you see? It's money to them: it's what brings guests to the hotel, day trippers to the island . . . It gets grants for building the cafe and restoring Hector MacKay's house . . . even a television company making a programme. Everyone's buying it. They're not going to let someone like you try to rewrite history and take it away from them.'

For a while each of them watched the sea.

'At least let me give you a lift to civilisation,' she said.

Cal thanked her and asked if he could be dropped at the hotel.

'That wasn't exactly what I meant.' The hotel belonged to the Raes. Of course.

On his way round the car to the passenger seat he noticed his rucksack in the back seat. 'I thought

234

you might need it,' Ellie said after he closed the door.

Cal asked, 'You know about my grandfather?'

'Oh, I've heard the story all right.'

'You don't believe it?'

She shook her head. 'No, not the one they've told me.'

A young woman with a 'can't you bother someone else' expression was at reception when Cal entered the hotel's small lobby. 'I'm looking for Rachel Newby,' Cal said. She didn't speak but pointed to a corridor beside the stairwell behind her desk. Cal followed the passage to a lean-to sun-room in which there were a dozen tables. Four were occupied; three by couples and the last by Rachel, on her own, her back to him, beside an overgrown jasmine. She was in jeans, walking boots and a fitted cream jersey.

'Nice shower?' he said, pulling out the seat opposite her.

'Actually,' she replied, smiling up at him, her left hand touching her wet hair, 'I've been swimming in the sea.'

He picked up a cup. 'Do you mind?'

She shook her head. 'Help yourself. I've had all I want.'

He reached for the coffee, poured half a cup and gulped it to stiffen his resolve while Rachel watched him.

'Well, go on, tell me, how was your night?'

'Two of Douglas Rae's men dismantled the cairn.'

'God, when?'

'Early this morning.'

'But you only built it last night.'

Cal poured more coffee.

'Rae saw me. He watches the island from his house. He's got a telescope trained on it.'

'What are you going to do?'

'I don't know.'

She sensed his evasion. 'I'm not pumping you, Cal.'

'It's not that, it's this situation. Well you know what I think about it.' Then, as if conceding something to her, he told her about Sandy MacKay's body beaching on the Lofoten Islands and the unexplained mystery of how he got there.

'What do you think happened?' Rachel asked.

'I don't know, but not what the records say. That's one of the reasons I wanted to see the logbook for myself.'

Cal rubbed his hands across his face. He was tired and his eyes were prickling and sore.

He wanted to get it over with. 'Listen Rachel –'

But she interrupted him. 'Please, Cal, there's something I'd like to say.'

'Ok.'

She looked out of the side window.

'I was wondering . . .' Her voice caught and she coughed to clear it. 'Will you think about something?' Cal made to reply but nodded instead.

'It was good yesterday wasn't it?'

Cal nodded again. 'Yeah,' he said guardedly.

'We don't fight when we're together, do we?' She looked up at him, hoping to find confirmation. 'We only ever argue when we're apart.' He noticed her use of the present tense when he would have used the past.

She dropped her eyes. 'Can't we be together again, at least give it a try?'

He could have asked for time to consider it, to let her down gently. He could have said he didn't think it would work. He could have talked about their differences: how he was happiest when he was alone, walking the tide line; how she was happiest when she was busy, with people around her. Instead he told her what he should have told her when they split. 'I had an affair, Rachel, when we were together. I should have told you. I'm sorry.'

Now she was staring at him, angry. 'Who, Cal? Who was it?'

He shook his head. 'It doesn't matter who Rachel.'

She jerked her head stiffly away. She didn't speak for a while, but Cal knew she was crying. Her shoulders were shaking gently.

'Nobody you know . . .' he tried.

'You let me think it was my fault,' she said eventually. 'When? When did it happen?'

'There's no point Rachel . . .'

He could have repeated what he had told her

when she read his note asking her to leave. She had rung him demanding an explanation and he had accused her of abandoning him, of putting her 'precious career' before him. He believed it then because it suited him. It gave him a justification for his behaviour. Now he said, 'I'm sorry. It wasn't anything you did.'

He could have said something else in mitigation, about him being the wrong type for marriage, for putting down roots with another person. Instead, he stood up to leave. 'I'm sorry.'

As he went back along the corridor to the reception desk he wondered why he'd thrown her away a second time.

The woman at reception said, 'Did you find her?'

He didn't answer. When the front door swung shut behind him, she said, 'Suit yourself, why don't you?'

CHAPTER 18

There was another passenger on the Postbus back to Lairg, and another driver. Cal didn't catch either of their names but they seemed to know each other well enough to chatter about their respective families for the entire journey. Cal leaned against his door, watched the scenery go by and thought of Rachel, wondering if he'd ever see her again, surprised that he minded. The train from Lairg left on time, with a party of noisy schoolchildren in his carriage. He changed at Inverness and slept most of the way to Edinburgh. When he awoke, he was crossing the Forth Bridge. He opened his phone and scanned his emails. There was a message from DLG. 'Hey, switch on the news NOW.'

'I'm on the train. Why?'

The response came immediately. 'Cal, get this. Remember the two matching feet, the one from Shetland and the other from East Lothian. Well, there's this cop on the news saying they were wearing odd shoes. How weird is that?'

'What type of shoes?'

'I've got it: the left foot from East Lothian was

wearing a Nike Air Max 360, the Right foot from Shetland a Nike Air Max 95. Both were American size 8.5, the same as British size 8s, men's.'

'Thanks.'

Before the train pulled in to Waverley Station, Cal rang his parents' home. The tenants were called Jim and Annabel Richards. He hoped the husband would answer. Jim was an easy going man, less likely than his wife to mind Cal rummaging around in the back room for an hour or two. After four rings the phone switched to answer. Cal left a message. 'Hi, it's Cal, Cal McGill Can you return my call?' He left his mobile number.

He rang again from the taxi rank and again on the cab ride south to Newington. He got no answer. He left another message just in case. It was early evening. Perhaps they were out. Perhaps they were away. The taxi pulled up outside the house, a Victorian semi-detached villa with a rectangle of lawn in the front garden and a laburnum tree. The knot of rope from his swing was still there. It had cut into the bark and become enveloped by it.

'Are we just going to sit here?' The taxi driver sounded weary.

'I'm waiting for someone.' Cal replied. 'If that's all right . . .'

'Fine by me, you're paying.'

Cal had keys, but he didn't like to use them without Jim or Annabel being there. He rang again and it went to answer. He'd give them another ten minutes before letting himself in. Then he saw he had voicemail. Maybe they'd rung when he was calling them.

'Mr McGill. This is Helen Jamieson. I've emailed too. Can we meet?'

He switched to email. Hers was the only one unread in his inbox. It was the same brief message. 'Can we meet?'

He replied. 'Ok. Where? When?'

Her response arrived as he watched. 'Tomorrow? 2pm? Your flat?'

Maybe she'd return his computers.

The smell was different, and the atmosphere. This part of the house used to be dank and musty, chill like an abandoned basement. At night it became a threatening underworld, a stairway of acid lagoons descending into the sulphurous centre of the earth where a monstrous creature lived, a thrilling place for an only child with too much imagination.

This was where he came on winter evenings after his tea when it was black dark. He would run up the front stairs, across the landing to the swing door which opened on to the back room and the old bathroom. The passageway at the top of the back stairs was his fortress. From here, he repelled the creature on its raids up the stairs and from here he launched his own raids down them.

Now the back porch smelled of fresh paint.

Cal let his hand run against the wall as he climbed the back stairs. The surface felt dry and papery, not the damp he remembered. Stepping on to the landing he expected the hardness of old linoleum but it was deep soft carpet. He misjudged the height of it and stumbled, steadying himself on the banister. At least *it* was still there.

His father had asked the letting agent to organise decorators between tenants. He was abroad and busy he'd said though the truth was he didn't want the house to change and couldn't bring himself to make the arrangements or to witness the make-over. A 'magnolia paint and beige carpet job' he said apologetically to Cal knowing his son felt the same way. Their memories of his mother were bound up in the house. She was in the haphazard detail of every room, the way the books were stacked in the sitting room; the claret paint in the hallway; the pulley she loved over the old Aga in the kitchen ('Tenants don't want cooking smells on their clothes, or knickers drying above the soup. Sorry,' the agent told Cal firmly when he'd protested at a 'site meeting' to discuss the plans. Cal had never been back.)

Now, everything was bland, without memories, for strangers who paid to inhabit a living space, to use his parents' furniture and to move it around to places and rooms it didn't belong.

Cal resented creeping round the house like a thief. This was home even if it didn't smell like it anymore, where his mother lived and died, the first of these in happiness, the second in pain, though she never cried, at least not in their presence. Cal had heard her one night when she thought the two of them were out; his father at a dinner; him at a student party. He had come back early because of her and opened the door to her wailing, not crying exactly but a keening which rose and fell with her breathing and which came from the downstairs bedroom they'd made for her in his father's study. He listened to it until he'd felt furtive, then he shut the front door, purposely loud, to give her time to compose herself. The keening stopped immediately. She died a week later. He was seventeen, which hadn't felt young before her death. It did afterwards.

His father's disintegration followed. He took compassionate leave from teaching, then sick leave. He slept during the day, in his clothes, and paced his study at night, talking to her, Cal assumed, though he never went near enough to the closed door to hear properly. The change in his father surprised him more than the death of his mother. He was uncommunicative and padded about the house unkempt and unshaven. After months of it, Cal came downstairs one morning to find him washed and dressed with breakfast on the table. He announced he was enrolling with VSO to teach in Papua New Guinea for two years.

'It'll mean the house being rented while I'm away.' Embarrassed, he added, 'You wouldn't want the responsibility of a big house like this. I thought

243

we'd split the rent money and you'll be able to lease a small place of your own.'

Cal moved into student lodgings during the term. In the short vacations he went on research trips to the west coast and the islands, or stayed with friends. In the summers he went to his father, paying for his trip with the rent money.

On one of these visits, a beach holiday in New Zealand, his father had said he didn't think he could go back to the house in Edinburgh.

'Why not?'

'Oh it's too full of memories.'

'Why don't you sell it?' Cal had said.

'No I couldn't. I'd be betraying her. She loved that house.'

His father looked at him, his mouth flinching, with an expression of desolation. 'Anyway it's all that's left of her.'

It was then Cal understood his father couldn't go home. He'd become displaced, as Cal's mother had been in childhood, as her mother Ishbel had been in pregnancy, and as Cal now was, standing on the gloomy back landing of his family home like an intruder. If displacement was his family's inheritance it was a legacy which originated on Eilean Iasgaich with Uilleam Sinclair's death.

In the gloom at the top of the back stairs, Cal fumbled for the padlock which he'd fitted to the store room door after helping his father carry boxes of his and his mother's possessions to it. The lock was stiff: Cal had to twist the key four times back and forwards to open it. When he opened the door, the room was dark and smelt dusty; the closed shutters prevented the city outside from penetrating. Cal flicked on the light, a bare cobwebbed bulb dangling from the ceiling above the corner fireplace. Along the wall to the right were two rails of bagged clothes, his mother's. In front of them were her personal things, packed away in large cardboard boxes.

In one of these boxes were three old photograph albums, square and squat with thick card pages and filled with sepia prints of family groups: the men with serious faces in tweed suits, watch chains and pigeon chests; the women, modest in hats, jackets and long skirts, with thin smiles, their lips pursed together; the children miniature versions of their parents, except for the mischief in their eyes. These were the Stewart forebears, his grandmother Ishbel's family, merchants and shopkeepers from Aberdeen.

In the same box, he remembered, had been two ledgers with lined pages bordered with vertical columns in black, blue and red inks for entries of pounds, shillings and pence. These were Ishbel's journals. He hadn't known of their existence until his father found them in his mother's chest when they were packing up the house. Cal flicked through a few pages before wrapping them in newspaper and storing them away – there had been too much else to do that day. All he could recall was his grandmother's hand-writing which was neat and plain apart from her capitals which she drew with flamboyance. T appeared to be a favourite. When it was the first letter of a diary entry she gave the cross stroke a looping flourish which became a cloud with the rays of the sun shining through it, or spots of rain falling from it. Cal had wondered whether it illustrated her mood that day, or the weather. But he hadn't been curious enough to go to the bother of unpacking her journals again, especially when tenants moved in.

Now he wanted to find them for the light they would shed on Eilean Iasgaich and the injustice done to his grandfather, his grandmother and the two generations which came after them. It was time for the truth to be told.

The first box he tried contained some of his mother's books. The next had the contents of her roll top desk, legal papers mostly. Cal's fingers fumbled clumsily at the tape of the next box. He opened the lid and inside was her wool, layered in colours, red on top, blue underneath, white, green and brown below; skeins as well as balls. He had packed it that way to protect the photograph albums and the two ledgers at the bottom. Cal emptied out the wool and removed the books one at a time, taking off their newspaper wrapping. The journals were identical in size and appearance with black covers and triangular red flashes at the top and bottom corners. The spines were matching red. Inside the front covers, on the facing pages, in printed handwriting and blue-black ink, his grandmother had written her name and the dates each of her journals spanned. In the first ledger, she'd written 'Ishbel Stewart 1939–1941', and in the second 'Ishbel Sinclair 1941–1943'. 1941 was the year she married Uilleam Sinclair.

Cal turned to the next page of the second ledger. The writing there was neat and economical, as he'd remembered it. Each day began with the date and a colon, followed immediately by his grandmother's trademark flourish on the first capital letter. Cal read the first entry. It was October 22, 1941.

'This is my first day on the island. My Uilleam carried me from the boat and Mrs Sinclair (I daren't call her Margaret though she urges me to do so) was there to welcome me. The others were fishing or working the land and too occupied to greet me, according to Uilleam, though I know when he is trying to protect my feelings. I will work hard, be a dutiful wife and with God's assistance I shall be accepted here.'

The next entry was October 24. 'I must be patient. I must persevere. All will be well, I am certain of it. Uilleam is by my side and I pray to God.'

There were five entries on the first page. The last was dated October 28. 'I have lived in dread of this day. Uilleam has gone to sea. He assured me he will be back soon. He did not say so but I overheard the other women talk of 10 days perhaps more. Our neighbours are the MacKays: the mother is called Ina, her daughter is Grace Ann and the boy is called Sandy. The boy is a delight and visits Uilleam often but neither Mrs MacKay nor Grace Ann will address me. Indeed Mrs MacKay shouts names at me. Mrs Sinclair told me it was on account of my marriage to Uilleam. Mrs MacKay had expected Uilleam and Grace Ann to marry, as had Mrs Sinclair 'though it is of no importance to me if you do your duty and provide Uilleam with a son and me with a grandson'. Mrs Sinclair had provided a male heir for the Sinclair croft and a share-holder for the boat, now the duty was mine.'

Cal let his eye run down the entries on the opposite page. They were more of the same; his grandmother missing Uilleam and wishing for his safe return; and hurtful confrontations with Mrs MacKay.

Cal turned the pages until he came to 1942. The writing was the same but her tone more despairing and there was an enigmatic reference in March of that year. 'If only I could persuade Uilleam to come with me, we would be content, I know we would.'

In May she recorded the day the Eilean Iasgaich arrived in its new livery as an anti-submarine trawler. 'I am so proud of Uilleam and frightened for us both. When I saw the boat with its fresh paint and its gun, the men lined up on deck and my Uilleam among them, I became sick with worry. I would have cried all night except that Uilleam would have heard me.'

There was a brief burst of euphoria on July 23. 'I am pregnant as I suspected though I didn't dare to write it here until now. The doctor has come and I can expect our baby before next spring. My prayers have been answered, though Mrs Sinclair told me that her prayers had not, not yet, and she would not be celebrating until she knew it was a boy because 'if it is not it will have been nine wasted months'. Uilleam is at sea. I will go to the hill every day and watch for the boat returning so I can be first at the pier.'

Then on July 24 she wrote, 'I hate this island and the people on it. Some person has nailed a rabbit's skin to the door of our house. Mrs Sinclair said it was the Raes who have desired the Sinclair croft for more years than she can remember. They want to frighten me, she said, to make me lose the baby or leave the island. I told her firmly, 'I will do nothing of the sort'. The talk is that it was Murdo Rae's doing – a man who has never said a word to me, kind or cruel, not in all the months I have been here. Nor does he speak to Uilleam even though they work side by side on the boat.'

Cal turned hurriedly to September 29, the day Uilleam was washed overboard, forgetting his grandmother did not hear news of it until later, when the boat returned to the island with seven men missing.

'The baby kicks me mercilessly. It must be a boy. Pray God that it is.'

Cal found the entry he was looking for on October 7. It was brief and underlined with two lines of black ink. 'Uilleam is gone. I cannot bear to write another thing this cruel night in this cruel place.'

The following day her journal seemed to bring her comfort of a sort, because the entry was long, filling almost a page. She wrote of Mrs Sinclair 'screeching and howling' all night, of hiding her own grief because she didn't feel comfortable displaying it. She was a 19-year old who had known Uilleam for so short a time and 'what comparison was that with a mother who had borne him, raised him and loved him all his life'. She added, 'though who could have loved Uilleam more than I?'

Ishbel related how she went out intending to climb Cnoc a' Mhonaidh to be alone in her misery and to scan the sea 'to look for Uilleam'. She had collapsed, exhausted by her grief, before reaching the hill, when she was surprised by Grace Ann MacKay. 'She embraced me and said tragedy had now brought us together. "Our men are dead and we must be strong for each other." She apologised for the way she had been. The hurt of Uilleam's marriage had set her against me and him though now it shamed her. She said she had loved Uilleam too but he had not loved her as he loved me. We hugged and cried and I said how sorry I was about the loss of her fine brother Sandy and for Hamish Sutherland who had to bring the dreadful news to our door. Grace Ann looked surprised and said it was surely Hector MacKay. I told her I was certain it was Mr Sutherland and she let the subject pass. When I returned to our house, I asked Mrs Sinclair about it. "Grace Ann said I must be mistaken about Hamish Sutherland but I wasn't, was I?" "No, Ishbel you were not. Hector MacKay went to the houses of all the other dead men."

'"Why didn't he come to ours?"

'"Because of something that Uilleam has done."

'"What has Uilleam done?"'

Ishbel recorded that Mrs Sinclair left the question unanswered and became uncontrollable with grief.

'October 9: Grace Ann visited today and made her condolences which we returned, for her brother Sandy who was like a younger brother to dear Uilleam. All three of us cried and when we were finished I asked why it was that no-one else had come to our door when I'd seen mourners visiting other houses. Grace Ann said she didn't know but Mrs Sinclair said, "Why do they blame Uilleam for your Sandy's death?"

'"Why would they indeed?" I said in innocence.

'Grace Ann replied, "It must be mistaken Mrs Sinclair for they died together, one 16, one 21, two brave young men."

'Mrs Sinclair persevered, "They say the depth charge breaking loose was Uilleam's fault because the repair to the rack was his and he should have been the one to secure it."

'"He did, with Sandy."

'"They say Sandy went to it first and when Uilleam followed him Sandy had already been swept overboard."

'Grace Ann said something about war being to blame, but this knowledge shocked me. Is this why we are being treated like outcasts?'

'October 10: Hamish Sutherland came to the door but refused Mrs Sinclair's invitation to enter. He said – and I will remember these words until I die – "Mrs Sinclair, you and your daughter-in-law will not be welcome at the memorial service for the men who died." Mrs Sinclair remonstrated with him. "Wasn't Uilleam one of the crew, one of the men who died?" "He will not be remembered Mrs Sinclair, for what he has done." Until that moment neither of us knew of the memorial service. What has my sweet Uilleam done?'

After that Ishbel's dairy entries became fewer.

'November 20: A curious incident with Grace Ann. I saw her walking the path to Cnoc a' Mhonaidh and, not having anything better to do, I went after her hoping for some company. I followed the path all the way to the sheepfold but there was no sign of her there. When I encountered her later, I asked, "Grace Ann, was that you I saw on the path to the hill this forenoon?" She replied, "Indeed it wasn't Ishbel. Why would I be going to the hill when I have work to do?" Her manner was offhand and she wouldn't look me in the eye. Then she excused herself and hurried away indoors. Why, suddenly, does she want to avoid me when she has been so kind since the news of our bereavements? I have searched my memory for occasions when I might have offended her though I can think of none.

'December 14: I am leaving this place. This is my final day; the last I will have to put up with these unfeeling people, the last I will have to listen to Mrs Sinclair telling me my duty to Uilleam is to remain here, to give birth to his son here and to secure the tenancy for the Sinclair family.'

'February 24 1943' – it was the first entry of that year – 'Eilidh was born today. She is 7lbs 3oz and lovely in every way with Uilleam's mouth. I am entranced by her.'

'March 7: Mrs Sinclair called at the shop. She is leaving the island. She is disappointed in me "because your duty was to produce a boy and you failed and now my life's work is wasted. The Raes have your husband's inheritance and may it curse them and you". I asked her to accompany me upstairs to see Eilidh, her granddaughter, and she replied "a girl is of no use to me," and she turned and left the house for Thurso, to stay with her sister.'

The next entry was September 29, 1943. It was at the top of a page, three lines of text. The remainder of the page was empty.

'I took Eilidh to the hill and we looked across the sea for Uilleam, this being the first anniversary of his death. I will do the same every year. I prayed for Uilleam, and also for Sandy. My comfort is that they are together in death and my blessing is Uilleam's child, my sweet daughter Eilidh, whose nature is as kind and loving as her father's.'

Cal read it again. Had she not known Sandy's body was buried on the Lofoten Islands? The diary entry suggested she didn't. According to Grace Ann, Sandy's mother had received the letter five months before. Surely Cal's grandmother would have made reference to it if she had known.

He turned the remaining pages of the ledger. They were empty. On the inside back cover he noticed a flap for documents and tissue poking from it. He pulled it out and a curl of white-blond hair dropped out. It fell on to the ledger. Cal touched it, wondering whether this was grand-father's hair, or his mother's, though she had been dark like Ishbel.

CHAPTER 19

It was less than a mile from his parents' house to The Mound, the man-made rampart which links Edinburgh's Old Town to the Georgian New Town. Cal was at the bottom of the slope by the Royal Scottish Academy when it began to rain and he hailed a passing black taxi. The driver, a retired male nurse working night shift for holiday money, attempted conversation, moaning about the digging up of Princes Street for trams that nobody wanted. Cal made occasional sounds of agreement, for the sake of politeness and because he didn't want a discussion. When the taxi arrived at The Cask, it was almost midnight and the driver said, without irony, 'Thanks for the natter chief, God bless'. Cal paid him and hurried inside, holding his grandmother's journals close to him to shield them from the drizzle.

One of the teenagers who lived the floor below passed him on the stairs. Cal said, 'All right?' The boy didn't reply and Cal carried on to the top landing, taking his key from his pocket, forcing it into the lock – Ryan or whoever had ransacked the place had damaged the alignment. As soon as he opened the door he smelt it: a pungent, feral odour. The hairs on his arms bristled. Someone or something was in his flat. He kicked the door shut with a bang, kept off the light and dropped his grandmother's diaries on his work table to free his hands. He hurried to his left. Now he was passing the spiral staircase to the roof. Was an intruder waiting for him there? At any moment he expected to be jumped, a knife cutting into him. When he reached the bathroom his heart was drumming. He closed the door, snapped shut the bolt and offered up a prayer that whoever was in his flat wasn't in the dark of the locked bathroom. With him.

He listened, his shoulder against the door, his legs braced. After a few minutes, he shouted, 'I'm calling the police . . .' Perhaps it *was* the police, he thought ruefully; another of Detective Inspector Ryan's extra-judicial surprises. Still there was no sound from the other side of the door. 'I've got no money,' he called out.

'. . . Or drugs.'

Or computers, his only possessions of any cash value, thanks to Ryan and Detective Constable Helen Jamieson.

'Ok, time's up. I'm ringing the police now.'

'Help me, please help me.' It was a young woman's voice; pleading with him.

'Who is that?'

'My name is Basanti, Please help me.' Her voice sounded foreign.

Cal listened at the door before shouting, 'What do you want?'

He couldn't hear all of her answer, but it ended with her begging him not to call the police. 'Please.'

'Are you on your own?'

'Yes.'

'Go to the back of the room,' he instructed. 'Turn on the light by the door.'

He heard her moving and the snap of the switch.

Then he opened the bathroom door, a fraction at first, his shoulder against it, certain this was the biggest mistake of his life. When he saw her she was at the far end of his work table, still walking backwards. Her clothes, baggy black jeans and grey hoodie, were stained and dirty, her dark brown hair cut short and ragged. Cal opened the door wider and she lifted her face at the movement, revealing hollowed cheeks and scabs on her cracked lips. Cal noticed this though not the knife behind her back which she'd taken from his kitchen drawer and which she kept hidden from him. Just in case.

'What do you want?' he said climbing the stairs from the bathroom and she told him about her friend whose body was fished out of the sea off the Argyll coast three years ago; the girl whose death was recorded in a newspaper cutting on his wall. 'Please help me. There's no-one else I can go to.' She apologised for frightening him, for being in his flat.

'How did you get in?'

'I climbed the ladders at the back of the building. I got in by the door in the roof. It was unlocked.'

She said she'd waited for him, for three nights now. She'd seen her friend's photograph in the background of the newspaper pictures of Cal. 'You must help me find the men who killed her?' It sounded authentic, particularly when she called the dead girl 'Preeti' and she added with a tremble of emotion 'she's from the Bedia tribe, like me.'

In the end what could he do but take her at her word? He sighed. 'Can I trust you?'

She nodded.

He watched her, making up his mind. Then he went to the kitchen alcove and picked up the kettle and held it up. 'I need some coffee. What about you?'

'Thank you.'

Suddenly she looked very young.

'How old are you?'

'Seventeen, I think.'

Cal registered her uncertainty, but didn't pick up on it. 'Listen, have a seat and I'll bring this over. Milk? Sugar?'

She shook her head.

While he waited for the kettle to boil she sat cross-legged on the hearth stone and slid the knife behind a pile of books.

When Cal joined her, handing her a mug, he hooked his foot round a moulded plastic chair, one he'd salvaged from a skip, and dragged it towards him. He sat about two strides from her, closer than he'd intended. The smell from her was strong: sweat, damp clothes and terror. Putting his mug between his feet, he said, 'So why do you think your friend was killed?'

'I didn't know Preeti was dead until I came here and read about her.' She glanced up to the map and the newspaper cutting of Preeti beside it.

A tear ran down her face. It sparkled in the bright overhead light. 'She died three years ago . . .' She turned her head away from Cal towards the window. The back of her hand brushed her cheek. '. . . She must have been so frightened.'

A tremor passed through her.

Cal asked, 'Could it have been an accident . . . ? The police don't know what happened to her . . .'

Basanti didn't answer and Cal turned on a lamp and went to the door to switch off the overhead light. 'That's better.'

The glow from the lamp cast shadows on the floor where Basanti sat. They seemed to comfort her and draw her tension so that when Cal sat down again and asked, 'How did you know Preeti?' she told him about the Bedia and the tradition of selling daughters into the *dhanda*, the sex trade. 'The Bedia are a warrior tribe. The *dhanda* is more honourable for Bedia girls than domestic work.' Her tone of voice made it clear she didn't believe this any more.

'Your parents sold you?'

'Preeti, too. We are from different villages. Our families were paid 60,000 rupees, for each of us.'

She glanced at Cal, as if expecting him to be impressed, but he didn't react. She tried to make him understand. 'For our virginity . . .'

'They sold your virginity?' Now he got it. 'My God.'

'Yes.'

She told him about the shiny black car, about Preeti holding her hand and looking after her even though she, Basanti, was the older girl and Preeti the younger.

'How old was she?'

'She was thirteen and I was fourteen.'

Basanti's hands clutched her coffee mug. She hadn't drunk from it. Cal asked if she would like something else instead and she shook her head. The warmth from the cup seemed to be sustaining her.

'We were taken to a city, Mumbai I think, and then to an airfield where there were other girls we didn't know, and then to a port where Preeti and I were put on a ship. I don't know about the other girls. We never saw them again.'

Gradually the story tumbled from her, with Cal interrupting with questions or comments when her voice tired with the effort of it or when it cracked with emotion. She held her head down. Occasionally her voice would waver as though she was crying. Cal imagined that was why she hid her face from him. It allowed her some dignity, what little of it she had left. She told Cal how Preeti and she had been kept on the ship for weeks, months – 'We lost any sense of time passing so I began scratching the days on the paint in our cabin and when we were taken ashore there were twenty seven scratches.' That was the last time she'd seen Preeti. 'We were taken ashore in a small boat, tied and blind-folded and carried from the boat . . .'

Cal helped her. 'Where were you taken?'

'I don't know. It was a room without windows.'

'And Preeti?'

'I don't know what happened to her. She was behind me, being carried when we came ashore . . . I never saw her again.'

'I'm sorry,' Cal said.

She sighed. 'Then the men came . . . for sex.'

She stopped again and Cal tried to make it easier for her by saying 'only tell me what you can.'

'Until this one night when I was taken outside. There was something going on. The man carrying me was running across rough ground – he was frightened. He tied me to an iron ring and left me. Then I heard shouting and sirens. By the morning I'd worked off my blindfold and that's when I saw the hill and the tree.'

She paused again. He wanted to ask, 'What hill and tree?' but before he could she said, 'The man came back for me and I was put in a van and taken away to a city. My new owners told me I'd been sold to them. I was their property. They said they could kill me if they chose, or sell me. I was theirs. They could do what they wanted with me.'

She knew now the city had been Glasgow.

'How long were you there?'

'I don't know. Many months, years, I don't know. I escaped nine days ago.'

'And you've been living rough since then?'

'There's nowhere I can go. The men who own me will be looking for me – and the police will send me back to India and my family and I'll be put in the *dhanda* again by my uncle to pay my father's debts.'

'The police will want to know about Preeti and you. The men who have done this are criminals. They'll want to find them and bring them to justice.' Cal thought it ironic he'd turned advocate for the police.

Basanti shook her head. 'You don't understand. I stabbed a man, when I escaped. I think I've killed him. Blood was coming from his neck. I can't go to the police. I've got to find who killed Preeti.'

'The police can do that.'

'Won't you help me?'

'I'm not that kind of investigator.'

After a pause, he said, 'There was something you mentioned earlier – a hill and tree?'

She unbuttoned her shirt at her midriff and slid her hand round to her back, pulling out a sheet of paper which had bent to the shape of her body. She put it on the floor and pressed it flat before handing it to him. It was her drawing of a hill with ridged flanks and a flattened top rising from a plain. Half way up its left side a tree leaned at forty-five degrees.

Cal studied it. 'This is what you saw?'

'Yes. This is where Preeti and I were taken ashore. This is where I last saw her.'

They talked for another hour, perhaps more, until the gap between his questions and her answers grew wider. Eventually, Cal said, 'I must get some rest. Then I can think more clearly. It's been a long day.'

Rachel was on his conscience too.

Basanti nodded.

'There's a bed,' he said. 'You have it. I'll sleep here, in the armchair.' He wanted to add, 'You can wash. There's a shower,' but he was concerned she would take it wrong.

She didn't respond and Cal said, 'Well I'll let you think about it.' He stood up and went to the other side of his table and opened a map. 'How long was the car journey when you were taken to Glasgow?'

'I don't know. Two, three hours maybe. Maybe less.'

'Let's say a maximum of two forty or two fifty kilometres.' He drew a circle with Glasgow at its centre.

'And you were close to the sea when you started?'

'Close; a short walk.'

Cal studied the map again. The circle he had drawn included much of the Scottish coastline, west as well as east. Only the far north-west and north-east, Sutherland and Caithness, were outside the circle. The circumference ran south of the

English border too. It included Blackpool on the west and Newcastle on the east. Her drawing – a hill and a tree growing from it at a peculiar angle – and 13-year old Preeti's body were the only other clues. They pointed to Scotland, somewhere along the west coast. But where? Had Preeti also been sold again and taken to Glasgow before being drowned?

While he'd been studying the map, he'd sensed Basanti moving but hadn't paid her any attention, hadn't even said good night, in case she became self-conscious about taking his bed. He turned off the desk light and sat back into his armchair. Out of the corner of his eye he saw Basanti go from the bathroom up the spiral stairs. On the landing by the half door to the roof she lay down on the bare wood. What he didn't see was his kitchen knife on the boards by her; her hand beside it, protection if she needed it.

It was late morning when he was woken by his phone. He looked at the screen, didn't recognise the number and let it ring. He stretched and coughed and glanced at the top of the spiral staircase. Basanti wasn't there. He thought she might have used the bed when she'd seen him dossing down in the armchair, but she wasn't there either. Nor was she in the bathroom; the door was open. He went back to his chair. On the table beside it was her drawing and a scribbled note. 'Thank you.' Was she coming back?

His phone rang again. It was the same number as before.

'Hello.'

'Am I speaking to Cal McGill?'

'You are.' He didn't recognise the voice.

'I'm Eleanor Ritchie, a nurse at the Royal Infirmary in Edinburgh. There's a patient here who's asking for you. Grace Ann MacKay.'

'Is she all right?' He hadn't realised she was in hospital.

'The thing is she says she hasn't got any next of kin . . .'

'I'm not next of kin,' Cal said in case that was what the nurse was checking.

'It's awkward when it's like this . . . she's most insistent that she sees you. She had your phone number with her.'

'I visited her a few days ago . . .'

'She mentioned it. There's something she wants to tell you.'

'I've got an appointment this afternoon.' He thought he wouldn't say it was a visit from the police. 'I can come after that.'

'Good, I'll tell her. It'll calm her.'

'What happened?'

'She's had another stroke, a bad one. I wouldn't leave it too long Mr McGill.'

CHAPTER 20

Detective Constable Helen Jamieson knocked once on Cal's door. She heard the padding of his feet and pulled the sleeves of her jacket straight, one at a time with a precise jerk of the cuffs. The jacket was cerise with white stripes and a matching cerise skirt which was a little too tight. She'd bought it the night before, after announcing to herself in the changing room mirror 'it's time you were good to yourself Helen.' She was an 18, but the skirt didn't come bigger than a 16. The shop assistant said, 'It makes you look very summery' and it did. It'd give her a target, a reason for slimming, something to aim for.

'Hi,' Cal opened the door. His hair was wet and he was wearing a blue shirt which was hanging outside his jeans. He was barefoot. 'Sorry, late start.' He held the door open for her. 'I was hoping you might be returning my computers.'

'I might be.'

'You don't sound sure.'

'Well, it depends.'

'On what?'

'Helping a police officer with her inquiries . . .'

'Ok'. But it was a wary 'Ok', one that was waiting for the catch. 'Sorry about the seating arrangements. Wait there a moment.'

He went to the sleeping area (his bedding looked every bit as untidy to Jamieson as on her previous visit.) 'It's more comfortable than it looks,' he said, returning with a plastic chair and putting it down near her.

'Coffee?'

'Please, black.'

Cal put the kettle on a camping stove. Jamieson would have been amused by his rudimentary kitchen equipment if her hips hadn't been bulging over the moulding of the seat, making her feel fat when she wanted to feel attractive, for once.

'Is this about the gardens?' he asked, suspecting it wasn't. Dr Tim Lenska, his director of studies at the Scottish Marine Institute, had emailed about a policewoman called Jamieson asking questions about the severed feet. He'd mentioned Cal's name to her. He hoped Cal didn't mind. Cal didn't.

Jamieson seemed startled by the question. She thought Cal had seen her trying to smooth away the bumps and ridges in her new skirt. But Cal wasn't looking. He was spooning instant coffee into two mugs. 'No, that's still with the Crown Office,' she said. It wasn't her job to let him know he wouldn't be prosecuted. Even the Environment Minister had refused to make a formal complaint.

Duplicitous prick Ryan had called the minister.

It takes one to know one sir.

Jamieson shifted again in her seat, to make herself more comfortable and, well, thinner if at all possible.

'So you want me to help you with the severed feet?' Suddenly he was there in front of her, holding a mug out.

The chair dug into her in all the wrong places.

She managed to take the coffee without it spilling and sipped at it, waiting for composure, aching for elegance.

Please. Just for a day, just for an hour.

'What makes you think that?' she asked eventually.

'Well, I imagine someone's been going around the marine scientists in Scotland asking questions.'

'So now you're psychic too.'

'Not psychic; Dr Lenska's been in touch.'

'Ah.'

Cal went on. 'You see I'm the only one doing this work in Scotland. There are some guys in the States, but their focus is mostly the Pacific. The best known is someone called Curtis Ebbesmeyer. By comparison to him I'm just a nerd.'

Jamieson warmed to Cal's chattiness and modesty. Men, in her experience, wasted few if any words on a plain woman. Her male colleagues – and some of her female, too – regarded her with lofty pity. They spoke to her as little as they could and spent as short a time in her company as possible within the boundaries of rudeness; and sometimes beyond them. After some of these encounters, she'd thought of preparing a stock letter of apology, copies of which she would keep in her bag for instant distribution. All she'd have to do would be to fill in the relevant name.

'Dear so and so,

'Someone of your stature is entitled to expect to be in the presence of beauty. I apologise for imposing my plainness on you.'

Ryan was like that. Cal wasn't. He had kind eyes without any hint of pity or contempt, or, she noted with regret, a hint of anything else. Still.

'Isn't Ryan in charge of the investigation into the feet?' Cal had read his name in some of the press reports. His expression told Jamieson it was a big problem.

'He doesn't know I'm here.' Jamieson watched his reaction. Was she being too trusting?

'So why are you?'

'Because we have a common interest . . .' Jamieson stopped mid-sentence.

'Go on,' Cal said.

'Both of us would like to find out how those feet washed up in Scotland.'

'Sure, yeah, ok.' What was so difficult about saying that? 'Is that it?'

Jamieson hesitated.

'And neither of us wants Detective Inspector Ryan to get the credit?'

She didn't need to tell him the risk she was taking. Her agitation did that.

'Ok.' He spoke slowly, keeping his eyes on her, letting her know he understood what she was saying, what was at stake.

'So you want to screw Ryan?'

'Yes, in a manner of speaking.' She laughed nervously.

Helen Jamieson screws Ryan. It was a sentence she'd never considered before.

Cal shrugged. 'Sounds good to me.' He leaned across his table and grabbed a pad of paper. 'What do you want me to do?' Jamieson relaxed. 'Tell me where the feet started from.'

'Oh that should be easy.' His tone said it wouldn't be. He turned to a clean page. 'Ok, we'll make some preliminary assumptions to narrow the search. We can expand it later if we have to.'

Jamieson let a little smile of relief flicker across her mouth. Sweat beads had gathered on her top lip. She nodded. 'Ok.'

'Let's take it these two men went into the sea same time, same place – both of them wearing trainers, two of the feet beaching in Shetland, the other in East Lothian. In view of the prevailing currents, we can rule out the east coast of Scotland as the starting place.'

He began writing, talking to himself as he did. 'Search area: Land's End in the south, up the west coast to the north of Scotland.' He glanced at the map behind him. 'Then take a line from Duncansby Head by John O'Groats north-east to St Magnus Bay, Shetland.' He looked up again. 'Then extend across the whole search area to the 13th meridian west.' He checked. 'That should do it: it takes in Ireland and the sea to the west of the UK.'

When he put down his pen he said, 'It'll have taken a minimum of two months for adipocere to have set in and for disarticulation to have happened. Then there's the time these feet have been drifting at sea. Let's start by going back a year, to last May.'

He tore the paper from the pad and handed it to her. 'It's a lot of ocean.'

'Is that all?' Jamieson said.

Cal responded to her amused sarcasm with a smile.

'Oh and I'll need trainers, like the ones that were found.'

'We're putting it out they were Nikes but they were counterfeit.'

Cal's eyebrows rose. 'Really? I'll need them, for buoyancy tests. How they float affects the speed as well as the direction of travel.'

'I can probably let you have them for 24 hours, no more.'

'That'll do.'

'Anything else?'

'My computers . . .'

'They're in my car.'

Cal said, 'Thanks.'

'I don't know why you're thanking me.'

'By the way,' he said, 'with these feet, all I can give you is a range of possibilities, the approximate direction of travel and some incidents worth examining in more detail. It's an imprecise science, not like DNA or fingerprinting.'

'A range of possibilities would be good.' Jamieson stood up and brushed the sides of her skirt with the flat of her hand where the chair had left tracks in it. 'Another thing. Can you keep in touch with me by email? I've set up a new account.'

'What's the address?'

'It's Bembo1@23comely.co.uk'

They exchanged glances. Bembo was the New Zealand harpooner in Herman Melville's book *Omoo*.

'It can't be my work email,' Jamieson said. 'Address me as Bembo when you're emailing, don't use my real name.'

Cal said, 'You don't like Ryan, do you?'

She didn't answer. She didn't need to.

He smiled. 'And since we're doing each other favours . . .'

He took the cutting from the wall and let Jamieson read about the dead Indian girl. He explained why he was breaching a confidence – 'it's too big, someone in the police needs to know' – and then he told Basanti's story and showed Jamieson her drawing.

Jamieson listened and at the end she said, 'We'll find them. You tell her that. Tell her she can trust me.' Her voice was cold, determined. It was one thing men treating her badly; quite another them molesting children, even touching a hair on their heads.

Cal said, 'I don't think she's ready to trust anyone yet.' Then, running his hands through his hair, he said, 'God, I don't even know I'm going to see her again.' He showed Jamieson the note Basanti had left him that morning.

'If she does come back see if you can persuade her; even if she'd speak alone to me, here.'

He shook his head. 'She won't, not yet. She's worried about being deported. She's illegal. She thinks she's killed a man.'

'Tell her none of that matters . . .'

'In a day or two perhaps, when she's more settled, if she returns . . .'

Cal went with Jamieson to the car and unloaded his computers from her boot. She helped him carry them to the lift. 'You'll send me a copy of that drawing of the hill,' she reminded him.

'I'll scan it in now.'

Jamieson nodded. 'They're scum.'

'Who are?'

'Men who treat young girls like that.'

Jamieson was almost at the door when Cal shouted after her, 'She'll come back. I've just realised.'

'Who will?'

'Basanti.'

'How do you know?'

'She wouldn't go, not without her drawing.'

CHAPTER 21

'Your visitor's here.' Nurse Eleanor Ritchie stroked the back of Grace Ann MacKay's veined hand. It was resting outside her blankets on a book with worn black covers and faded gold lettering. Cal recognised it from his visit to her bungalow. It was her Bible. The nurse lowered her voice. 'She won't let go of it; she had it with her in the ambulance.' Eleanor regarded her patient with affectionate indulgence. 'She'll be so relieved you've come.'

'Should I get a coffee or something?' Cal asked, 'And come back when she's awake.'

'She'll murder me if you do. She was most insistent I woke her as soon as you arrived.' She rubbed the old woman's hand once again. 'Grace Ann, your visitor is here. Cal's here, Grace Ann.'

Grace Ann stirred, opened her eyes and shut them again.

'She'll just be a wee bit disorientated.'

The nurse was jolly and small with blonde hair cut into points under her angular chin. 'Just call me if you need anything. I'll be over there.' She indicated the nursing station in the middle of

274

the ward opposite the four bed bay where Grace Ann was lying. The other beds were empty. Eleanor straightened Grace Ann's bedding. 'I'll do her pillows if she wants to sit up. Just give me a call, ok.'

Grace Ann's throat rasped. 'Cal, is that you?' The effort of it made her cough. Cal noticed the skin below her eyes was puffy and black.

'How are you?' he replied.

She coughed again. 'It doesn't matter about me,' she croaked and the dryness caught at the back of her throat. Cal suggested a drink and she shook her head. 'No.' The rasp became stronger, setting off a sequence of hacking coughs. Her face turned purplish-grey and she began to choke.

'Nurse,' Cal shouted but Eleanor wasn't there. He picked up the glass of water on the bedside table, hesitating before slipping his hand behind her head and lifting. 'Here, have a drink.'

Her neck was thin and bony against his palm. It felt fragile, breakable, and he worried about pushing too hard. When she'd taken a sip followed by a gulp which spilled out of her mouth, her coughing stopped and Cal lowered her head and removed his hand.

She mouthed 'Thank you', but no sound emerged. Her eyes were fixed on him. They were rheumy and pleading.

'Rest for a bit, then we'll talk,' Cal said but she shook her head.

She coughed again. 'I have something you must

see.' She held up her Bible but the drip at her wrist prevented her from handing it to Cal and he took it from her. 'Open it, inside the back.'

Cal opened the leather back cover revealing a folded sheet of writing paper. He held it up to Grace Ann. 'You want me to see this?'

She nodded, her eyes never leaving his face. Now she looked fearful.

He unfolded the paper which was filled with writing, black letters sloping backwards. One word was at the top: Archangelsk. It was dated 25 September 1942.

'My Dearest,' he read it out loud.

'I miss you more than I can express. My love, I am so proud of you and of our unborn baby. I think of you every hour and every minute I am away from you.'

Cal stopped and glanced questioningly at Grace Ann. 'Please,' she said, 'Finish it.' When he hesitated, she said 'please' again with such anguish that he continued reading to calm her.

'The voyage here was dreadful for its loss of ships and men and, my love, I am apprehensive of the return. Five of our own crew were lost on the outward journey – though you will know of this by the time you receive this letter. By God's grace Sandy is not among the dead. He has been my strength in all our difficulties, and I his. We share our clothes and our food and we are wearing each other's watches so that if I die he will bring mine to you as a token of my enduring love, and if he dies I will bring his to Mrs MacKay and to Grace Ann. Knowing this gives each of us the strength and determination to survive. But if neither one of us returns we will have something precious of the other's to accompany us to our deaths and to comfort us in our solitariness. I am writing you this letter to let you know that I am as reconciled to my fate as any man can be. The good Lord willing, it will be to spend the rest of my days with you and our child.

'With all my love, my dearest,

'Uilleam'

Cal scanned hurriedly through the post script before reading it aloud too.

'PS: I am giving this letter to the safe keeping of a Canadian pilot I have met here. He will send it to you when he returns to his squadron's base in Yorkshire at the start of November. With God's protection I will be home with you before it is.'

Cal said, 'My grandfather wrote this?' It was an accusation as well as a question.

Grace Ann flinched. 'Don't judge me, Cal. I was so in love with him.'

Dark shadows seemed to underscore the translucent grey of her skin. She had the same pleading expression which Cal noticed earlier. Now he understood it. She wanted his forgiveness.

'Where did you get it? Do you know what this means?'

Grace Ann flinched again. 'I do.'

'My grandfather is buried in the Lofoten Islands, not your brother Sandy.'

'I know.' She swallowed. 'Please Cal.' Tears were beginning to tumble across her cheeks. 'It's been so hard for me to give him up. Please try to understand. I was so young.'

Cal's exasperation was rising. 'Who have you given up?'

'Uilleam, your grandfather . . .'

Cal glanced behind him at the nurses' station in case his raised voice had attracted attention. 'How long have you known?' he asked, repeating it with emphasis to make sure she heard him. 'How long?'

Grace Ann closed her eyes and turned her head away.

'Since 1943, when my mother received the letter from the Admiralty saying Sandy's body had been found; I've known since then.'

'This letter, where did you . . . get it?' He almost said steal.

Still she couldn't bring herself to look at him, to see his contempt. 'A few weeks after the *Eilean Iasgaich* returned from Archangelsk in October 1942,' she sighed. 'I was collecting the island's letters from Eastern Township and I recognised his writing on the envelope. I knew it was wrong but I couldn't stop myself.

'I was 18, Cal. I was desperate for something of his. Ishbel had everything else. Is it so hard to understand why I wanted his letter?'

Cal's eyes met Grace Ann's staring, willing him

278

to forgive her teenage passions. 'I loved him Cal more than anything else in the world. Ishbel had his baby. I had his letter. Was that so unfair?'

'But it was written to my grandmother.'

Grace Ann didn't reply immediately. 'I've had it on my conscience for so long.' She wheezed and her lips spread across her sunken face in a grimace of contrition.

'Why didn't you say something when the Admiralty letter arrived the following year? You knew my grandfather had been wearing Sandy's watch when he died.'

'I couldn't. I couldn't do that to my mother. I couldn't tell her that it was Uilleam in the grave, not Sandy. His death destroyed her. Her only comfort was the knowledge he was buried.'

'So you kept it to yourself.'

'I had to. And afterwards too . . .'

Neither of them spoke, then Grace Ann said, 'When I saw your photograph in the newspaper I knew it was time. It's been on my conscience so long. When you visited me I couldn't tell you. Your eyes are so like Uilleam's. To see them hating me . . .' Her head rolled back across the pillow.

He spoke slowly, trying to make her realise what she'd done. 'My mother died not knowing her own father's body had been found and buried . . .'

Grace Ann cowered as though every word was striking her. The sight made him stop mid-sentence. Losing his temper with an old woman on her death bed wouldn't make it right for his mother.

Grace Ann began to cough, a rasping dry noise and Eleanor, the nurse, arrived bustling at her bedside. She took the glass of water from Cal. 'Have a wee drink, Grace Ann.'

She turned to Cal. 'Maybe she should have a rest now.' The nurse brushed Grace Ann's cheek with the back of her fingers. The old woman's eye lids fluttered and her lips stretched in a tired grimace. 'The letter, take it.'

Eleanor whispered over her shoulder to Cal. 'She's tired, the old soul. I think it'd be better if you went now.'

Cal laid Grace Ann's Bible on the bed and said his thanks to the nurse. On his way out of the ward he held the letter to his chest. His possession of it provoked a feeling of unexpected melancholy. His 19-year search for his grandfather was over: his constant and loyal friend since boyhood found and laid to rest; a collection of old bones in a Norwegian grave. Cal felt he had lost his companion.

Outside the ward was a rest area. He sat there, reading the letter once more, wondering how his grandfather had washed ashore on the Lofoten Islands and where he'd gone overboard. Wherever it was, it wasn't to the south of Bear Island as his grandmother and his mother had been told. There was only one explanation. The *Eilean Iasgaich* must have steamed close to the Norwegian coast south of the Lofoten archipelago before he went into the sea. If it had, the boat would have been within range of German coastal batteries and air patrols. Why, he puzzled, would Hector MacKay, the skipper, have taken such a risk?

Was the answer contained in the log book, the page he hadn't been allowed to see?

On the bus from the hospital, he read the letter again and thought about the gravestone which bore Sandy's name. Should it be changed? Thinking of his grandfather's fondness for Sandy he decided the inscription should remain as it was: Sandy's name on the headstone; Uilleam's body in the lair; the two of them together in death, as they had been in life.

The bus stopped at St Andrew Square in the centre of Edinburgh from where he walked along Princes Street, to a branch of *Gap*. He bought jeans, a pair of linen trousers, two white tee shirts, two cotton shirts and a cotton jersey. A female shop assistant helped him choose. As an afterthought, he also bought socks, two packs. The assistant saw him looking nervously at the underwear stand. 'Is she about my size?' she asked. 'A little bit taller and slimmer,' he replied and then worried he'd made it sound as though the assistant was short and fat. 'About the same,' he corrected himself. She reacted with good humour. 'How many?' she laughed. 'They're in packs of two.'

'Three packs, I guess: how many do you think?'

He walked home through the New Town and then took a brief diversion to Inverleith Park where he watched after work football games, reflecting on his grandfather and Grace Ann. Had he loved her? Had he given her the impression they would be married? Had Ishbel been a coup de foudre for him? Cal thought of Rachel too, of how they'd been at the beginning. Could they be that way again?

By the time he was back at his flat, it was late evening. The door to the roof was open and Basanti was sitting there, half in, half out, resting against the jamb. She smiled at him and apologised for taking some of his paper. She was trying to draw the hill and the tree again, to make it a better likeness. 'You're welcome,' Cal replied. 'Anytime,' he added, trying to let her know how relieved he was she had returned. 'Really, make yourself at home.' He left the *Gap* carrier bag on the bottom of the stairs. 'Just a few things; I thought you could do with them.'

He turned away before she could say anything, hoping to make it easier for her to accept his gift. At the long table he switched on his computers and while he waited for them to flicker into life, he picked up the frame with his grandfather's photograph. He regarded it thoughtfully before flipping it over and prising open the back with his thumb nail. Into the slender aperture he slid his grandfather's final letter to his grandmother, resolving as he did so to find a picture of Ishbel from among his mother's belongings to replace the photograph of the Ardnamurchan gravestone. Then he clipped the back shut, slid the two brass fasteners into place and returned the frame to its place on the table.

The sound of the bathroom door closing made him look up. He heard running water. Basanti had turned on the shower. The bag of clothes had gone from the bottom of the stairs. While he waited for her to emerge, he logged into his email account. There was only one new message in his inbox. It was from Jamieson. She had written 'Nail the bastards' in the subject box. She thanked Cal for scanning and sending Basanti's drawing. Cal deleted the message and began searching through websites with pictures of the west coast of Scotland – Google produced 4,520,000 results. Then Basanti was standing in front of him, clean and in her new linen trousers and a blue cotton shirt. Her hair was wet and glistening.

'Thank you,' she said, breaking into a smile, which began uncertainly and lopsidedly at the edges of her mouth before widening into a grin of girlish pleasure. The instant it did she dropped her head, now shy in case he mistook her delight for immodesty.

Cal almost said something about how lovely she looked but settled for, 'Are you hungry?' Hadn't she had enough unwanted attention from men?

Basanti nodded.

Cal went to the kitchen, put water into a pan and poured in a bag of easy cook risotto. After adjusting the heat he went back to his table. 'Now . . .'

He pushed one of his computers across the table and swung it round to her.

283

'Do you know how to work this?'

'Yes,' she said, and then more warily, 'One of the men taught me – he used to bring a laptop when he visited me.' Her eyes filled with sudden alarm. What would Cal think: that she had colluded with one of her abusers? She glanced at him, expecting to find a look of disapproval, but Cal didn't react. He continued to open up pictures and discard them. 'Think you can do that?'

'I think so,' Basanti replied, trying it herself.

'If you find a photograph like your drawing let me know.'

Cal returned to the kitchen where he stirred the risotto, chopped parsley into the pan, and grated parmesan over it after the grains and water thickened like porridge. When he came back with the plates, he asked, 'Recognise anything?' She shook her head so he went to the other side of the table and sat opposite her. 'Would you mind if I sent your drawing to some people I know? They might be able to help.'

'If you think it is all right?'

She went back to searching the pictures, taking small mouthfuls of risotto as she did so.

Cal sent an email to his Omoo contacts. 'Does anyone know this scene, probably west coast Scotland?' he wrote, attaching Basanti's drawing.

It was late when Basanti complained of tired eyes and asked if she could carry on going through the photographs the next day.

'I'm sorry. You must be exhausted.' Cal had put

284

a key beside him, Rachel's key. It was tied with a piece of blue ribbon. He slid it over to Basanti. 'It's for the flat. It means you can come and go as you want. Well I suppose you do anyway.' She shook her head, refusing it. He didn't press her. He'd leave it on the table and she could use it or not as she chose. 'Have the bed, Basanti. I'll be sleeping there.' He nodded at the armchair beside him. 'It's comfortable. I sleep there often when I'm working late.'

'Thank you, but I prefer to be up there.' She pointed to the door to the roof. She needed to be near an escape when she was sleeping, he realised. Being held captive for so long had done that to her.

'Take a pillow at least.'

He went to the cupboard by the bathroom door, pulling out a sleeping bag and a pillow. He put them on the bottom of the stairs, apologising for not having a clean pillow slip.

'It doesn't matter, really.' She sounded amused.

When Cal returned to his chair, she said good night. Cal grunted in acknowledgement. At the foot of the stairs, she stopped and turned back to him, self-consciously. 'Thank you,' she said. 'I don't know what I'd have done . . .' Her voice trembled with emotion.

Cal waved his hand dismissively. 'No bother, really.' Then he said, 'You're welcome.'

Basanti picked up the sleeping bag and pillow and carried them up to the wooden landing. She unrolled the bag on the boards and lay down on top of it in her clothes. She put the pillow under her head. Cal watched her briefly before an incoming email distracted him.

It was from Mack, the leader of the Omoo group. 'Do you have any more clues?'

Cal replied: 'Not really. I'm not even 100 percent sure it's west coast?'

Mack: 'What's the story?'

Cal wrote two versions of his reply before settling on, 'It's a favour for a friend of mine. She wants to find the hill again. She's in Scotland, revisiting her childhood holiday haunts.'

He dozed, lying back in his chair. At intervals during the night he woke to check on Basanti. Her back was to him; her face towards the roof door. Finally, he fell into a deep sleep which was broken by sunlight warming his face and the screech of gulls outside. The first thing he did was to look for Basanti, but she was no longer there. The sleeping bag was folded on the landing with the pillow on top of it.

He went to the table. She'd left him a scribbled note. His key was on it. 'Thank you' was all it said.

CHAPTER 22

The counterfeit Nike trainers arrived by motorcycle courier after 9am. Jamieson emailed using her Bembo address. 'Return them in 24 hours, quicker if you can. Use the same courier company.' She gave its phone number and her account details. Cal filled his kitchen sink with some sea-water he had collected in buckets from nearby Granton harbour and put in the shoes, weighting each one with tide-smoothed stones he'd brought back from beaches around Scotland.

By late morning Bembo had emailed three more times.

The first email enclosed attachments from the Coastguards detailing emergency call-outs at sea for the relevant dates in Cal's search area, 28 involving loss of life. Twelve bodies were still missing, all of them men. Two of them died sea kayaking, only one of whom was definitely wearing trainers. Two other men drowned after their fishing boat capsized, but neither was wearing trainers, according to the police. The remaining missing men died in two separate incidents off the west

287

of Ireland, but there were no reliable reports about their footwear.

The second email listed double suicides. There had been six, pacts by desperate people throwing themselves into the sea together, but only one involving two men. One of the bodies had been recovered and neither had been wearing trainers. (They'd taken their shoes off. 'Suicides do,' observed Bembo, 'and spectacles.')

The third email listed estuary drownings: there had been 14 and all but four of the bodies had been recovered. Three of the missing bodies were men, two of whom had been wearing trainers. Both had drowned in the Clyde estuary, a day apart.

'How do we know two night-time cockle gatherers weren't swept away at high tide in Morecambe Bay and no-one saw them?' Cal asked.

Bembo: 'We don't.'

Cal opened a can of tuna for lunch, tipped it into a bowl, mixed it with mayonnaise and toasted pitta bread. After his first bite he glanced up at where Basanti had left the sleeping bag and pillow. He took another bite then climbed the spiral stairs, apprehensive about her finding him there, on what was her territory, her sanctuary. He listened for her and pushed on the door. The roof was in bright sunshine. His plants were in the gully to his left. To his right, underneath a chimney breast was a cardboard shelter. Basanti was sitting at its entrance, drawing. She started when she saw him and Cal regretted his impatience.

'I was concerned about you,' he said.

'I was going to tell you,' she said, looking embarrassed as though he might think she had spurned his hospitality. 'I can't be inside when it's daylight. I've been locked away for so long I have to be outside, or I feel trapped,' she tried to explain.

Cal said she must do whatever suited her.

'When it's dark I'll come in again,' she said.

'It's ok, really.' He noticed some bread and fruit at her side, and she saw him noticing. The fruit was overripe and the bread was crushed in its wrapping. She had scavenged it from the rubbish bin at the back of newsagents before dawn. He left before he made her any more ill at ease. 'See you later then,' he said.

Cal spent the remainder of the afternoon keying information from Jamieson's Bembo emails into his computer and launching tracking programs, each calculating the probable course of a disarticulated foot floating away from any coordinate where he had a report of an unrecovered body going into the sea. The program automatically selected the relevant weather and ocean current reports from Cal's database.

Soon after 5pm Bembo sent him details of scores of maritime accidents, mostly minor, where there had been no reported loss of life. He had asked her to provide this information. Cal searched through them for those which involved impact between two vessels – most involved yachts and small boats – or unexplained contact between bigger boats or ships colliding with unidentified floating objects, usually flotsam cargo.

Bembo: 'Why do you want all this? Shouldn't you be concentrating on missing bodies?'

Cal: 'A ship at night can run over a small craft without knowing what it's done. Say a tanker runs over a drug smuggler's speed boat or a people trafficker, who's going to report it missing?'

By 9.30pm he'd inputted the coordinates of dozens more incidents for tracking. He switched on his lamp and yawned. Soon after, the door to the roof opened and Basanti came to sit in the chair opposite him. 'It's dark outside,' she said, explaining why she'd come indoors. 'I'd like to look at some more pictures now?'

He switched on the other computer and reminded her how to access the sites he had bookmarked. 'Maybe today we'll find it, Basanti.'

She said, 'I hope so.' Then she started searching.

For the next two and a half hours, they worked at their separate computers, with Cal taking a break to bring her coffee and a slice of cold pizza. She hadn't asked for it but she ate it. Soon after midnight, Cal's monitor screen of thumbnail icons – one for each of his computer tracking exercises – showed 49% beginning to veer off course, with 23% going north of Shetland, 14% washing up on the west coast of Ireland and 12%, mostly those incidents within a mile or two of the UK, beaching on the Welsh or Scottish west coasts. He fell asleep in his chair. When he woke later,

Basanti was no longer at her computer. She was curled up on the landing by the roof.

On his way to bed he stopped by the Belfast sink and removed the stones from the shoes now that they were saturated with sea-water. One by one the trainers rose to the surface where they floated, sole up. Cal knelt down and scanned across the surface. None of the shoes floated higher than the others. He checked the fake Air Max 360 in particular. It had come ashore in East Lothian. He pushed it under the water and let it rise again. It settled like the others; flat in the water.

He went back to his desk and emailed Bembo. 'Increased exposure to wind does not explain the extra distance travelled by the counterfeit Air Max 360. It sits no higher above the surface of the water than the Shetland shoes. The explanation for it beaching earlier has to do with the timing of disarticulation. The Air Max 360 foot must have disarticulated and floated free some days/weeks before the others. I am still working on the theory all three feet disarticulated in approximately the same place.'

He took the shoes out of the sink and left them to dry on his bathroom towel rail.

He woke soon after 6am, stumbling out of bed, looking for Basanti, but dawn had long gone and she had gone with it. He slumped into his chair and tapped the return key on his computer. The grid of icons came up showing most of his simulations had gone off course, leaving 8 within his margins of tolerance. He'd entered two instructions: the drift track from any of the starting coordinates had to pass within 32 kms of Shetland or be in the North Atlantic Current waters which flood into the North Sea through the Fair Isle gap between Shetland and Orkney.

He composed an email to Jamieson.

'Dear Bembo, you should concentrate on these incidents from last year and one (number 8) from earlier this year:

1. May 13: Submarine reported night-time collision with unidentified 'contact' in The Minch. 58°15'N, 5°45'W.
2. May 29: Unconfirmed report of yacht capsizing, west of Dingle Bay, Eire. 52°01'N, 10°58'W
3. July 23: Drowning of father and teenage son rescuing a dog, Aran Islands, Eire. 53°07'N, 9°55'W
4. August 16: May Day emergency. Two sea kayakers lost following collision with cruise ship, west of Tiree, 56°31'N, 7°05'W
5. September 4: Grain carrier ran aground Achill Island, Eire. Five men lost overboard. 54°N, 10°12'W
6. September 24: Prawn boat sunk off Western Isles. One body recovered, two missing. 57°16N, 7°31'W
7. October 26: Oil tanker struck unidentified object west of Benbecula. 57°28'N, 8°12'W

8. February 7: Bulgarian coal ship. Three
   men lost overboard west of Eire. 53°16'N,
   12°18'W

'Please check with aviation authorities, UK and
Ireland, about aircraft incidents for the same
general search area as before.'

He made coffee, two teaspoons of instant and
half a mug of hot water poured from the tap,
and spent the next two hours inputting more of
Bembo's data – his reserve list of possibilities. He
watched the simulations begin, pulsing dots
tracking slowly northwards on miniaturised ocean
maps, before going for a shower. When he emerged
from the bathroom ten minutes later his phone
was ringing. It was a number he didn't recognise.
There'd been three missed calls. He answered it,
with misgivings. 'Hello.'

'Is that Cal, Cal McGill?'

It was the nurse from the hospital. She apologised
for 'troubling him' as she put it.

She wasn't, Cal reassured her. 'How's Grace
Ann?'

'She passed away this morning, poor soul.'

'I'm sorry.' It came out automatically. He didn't
feel anything for her now, not after what she'd
done, though something about the fierceness of
her love for his grandfather had impressed him.

'It didn't seem right for an old lady to die like
that and for no-one to be told.' She was still
apologising for ringing.

'It's all right,' Cal said.

'She never spoke again, not after your visit. She closed up, didn't say another word, the poor dear . . .'

'I didn't know.'

'Seeing you, it was the last thing she had to do. That's all it was. You come across it all the time in my job.'

'Yes, I suppose you do.'

After they said goodbye, Cal collected up his grandmother's journals, his laptop, the photograph frame with the picture of his grandfather and a chart of the North Atlantic. He packed them carefully into his backpack, zipped it and placed it by the door, along with the counterfeit trainers which he put into a carrier bag. He rang the courier company for their collection and climbed the spiral stairs to the roof. Basanti's shelter was empty. The clothes he had bought her were neatly folded beside a growing pile of drawings of a hill with a tree on its left flank. He took a clean sheet of paper and wrote on it, 'Have to go away for a day or two, something I've got to do. I'll ring. Make yourself at home.' He added his mobile phone number and his email address, username and password with instructions for opening his google-mail account. 'If you can't reach me by phone – the signal can be unreliable where I'm going – send me an email instead. I will pick it up when there's reception.'

He put his message to Basanti on the computer

keyboard she'd been using and dug into his pocket for some money. He unfolded the only two notes he had, £20 and £10, and put them beside the message.

The buzzer went. It was the courier company.

As he was leaving his flat, he turned back, going to the gantry of shelves where he kept his collection of flotsam and jetsam. He picked up a large black Mary's Bean, the seed of Merremia Discoidesperma, a tropical vine of the Morning Glory family. He'd found it on Orkney's west-facing coast, at the tide line, concealed under sea-weed, the day he'd met Rachel.

He dropped it into his pocket, went downstairs, handed the shoes to the waiting courier and rang for a taxi to the station.

He slept on the train waking an hour before Inverness. He tapped the return key of his laptop which was on the seat beside him. There were three emails generated automatically by the computer in his flat. Each contained a map and a blue line tracking the Atlantic to the west of Ireland and the Outer Hebrides towards Shetland and the Fair Isle gap. They were the successful simulations from his second run. He emailed the details to Jamieson, with the suggestion that they take a lower priority than the first list of eight because he had widened the margin of error.

An acknowledgement arrived in his inbox three minutes later. 'Thank you. Aviation data will follow shortly. There are no recorded crashes or planes ditching in the search area for the relevant dates, though there are a number of unexplained 'incidents', reports of bright lights in the sky, UFOs etc.'

When the train arrived at Inverness, Cal changed platforms and caught the local service to Lairg. He copied the 11 successful simulations, eight from the first run and three from the second, on to a single ocean map. Each dotted line was a different colour; each showed the probable course of a floating shoe containing a severed foot. The track from simulation 10, one of the second group, was coloured purple. It started at 55°51'N, 10°48'W, north-west of Eire, and travelled north-east before passing through 57°28'N, 8°12'W, another of his starting coordinates from the first batch. One line then merged into the other as they followed exactly the same course north and then east to the south of Shetland.

Cal checked the two incident references. On October 6 the previous autumn a container ship sent out a May Day call reporting it was listing after some of its load slipped in a south westerly gale. Later it reported the emergency a false alarm. It had secured its containers and would ride out the storm at sea before proceeding across the Atlantic to New York. Twenty days later an oil tanker struck an unidentified object which was large enough to inflict a sizeable dent in its hull. Cal measured the distance between the two sets of coordinates. It was about 250kms. The current off the west of Scotland moved at between 10–15kms a day. If a container had fallen overboard on October 6, it was plausible Cal thought for it to have travelled 250kms in 20 days, at 12.5kms a day.

He emailed Bembo. 'Pay attention to a connection between possibilities 7 and 10. You're looking for a container going overboard on October 6 and the tanker colliding with it on October 26.'

Bembo: 'Do containers float?'

Cal: 'They can do, yes. Check the loading and offloading manifests for discrepancies and also check satellite tracking data. Some companies which own containers put tracking devices in them.'

'What are you getting at?'

'Call it a gut feeling.'

When he'd found the Mary's Bean, a surfer in a wet-suit passed him on the beach. 'Wow what's that?' she'd asked, her smile rippling from the edges of her mouth to small vertical dimples on each cheek.

He told her the folklore of Mary's Beans; how they were good luck charms; how they were also known as crucifix beans because of the cross etched on one side; how pregnant women prized them for their beneficial influence on childbirth; how currents carried them from Central America across thousands of miles of ocean, their hard outer casing protecting them from sea water, their internal cavities giving them buoyancy; how he'd searched beaches in the Outer Hebrides, Orkney and Shetland for just this discovery; how he'd found other tropical beans but this was his first Mary's Bean.

They walked back up the beach together, him asking about surfing; her rubbing at her hair to dry it and answering his questions with a mixture of enthusiasm and self-deprecation. 'I only came in because I didn't want you watching me fall off another big wave.' They stopped where the sand gave way to grass, neither one of them knowing quite what to do next. She laughed at their sudden reticence. 'Hi, I'm Rachel Newby.' She'd held out her hand. 'I'm from London. I work for a television production company. And you?'

They spent the weekend camping together on the beach, his sleeping bag and her tent side by side. After the first night, one or other was empty. When it was time for them to part – she was attending a concert at the St Magnus Festival in Kirkwall before flying south to London – they kissed and Cal gave her the Mary's Bean, awkwardly, self-consciously. She understood the gift's emotional significance even though Cal left it unspoken (typically, as she would discover). It was to be a symbol of the bond between them, of the good fortune which brought them together, which made their marriage five months later on the same Orkney beach in a wild November gale seem as though it had somehow been arranged, even ordained, by nature.

'I'll keep it, always,' she said, 'Always.' Thereafter, when they were apart, either because of his work or, as became mostly the case, hers, she slept with her fingers folded around it. Gradually, the Mary's Bean changed into being a symbol of everything that separated them instead of that which bound them together.

Shortly before their second anniversary, after another fractious phone call, the third in as many days, Rachel rang late one night from New York where she was working. She was sorry about what was happening to them; she worried she wasn't the right partner for Cal; she didn't like to think of him being unhappy; did he want to take time out? He responded by accusing her of dishonesty, of preparing her pretext for deserting him. Rachel didn't argue. She was tired of arguing. He was wrong was all she said.

Another long period of silence followed, during which he went to Knoydart and met Catherine Sale, who was compiling a botanical map of the peninsula. They were together for two weeks, becoming lovers, before Cal returned to Edinburgh. Rachel's work took her to London and then to Madrid, while Cal went to North Uist with Catherine. The flat was empty and cold when Rachel visited Edinburgh for a long weekend before another working trip to New York. She hoped Cal would be there. Instead she found a brief letter asking her to go. 'You're never here. I'm sorry I can't live like this. It's over, please leave' were the only reasons he gave. She put her keys on his table, packed her clothes and left the Mary's Bean on the shelf along with his other beach discoveries. She wrote a label for it, just like all the others in his collection.

'Skaill Beach, Orkney, West Mainland, 18 June 2005'.

'Where's Jamieson? Get her in here now.' Detective Inspector David Ryan barked his instruction to Joan, his PA, through the open door of his office.

'Yes Mr Ryan.' Joan cupped the phone to prevent him overhearing her. 'Helen, he wants to see you and look out – he's raging.'

Jamieson was in the detectives' room. She closed her lap top, locked it in her drawer and gathered up her case file. It was 13.50. The conference call with the detectives from Shetland was scheduled for 14.15. What was Ryan panicking about now?

Jamieson winked at Joan as she passed. Joan held in her smile because Ryan was looking at her, drumming his fingers on his desk.

'Good afternoon sir. You asked to see me.' Jamieson stood just inside the doorway from habit forged by Ryan saying daily, sometimes twice daily, to her 'I can hear you from there Jamieson.' As if ugliness was catching on closer contact.

'Have you seen this, Jamieson?'

Good afternoon Detective Constable Jamieson. How are you today? I'm well thank you sir. I'm following some good leads sir. Well done Jamieson.

'What sir?'

'This statement from Nike . . .'

'No sir. I haven't seen it sir.'

'They're saying the trainers are counterfeit.'

'Yes sir.'

'You don't seem surprised Jamieson.'

'No sir.'

'Did you know they were counterfeit?'

'Yes sir.'

'What are you playing at Jamieson?'

'Nothing sir.'

'As senior investigating officer don't you think I should be told something like that?'

'Yes sir. I do sir. I did sir.'

'You're a liar Jamieson. I'm not a fucking imbecile.' He banged the desk with his fist.

No sir and neither am I sir.

'It's in my report, on page 2. Didn't you read it, sir?'

Ryan blinked.

'If that's all, sir, shall I come back for the conference call?'

'No.' His eyes narrowed as if he was seeing something for the first time. 'No, I don't need you for the call, Jamieson. Brief me on what you're doing.' Jamieson opened her file.

'Here's a list of all the inquiries I've initiated, sir. There are rather a lot of them as you can imagine.' She glanced at the page and was about to approach Ryan to hand it to him when he said, 'Give it to Joan on your way out.'

'Yes sir. I thought you wanted me to brief you sir.'

'Well get on with it. I don't have all day.'

'I've worked through the DNA databases north and south of the Border. There are no matches with the feet, at least none with any of the missing people for whom we have a DNA sample.'

'So what are you doing now?'

'I'm running checks on a variety of different maritime incidents to the west of the UK. They're a combination of suicides, drownings, shipwrecks, collisions, you name it we're investigating it sir.'

'Any leads?'

Yes sir.

'No sir. It's like searching for a needle in a haystack sir.'

Ryan's look was withering and contemptuous. 'You'd better find it, Jamieson.'

'Yes sir.'

He sneered at her. 'Have you ever heard of something being career-changing?'

'Yes sir.'

'Well this is career-changing for you, Jamieson. If you let me down . . .'

And for you sir

'. . . Now get out of my sight.'

'Yes sir.'

Later in the afternoon, Jamieson walked by Ryan in the corridor outside the detectives' room.

'Very elegant sir.' Ryan reared back at the idea of Jamieson paying him a compliment on his new blue suit. 'What?'

'Very elegant sir, the press statement saying you were aware the shoes were counterfeit and you were keeping it confidential for operational reasons.'

'Get out of my way Jamieson.'

Yes sir, no sir, you can fool Joe Public sir but not the SCDEA's interviewing panel, sir.

CHAPTER 23

The tide was full and the creel boat nudged against the low bridge spanning the Kyle between Tongue and Eastern Township bay. The skipper looped the mooring rope round an iron railing and pushed his red woollen hat off his forehead. The time was 5.18 in the evening. The hotel van was due at 5.30. He stretched and pushed back his shoulders. For a blissful moment the ache low in his back went away but when he bent to pick up the next box of lobsters it stabbed at him again and he screwed up his face. With a heave and another spasm he raised the box shoulder high and slid it on to the side of the road. Back pain ran in his family. His grandfather had it. His father had it. Now he had it. The other family legacy was his name, Hector MacKay, though he'd managed to rid himself of some of its burden of expectation. Everyone called him Red after his hat which he wore indoors and out, winter and summer. His surname and back pain had proved more dogged inheritances. When he got lonely, which was seldom, he consoled himself with the knowledge that he would pass on neither to a son.

He was childless and a widower and likely to remain so though he was 38 years old and good-looking. His hair under his red hat was blond and curly; his eyes were blue, his nose aquiline, his cheek bones prominent and his cheeks concave. The women of the crofting townships found two faults with him. One was forgivable: his height. He was five feet seven inches which was judged disappointing for a man with such fine features. The other was not. His young wife had killed herself, an overdose of pills. Some said his cruelty was to blame; others that he had administered the dose himself.

In the aftermath of her death, while he was still unwelcome in the community, he encountered God. He found him in nature, in the seas, the landscape, the birds, and the whales and dolphins which slipped like oil on late summer evenings across the bay by his home. Over time, he abandoned his Bible and stopped praying. The less he asked of God, the more he felt his presence. He was everywhere. Late one night he found a name for this type of religion. He was, according to 'Amos', an American internet chat room acquaintance and sometime evangelist, a pantheist.

Red looked up pantheism in a long undisturbed *Oxford English Dictionary* and found a definition to his liking: 'The belief or theory that God and the universe are identical (implying a denial of the personality and transcendence of God); the doctrine that God is everything and everything is God.'

305

(If God is not transcendent, he thought, why had the *OED* written God with a capital G?)

By the time he had heaved the fourth and last of his shellfish boxes on to the roadside, Kenny, the driver of the van from the hotel, was opening the boot doors. 'Good catch today Red?'

'I can't complain.' Red pushed his shoulders back and pulled a face.

'Back getting to you again?' Kenny shook his head in amusement at Red's contortions. For as long as he'd been collecting Red's catch, seven months on and off, he'd been complaining about his back.

'It's been murder today.'

Kenny swivelled his San Francisco Giants baseball cap back to front, stuck his hands in the pockets of his blue overalls and spread his legs in an 'I told you so' stance. 'Don't blame me.' Kenny, the hotel's trainee chef, had offered to crew for Red three mornings a week when he wasn't working in the kitchen.

'Yeah, yeah . . .'

'Just say when and I'll do it.' They both knew it wouldn't happen. Red enjoyed fishing as much for the solitude as for the catch.

'Chef's looking for two boxes of prawns tomorrow, and a dozen crabs, good big ones. There's a special do on.'

Red screwed up his face again. 'I'll see what I can do. I've got a physio appointment in the morning which'll delay me no doubt.'

Kenny was accustomed to Red's grumbles and pessimism. 'Same time, same place tomorrow.'

'If the body's willing. The tide'll be good for landing here for a few evenings yet, then it'll be back to the old pier.'

'Is the road fixed?'

'They say it will be. They were working on it today.'

Kenny snorted. 'Sure thing it won't be. See ya tomorrow Red.'

Kenny turned the van in the middle of the bridge and sped away westwards. As the sound of its engine faded, squealing brakes from the other direction made Red turn. A lorry juddered twice before stopping. Bellows of distress came from the cattle it was carrying in the back. Their hooves slithered on the wet, dung-slicked corrugations of the floor as the animals fought to keep their balance. A youngish man with short dark hair and wearing jeans dropped to the road from the passenger door. He reached into the cab for a backpack, slammed the door and banged on it with the flat of his hand. The driver let out two loud blasts of the horn in answer before accelerating slowly away, the engine straining under its load, the cattle still bellowing.

Red looked at him with curiosity.

'Hi, can you help me?' the stranger said, politely.

'I'll do my best, I'm sure.'

'I'm trying to get to Eilean Iasgaich tonight.'

Red was loosening the knot on the rope securing his boat. He studied the younger man's face. 'Are you now?'

Red didn't need to ask the next question. His expression did it for him: why?

Cal shrugged. 'I was wondering if you might be going that way.'

Red kept on staring, his eyes narrowing a fraction, his face giving nothing away. 'Well that depends doesn't it?'

'On what?'

'I guess on why you want to go there.'

Cal looked towards the island and back at Red. He recognised him from his first trip to the island. Red had been moored in the same place at the bridge when the *Rib* had gone past. He decided to take a chance.

'Uilleam Sinclair was my grandfather.'

A look of understanding passed from Red to Cal, a silent acknowledgement of a shared heritage, of Cal's right to visit the island without having to answer any more questions. Red said, 'Aye, that'll do. I've heard of him all right.' He pulled on the rope and the boat nudged back against the bridge. 'Jump in.'

'Thank you.' Cal handed down his backpack and Red winced at its weight. Inside it were Cal's laptop and his grandmother's diaries.

'Bad back?'

'Don't get me started.'

Cal sat on the road bridge, his legs over the edge, reaching for a firm footing on the deck. He jumped and landed awkwardly.

Red grabbed him.

'Ok?'

'Thanks.'

'I'm Red, by the way, after the hat. My other name's MacKay.'

Cal said, 'I know.'

'And how would you know that?'

Cal told Red how Mike had pointed him out to the boat party.

'Did he now?' It seemed to tickle him, becoming a local tourist attraction. 'So you've been out to the island before?'

Cal said he had. 'A few days ago, my first visit . . .'

Red considered asking him another question but instead said, 'No, you're fine,' and started the engine. He asked Cal to gather up the mooring rope and the boat nosed out into the tidal stream. Cal joined Red in the wheel house. 'Nice old boat.'

'She suits me.'

'What's her name?'

'*The Eilean Iasgaich* . . .'

'After the trawler that went down in the war . . . ?'

Red nodded. 'You know the story?'

'Yes.' Another look passed between them.

'Tide's turning,' Red said and spun the wheel to starboard. The boat veered towards the wide mouth of the bay. 'So you'll know my grandfather was the skipper.'

'Yes, of course.' He hoped there wasn't any animosity in his voice.

Red didn't appear to detect any because he carried on, 'After his death, my grandmother and

309

father went to the new settlement.' He pointed east, to the headland behind which was New Iasgaich township. 'Over there, just beyond the point. The Norwegian government gave the land to the surviving islanders.'

Cal said, 'Does your father still live there?'

'No, he's long gone. He married an island girl and they lived there for a time, but he was a drinker and fell out with the neighbours, not to mention his wife, my mother,' Red shrugged. 'It can happen around here.' He laughed. 'And how. My grandmother was in her coffin by then and just as well for him, because he sold the house and his share of the island. He bought this boat with some of the cash. So the name is the only bit of the island we've still got. My grandfather's descendants are the only ones allowed to name a boat *The Eilean Isagaich*.'

'Where's your family now?'

'My family's me. I'm all that's left.' He glanced at Cal. 'Me, the boat and the house my father built over there to the west. You'll see it when we get to the island. There's no road in or out, only the sea.'

'Your father's dead?'

'The bottle did for him 17, 18 years ago.'

'I'm sorry.'

'I was at university in Glasgow at the time. We'd been estranged because of his drinking. When I went to the house after the funeral there were empty bottles everywhere, sheep and hen muck in every room. God knows how he lived like that.'

Cal wondered what happened to his mother: it sounded as if she was dead too.

'It's got a lot to answer for . . .' Red nodded towards the island. 'All those ruined houses. A broken human spirit in every fallen stone, I say.'

Cal kept his view to himself.

The island was close enough now for Cal to pick out the pier. Red was steering further to the west. 'D' you mind if I drop you in Seal Bay?'

'Anywhere's fine.'

'It's on the north of the island, more sheltered when the wind's blowing from the south-west. I've got some creels to drop along that shore this evening. You'll find there's a path up the back of the hill. It's steep but the footholds are easy enough.'

The boat swung round the buttress of Cnoc a' Mhonaidh and Cal searched the skyline for the site of his dismantled cairn. Red tapped him on the shoulder and pointed towards the mainland, at a small white house beside a banked crescent of grey sand. A high rampart of hills loomed behind it. 'That's where I live.'

'It's very pretty.'

'I'll be coming by first thing in the morning, an appointment with the physio.' He rubbed at his back and pulled a face. 'So if you're at the old pier, eight-ish, I'll take you into Eastern Township. Otherwise you can always catch the *Rib* later in the day.'

Cal said, 'Appreciate it.'

Scores of kittiwakes and fulmars launched them-selves off their nesting cliffs as the trespassing boat passed close by. Red pointed to a bay which was opening up. 'Seal Bay,' he shouted.

The boat slowed and Red said, 'The path goes up that gully, do you see?'

Cal said he did.

Soon the boat, its sides protected by buffers of old tyres, was nudging against a natural rock breakwater. 'See there, the mooring ring,' Red shouted to Cal. 'Put the rope through it.'

The ring was beside a line of footholds. Cal pulled the rope tight and knotted it. Red cut the idling engine. When Cal had scrambled out and was standing on top of the rock, Red squinted up at him. 'It was the trawler that did for this island, the money it brought. Other islands had a sense of community. They needed it for survival. But Eilean Iasgaich was different. The boat made people greedy.'

Red paused. 'It wasn't right.' Then he said, 'We're not all proud of our past, you know.'

Cal understood it as Red's way of acknowledging his grandfather and the wrongs done to him. Cal inclined his head to signal his appreciation. 'Thanks . . . and for the lift.'

Red shrugged again. 'You're welcome.' He gestured for Cal to throw the rope back on to the deck. When he did, the boat drifted away from the rock. Red said, 'Maybe pick you up tomorrow . . .'

Cal raised his right hand and turned towards Cnoc a' Mhonaidh.

The path from the bay passed below an overhang before veering right and uphill. Cal followed it until he emerged on the north-west shoulder. From there he struck out across a grassy bank, taking care not to break the sky-line. After a hundred metres he settled into a patch of heather, hidden from the mainland, a place to watch the sunset and to wait for night.

The sky to the west was tinged copper-pink when Cal stirred himself five hours later. Looking east, it was as if a sooty cloud had settled over the island, as dark as it got at this time of year, but sufficient in Cal's view to render Douglas Rae's telescope more or less blind. He stood, hooked his backpack over his left shoulder and climbed uphill through snagging stalks of heather. On the plateau of Cnoc a' Mhonaidh he stopped, knelt and peered into the gloom until he was sure of his bearings. From there his descent to the westernmost of the ruined island houses took him no more than twenty minutes. He slipped a number of times on the steep gradient, finally reaching the bottom of the hill by sitting and sliding on the damp grass and bracken.

Once on the flat, he veered left along the bottom of the hill until he found the stone foundations of the grassed-over track. He followed it, passing the forlorn dark shapes of abandoned houses. At his family's old home, he stopped and searched the debris by the doorway for a small stone. He found one which was rounded and rubbed it between his fingers before putting it in a pocket. Then he continued along the track, sometimes disturbing sheep which had taken night refuge in one of the ruins he was passing. Their hooves clattered against slate and corrugated iron as they ran off. Their lambs complained shrilly as they bolted after their escaping mothers.

Soon he was at the bottom of the slope by the museum. He worked his way around the building, pulling at the padlock, rattling the door latch, testing the two front windows for movement. At the back he found a small window with pebbled glass which was open a few centimetres. He heaved at it with both hands until he'd forced it down. He took his backpack off his shoulder, rummaged inside and removed a carrier bag which he stuffed inside his jacket. Then he hauled himself on to the sill and put his right leg through the gap. The rest of his body squeezed after it.

Inside, by the faint glow of his mobile phone, he made out a toilet to his right. He jumped down, pitching forward when his feet hit the tiled floor sooner than he expected. He swore, picked himself up, and using his phone again fumbled for the door and the light switch beside it. He flicked it on. When he opened the door a few centimetres, a shaft of light fell across the museum's counter, the two display cases in the centre of the room and the window beyond them. Immediately he switched off the light. In the dark he walked towards the right hand display case and lifted the lid. He used the light from his phone to locate the logbook which was in the centre of the cabinet. Cal put his phone on it and slid one of his hands underneath the book, supporting its open covers with his splayed fingers. He removed it, closed the lid and went back to the toilet. Shutting the door he turned on the light.

He read the entry at the open page – it was the one he had seen before. Then he teased at the unopened pages with the nail of his index finger until one sprang clear. He turned it slowly until he could see all the writing on it. The entry was for September 18, 1942. It recorded the Eilean Iasgaich's position and progress but nothing about the crew, or their recent losses.

Cal separated the next page, the next and the next, turning each one slowly. The entries were similar in each case: Hector MacKay recorded more details about the boat's position and the weather but like the September 18 entry none made mention of the crew. After 12 pages he came to 29 September 1942, the entry he wanted to see. It was different, as he expected.

The skipper had written, 'Please God, when will this ordeal end? This forenoon at 72° 30'N, 18°03'E we lost young Sandy MacKay swept overboard in the westerly gale which has been blowing hard all day. May God be with him and bless him. Uilleam Sinclair went with him, also lost overboard.'

Cal read it again, wondering why Hector MacKay had omitted to write 'May God be with him and bless him' after recording Uilleam's loss when he had done so after Sandy's.

The difference in the text struck him too. The writing recording Sandy's death was large, as it had been in the earlier entries. But in the short final sentence, marking Uilleam's, the writing was smaller; the ink blacker; as if it had been added later.

Cal photographed it with his mobile, checking it was in focus before returning the phone to his pocket. He lifted the next page which opened on to three short stubs. The neat edges suggested a knife or scissors had cut these pages away. After them were a dozen or more empty pages.

Cal turned them all before going back to the stubs. He ran his finger along their straight edges as if touching them might somehow reveal what Hector MacKay had written there and why they'd been removed. Then he closed the book slowly, trying not to force it. He took the carrier bag from his jacket and slid the book in, wrapping the plastic round it three times to protect it. He zipped the bag into his pocket and opened the toilet door wide letting the light flood across the room to the window which faced towards Douglas Rae's telescope. Cal left the museum the way he had entered it.

CHAPTER 24

The last remnant of the sun's pinkness has gone from the undersides of the clouds; it has become night. What is happening to me, Basanti asks. Why do I feel this vulnerability, this dread, now? Why, of all times, now?

She is sitting on the roof, her legs folded at her side, her body tilted, her weight resting on her right hand, her fingers pressed against the lead flashing of the roof's gully.

Why is she here when she should be inside, searching for the hill and the tree, in Cal's apartment, at his table, with the only man she has met in this frightening place who wants nothing from her and who doesn't regard her in that lascivious male way. Why now? Has her escape from the *dhanda*, wearing new clothes (she feels the texture of her linen trousers) somehow weakened her?

She considers the possibility, a flush of shame making her face suddenly hot. It cannot be, she says. Isn't she the daughter of warriors? Blood and honour demand retribution. Isn't this her Bedia obligation? She goads herself with what she believes is her heritage. Yet she feels a debilitating weariness, a sense that this has gone on too long, even though she knows it cannot end until she has avenged her friend's death and the many crimes she herself has endured.

She stands, turns, and walks slowly towards the steps leading to the door into Cal's apartment. She opens it slowly, now worrying that Cal will be offended by her delayed arrival. Night is more than two hours old. He will have been expecting her. Has he cooked for her? Does he think her ungrateful? Now she scolds herself for lacking consideration. So when she sees the room in darkness, she experiences a fluttering of relief. Thank goodness I have not let him down, she thinks. Her light-headedness lasts only until she reaches the bottom of the stairs. From here, in the glow of the street lights, she can see the note he has left, his handwriting in big legible letters. Some money is beside it resting on the keyboard she has been using. She walks towards it, reads the message and emits a howl of anguish.

The sound is as strange to her as the immediate and abject despair from which it has sprung. Why is she behaving this way when finally she is safe? She lets her head fall and covers her face with her hands, trembling. A flood of tears soaks her face and fingers. She has not cried at all since she laid her head in Preeti's lap in the car taking them from their villages. Now her crying is for everything that has happened in between: the loss of child-hood, the daily degradations, the vileness of the men, Preeti's death; the unrelenting savagery. She has not allowed any of this to touch her until tonight. Didn't Preeti tell her to be brave? Didn't Preeti suffer the same, worse, for all Basanti knows, with uncomplaining fortitude?

She continues to weep beyond any consoling for twenty minutes, longer. After her tears have stopped, her sobbing and whimpering continue. When, finally, she exhausts these too she sits, eyes closed, the pads of her fingers pressing gently against her swollen face. She shakes her head as if she cannot believe what has overcome her. A small act of kindness, the first for so long – the clothes Cal bought for her – penetrated her emotional defences. Then his unexpected absence for a day or two, maybe more, (his message doesn't make it clear) has dismantled them completely. She is dazed by it. After all the hurts she has borne with such resilience how has she allowed two such small events to devastate her so completely?

In her bewilderment, she feels more alone now than ever, more exposed to danger, though she is rational enough to know that neither can be true. Still, it alarms her because to avenge Preeti, she must be like those who killed her young friend, merciless, murderous. She must be the way she was when she was in captivity: without emotion.

She reads Cal's message again, this time without tears. He has written down his mobile phone number, also his email address, with his password and instructions for logging on. 'If you can't reach

319

me by phone – the signal is unreliable in the north of Scotland – send me an email instead. I will pick it up when there is reception.' She turns on the desk lamp and the computer. While she waits for it to warm up she walks to the window and looks out into the darkness. She sees little apart from street lights and the silhouetted bulk of the deserted flour mill across the wasteland opposite.

What she cannot see is the man who is watching her. He is in the shadow of a wall on the other side of the road. As soon as he sees her he holds his cigarette in the cup of his hand in case she notices the burning tip. When she leaves the window he takes a puff from it, exhales, drops the stub to the ground, and grinds it with the toe of his boot. He flips open his phone and rings a number. 'It's her.'

Another voice replies. The tone is questioning.

''Course I'm sure,' the first man says. 'The light went on and there she was.'

Another question.

'I dunno. Only saw her. There could be others up there.'

Another question.

'I dunno why she's only turned the light on now. Maybe she's been asleep.'

The other man replies and the watcher sneers.

'Mind she'll get a slap if she's been giving it away.'

Both men guffaw.

Then the watcher asks, 'How long?' After the reply, he adds, 'Soon as you can.'

The watcher puts his phone into his pocket and brings out a pack of cigarettes. He takes one out, puts it in his mouth, glances up at the window, and turns his back before lighting it.

Basanti is examining a photograph, the sixth in this folder that Cal has stored for her. The previous five were also of hills, but unlike this one they were the wrong shape: too rounded, too steep, too flat, too wooded or with different combinations of features she doesn't recognise. The sixth one has a familiarity to it, though there is a single ledge on its right side where she remembers a ripple of descending ridges, like rolls of stomach fat. Also, there are occasional trees dotted across it but she recalls only one tree. Could her memory be faulty? She tries to imagine it at different angles. Could this be it? She begins to think so. She reaches for a copy of her drawing which is lying on Cal's scanner and she holds it beside the screen for comparison. There are similarities but also differences. She reads the caption. Knoydart.

She goes to Cal's map and looks for the name, tracing her finger up and down the Scottish coast line. There are so many strange names that she doesn't find it, but she decides to tell Cal. Sitting back in her chair she reads his message again. She follows his instructions: first type 'gmail' in the search box; click on 'gmail: email from Google', enter 'flotsamandjetsam' in the username box and 'caladh1' in the password box. Then hit 'return'. Cal's inbox appears in front of her and she notices the most recent message is from someone she has heard Cal mention – DLG. The first line of his email begins 'The hill. This is it.' She hesitates but clicks on it. A photograph appears in front of her, of a hill and a tree.

Staring at it she lets out a shocked cry. Then she writes DLG's location details: 'North-east of Seil Island, on the mainland, a mile or two from Kilninver, south of Oban'. She returns to the wall map and traces her finger along the coast again. She finds Oban, then Kilninver. Below them and to the left, in the blue of the sea, there is a pin marking where Preeti's body was recovered. Basanti remembers Cal telling her the police thought Preeti had gone into the sea further south still (he'd mentioned the Clyde Estuary as a possibility) and had drifted up the coast with the current. Oban and Kilninver are further north, in the wrong direction. This discrepancy puzzles Basanti. She returns to the computer screen but there is no mistaking the photograph. It is the hill. The tree is there just as she remembers it. Basanti wishes Cal was there to explain the significance of the discovery to her. Then she is glad he isn't.

Isn't this her score to settle? Preeti will be her companion, her guard.

Now she breathes more slowly. She feels her old emotional coldness returning. She welcomes it as a reliable and strong friend. She takes Cal's money from the table, clicks to shut down the computer and as she does so notices the lettering of DLG's email in Cal's inbox has turned from bold black to something lighter. He will know she has read it, she thinks. She feels a pang of regret. Will he think she was prying? She hesitates for a moment wondering whether she should send him an explanatory message but she decides not to. After all, he will understand why she had to look at it.

She switches off the table lamp and the watcher outside sees the light go out. It's good, he decides. Perhaps, she'll be sleeping when we come for her. Perhaps she'll be screwing a guy. Either way she'll be distracted.

He smirks with his thin lips.

He's now looking forward to having her. She has to be taught a lesson. All the girls do sooner or later. He'll ask the boss to let him have her first.

He imagines what he will do her. What *won't* he do to her? It's his payback, he reckons, for standing out there all day, in the cold. The boss'll be here soon, any minute in fact.

Basanti goes to the roof, takes off her new clothes and leaves them folded tidily inside her shelter. She puts on her old green shirt, baggy black jeans and the grey hoodie. She folds the money and slides it into the back pocket of her jeans. Then she slips her hand under a loose slate and brings out Cal's kitchen knife. She cuts a rectangle of cardboard, about the same length as the blade and folds it around the sharp steel. She places it in the zip-up pocket of the hoodie and feels through the fabric to make sure the blade is still in its rudimentary sheath. She goes into the darkness, exhilarated by her sense of purpose, by her determination for revenge. Finally, she will be the warrior she was born to be. She shivers when a breeze touches her cheeks. It is not the cold, but excitement at the prospect of retribution.

At the top of the fire escape, she watches for movement below. She waits for a few minutes, not because she expects anyone to be there, but because she knows she must take nothing for granted. She has trained herself to be careful. She stalls again at the landing above the ladder and listens. Then she drops silently to the ground and crouches. The corner of the building is twenty metres away. When she reaches it she watches again before walking in a long pool of shadow under the gable wall which stretches to the street. Half way along it she stops suddenly. She crouches and lies flat. There is a tiny ember of light which has just flared brighter. It is a cigarette. The light moves. It fades. It moves, then burns bright red again.

She studies it with the concentration of a raptor. From the roof she has watched dog-walkers stop for a cigarette while their animals range across the waste ground. She imagines this is one of them. She waits. She has time.

A car pulls up, inserting itself between Basanti and the burning cigarette end. She hears two male voices, perhaps three. She hears McGill's name. Suddenly the car swings down the lane towards her. Its lights are about to expose her. She cannot risk being trapped against the wall so she breaks across the lane, across the beam of light, into the bushes on the other side. She hears a cry, a man's voice. 'It's her. Get the tart for Chris'sake.'

She hears a door slam. She scrambles over a wall and jumps to the pavement below. She runs away from danger, past the newsagent shop where she scavenges fruit.

Only one thought occurs to her. Has Cal betrayed me? Is that why he had to go away so quickly? Who else knew I was here?

As she reaches the corner, she looks back. A man is pursuing her. He is young and fit. He is gaining on her. She runs fast, as fast as she can. Ahead of her, an office worker in a suit, carrying an executive case, is crossing the road. He steps on to the pavement and approaches her, going slower as he tries to work out what this is coming towards him. When he realises it is a girl he relaxes a little.

Basanti pleads with him.

'Help me, I'm in danger,' she cries.

But the suit steps back from her. His attention switches to her pursuer who is rounding the corner. He realises her danger will soon be his danger and he mutters 'I'm sorry, I can't'. As he steps off the pavement to go back to the other side of the road, he adds, 'my wife . . .' as if in those two words there is an explanation of some kind for abandoning a distraught girl who has just begged him for help. The suit is hurrying now, putting distance between himself and her, between his conscience and the scene of his cowardice.

At the top of the road, the suit stops and watches. The girl has fallen to her knees. She has her back to her pursuer who stops just short of her, seemingly to catch his breath. He bends, straightens, steps towards her, and lifts her easily with one bare arm hooked around her torso. Everything accelerates after that. There is a flash of silver. The man screams and curses. The girl falls to the pavement. The man sits back heavily beside her. He shakes his head and he grabs at her with his other arm. She swipes at him again. There is another flash. And another. The man slumps, his head lolling in the gutter. There is a squeal of tyres. A car speeds downhill. A door opens before it stops beside the fallen man. Another door. Two hooded figures jump out. The doors slam. The car races away. The man with the lolling head has gone.

What has happened to the girl the suit is not sure. Has she made her escape when his attention was drawn by the squeal of tyres? Is she in the car too?

The suit clutches at his executive case and hurries up the road. He feels his ordered world hanging by a precarious thread. He thinks about ringing the police, anonymously, but rejects the idea. If he uses his own phone, his number will be logged.

Better keep out of it, he thinks.

Play it safe.

Not my business.

He imagines what might be the cause of what he has just seen: a prostitute cheating on her pimp; a drugs mule double-crossing a dealer. It happens. It's low life. Other people. The more he convinces himself it belongs to a different milieu to the one he inhabits the safer he feels and the more certain he becomes he played it right. By the time he is putting the key in the lock on his mahogany front door he is congratulating himself on his instincts and he decides not to mention it to his wife, in case she frets about him. She's always fretting about him, given half a chance.

Basanti is crouching between parked cars in a second-hand garage forecourt. She is watching the road in a car's wing mirror which she has tilted towards her. She is breathing heavily. Her shoulders rise and fall with her gasps. The knife is on the tarmac beside her. She picks it up and wipes the blade clean with the cardboard sheath before replacing it in her pocket. She looks at the wet blood stain on her sleeve and is pleased she isn't wearing her new clothes.

Her head is full of only one thought. Cal has betrayed me. Who else knew where I was? It's a question she keeps asking herself.

Cal didn't sleep, didn't want to sleep, didn't even feel tired. He sat on the cliff watching for the white 'v' of the *Rib*. Every so often, he glanced back

327

towards the museum and the light shining like a beacon from one of its two front windows, and then looked towards the mainland again, at the sheltered stretch of sea between him and it. The *Rib* would come. He was sure of it, at first light if not before. He felt excited at what was about to happen. Wasn't he *this* close to solving the mystery of his grandfather's death?

He knew now that Uilleam hadn't died on September 29th, 1942, not if the coordinates in Hector MacKay's logbook that day were correct (and he had no reason to doubt they recorded accurately Sandy's death). Not if Uilleam's body washed ashore on the Lofoten Islands, which it had. Somebody must know what Hector MacKay had written on the logbook's missing pages. Somebody must know why Uilleam's name had been added later to the September 29th entry. Somebody must know the truth.

Just after dawn he went to sit on the top step above the pier, where his great-grandmother and grandmother waited for Uilleam when the *Eilean Iasgaich* returned home in its new livery as an anti-submarine trawler. He hadn't been there long when a white bow wave began to spread across the Kyle. The *Rib* was coming. Cal nodded when he saw it, wishing it closer. The sooner this started the better. His only misgiving was Rachel. How would she react? If this played out the way he expected, there'd be media. The story would be everywhere: his notoriety as the eco-warrior who raided the gardens of politicians would make sure of that. He was relying on it. Would it wreck Rachel's documentary, or make it? He wasn't certain which it would be. All he could do, he persuaded himself, was to fight this in his own way. After all, it was his battle, not hers, his territory. Hadn't he warned her?

He watched the *Rib*. As it approached the base of the cliff, he made out three people on board. Two of them were wearing uniforms. This turn of events pleased him. It was better than he expected. He stood as the *Rib* reached the pier. Two policemen climbed towards him. Douglas Rae, he noticed with interest, remained behind on the boat.

CHAPTER 25

'He has confessed; everything, all of it, *tutto*.' Enthusiasm was running away with Inspector Giancarlo Costantini of the anti-mafia police in Calabria. 'This Anglo-Italian collaboration of ours has got the gangsters on the run.'

Detective Constable Helen Jamieson considered correcting him (*Scottish-Italian, Inspector C*) but she let it pass. 'We have them bamboozled, Giancarlo.'

Inspector Costantini sounded perplexed. 'Indeed we have.' The safest thing for him to do was to agree with this British detective who used strange-sounding English words.

Jamieson loved saying *bamboozle*. The effect always pleased her. 'We have, Giancarlo, bamboozled them good and proper.'

Inspector Costantini hummed uncertainly, a nasal sound like a bluebottle caught in a glass tumbler.

'But it's important you remember, Giancarlo.'

'I do, I do, Helen.'

'There are some loose ends here in Scotland.'

'You have gangsters of your own?'

'A very bad man, Giancarlo, who's got what's coming to him.'

'You'll be . . . *bamboozling* . . . him too?' Inspector Costantini surprised himself by flourishing the word with even more flamboyance than Jamieson.

'I hope so, Giancarlo. I do hope so.'

'Good for you, Helen Jamieson.'

'Good for Cal McGill you mean.'

'*Bravo* your Cal McGill. *Bravo* for his computer program. *Bravo* for sharing it with us. *Bravo*, Helen Jamieson!'

'*Bravo*, indeed. But not a word about me or collaboration with police in Britain.'

'Not a word, Helen Jamieson.'

'I have one more request.'

'Please. I have a – how do you say – a rule.'

'What's that?'

'Always to say yes to a woman, whatever she asks. It is a man's privilege. No?'

Would he say yes? Would he really if he saw her?

'Not a word to your media, not for 24 hours,' she said.

'Not a word about Anglo-Italian police co-operation, not ever, not a word about Helen Jamieson, my lips are sealed, and not a word to Italian media for 24 hours. How do you say . . . your wish, my command?'

'Giancarlo is a man of his word.'

'Indeed he is Helen Jamieson.'

A man of chocolate smooth words

The case was wrapped up, or as wrapped up as Jamieson or anyone else could make it. Perhaps someone more important than her, the Chief Constable, the Prime Minister, Scotland's First Minister would decide it was worth spending hundreds of thousands of pounds recovering the container from the sea bed. Perhaps, though Jamieson doubted it. After so many months and the storms of winter the container had probably broken up, the debris scattered, the bodies dispersed, limbs slowly disarticulating, fish scavenging the remains. What would there be to find? Even if the collision with the oil tanker had only holed the floating container, causing it to sink more or less intact, whatever remained of the bodies would be unrecognisable.

As Giancarlo said, 'The Mafia don't keep records and people are disappearing from Eastern Europe and North Africa all the time. It is *impossibile*.'

Whatever the cost of a salvage operation, it would be a lot of money to spend on recovering 10,000 pairs of saturated counterfeit Nike trainers. Jamieson corrected herself: 9,997 pairs since she was looking at three unmatched trainers on her desk. Whether more feet would surface depended on how many of the container's illegal human cargo helped themselves to free samples. There were thirteen men, all from Algeria, according to the Italian warehouse clerk who confessed all after he was offered immunity from prosecution by Inspector Costantini. Jamieson picked up the shoes one by one and locked them away. They had provided the final piece of evidence. The stitching and the labels were an exact match with the Chinese-made counterfeit Nikes found by Inspector Costantini's men when they raided a cargo clearing warehouse at the Gioia Tauro container port, on the knuckle of the toe of Italy.

Thanks to Cal McGill the case was solved, though 24 hours earlier Jamieson was cursing him for raising her hopes. The cargo manifests from Gioia Tauro and New York, respectively the home port and final destination of the container ship, matched. 1257 containers were loaded at Gioia Tauro, 460 were unloaded at Liverpool and the remainder at New York, the intended destination of the counterfeit trainers and the illegal cargo of Algerians.

The satellite tracking report provided the breakthrough. Inspector Costantini had sent the data company the coordinates of the container ship's May Day call and the oil tanker's collision 20 days later. Prompted by Jamieson, he had asked for the details of any containers which had travelled from the first set of coordinates to the second set between October 6 and 26 last year.

The response was what she wanted. 'There was a container following that course but the owners informed us the tracking device was malfunctioning. They contacted us on October 8 and the last signal we received from it was on October 26 at 57°28'N, 8°12'W, the last of the two coordinates you sent us.'

The collision with the tanker had brought an abrupt end to the tracking device's signals.

Revenge time sir.

Jamieson lifted the half-closed lid of her lap top and opened her Bembo hotmail account. She clicked on 'new mail' and typed rosie.provan@ thereportingfactory.co.uk.

'Dear Rosie, I read your story on Cal McGill and enjoyed it very much. Would you like a story about him which is even bigger?'

Rosie replied, 'Dear Bembo, Bigger than him being charged with theft and breaking into a museum?'

'Dear Rosie, I don't understand.'

'Dear Bembo, Cal McGill is in custody. He broke into a museum on an island called Eilean Iasgaich and stole its most precious artefact. Is your story bigger than that?'

Jamieson stared at the email, mouth gaping. *Cal McGill what have you done?*

Detective Inspector David Ryan held his face in his hands. 'Fuck, fuck, fuck.'

Joan, his PA, at her desk across the corridor from Ryan's open door, inquired, 'Is there something the matter Mr Ryan?'

'Nothing you should be worrying about Joan.' Ryan glowered at her. 'Get me Detective Constable Jamieson, now.'

'Yes Mr Ryan.' He had spent the morning reviewing the '20 front runners' – Jamieson's description of them. He could see why she'd chosen them. Most involved missing bodies, suicides or yachting accidents of one kind or another, but in only three cases were the missing people definitely wearing trainers. The investigation was being buried under mountains of paper, missing people files, marine accident reports, and with all the television coverage, dozens of random calls from worried relatives saying 'My so-and-so was wearing trainers when he left home x years ago. Do you think the foot could be his?'. Every day brought so many new lines of inquiry forty officers were working full-time on the case. There had been moments in the last few days when Ryan had wondered whether Cal McGill could be useful, if only to narrow the scope of the investigation. But no sooner had the notion come into his head than he rejected it. McGill was a troublemaker; what's more a troublemaker who had no reason to do him or the police any favours. Now Ryan thanked God for his instincts. He'd heard about McGill's arrest on the police grapevine.

Jamieson knocked on his open door.

'Come on in,' Ryan stood up. 'Take a seat.'

Jamieson hovered by the door with an expression of bemusement. She looked behind her in case someone else was there, but there was only Joan across the corridor, cowed and at her desk.

'Do you mean me sir?'

'Yes Helen. Of course I mean you.'

He called me Helen.

'Thank you very much sir.' Jamieson walked

nervously to the chair in front of Ryan's desk and slid sideways into it. Her hips caught on the arms. She pushed down and her bottom hit the seat with a thump. She blushed.

'This is what we're going to do Helen.'

'Yes sir.'

'I'm going to solve this case in the next seven days.'

'Are you sir?'

Jamieson knew what happened in seven days. Joan had told her. The date of Ryan's SCDEA interview had been brought forward.

'Yes, Helen.' He smiled at her and leaned back in his chair, throwing his arms wide. 'Look Helen. I know we don't always see eye to eye . . .'

'If you say so sir.'

'But we have to put aside personal differences here.'

'Yes sir?' Jamieson's voice lifted quizzically.

'We're in this together Helen. We're a team.'

'Yes sir.' *No sir.*

'I just wanted you to know that.'

'Thank you sir.' *No thank you sir.*

'So you'll do your damnedst to get a result in seven days? No stone unturned, eh, Jamieson . . . Helen.'

'Yes sir.' *I've got a result already sir.*

'Good girl.' Ryan's smile withered.

Fuck you sir.

Out of habit Jamieson angled her body when she stood up but her hips still stuck on the chair's arms. She was at the door when Ryan said, 'Have you heard about McGill?'

'Yes sir, just now sir?'

'I knew he was no good.'

'Yes sir.'

'We'll come under fire I'm afraid.'

'Will we sir?'

'We had him in custody a week ago.'

'I suppose we did sir.'

'The media will be blaming us for letting him go.'

'I suppose they will sir.'

Not us sir. You, sir.

'But thank God we didn't use him on this case, eh Helen.'

'I guess so sir.'

Jamieson regained her composure as she walked along the corridor. Cal's arrest had thrown her but it didn't really change anything.

When she returned to her desk she emailed Rosie Provan.

'Dear Rosie, Yes, it's bigger than theft, much bigger. Details will follow.'

CHAPTER 26

The Eastern Township hotel bar at lunch-time was buzzing. The talk was all about Cal McGill's 'bad blood'. Hadn't his grandfather caused the death of a teenage lad called Sandy MacKay, one of the brave men of Eilean Iasgaich? Hadn't McGill's grandfather's name been left off the Eilean Iasgaich memorial because of it? No-one could remember the exact details of the story, except that young Sandy had been swept overboard because of Uilleam Sinclair's negligence. The reporters listened and took notes. There were three of them, two from local weeklies and one from Aberdeen, the Press and Journal. More were on the way. BBC Scotland was sending a crew. The hotel had taken the booking. Cal McGill was big news after his exploits in politicians' gardens. What was he doing stealing a wartime logbook from a museum? It didn't fit.

The bar's lunch-time regulars didn't seem to have the answer, but it didn't stop them speculating if there was a prospect of another round of drinks and the reporters were paying. None of them noticed a man in a red woollen hat leaving

338

his coffee untouched as he listened to the chatter then hurrying from the bar.

Audrey Gillespie saw him.

She was sitting, as she usually did at lunch time, at the round table by the fire. She was eating her toasted cheese sandwich and drinking IRN-BRU. She'd never spoken to Red MacKay but she knew him, by his hat, by township gossip and by the file in her employer's office.

It was time for her to go, too. She had to be getting back to work.

Outside the bar, she saw Red MacKay crossing the field, the short cut to the pier. He was walking quickly. Audrey wondered if he was rushing to catch the tide, but she looked at the Kyle. The tide was still full. He was a rule unto himself, so she thought nothing more of it, instead worrying that she was going to be late. Her boss liked to start the afternoon at 1.55pm with a cup of coffee. She walked quickly along the road to the premises of Alexander Mackenzie & Partners. She went in, glanced at the clock – it was 1.53 – and put her bag down on her desk in reception. When the water had boiled she stirred in one level teaspoonful of Gold Blend, dropped in a white sugar lump and carried the cup and saucer to the closed door opposite. The name plate on it said Mr Robin Mackenzie, senior partner. It made Audrey smile because he was the only partner. She knocked, taking care not to spill the coffee. 'Come, Audrey.'

Mr Mackenzie was sitting at his desk with tidy

piles of legal papers balanced on either end of it. He was a small man with thinning ginger hair, a freckled face and a long nose, at the end of which he perched his computer glasses. He squinted at Audrey over them, the look he always gave her, not quite approving, not quite disapproving but always closer to the latter than the former. 'Ah Audrey, my coffee.'

'Have you heard what's happened?'

'Enough for my purposes I think, Audrey.'

He was always trying to stop her relating gossip about clients. There were some things a family solicitor in a small community was better off not knowing, he would tell her. On this occasion Audrey thought otherwise and told him everything she'd heard: how Cal McGill, the man who broke into the museum, was Uilleam Sinclair's grandson. Wouldn't Mr Robin want to know about it? Wouldn't he want to hear what the reporters were asking? Wasn't Uilleam Sinclair's name on a big enamelled box in the back room, one of the dozens he made her dust once every quarter? 'Nothing happens for months around here then this!'

After her tumble of words, he held up his hand. 'My coffee please, Audrey. Are you going to give it to me before it gets cold?'

'Oh Mr Robin I got quite carried away with myself.'

'Mmmh.' There was that look again. She put the cup down. 'Audrey.'

'Yes Mr Robin.'

'Has there been much talk about Uilleam

Sinclair?' She screwed up her expressive face with a frown of concern. 'Yes Mr R, they say Cal McGill's bad blood comes from him.'

Mr Mackenzie let out a little sigh of exasperation. 'How many times must I tell you Audrey?' He looked at her sternly.

She put a hand to her mouth. 'Sorry, Mr Robin.'

Audrey sometimes called him Mr R when she forgot herself, though she wasn't sorry at all. She pitied her employer, the way no-one, apart from her, ever called him anything but Mr Mackenzie. She'd never heard anyone use his first name. No-one in the township did. None of his clients did. No-one at home did because there was no-one at home. He was unmarried without any close family. Audrey thought the least she could do was to show him a little familiarity, because it pained her to think of a life like his without it. So sometimes she called him Mr R.

'Oh, there's something else.'

'What Audrey?'

It was unusual for Mr Robin to encourage her like this.

'Well,' she said, enjoying the moment. 'There's another bit of news. There was some talk about an old woman called Grace Ann MacKay.'

'What of her?'

Audrey knew Mr Robin would be interested. Wasn't her name also on one of the boxes? She knew all the names off by heart now. What else was there to do when she was dusting?

'Well,' she said. 'She's died, from a stroke. She lived in the Borders apparently though no-one's seen her or heard of her for years.'

'Thank you Audrey. Please close the door behind you.'

When she had gone, he reached into the top drawer and removed a key. He went to the door behind his desk, unlocked it and turned on the light. His back room, as Audrey referred to it, or the client repository as it had been called by the partners of Mackenzie & Partners since Mr Robin's grandfather Alexander founded the firm in 1926, was shelved from floor to ceiling. Every shelf was packed tight with black tin boxes, about two feet high and eighteen inches across. Each had a lid and each was tied with red ribbon. The names of the clients were also enamelled in red. He went to the box which bore the name Hector MacKay and his dates, 1891–1944. He lifted it down to the floor, untied the bow, blew away the dust ('That girl,' he muttered) and removed the lid. He took out a buff-coloured file and returned the box to its position on the shelf. Four away was another box which bore three names and dates Ina MacKay, 1896–1943; Alexander (Sandy) MacKay, 1926–1942; Grace Ann MacKay, 1924–. Mr Mackenzie made a mental note to add the date of Grace Ann's death and left the room.

He put the key back in his drawer and opened the file, taking from it a single typed sheet of paper and a long white envelope which had broken red

342

sealing wax on the open flap. He read the paper briskly – he didn't need to take his usual lawyerly care because he'd read it many times before. Satisfied with it, he went into the outer office.

'Audrey, I want you to copy this.' He gave her the sheet of paper. 'And on your way home this afternoon append it to the notice boards in Eastern Township, the store, the hotel bar and outside the community centre.'

'Yes Mr Robin.' As he returned to his office she noticed he was carrying an envelope with red sealing wax and wondered what it was.

Soon after 4pm, when the last appointment for the day had ended, the phone went. Audrey answered. It was Red MacKay, asking to speak to Mr Mackenzie. She put him through. The call lasted ten minutes. Audrey logged it as usual on Mr Mackenzie's client time sheet. As she was doing so, her employer left the office, suggesting she lock up early. 'On reflection, Audrey, the sooner you put up those notices the better.'

Cal McGill was already in the police interview room, his back to the door, when Mr Mackenzie was shown in. He pulled out a chair, put his case on the table, snapped open the locks, lifted the lid and sat down.

'Well, young man it looks as if you're going to need some legal assistance.'

'I didn't ask for a lawyer, did I?'

'Red MacKay thought you might need one.'

343

Cal didn't reply.

Mr Mackenzie took an A4 notepad from his case and the envelope he'd taken from Hector MacKay's box. 'My grandfather represented your great grandfather Robert Sinclair in a dispute about grazing rights in 1929. My father was the executor of your great grandmother Margaret's will.'

Cal watched the lawyer who held out his hand. 'I'm Robin Mackenzie, of Alexander Mackenzie & Partners. We've represented your family many times over the years, as we have all the families from Eilean Iasgaich. I'm here to help you, if you're agreeable of course.'

'And if I'm not?'

Mr Mackenzie considered the possibility. 'Well, I'd advise you against it,' he smiled contentedly at his dry, legal humour. As Cal was about to reply, he held up his hand to stop him, 'Bear with me for a minute, yes?'

Cal shrugged.

Mr Mackenzie said, 'What do you know of your grandfather, Mr McGill?'

Cal said, 'A bit . . . quite a bit, but I'm missing some pieces.'

Mr Mackenzie reached for the envelope with the broken sealing wax and slid it across the table. 'In that case, these might interest you. Old Hector MacKay, the skipper of the Eilean Iasgaich, left them behind. They're pages from his log, the one you took from the island's museum. I imagine these are what you've been looking for.'

Cal opened the envelope and removed some yellowing paper which was folded over. He pulled apart the sheets. The first was dated September 30th. 'Arrived Vaeroy, to the south of the Norwegian Lofoten Islands, to shelter from the storm. We pray for all our lost brothers and comrades, young Sandy MacKay being the most recent of them. May God grant them all peace.'

The next was dated October 1st. 'Another day at Vaeroy. Storm force westerlies. Uilleam Sinclair has been banished from our company. Sandy MacKay's death has broken us and there is talk of vengeance among the crew, what is left of us.'

Cal looked up at Mr Mackenzie.

'Read on.'

Cal looked at the third page.

'October 2nd: The storm abated and we sailed at dusk, using the last of the light to navigate from Vaeroy. Sinclair sighted two German airmen in the water and we left them where they were for our five crewmen who were shot and killed by their planes. God knows, their deaths have turned us into cold hearted creatures. Sinclair jumped overboard and swam to them to force us to turn the boat. God help us all. We are in the grip of madness.'

Cal asked, 'What does this mean?'

'They sailed on.'

'And left him in the water.'

Mr Mackenzie nodded. 'Yes.'

'To die.'

'Yes.'

'My God.'

Cal read the pages again. 'Where have these come from?' he asked when he'd finished.

'Hector MacKay deposited them with my company in November 1942.'

'And you've been keeping them secret?'

'My grandfather, who was the senior partner at the time, didn't know they were there until 1945, the year after Hector's death. His widow, Mary, found them when she came to my grandfather's office to go through her husband's effects. According to a note my grandfather left, she'd put it off and put it off but what with the ending of the war and the island being abandoned he persuaded her it was time for her to put things in order, if you understand me.'

'Didn't they realise what these pages meant?'

'Oh yes, they did. Mary MacKay wept – cried for a month according to my grandfather. She had to revise her view of her husband, a man she and everyone else for that matter held in admiration. It was painful for her. She asked my grandfather – and my grandfather agreed, to his discredit – to keep the pages secret. You see the widows and the families had nothing left of their husbands and fathers but their reputations and their bravery. They were destitute, forced to leave the islands, and their only hope was help from the Norwegian government and the money from a public appeal. My grandfather and Mary MacKay agreed it should be kept secret for the well being of the community.'

Mr Mackenzie coughed with embarrassment. 'You have to remember these families were my grandfather's clients. He thought it his duty to protect their interests.'

'So was my family.'

'Yes indeed, though the Sinclairs had left the island before then. My grandfather's view, if I can speak for him, is that your family were former clients. He told my father that he'd wanted to make it public after Mary's death but by then the myth of the 'Brave Men of Eilean Iasgaich' had taken such a hold that it had become impossible. It was easier to let the lie go unchallenged, though there was a caveat. My grandfather told my father, and my father told me when I took over the company, that if ever again the story of Uilleam Sinclair attracted public attention we had a duty to reveal the truth. My grandfather wrote a simple account of the events, setting out the circumstances of Uilleam Sinclair's death and this afternoon it was put up on notice boards in the village.'

He passed it to Cal who said, after reading it twice, 'They murdered him, didn't they?'

'In a manner of speaking they did, even if they didn't strike a blow. They left him knowing he would die, and the two Germans with him.

'My grandfather's view, told to me by my father, was that young Sandy MacKay's death broke them. He was the boat's talisman. They wanted to avenge him, and the others who had died, and your grandfather was the target of their desire for revenge. As you probably know, the Sinclairs and the Raes and the MacKays had been at odds for years.'

'But they continued hating him even though they killed him.'

'In my grandfather's view . . .' Mr Mackenzie weighted his words with lawyerly gravitas. '. . . Their loathing of Uilleam grew after his death.'

'But why?'

'They'd made themselves hateful for what they did to him. The manner of his death ate away at them and as time went by they despised him all the more for it. They passed it on to their wives and their children, but not the reason for it. Your grandfather was a wronged man, Mr McGill, a brave man.'

CHAPTER 27

Detective Constable Jamieson was woken by the beeping of her digital alarm at 6am. She sat up, ran her fingers through her hair and went to her wardrobe. Her winter overcoat was on the hook behind the door. She slipped it from its hanger, put it on over her pink silk pyjamas, slid her bare feet into some mules on the bottom shelf of her shoe rack and took a £20 note from her purse on the dressing table. Her flat was a block from the 24 hour store. Half way there two labourers nudged each other and pointed to the pink pyjamas showing beneath her coat.

One of them whistled and the other shouted, 'any time you're lonely.'

She wriggled inside her coat, trying to pull it down, and pushed open the door of the shop. The newspaper stand was beside the counter. She took one of each title, glancing at the front page headlines as she put them by the till. A middle-aged man with sandpaper skin and bad teeth came to stand behind her. 'Empty day ahead, luv?'

Jamieson turned to give him a piece of her mind but thought better of it. She paid the shop manager

349

and returned to her flat, where she kicked off her shoes and fell on to the sofa, the newspapers still in her arms. The headlines were different from the Italian editions she had read on the internet. They put the stress on anti-mafia police rolling up a counterfeiting and trafficking gang, whereas the British papers went strong on Cal McGill assisting the Italian police to solve the mystery of the severed feet. *The Telegraph*'s front page splash heading was 'Amateur ocean detective solves severed foot mystery' with a sub deck 'Scottish Police humiliated by PhD student in custody for theft.' Jamieson scanned the other front pages. Rosie Provan had by-lines in all of them. Most of the papers also ran inside pages of coverage: the story of Cal McGill's grandfather left to die by his crewmates also made it big in the tabloids. Jamieson was reading the details with a growing sense of outrage when her phone rang. It was Ryan's number, the call she'd been expecting.

'Have you seen the papers, Jamieson?'

'Yes sir, just reading them. I was going to ring you. It's bad for you isn't it sir?'

'This is your fault Jamieson. I blame you . . .'

'Well, I did suggest we use McGill sir.'

'Don't mess with me Jamieson . . .'

'No sir.'

'You're way out of your league.'

'Am I sir?'

'You're finished Jamieson.'

'I sent you a memo sir.'

'What?'

'Joan put it on your desk sir. Perhaps it was under some other papers and you didn't see it. I've got a copy if you'd like one.'

'What are you talking about Jamieson? What memo?'

'The one about McGill, sir, where I proposed using him to prioritise our investigations sir.'

'Are you trying to fuck with me, Jamieson?'

'Definitely not, sir.'

'Your career's going nowhere, Jamieson.'

Ryan cut the call.

Neither is yours sir.

Ryan slid open the glass door to the balcony outside his bedroom. He leaned against the frame and took a pack of cigarettes out of the pocket of his white towelling dressing gown. He lit one and drew the smoke deep into his lungs before letting it leak away in short puffs from the side of his mouth. Jamieson had pulled a stroke. He hadn't seen that coming. He inhaled again before dropping the cigarette on the decking and going back inside.

The *Eilean Iasgaich* bumped against the tyres hanging from the side of the pier. Red MacKay threw a rope and one of the reporters waiting for the *Rib*'s scheduled sailing to the island from the nearby slipway said, 'Want a hand?'

'Thank you, could you tie it round that post?' Red collected his bag and climbed out.

'It's a lovely day.'

Red looked around as if he hadn't noticed until then. 'So it is. Going to the island?'

The reporter nodded. 'I thought I might as well see the scene of the crime.' Red pursed his lips. 'Have a good trip.' He walked into the township, clutching a brown envelope in his right hand. Janice, the physiotherapist, saw him as she was going into Rae Family Stores and held back for him. 'We're not used to seeing you twice in a week.'

Red smiled. 'Things to do,' he said and walked on. Janice stared after him as he went into Mackenzie's, the lawyers. She'd never been able to make him out. Nice enough man, though a bit odd living alone like that.

Audrey was at her desk, engrossed in the Eastern Township chat-room on the internet. She wanted to let Mr Robin know what people were saying about him but he would only give her one of his looks and say 'Mmh.' Audrey was becoming outraged by all the cruel comments, on Mr Robin's behalf. Interfering busybody was the least of the insults being levelled at him. Some people, clients among them, criticised him for bringing disgrace on a fine group of men who died for their country. 'Betraying them like Judas,' said one. Others were alarmed at the effect on the local tourist industry and one accused Mr Robin of cruelty of the worst kind, raking over old coals and bringing suffering to all those fine families. Audrey was contemplating writing under a pseudonym to defend her employer when the bell on the door went. She sighed with irritation at the disturbance. Then she saw who it was.

'Mr MacKay, isn't it?'

'Is Mr Mackenzie available?'

'I'll inquire.'

She tapped in Mr Robin's number. 'Red MacKay is here to see you Mr Robin.' Red could hear Mr Mackenzie's weary reprimand. Audrey flushed and glanced up at Red with embarrassment before speaking into the phone. 'Mr Hector MacKay is here to see you Mr Robin.'

She put down the phone. 'He'll see you now Mr MacKay.'

An hour and twenty three minutes later – Audrey kept the precise time as usual – Mr Robin put his head round the door.

'Cancel my appointments this afternoon, Audrey, and ring a car hire company would you?'

'Yes Mr Robin.'

'Tell them we'll need a driver too. Give them my mobile number and I'll tell them when and where.'

'What's the destination Mr Robin?'

'Edinburgh.'

Mr Robin returned to his office closing the door behind him and Audrey made a note to deduct 34 seconds from Red MacKay's bill because, strictly speaking, her conversing with Mr Robin wasn't 'client time'. Twenty six minutes and 22 seconds later Mr Mackenzie opened the door, and held it for Red. 'Mr MacKay and I have an appointment out of the office Audrey. If anyone wants me I won't be available until tomorrow.'

'Yes Mr Robin.'

Red MacKay had his woollen hat in his hand. Audrey hadn't seen his hair before. It was blond and curly and made him look rather dishy. She smiled at him but he didn't seem to notice her. At lunchtime in the hotel bar, Audrey was telling her story of Red MacKay's hair when the group of reporters and photographers in the table by the window began running for the door.

'What's up?' Audrey asked the short scruffy one in jeans and black corduroy jacket who had offered to buy her a drink the day before.

'Dunno yet, but something's going on at the police station. McGill's lawyer is holding a press conference in the car park at 2.30pm.'

'Mr Mackenzie?' Audrey asked.

'Yup that's the bloke.'

'He's my –' But before Audrey could finish the sentence the door slammed shut.

The reporter who had gone to Eilean Iasgaich made it back with ten minutes to spare. Mike nosed the rib up to the slipway, registering surprise that Red's boat was still moored at the pier and wondering what had kept him. It was unusual for him to spend much more than an hour or two in the township. At 2.30 Mr Mackenzie, in his tweed suit and with a severe expression, came out of the police station accompanied by Chief Inspector

Donald Findlay. Mr Mackenzie waited for the reporters to settle.

'I will read out a short statement and then the Chief Inspector will also read out a short statement. I will answer no questions.'

He coughed and composed himself. 'My client Mr Cal McGill was released without charge this afternoon after new information came to light. Thank you.'

One of the reporters shouted, 'What information? Either he broke into the museum or he didn't.'

The Chief Inspector stepped forward and held up his hand. 'Gentlemen, gentlemen . . .'

'I have a short statement to make and like Mr Mackenzie here I will not be answering questions. The charges against Mr McGill have been dropped. As of this time police inquiries into this incident are at an end.'

He put his arm round Mr Mackenzie to guide him back to the police station door. 'Thank you, gentlemen.'

The reporters did not notice a chauffeur driven hire car with a male passenger leaving the back of the police station and taking the road to Whale Back Beach, or an old fishing boat steaming up the Kyle, a man in a red hat in the wheelhouse.

Before 4pm, when Audrey went to post some letters, the story was beginning to be pieced together. Red MacKay had been seen going into Mr Mackenzie's office by Janice, the physio. There had to be some connection, particularly as Red never came into the township more than once a week. Not until today.

A crowd had gathered in the post office and when Audrey appeared through the door the questions came at her thick and fast.

'I don't know anything, I swear.'

Someone shouted 'Leave the lassie alone' and they resumed their discussion among themselves.

Mr Mackenzie returned to the office two minutes before 5pm. Audrey was locking up.

'Are you going home early, Audrey?'

'My watch says 5pm Mr Robin.'

'The office clock is the clock we work by Audrey.'

'Yes Mr Robin.'

She didn't know whether to go or to sit at her desk. Instead she said, 'Mr Robin?'

'Yes, Audrey.'

'People are saying . . .' She hesitated because she knew what Mr Robin thought of 'tattle' as he called it. 'Mr McGill will want his grandfather's name carved on the memorial now that he's a hero too.'

Her employer frowned. 'I cannot imagine it, can you Audrey?'

'No Mr Robin, I wouldn't want my grandfather's name to be on the same memorial as the people who left him to die.'

'Quite so, Audrey.'

That evening, the hotel bar was fuller than usual.

The drink and the gossip were flowing. Laura, one of the bar staff and the sister of a police officer, told the manager, in hushed tones, that Red MacKay had letters proving he was still the legal owner of his grandfather's log. He'd told the police he wouldn't be pressing theft charges against Cal McGill. Indeed, that very morning he'd asked Mr Mackenzie to transfer ownership of the log to McGill. 'You can't steal your own property can you?'

Jimmy Probert, an incomer who lived on the other side of the Kyle, was huddled in a corner with a reporter.

'That's worth another drink son. It's gold I'm giving you.'

His 'woman' was a cleaner at the police station. All the cops were talking about it, how Ellie Rae had gone against her husband Douglas. 'There'll be trouble in that house tonight, there will.' According to Jimmy, Ellie Rae had visited the police station that morning and had spoken to the Chief Inspector. 'She's a trustee of the museum,' Jimmy explained. 'There are only two of them, Ellie and Douglas.'

'So what?' the reporter said.

'Well she told the police she'd take the stand for McGill if he's tried on a charge of breaking into the museum.' Jimmy hadn't known this but descendants of the islanders had always been allowed special access to the museum. It had been opened up on a number of occasions outside normal hours. Apparently Ellie Rae had told the Chief Inspector that as far as she was concerned the same rule applied to Cal McGill, even though he hadn't sought permission in advance and had entered through an open window.

'The cops gave it up after that. The trial would be a farce, Douglas and Ellie Rae quarrelling from the witness box.'

Jimmy tapped his empty glass on the table top.

'Ok, Jimmy, you've earned it. What'll you have?'

Jimmy smacked his lips together, 'A whisky would be grand.'

Back at the bar, the manager came from the office with a print out of a BBC Scotland story. He told Laura about it. 'McGill's offered to loan the log back to the museum on condition that it is kept open at September 29, 1942, the day his grandfather's death was recorded incorrectly by old Hector MacKay, and that the three missing pages are displayed beside it.'

CHAPTER 28

They were the verbal equivalents of old-fashioned mile marker stones on the road south. Every minute or two, the driver would offer up a comment to tempt Cal into conversation. 'Haven't had such excitement round here for years. Not that you found it exciting I suppose.' After each remark he would glance in his rear view mirror and study his passenger's reaction. Cal didn't respond until the driver said, 'You'll be in line for compensation I wouldn't wonder.'

Cal snapped back, 'Look, why don't you pretend I'm not here and I'll do the same for you?'

'As you wish,' the driver said, his jaw tight with offence. He added 'Sir' as an afterthought and loaded it with disrespect.

From the police station, the car had taken Cal to Whale Back Beach, named after the long curved hump of rock at its northern end which resembled a cetacean on its way down after breaching. Rachel, according to Mr Mackenzie, had asked to see him there. 'Not the hotel?' Cal had asked, but Mr Mackenzie informed him that old

Mrs Rae and Douglas had banned him from all their properties in Eastern Township, including the hotel. Anyway, Mr Mackenzie continued, feelings were running high in the local townships, both for and against Cal. In Mr Mackenzie's considered view, it would be judicious of him to leave the area as soon as possible 'to let tempers cool'. Under the circumstances, he continued, the beach was as good as anywhere if 'what you require is a quiet discussion without unwanted interruptions or perhaps some hostility'. Cal didn't know what Rachel had in mind, so he said nothing.

The driver parked in a turning circle at the road end. From there, the beach curved in a shallow crescent towards the north. Cal saw Rachel immediately. She was alone, walking below the tide line, occasionally stopping to pick up shells. When she saw Cal approaching, she stopped. The shells fell from her hand on to the sand. Cal waved, but she didn't wave back. Then she turned away from him and Cal worked the Mary's Bean between his fingers, like she used to, feeling the patina of its woody surface, wondering if she would accept it back as a token of friendship, now that there were no secrets between them.

When he came close to her, he said, 'Hi.'

She knelt to pick up one of the cockle shells she'd dropped.

'Why didn't you tell me you were going back to the island?' Still she didn't look at him.

'I didn't think you'd want to know . . . it'd implicate you.'

'So you were being considerate?'

'That's not what I said.'

Rachel stood and flashed an angry look at him before turning away again.

Cal tried again, 'I'm sorry if it's been difficult.'

'Everything is all over the newspapers, the television news bulletins, everything we've filmed.'

There was more she wasn't saying. Maybe her bosses were kicking up about it. Maybe her job was threatened.

She stared at him, shaking her head as if he just didn't get it. 'You never cared about me, you never wanted what I wanted did you?' Her voice was heavy with disappointment and betrayal.

For a moment Cal considered trying to console her. He'd give her the Mary's Bean. He'd remind her of the first time they'd been alone on a beach, Skaill Beach, Orkney, where he'd found the bean, how it had been a symbol of his commitment to her, how he'd meant it at the time, but things hadn't worked out the way he'd expected, how it could stand for something different now, something more durable. He'd rehearsed a little speech in the car, not sure if he should say it, not sure what he should do, knowing that he had to do something, or nothing.

The bean remained in his pocket, his hand clenched around it. Seeing her now, distant and angry, he realised she wouldn't want it.

He said nothing. (What was there to say if he couldn't give her the bean?)

'I can't do this,' Rachel said after they'd be standing like that for seconds which were as long as hours. She came close to him, hitting softly at his arm twice with her clenched fist.

All he could think of saying was 'sorry' but what was the point? So he didn't say anything. After a while he turned to look after her and she was already at the car. Then she went behind a grassy dune and was gone.

Cal walked along the tide mark to the rock shaped like a whale's back. The movement of the sea made him wonder. Should be throw the Mary's Bean back, let it continue its journey? Instead he pulled at a clump of pink thrift, snapping the flowers until each of his hands was full of them. At the neck of the rock, where it dipped into the sea, he dropped the handfuls one after the other into the water, and watched as the two pink rafts separated and drifted on the tide away from him. He remained there until he couldn't see them anymore.

His driver had observed it all, leaning against the car, smoking a cigarette. He'd kept his curiosity to himself until Altnaharra, half way to Lairg. 'Pretty girl, she was crying you know.' Cal hadn't replied. Then the driver mentioned compensation and Cal had snapped at him. After this exchange, the driver raised the glass partition between them and Cal had called Basanti. He let his phone ring until the answer phone cut in. By the Dornoch Firth he was calling every five minutes. It was daylight. She'd be outside, somewhere: on the roof. Still he rang until he was overcome by the dread that something awful had happened to her. It occurred to him first when he checked his emails. There were dozens of them: from journalists or radio and television producers, wanting him for interviews. The odd one out was a two day old message from DLG. DLG had copied it to everyone in the Omoo group.

'One of the Omoo guys says he sees that hill and tree every morning from his bedroom window. It's north-east of Seil Island, on the mainland, a mile or two from a village called Kilninver, south of Oban. There's a headland with a single track road into it. I'm attaching a photograph. It was taken from his house on the south-east corner of Mull looking across the Firth of Lorn. Sorry about the quality.'

Even with the pixilation, there it was: the hill with the top cut off and ridged sides, looking smaller than in Basanti's drawing because it was set in a larger landscape. The tree, frozen in the act of toppling, was on its left hand flank, just as she'd drawn it.

As he examined it, his thoughts turned to the currents there. What if Preeti's body hadn't floated north with the currents as the police had assumed at the time? What if the opposite had happened? There were strong tidal streams to the north of Corrievrechan, the famous maelstrom between the islands of Jura and Scarba. One of these flowed from the Firth of Lorn, past some small islands called the Garvellachs, towards Scarba. It was here, in an area of sea where a whorl of currents trapped flotsam, that Preeti's body had been found. What if she had gone into the sea north of Scarba, not many kilometres to the south of it, as the police had thought? The hill with the single tree growing out of its flank was to the north. Cal rang Jamieson's number but it went straight to answer. He left a message asking her to ring him urgently and forwarded DLG's email.

When he went back to his inbox, it occurred to him his other emails were in bold black type, but DLG's was not before he clicked on it. Somebody had already read it. It had to be Basanti. Had she logged on to his email account? Had she followed the instructions he had left her? He rang her again, and again, willing her to answer; talking out loud; accusing himself of letting her down too, Rachel first, now Basanti.

When it was dark he'd be certain, when she came in from the roof. If she didn't answer then he'd know she'd gone to the headland overlooking the Firth of Lorn to find Preeti's killers. But he couldn't wait till dark. She had a two day start on him. Cal tapped on the glass partition. The driver lowered it electronically. 'Take me to the Argyll coast, south of Oban.'

'Sir.' It was still laden with disrespect.

The 06.45 bus from Edinburgh had arrived in Oban on time at 11.20. Basanti inquired about Kilninver and whether any services went there. A man in uniform who was leaning against a parked bus reading the *Daily Record*'s racing page, answered without looking up. 'Stance 3 at 1.30pm.'

'How much?' Basanti asked.

He replied in the same bored monotone. '£2.80 single; £5.60 return.'

Basanti went to the nearby railway station where she bought a cup of tea and a salad sandwich. She walked back along Queen's Park Place where she found a discreet bench overlooking the sea. She ate her sandwich and watched the Caledonian Mac-Brayne ferry, painted white and black with a red and black funnel, leaving for the island of Mull.

Her composure pleased her after her close encounter at Cal's flat. It was how she wanted to be, how she must be, not caring whether the man she'd stabbed lived or died. Nothing mattered now apart from avenging Preeti.

At 1.15pm she walked back to bus stance 3. She paid the driver the single fare and asked him how far it was to Kilninver. 'About ten miles,' he replied. She sat at the back on her own. The other passengers, four of them, sat two by two behind the driver. Basanti was first to alight. As she stepped on to the pavement a woman and a child passed by and Basanti showed them her drawing of the hill and the tree. The woman pointed to a rounded hill with a flattish top a kilometre away before examining the drawing again.

'Right enough,' she said, looking at the hill a second time. 'That's it from the other side.' Unasked, the woman gave her directions – the best way was 'down that wee lane' to the coastal path. 'The path's longer than the road but it's a lovely walk.'

Basanti chose the path.

When she reached the sea, she sat on a rock and watched the waves, wondering how water as blue and as lovely could have killed Preeti, how beauty like this could have destroyed beauty like hers. A shiver passed through her at the sea's disregard for the life it had taken. She clutched at her pocket, finding reassurance in the hard shape of Cal's knife.

A few hundred metres further on, the hill began to reveal its familiar side to Basanti. The memory of everything she had suffered rooted her there momentarily. She shuddered, suddenly uncertain about the strength of her will to keep going. She glanced behind her and let out a muffled cry. A man was following her. He was 400 metres away but she recognised his build and shape.

He knew I was coming.

Suddenly she could smell him again: the bitterness of his sweat, the foulness of his breath. She continued along the path, running fast now, down into a dip until she was concealed from him. She peered through the rim of grass and she saw him again. He had stopped on the top of the rise. He was alert and watching, a predator waiting for prey to break cover. Under cover of a sand bank, Basanti ran towards the beach. Her footfalls jolted her ribs, expelling air from her lungs which made a plaintive moaning sound as it passed through her throat.

How did he know I was coming?

Cal had read DLG's email.

Cal had betrayed her again.

Cal.

A woman was walking along the shore towards Basanti. She wore denim dungarees and a cap and had a red bucket in her hand. A white and tan dog ambled ahead of her, sniffing at shells and seaweed.

Basanti looked at her and back at where the man had been. If she ran to the woman across the shingle beach the man would see her. If she didn't, the man would find her when the woman had gone. Hadn't only men touched her, harmed her or betrayed her since she left India? She ran to the woman.

The dog barked when it saw Basanti, bouncing up and down on its front legs, as if held back by an invisible lead.

'Please help me,' she gasped.

The woman ordered her dog to be quiet. A sympathetic smile stretched across the ruddy fleshiness of her face. 'What's wrong, pet?'

'There's a man.' Basanti glanced nervously behind her. She could see the sweep of heather and grass back to the base of the hill. But no-one was there.

'Is he following you?' the woman said, looking too.

'Yes. He was there.' Basanti pointed to the rise where she'd last seen him.

'Well, why don't you come with me?' the woman said. 'I'm finished here.' She swung her bucket full of mussels. 'My caravan's up that way. The road's just the other side. You'll be safe with me.'

Basanti kept on looking behind her as she and the woman walked side by side. The woman told her about her dog, Alfie. He was a terrier, a Jack Russell, four years old, and 'always hunting, rabbits, mice and rats, you name it'. The beach narrowed and a path forked left from it between two sand dunes. The woman, who said her name was Barbara, went first. Basanti followed. They emerged on to a flat, sandy piece of ground over-looking another bay where a small boat was moored at a short wooden pier. The beach round the bay was shingle. There was a cottage close by it and another across a flat of heather, closer to the hill.

Basanti's heart beat loudly. This had been her prison.

'The caravan's along there.' Barbara nodded towards a single track road which was just coming into view. Basanti yelped in fright. The man was on it, running towards them. Every so often he stopped to search the surrounding terrain. He had binoculars round his neck.

Basanti said, 'That's him'. She felt for her knife.

Barbara put a reassuring hand on Basanti's arm. 'You're all right with me, pet.'

The man saw them and ran in their direction. He was big, at least six feet, and broad, the same build as the man who'd carried Basanti when she'd last seen the hill. Barbara felt for Basanti's wrist and held it tight.

'It's ok,' she said, reassuring her. 'He'll be looking for a lost dog or something.'

Basanti tried to shake off Barbara's grip. But Barbara squeezed tighter, preventing her from putting her hand in her pocket.

The man stopped a few metres in front of them, panting; his face screwed up with the effort of running. Barbara said to him, 'What are you waiting for? Take the little bitch.'

She yanked her arm and propelled Basanti forward. She sprawled on the ground at the man's feet. 'Watch out,' Barbara said, 'She's got a knife.'

It was 8pm before Cal's driver parked on the verge by the single track road to the headland. From the landward side, the hill was a series of ascending

369

humps and knolls with occasional trees scattered across them. But on its right flank, Cal's present view of it, there was a single tree, a Scots pine, at a precarious angle of 45 degrees.

'There's no need to wait,' Cal said getting out of the car.

The driver didn't acknowledge Cal or alter his expression. When Cal slammed the door, the car swung back towards Kilninver and Oban. Would a tip have made their parting any more amicable? Cal started along the single track road to the coast. About half way there, the road passed a disused quarry. In it, were a rusted white Volkswagen and a mobile home supported on foundations of brick. A woman sat on a boulder beside the caravan steps, picking mussels out of a bucket and scraping seaweed and barnacles off them with a pen knife. She wore a man's blue and brown check shirt, patched denim dungarees and a denim cap. A dog yapped repeatedly from inside the caravan.

'Anything I can help you with?' she called out to Cal. She squinted at him in the setting sun, covering her eyes with the hand which held the knife.

He stopped a few paces from her. 'Lovely evening.'

'So it is.' She continued to regard him, her fleshy face inquisitive, waiting for Cal's answer.

'I'm looking for a friend,' Cal ventured. 'We'd arranged to meet up here. We're walkers.'

'Lots of walkers round here,' she said, picking up another mussel but continuing to stare at him.

'Any down there?' Cal gestured towards the sea.

'There wasn't half an hour ago, when I was collecting these.' She sounded Geordie.

'Well I'll take a look.' Cal said, 'Thanks for your help.'

She watched him for a moment before continuing to scrape mussels.

Inside the caravan, the man took his hand away from Basanti's throat. She tried to shout, to warn Cal, to beg forgiveness from any god who would listen to her for suspecting him, but the gag filling her mouth choked her. The terrier stopped yapping and went to sniff at her shoes and trousers. The door opened and Barbara said, 'Make sure the knots are tight. We've got work to do.'

The man yanked at Basanti's wrists, checking the rope, before following the woman out of the door. A padlock snapped shut after it had closed.

His smell remained behind.

If not Cal, then who?

The road stopped at a turning circle some 200 metres from the shore. The hill was now further inland and up the coast from Cal and he struck out across aromatic bog myrtle towards it, following a sheep's trail up an incline. Over it two cottages came into view. Both were modest, two-roomed 'but and bens' with slate roofs. The nearest was down by the sea, beside a shingle beach with a pier and a boat moored at it. The second cottage was further from the bay, closer to the base of the hill. Was this where Preeti and Basanti had been brought ashore and imprisoned?

The first cottage was enclosed by a wire fence and had the appearance of being unoccupied. The gate to the front door was padlocked and the gravel path was overgrown with grass and weeds. Cal climbed the fence and looked in the nearest window. It was a sparsely furnished sitting room with one sofa, an arm chair, a cheap coffee table and a standard lamp with a fabric shade frilled at the bottom. He tried the door before going on to the next cottage which had a similar atmosphere of neglect. From here the hill was almost as Basanti had drawn it. Half of the Scots pine was now visible on its left hand side.

The path stopped at the second cottage but Cal tramped across heather until the angle of the hill was exactly as Basanti had seen it, with the leaning Scots pine fully in view. He found what he was looking for off to his left, after a couple of hundred metres. Here, there was a depression in the ground with a large lichen covered boulder at one side of it. Attached to the boulder was a rusted ring sunk into cement in a crevice of rock. He touched it as if the warmth of his fingers might coax it to impart its story.

This was where Basanti had been taken that night.

This was where she'd seen the hill.

By now it was dusk and Cal cut across the headland to the sea, stopping only when he reached the little bay by the first cottage. The gravel beach crunched under his feet as it had for the man who carried Basanti ashore. Cal inspected the boat which was wooden, again as Basanti had recalled it. As the sun dipped behind Mull, he sat on the end of the short pier, listening to the lapping of the sea.

He remained there until it was dark and then he tried to ring Basanti. If she was still in Edinburgh, she'd be inside his flat now. He was tapping in the number when he noticed his phone had no signal. He continued to walk around the bay glancing every so often at his mobile: still no signal. He swore and resolved to wait for her there, in case she was on her way. At a part of the bay where the sea had eroded the bank, spilling a chute of sand across the gravel, he sat down. He watched the rise and fall of the waves and the pink sky fading on the horizon, fighting tiredness. Somewhere out there, three years ago, a ship unloaded its cargo of two virgin Bedia girls for something unimaginably awful.

Cal was dreaming. Hands held him by his legs and arms, tying them with rope. A knee pressed into his chest. A cloth was being forced into his mouth and he choked. Now it wasn't a dream. He was turned on his front, a blindfold tied tight around his eyes. There were two of them holding him, one his legs, one his torso. They carried him across the gravel, their feet crunching into it. He kicked and twisted but they held him. He attempted to scream but only a low, muffled grunt made it past the gag. Then he was in the boat. Another rope was wound round his body and legs and tied under the bench seat, stopping him from moving. He heard them go back across the gravel and he strained at his knots until they cut into him. Then he heard their feet approaching. Something was put on to the seat beside him. He felt the warmth of another body and a tremble of fear through cotton clothes. Basanti. Cal jolted with the shock of her. He fought against his ropes. He tried to shout.

Soon the boat was out at sea, rolling with the swell. They came for Basanti first. He heard them untying her ropes, her pleas for mercy after they removed her gag, her begging Cal for forgiveness, her prayers for Preeti and their families, then his own screaming but only a strangulated squeal emerging. Then they took off Cal's blindfold. There were two of them. They wore balaclavas, with only their eyes showing. Did they want him to witness what they were about to do? The taller one held Basanti under her arms; the other gripped her legs. Cal saw the fright on her lovely young face, her silent pleading for Cal to help her, and then she was gone, tumbling into the sea, a cry of terror, followed by a splash. He saw Basanti's face once more, lit dimly by the sea's phosphorescence, before it was lost in the darkness. Cal prayed she wouldn't scream again and she did not.

Now they started on Cal, working silently and methodically, untying his knots. They left the ones at his wrists till last, as he was being lifted up, as Basanti had been. He kicked out but he was held tight by strong hands. The gag was pulled from his mouth. He saw a shirt cuff: the same check the woman by the caravan had been wearing. Next he was in mid air. Then he was in the water, the cold shock of it making him gasp. His mouth and nose filled with it. When he surfaced the sound of the boat's engine was faint and distant. He shouted for Basanti: the soft syllables of her name a small sound in a vast blackness. He listened for a reply but none came. Between calling and listening, he swam back towards where she had gone into the water.

But the further he went, the more disorientated he became. The waves were bigger now and he was tired swimming against them. When exhaustion overcame him he trod water, crying out her name, over and over, turning one way then another. Finally, he let out a scream of rage and frustration before falling silent. It was then he realised he was caught in a strong current, the direction of which he calculated from a single distant light on the Argyllshire mainland east of him. The sea was pushing him south-west, and quickly. He'd been dropped into one of the tidal streams between the Firth of Lorn and Corrievrechan. For Preeti and

Basanti it had been a drowning stream; and so it would be for him. He was too weak to swim across it or against it. It was pushing him further from land. All he could do was let it take him. Cal closed his eyes imagining his grandfather beside him, being his guide through the stages of drowning: the struggle after submersion, the physical exhaustion, the vomiting, and the loss of consciousness. After Basanti's death he tried to resign himself to it as his fate, his atonement for failing her.

A wave broke over him, filling his mouth with salt water and he surfaced again, choking. The sea was becoming a frenzy of little waves. A powerful downdraught buffeted him. Someone was shouting to him, a male voice, close to his ear, sliding a harness under his arms. Then he was free of the water. Hands grabbed at him. Then he was inside a helicopter. A survival blanket was wrapped around him, a mask placed over his face. A voice said, 'You had us worried there. We thought we'd lost you, would have done without thermal imaging.' The last thing he did before falling into unconsciousness was to call for Basanti.

When he came round he was in hospital. A nurse was checking the monitor screens and Detective Constable Jamieson was sitting in a chair beside his bed. 'We have signs of life,' Jamieson said. 'Welcome to the living, Cal.'

'Where's Basanti?'

Jamieson asked the nurse to leave them alone.

When she shut the door, Jamieson said, 'We've told the media that a 17-year old female is missing, feared drowned.'

Cal cried out, an echo of the scream that had stayed suppressed inside him since he felt Basanti close to him on the boat. Then he saw Jamieson was holding up a drawing of a hill and a tree on its left hand flank. 'Dear Cal, Thank you so much, Love Basanti' was written across the bottom of it.

'She wanted you to have it,' Jamieson smiled. 'She's alive. She's fine. We picked her up before we got you. You were a bit more difficult to find. You had us worried there. The current had taken you away. We cut it fine but we couldn't move any sooner because we didn't know if they had Basanti until she was taken to the boat.'

Cal looked uncomprehending. 'But you said she had drowned.'

'We've told the *media* she's missing feared drowned because we didn't want the men who abused her to think she's alive. Not yet.'

Jamieson told him the rest on the journey back to Edinburgh. She talked as she drove, though Cal wished she would do one or the other, not both. Most of the way her head was turned towards him instead of the road, or so it seemed to Cal. Quite quickly they settled into a routine. She briefed him on the investigation and he interrupted with warnings to her about sharp bends or slow moving tractors or caravans.

The man and woman, husband and wife, who had thrown Cal and Basanti into the sea had been arrested and charged with attempted murder and a number of child sex offences. The police expected to charge them with Preeti's murder in due course. They weren't saying anything but Basanti was in protective custody and looking through the mugshots of the country's worst sex offenders. 'There've been whispers before about children imported from countries like India or Bangladesh but we never had proof until now.'

'Why go to all that bother? Aren't there enough children here if you want to abuse one?'

'It's all about untraceability. Nobody notices a fourteen year old Bedia girl in India going missing. It happens every day, a young girl being sold into the sex trade. They're disposable when you're finished with them, and in this country they're exotic with a high market value.'

Cal drew her attention to a sharp left hander. Jamieson braked but less hard than Cal wanted.

'Think of this operation . . .' she braked again as the corner turned out to be longer than she anticipated, 'as a bespoke import business serving a market where rarity commands a premium price. The customers are paedophiles, sex tourists, the ones on the sex offenders' register we prohibit from travelling abroad because they'll go to Thailand or India to abuse children. So the children are brought here for them instead.

'In this case, Preeti and Basanti were installed

378

in underground rooms in the two cottages by the bay. The men spent a week on holiday, a weekend, even a day or two, and nobody was any the wiser. Even if the police had been watching what would they have seen? None of the men approached any children or young girls locally because they didn't need to. They had two captive in the cottages.'

Jamieson also briefed Cal on the police search for the hill.

'After you sent me Basanti's drawing a helicopter went up and down the west coast taking pictures of hills with a single tree on their left sides. There were six possibilities between Oban and Stranraer. The Scottish Crime and Drug Enforcement Agency has been coordinating rotating surveillance operations at them all.

'That headland was a favourite, though your phone call and the email you forwarded from DLG confirmed it for us. The landscape was right and so was the proximity of the bay to the cottages. As luck would have it we were at another site when Basanti went to it.

'And we checked back. Before Preeti's death, there had been a police operation to recover bales of cannabis washing ashore up and down the Firth of Lorn. God knows where they came from. We suspect that's why Preeti was dumped at sea and Basanti was taken outside and left chained to the rock. When the police cars came down the road to the headland in the middle of the night the alarm went up. Our friends must have thought it was a raid on the cottages. The quickest way of getting rid of Preeti was to dump her in the sea. They didn't have time with Basanti because the second cottage was too far back from the bay so they did what they could in the time they had.'

Now they were on the motorway and Cal was more relaxed. At least the road was straight. 'It makes a kind of sense,' he said, 'to throw someone alive into the sea far enough from land, or into a strong adverse current. So many bodies sink to the bottom and don't resurface for years if at all. If they do, they can drift for miles, sometimes thousands of miles, away from the scene, and who's to say they didn't just drown in an accident.'

They didn't speak for a while until Cal said, 'Thank you, by the way.'

'What for?'

'I saw the papers, about the severed feet, the way you cut Ryan out of it and let the Italians take the credit, and me.'

'It was a pleasure.' Jamieson beamed.

By now they'd left the motorway and were travelling through Corstorphine in West Edinburgh. A delivery lorry was edging out into the flow of traffic. Cal had seen it but Jamieson hadn't. 'Look out!' he shouted and then in pent up frustration he said, 'Just drive; please just drive.'

Neither spoke for a few minutes, though Jamieson continued to watch him. Finally, she said, 'Look, there's something you need to know.' She indicated

380

left and drove into the gates of a hotel beside the zoo. Two police cars and a taxi with its engine running were parked away from the hotel patrons' cars. Jamieson pulled up beside them. 'My boss wants to have a word.'

'Detective Inspector Ryan?'

'No, I've a new boss. Chief Inspector Richard Beacom.' She paused, 'I've been seconded full-time to the SCDEA, to be Basanti's liaison officer. I worked in an Indian orphanage in my 20s, so I was given the job. Basanti's probably one of the most important witnesses we've ever had. She'll be in witness protection for years, possibly the rest of her life. Change of name, the works.'

'Won't Ryan mind you going to the SCDEA?' Cal asked.

'He'll mind all right.' Jamieson whooped with the joy of it.

A slight man with long, swept-back greasy blond hair, a sharp face, small mouth, stubble and a slanting frown line on his forehead approached their car. 'That's him, my new boss,' Jamieson said. She lowered her voice. 'Doesn't look like much but wow he's hot.' Jamieson suddenly became flustered. 'I didn't mean in *that* way.'

'Obviously,' Cal said.

'Yes; obviously.' Jamieson laughed too, loudly. 'I mean if I had I wouldn't . . . well you know. And I haven't, obviously.'

'Obviously,' Cal said again which irked Jamieson. She opened her window. 'Hello, boss'.

'Introduce us if you would, Helen?'

He called me Helen.

Beacom, who was wearing a leather jacket, jeans and a blue shirt, opened the back door behind Jamieson and got into the car. Cal guessed he was in his late 30s.

'Boss this is Cal McGill. Cal, Chief Inspector Richard Beacom.'

The Chief Inspector leaned over offering Cal his hand. 'It's Richard by the way.'

His accent was Glasgow private school.

Cal nodded.

'There's something we'd like you to do,' Beacom said, 'if you feel up to it.'

Cal looked at Jamieson. 'It's your choice,' she said. 'Isn't it sir?'

'Yes.'

'What is it?'

Beacom said, 'The guys who run this child trafficking racket are trying to close things down. An address in Glasgow was firebombed last night – we think it's where Basanti was held. We've had reports of some of Basanti's clients – if I can call them that – being beaten up, baseball bats, razors, you name it, to stop them saving their own skins and blabbing if and when we bring them in. A couple of them are in hospital too scared to talk. The frighteners are going on. They're doing what they can to slam the door on us.'

Just in case Cal needed it spelled out, Beacom said, 'It's big. Child trafficking and sex abuse on an industrial scale. We need to get these bastards. Fast.'

He took a cigarette pack out of his jacket pocket and offered it to Cal. 'Do we share a bad habit?'

Cal declined.

'You don't mind do you Helen?'

'No Sir.'

Yes sir, but not if you call me Helen.

Cal said, 'What do you want me to do?'

'There's a chance . . .' Beacom elongated the word and spread his lips into a grimace to signal how small a chance it was, 'they don't know what we've got. We've told the media a seventeen year old female is missing, feared drowned. But we haven't said anything about you or about the two arrests we've made. We're assuming they know we've got their people from the headland, which is why they're taking precautions, but we're not sure they know you're with us. We don't even know if they're aware you were with Basanti in Argyll.'

He paused. 'Do you follow?'

Cal said, 'Yes.'

'Let's say they think their guys disposed of Basanti before they were arrested. Let's say they believe she's dead. So that leaves you as Basanti's only contact on the outside. They'll worry that she gave you dates, descriptions, whatever. They'll want to eliminate that possibility.'

'You mean eliminate me?'

'These guys are desperate . . .'

'But if they don't know I was in Argyll why would

they think I know Basanti at all? Why would they make a connection?'

Beacom glanced at Jamieson.

She said, 'Shall I, sir?'

He nodded.

'They were waiting for her at your flat.'

'When?'

'When she left it on her way to the bus station to go to Argyll. They were staking out The Cask. They almost got her too. If she hadn't taken one of your kitchen knives she'd be dead by now.'

'But nobody knew she was staying there,' Cal protested, 'apart from you.'

Jamieson ignored Cal's implication. 'And they were waiting for her at Kilninver. She walked into a trap. She's sure of it. They were expecting her.'

'But I didn't even know about Kilninver until she'd gone there?'

Jamieson glanced at Beacom who shook his head. The gesture said lead him there, let him discover the answer for himself, let him realise the mistake he made.

'Who else did you tell about her drawing of the hill?' Jamieson said.

'I emailed the Omoo crowd.'

Jamieson nodded, encouraging him along that line of thought.

'No way.'

'We think so. Whoever it was would have known as soon as they saw Basanti's drawing. He'd have known she'd been in touch with you.'

Cal put his head in his hands. 'Shit. And when DLG sent the email identifying the drawing they'd have seen that too. His email was copied to everyone in Omoo.'

'Do you know who it might be?' Beacom asked.

Cal shook his head.

'Basanti will get us the guys who abused her,' Beacom said. 'And maybe they'll lead us to other kids like her, though if we don't get to them soon we'll be pulling more dead bodies out of the sea. But Basanti never saw the faces of the guys who ran the show. We need to get to them a different way.'

Beacom leaned forward. 'Let me put a proposition to you . . .'

'Ok.'

'You're not exactly flavour of the month with people like me are you?'

'How do you mean?'

'How can I put this . . . the police have a few issues with you, trampling over ministers' gardens, assisting the Italians with the severed feet inquiry, breaking into museums. Do you think that's fair?'

'I guess.'

'If the guys we're after didn't know you were in Argyll, they'd think you were pretty high up the police grudge list. Which means they might not be expecting you to have protection. Which also means they might come for you if they think you're alone.'

'What do you want me to do?'

They spoke for another half an hour. Beacom was meticulous in his briefing, checking at every stage that Cal understood what was expected of him and the various contingencies for which the police had prepared: all of them as far as Cal could tell. 'Any further questions?' Beacom asked at the end.

Cal shook his head.

'Do what we've outlined and you'll be fine.' Beacom offered Cal his hand again. 'Good luck.'

Jamieson accompanied Cal to the taxi. 'You ok?' she said.

'Yeah.'

'But there was something different about him. 'You sure?'

'Yeah, I'm sure.'

In case Cal still wasn't convinced about the Omoo link, she said, 'It gave whoever we're after a perfect cover for sussing out remote sites for bringing trafficked children ashore, and for identifying isolated cottages. Whoever it is in the Omoo group might not be a ring-leader; he might only be a gofer but we need to find him. Ok?'

'Ok.'

She opened the taxi door. 'Be careful,' she said. 'They may be watching your flat. We don't think so, but it's possible. Stick to the plan and you'll be fine.'

Cal didn't reply.

Jamieson said to the driver, 'You know where you're going?'

'The Cask, in Granton.'

When the taxi was leaving the car park Cal realised he had no money for the fare. 'I've got no cash.'

'Don't worry mate. I'm not a cabbie. I'm a cop.' The driver pulled a face at Cal in his rear view mirror. 'So no tip then . . .'

CHAPTER 29

C al wrote the email as Chief Inspector Beacom instructed.

> *Hi Everyone,*
> *I'm home again, bruised and a bit battered after recent events. I assume you've read about them so I guess elaboration isn't necessary. Give me a few days to sort myself and I'll be back in action, relying on you guys for occasional assistance, as ever.*
> *Cal*

He read it through and clicked send.

He remained sitting at his computer looking at the twelve addresses of his Omoo contacts to which it had been dispatched. Which of them would it be?

DLG was the first to reply. 'Good to hear from you. Be in touch soon, all right?'

He wondered about the significance of DLG making no mention of Basanti's drawing of the hill and the tree. Did it signify something or nothing? Perhaps he didn't want to bother him with it so soon after his release from police custody.

Zeke was next. 'Welcome back. Take it easy now. Be good.'

Shorty was after him. 'What a tragedy about your grandfather. He'd be proud of you. I will light a candle and pray for him – and you.' Cal registered that Shorty was religious.

He ruled out Shorty.

And Zeke.

Zeke was in his 70s. He was infirm and hadn't been on an Omoo expedition to the west coast or the islands for many years.

What about the others? Cal knew little to nothing about them, except their Omoo names. He hadn't met them, didn't know who they were or what they did.

He waited at his computer for another reply. No more came. After a while, he wrote three emails. One was to Basanti; one to his father; the last, the longest, was to Rachel. After checking them and making corrections, he saved them into his drafts folder and wrote to Bembo. 'In case this goes pear-shaped please forward the three emails in Gmail drafts. Thank you. It was good knowing you. Look after Basanti won't you?'

He checked the signal of his mobile. Four bars. It reassured him. Now he had to wait for Jamieson's call.

While he killed time, he did as the Chief Inspector instructed.

He went to the window and stood there looking across the waste ground to the ruins of the old flour mill 200 metres away. He glanced down at the street. A bus was passing. He turned away.

Don't behave as if you're expecting someone.

He returned to his chair, checked for more emails. There were none. He pushed away his key board, leant back and rested his feet on the edge of the table. He remained like that, casting back, wondering, analysing. Which of them would it be?

When it grew dark he switched on his desk lamp. He went to the bathroom door and turned on the overhead light. He walked past the windows once more. He saw his reflection in the glass and the colourless silhouette of a fading city skyline behind it.

The waiting had taken away his appetite. But he looked in the fridge and along the kitchen shelves anyway. It was something to do. He boiled the kettle, put a teabag in a mug but didn't pour in the water. He didn't want a drink.

Don't keep all the lights on all the time. Mix it up.

At 11pm, he turned off the bathroom light and turned on his bedside lamp.

At 11.20pm he turned off his desk light.

At 11.55pm he turned off his bedside lamp.

His apartment was now lit only by the pallor of the street lights reflecting off the white of his ceiling. He pushed his armchair underneath one of the big windows in the living area. He sat back into it, making sure the top of his head was below the windowsill. His desk lamp was on the small table beside him. He checked the plug and pushed the table forward so the lamp's arc of light would leave him in shadow. He tested it once before turning it off.

His phone was in his hand. He checked it. Four bars.

Cal feels a sense of purpose; a mixture of determination and recklessness. Someone has betrayed him. It's time for him to discover who. One o'clock. Two o'clock. The hours pass. He's drowsy, falling in and out of sleep, waking at the sound of a car, or at passing pedestrians, their shouts and laughter drifting up to him.

When his phone rings he is asleep. He fumbles to answer it but instead, all thumbs and fingers, cancels the call. He swears. The phone rings again. It's Jamieson.

'They're here.'

'How many?'

'Four that we've seen. There's one in a car, one at the front door and two just going inside. So get out on to the roof now. Go.'

Cal says nothing. He cuts the call.

Don't mess about. Just get the hell out of there.

Chief Inspector Beacom is watching the monitors in the mobile police control centre. Two night vision cameras are streaming pictures; one is in an unmarked van parked along the street from The Cask. The other, which gives a view into Cal's apartment, is on the roof of the old flour mill.

'Can't see him moving?' Beacom stares at the second screen again.

He studies every dim detail. He can see the long back wall of Cal's living area, what looks like a group of posters, the front door to their right, the spiral staircase to the roof.

He asks for more zoom. He watches again for movement. He doesn't see any.

'Chris'sake Helen, is he still in there?' By now McGill should be climbing the spiral stairs. Beacom wishes he'd fixed a camera inside the apartment. But there was a risk the building was being watched.

There's always a risk.

'I don't know sir,' Jamieson replies. It means she thinks Cal is still inside. 'I'll ring again sir.'

It's really a question. She waits for his answer. Beacom is operating blind.

He doesn't know why Cal isn't moving.

He doesn't know where in the building the two men are.

He doesn't know whether they're close enough to Cal's door to hear a phone ringing. 'Do it,' he says.

Jamieson lets it ring four times before Beacom says, 'enough.' He is watching the second monitor again, asking for more focus on the door. He expects two men to burst through it any moment now.

He says under his breath, 'Get out, get *out* for Chris'sake, get *out*.' He takes a deep breath. 'What the fuck's he playing at.' He bangs his hand against the wall. 'Shit.'

He orders his waiting men to move on the driver of the car and the look-out by the front door. Another risk. Will they tip off the men inside before they've committed any crime?

Another group of officers has moved up to the back of the building. He gives the order for them to go on to the roof. None of this is what he wants. What he wants is to see the two men inside the building force entry into the flat. He wants them to commit a crime, any crime, before he makes his moves. Otherwise the advantage shifts from him to them. There's no law against visiting someone you email occasionally about flotsam and ocean currents, even if it is at 2.40 in the morning. There's no law against sitting in a parked car while your mate visits an acquaintance, or against smoking a cigarette in the shelter of a block of flats while you wait.

Beacom can't take his eyes off the second monitor. Will the camera on the old flour mill soon be relaying Cal's murder?

Beacom knows he cannot let that happen.

A call comes through. The driver and the look-out have been detained. Beacom gives the order for police to enter the front door of The Cask. He checks the progress of his men on the roof. Two minutes, he's told. Two minutes isn't fast enough.

'What the fuck's he playing at Helen?'

He's turning back to the monitor when the door bursts open. It's what he wants to see but not with

Cal still inside. This is his nightmare. Two shapes run through the open door, low and fast.

There's a smell, like petrol. Cal remains in his chair, below the window. He registers the landing beyond the swinging door is dark. The men have blacked out the lights. Everything goes quiet. Then Cal hears their breathing. They're crouching. There's a movement to his right, towards his bed and the bathroom. The other man stays where he is, watching. Cal is still. The darkness conceals him. A shadow moves left. The two men are together again. He hears their hurried whispers. Both men stand. There's the sound of liquid pouring on to the floor. Cal clicks on his desk lamp, lighting them both. They wear masks with slits.

The man on the right raises his hand towards the light. It holds a gun, but Cal doesn't move. The man can't see him. There's a crash of glass breaking. The man with the gun cries out and falls backward. His companion runs for the door. When he reaches the dark of the landing he flares a cigarette lighter, sets light to something which he lobs back inside. The air ignites before it lands. The flame races in front of Cal. He jumps up, pulls his table over to protect his papers and books. The photograph of his grandfather is in his backpack behind his armchair. He doesn't think about his computers. They crash to the floor. There are shouts outside, a tussle. Suddenly police are everywhere: at the door; on the spiral staircase. Two officers wearing goggles see Cal and hurry him from the burning apartment.

'Were you trying to get yourself killed?' Jamieson asked.

Cal said, 'I had some personal issues.'

'My boss has a few personal issues with you too. He'll kill you himself given half a chance.'

Cal shrugged, smiling weakly.

Jamieson said, 'You knew we'd have to shoot, didn't you?'

'No.'

'You'd be dead if we hadn't.'

He shrugged again, as if to say it didn't matter to him. 'Then you'd have had him for murder,' he said. She'd already told him the dead man was Mack, the leader of the Omoo group. How police were already taking his home apart, looking for clues. How they'd already found some email print outs addressed to Mack.

All Cal had said was, 'served him right, the bastard.'

'The other guy was muscle, doesn't seem to know anything,' Jamieson said.

Cal rubbed his face. 'I'm tired. I want a shower, a clean bed.'

'We've booked you into a hotel for the night.'

'When will I be allowed to get some things?'

'Couple of days . . . Forensics will need the place to themselves until then. I'll let you know, ok?'

Cal thanked her. 'By the way, there's an email in your Bembo account. Ignore it.'

Rosie Provan pulled at the cuffs of her calf's leather Armani bomber jacket. She unfastened and fastened the third top button. She couldn't make up her mind: too much cleavage, not enough cleavage. She shook her blonde hair and reapplied her lip gloss. Her taxi pulled into the parking bay in front of The Cask. The media pack had moved on and so had the story. It was everywhere, page after page of it: police raids on paedophile hide-outs; the secret double life of 'Mack' Crosby, the customs officer who moonlighted as a sex trafficker; the sordid twilight trade in child prostitutes; how the rest of the gang had operated offshore; how they'd gone to ground; how the police had leads to India, Albania and North Africa, places where children were cheap.

So far nobody in the media had got to Cal McGill. Rosie had tried his hotel but his police guard had turned her away like the other reporters. Unlike the others, she'd gone back every few hours. She'd phoned his father. She'd emailed Bembo, her mysterious and well-connected contact who told her about Cal solving the severed feet mystery. 'Can you help with access to McGill?' A day or two passed before Bembo replied. 'McGill's going to his flat this afternoon. Be there 2.30pm. Re the severed feet, you scratched my back. Re McGill, I scratch yours. Now we're quits. Bye.'

She was late. It was 2.34 when she paid off the taxi and walked towards the uniformed policeman at the door of The Cask. He was speaking to an overweight woman having a bad hair day, a bad everything day. (Rosie registered an involuntary internal gasp of disapproval. The woman's skirt was too tight *and* too short.)

Rosie wasn't sure what to say so she tried up-front and obvious. 'Rosie Provan from the Reporting Factory . . . to see Cal McGill.'

The officer asked for her ID. Rosie flashed her press card at him and a smile.

It irked Rosie the way the fat woman clocked her card too. (She was a paper bag job if Rosie had ever seen one.) What surprised her was the woman saying with a quiet authority, 'It's ok; let her in.' The uniformed officer pushed the door open, Rosie went inside and went to the top floor where another policeman was waiting by the lift door. 'Miss Provan is it?'

Rosie flashed a smile.

'He's expecting you.'

'Who was that, the woman at the front door?' She'd almost said 'fat woman'.

The officer said, 'That'll be Helen Jamieson.'

'Who's Helen Jamieson?'

'Detective Sergeant Jamieson; just been promoted.' He tapped his nose with an index finger. 'One to watch, I'm told.'

She couldn't be Bembo, Rosie thought; too subordinate despite her promotion; too ugly to have *that* kind of access and information. Whoever *was* Bembo had opened doors, had told the fat officer to let Rosie in. That was the way the world worked.

The policeman watched after Rosie as her high heels click-clacked down the landing, the lights flicking on ahead of her. Cal's door was ajar, like the first time she visited him, and as she approached she heard what sounded like someone moving furniture. Just like the last time. It was weird, like seriously weird, like oh-my-God weird.

She made to knock on the door but instead put her head through the gap. Cal was sitting on the floor, gathering up papers. She took in the scene: books and burst files scattered everywhere; the window behind him boarded up; that familiar smell, one Rosie recognised from the many flat fires she'd covered as a trainee reporter; a smell Rosie had grown to associate with poor people.

'Wow,' she said, 'Who said lightning never strikes twice?'

'Hello, Rosie.' Cal looked up at her quickly and then back at what he was doing.

'Hi.' Rosie took a step into the room, noticing the scorch marks on the wall, the bubbled paint on the skirting, the charred black floor boards, the water stains – had the blood been washed away? Keep it light and easy, Rosie. 'Well what's been keeping you busy since we last saw each other?'

Re-establish the relationship, Rosie.

Cal didn't reply.

In Rosie's view journalism was similar to warfare: it was all about taking territory. She glanced at Cal. This was a man who wanted to talk if ever she saw one, contemplative, solitary, in need of a friend. She crossed the room to his armchair and sat on an arm. After a long silence, Cal stopped sorting through papers.

'Why did you do that?' He spoke so softly, so accusingly, that it caught Rosie off-guard.

'What?' Rosie said.

'Take a photograph of my grandfather without my permission.'

'Oh I didn't realise.'

Now Cal stared at her with an intensity she hadn't seen in him before.

Rosie said uneasily, 'It must have been a mis-understanding. I'm sorry.'

'Stop the pursuit, Rosie. I'm not going to talk to you.'

She made a show of disappointment. 'I didn't mean anything by it.' Rosie pretended hurt at a false accusation.

'Goodbye, Rosie,' Cal said, starting to sort through another file.

Rosie shrugged. 'Ok.' She picked up her bag. 'Nice to hook up again.' She held up her left hand and waggled her fingers stiffly. 'Bye Cal.'

Rosie pulled the door shut and scribbled notes as she went along the landing. It'd make a story all right: Cal McGill, the sea detective, sitting in the wreckage of his life, in the apartment where Mack, the scout for the sex trafficking operation had been shot by a police marksman. She'd seen the scrubbed boards where the blood had been. Who needed an interview with colour like that?

When the noise of Rosie's heels had gone quiet, Cal wandered about the flat, distractedly picking up books, flicking over pages; touching some of the artefacts he'd collected, feeling their texture, searching for reassurance in them. For the next hour or two, he packed the turtle shell and his other flotsam and jetsam, including the Mary's Bean, into storage boxes. He gathered salvageable papers and books into piles and tied them with sash cord. Everything undamaged would be taken away tomorrow and stored in the room at the top of the back stairs in his parents' house. His computers were already packed for pick-up by a specialist data recovery company. A flat clearance company would remove the rest. Cal had put some books, maps and sea charts on his mattress. They were for his small backpack. His clothes went into his rucksack. He hooked it on to his shoulder; the small backpack hanging from his right hand, its straps trailing the floor. He opened the door and slammed it shut behind him.

Detective Inspector Ryan was at home taking 'a week off, to let the storm blow over,' as Detective Chief Superintendent Reynolds had advised. But politicians were still clamouring for heads to roll, in particular the Justice Minister's and the Chief Constable's. The *Daily Record*'s leader column asked, 'Does Edinburgh have the worst cops in the world?' In the last paragraph it said, 'The operation by the SCDEA to break up a gang of child sex traffickers contrasts with the lamentable performance of the Lothian and Borders force over the severed feet mystery. The case for amalgamation of Scotland's eight forces into one grows stronger by the day.'

Ryan waited for the call.

It came soon after 3pm, in time for the broadcasters and their early evening news programmes. 'David?' DCS Reynolds sounded distant. 'The chief is calling in an Assistant Chief Constable from Strathclyde to review your handling of the severed feet inquiry.'

Ryan put the phone down without speaking.

He rang Joan, his PA, to tell her to contact the SCDEA to withdraw his application.

'Any letters or emails I should know about?'

'There's one I've been asked to bring to your attention.'

'Who from?'

'Someone called Bembo. At least that's the name on the email address.'

Ryan hesitated. The name was familiar though he couldn't quite place it. 'What does it say?'

'It says . . .'

Like a host revealing the result on a TV game show, Joan waited. Jamieson had coached her, the two of them laughing at the thought of Ryan's expression.

'It says . . .'

'Get on with it woman,' Ryan barked.

'It says: Detective Sergeant Helen Jamieson is being seconded to the Scottish Crime and Drug Enforcement Agency with immediate effect.'

CHAPTER 30

Jamieson watched for Basanti's reaction. 'And him?' she asked, putting down a photograph of a bald man, with a goatee and a diamond stud in his left ear. Basanti stared briefly at it before turning away, as she had done with all the other mug shots Jamieson had placed in front of her.

'Well?'

It had become choreography; Basanti neither shaking nor nodding her head until she had looked away and Jamieson inquiring gently, 'Well?'

Basanti nodded.

'Do you need to look again, just to be certain?'

Jamieson asked her every time before removing the photograph and replacing it with another. Basanti's response was always the same whether she had recognised the man or not.

'No, I don't need more time.'

Jamieson wanted to say 'Are you sure? It's important,' though she never did. There'd be an opportunity for going through the photographs again when Basanti was stronger, in a day or two. What was important now was identifying the men, as quickly as possible, alerting the local police forces, locating the suspects, mounting surveillance operations, making arrests, discovering whether there were other girls like Preeti or Basanti held captive in safe houses for abuse by known sex offenders.

For the last three days, they'd spent an hour in the morning and an hour in the afternoon going through the photographs and by now Jamieson thought she had an understanding of why Basanti did it this way. These men had invaded her, in the worst cases multiple times over weeks. She didn't want to let them invade her again, even for a few seconds, even with their photographs. So she glanced at their faces for as long as she needed and no more before turning away. Jamieson wished Basanti would look again 'just to be sure'. On the other hand, if a man had done to Jamieson what these men had done to Basanti she wouldn't forget them either. Yes, it'd only take a glance, a second. You'd know them anywhere. However long you had to hold the memory. You wouldn't forget; not if you wanted vengeance, which Basanti did. Not if you'd been waiting for this moment, as Basanti had. You'd remember them, until you didn't need to remember them any more. Then you'd forget then. Then you'd want their faces out of your head, forever.

'Are you able to tell me what he did?' Jamieson asked.

Basanti shook her head.

There was a digital voice recorder between them

on the table under the walnut tree in the garden. They sat here every day because of Basanti's aversion to being indoors in daylight. (With the help of a psychologist she had started to walk through the house but only if the front and back doors were kept open.)

'Would you talk into the recorder?'

Sometimes she preferred to do it this way. Jamieson would leave her on her own and Basanti would spend five, 10, 20 minutes talking into the machine. She'd call Jamieson when she'd finished. 'Don't listen to it now. Please,' she'd say, always.

When Jamieson did play back Basanti's recordings, she'd cry. They were the worst. Unspeakable. How could anyone do that to a child?

On this occasion, Basanti said, 'Can we go for a walk, around the garden, see something pleasant?'

'Yes, of course.' Jamieson put the photograph face-down so Basanti couldn't see it and said into her police radio, 'We're just going for a walk.' A woman's voice acknowledged. The security guards were all women. The detectives who came to the house to collect the Basanti's statements, oral and written, were women. So were the psychologist and the cook. 'No men,' Basanti had insisted even though a woman had betrayed her at the last, on the beach. One woman, but dozens, scores of men. 'No men it is,' Jamieson said, imagining the expressions on the faces of the mostly male police taskforce which had been assembled to pursue Basanti's abusers.

No men didn't worry Jamieson.

The garden was about an acre, with a high boundary wall. Basanti chose the path which passed the lilac bushes and, as usual, she brushed her nose against the bluish purple flowers, breathing in their strong perfume. 'What's going to happen to me, Helen?'

Jamieson had suspected this was coming. The consul's report on Basanti's mother and sister had arrived that morning. Jamieson had read it first before giving it to Basanti.

'Nothing will happen, not if you don't want it.'

'I can't go home.'

'Can't you?' That had been the consul's opinion too, in a covering letter.

'My mother and sister are living with my uncle. If I go back to them he will force me back into the *dhanda* until my father's debts are paid.'

'What about the man who was going to marry you?'

'He wouldn't want me now. I am not a virgin.'

Jamieson regretted asking. 'Do you have any relatives here, in Britain?'

'No.'

'You know you can stay in this country, don't you Basanti?'

'Yes.'

'You'll be given a British passport, and a new identity in exchange for assisting us with the prosecutions.' There'd be money too, but Jamieson didn't know how much. The politicians were

406

wrangling. The Scottish government wanted the UK Home Office to pay because most of the men who abused Basanti lived in England; but the Home Office insisted Scotland pay because that's where Basanti had been abused.

'Where will I live?'

Jamieson answered a different question. 'I'm sure we could find an Indian family who would be happy to have you as a lodger.'

'No. No Indian family.' She was firm about it.

'Why, Basanti?' Jamieson held her hand.

'They will disrespect me, for what I have done. Remember I am a Bedia.'

As the conversation carried on Jamieson recalled what she had been like at 17, with no family, lost, in lodgings, unhappy, until she'd had the nerve to broach adoption with Isobel Dalgleish. 'We'll sort something out. I promise.'

Basanti was now sniffing the lupins whose dusty scent she also enjoyed. If Jamieson had been locked away for as long as Basanti she would also want to smell flowers.

While she watched her, she thought of her flat which no men ever visited, of her spare room, the room she'd moved into at the age of 17, when she gained a mother, and whether history could repeat itself.

Stop it Helen.

There were five gravestones, gathered together like sheep huddling against the northerly wind. After looking at each in turn, Cal knelt at the one closest to the fjord, a grey headstone grizzled with lichen and with a curved top. He touched it and brought from his backpack the small round stone he'd collected from 14 Eilean Iasgaich, and from his wallet, the photograph of the Ardnamurchan grave which had begun his search for his grandfather 19 years before. He pushed the photograph against the gravestone and secured it there with the stone from the Sinclair croft. His head drooped and he said under his breath, 'Known unto God'. He stayed there for the remainder of the afternoon, sometimes staring across at the jagged-edged mountains and the snow in the gullies; sometimes strolling along the shore; and sometimes kneeling among the familiar white flowers of Dryas Octopetala which had colonised this barren arctic landscape.